# Secrets of Time
# Finding Light

## SD Barron

SDC Publishing, LLC

SDC Publishing, LLC was established to promote and encourage aspiring writers and artists. It is a family oriented vehicle through which they can publish their work.

Contact SDC Publishing, LLC at allenfmahon@gmail.com

Or on the web at SDCPublishingLLC.com

This is a work of fiction. The events and characters described
herein are imaginary and are not intended to refer to specific
places or living persons. The opinions expressed in this manuscript
are solely the opinions of the author and do not represent the
opinions or thoughts of the publisher. The author has represented
and warranted full ownership and/or legal right to publish all the
materials in this book. No portion of this book may be copied or
reproduced without express written permission.

## DEDICATION


This book is dedicated to my husband, Kenneth Barron, Jr
and my children, Abby & Kenny.
Any inspiration for writing about love came from thoughts
of all of you.

# ACKNOWLEDGMENTS

My gratitude goes out to so many but especially my tenacious beta readers and loudest cheerleaders:

Elizabeth Rutrough
Dana Abney
Alden Baker
Ken, Kenny, & Abby

Thank you to my editor who can make one cry & smile at the same time:
Chuck Sambuchino

Thank you to Franklin County Historical Society for your library and inspiration for my 1958 Ferrum.

*The cover art is a photograph taken by SD Barron of a tree in her yard carved by Dwayne Hodges of Woodchucks Woodcarvings, Boonesmill, Virginia.*

# CHAPTER 1
## Tartarus, Emergent

Billy cracks his eyes open and swallows past the scorch in his throat. His muscles object like the rusted hinges on Mister Gravely's barn door in Fayerdale when he sits up. The old man ran the small stable where Billy worked occasionally. It sat next to the Pennymaker's general store where he also worked along with other odd jobs. The tiny town was nested in the Blue Ridge and slowly dying while he was there, but he managed to live a busy life. Despite the whirling memories that usually lack focus when he first transitions, images of his life and those he shared it with in Fayerdale sharpen more quickly than usual. All except one which, despite its blur, seems to wrap a blanket of warmth with an infusion of a soft vanilla fragrance around him.

He starts to swipe his hair back and stops short. "I see the three of you. Again." A heavy sigh collapses his chest while the three asps bound to his arm flicker a forked tongue greeting. "Well, I suppose we know where we have landed then." After adjusting the leather straps across his chest, he picks his broad sword up from the ground to sheath it behind his back. The dark demon marks have etched into his skin along with the glistening protective marks. *Everything as it has been before. So many times before.* The leather pants and boots fit almost like a second skin, and he is grateful for their comfort. One of nearly none in his underworld existence. He is armed to fight for nearly anything except for his own freedom.

Through the Tartarian mist he sees that his friends, Luke and Jeb, are across the Asphodel Meadow gathering the Demon King's conquests. They, along with a few others, were friends in 1720 Williamsburg. After Billy's original self, William, was cursed by the dark witch Resmelda Bigelow they all became a Circle of Souls bound together and enslaved to the Demon King, Paimon. *How many times have we lived and died now?* Billy swipes a hand across his bruised neck. The harvest in Fayerdale was not their worst, but its remnants incumber his usual robust gait, and he holds back a grimace while pushing through the pain to join his friends.

The chain binding the demon conquests rattles with Jeb tugging to urge them forward. Blood melds with rust as the cuffs twist with each conquest's step and swing of the iron links. Billy glances over at the group they are escorting and imagines seeing their souls cascade into the dismal mist of Tartarus creating a hiss from icy terror meeting fiery retribution.

A jolt of recognition fractures outward and electrifies his skin. "Missus Pennymaker," he whispers her name watching her pass. She brings up the end of the line of conquests, and her hollow eyes glance at him, but she says nothing. *What bargain could have snatched her soul?* He can think of nothing and runs his hand through his hair while taking a step back. *Sometimes you do not know what you think you know,* he reminds himself.

The judged souls follow the conquests. They will cross the Stix to transition to their next existence. Some are twitchy like caged birds. Others walk with mouths agape as though caught in one of Robert Ripley's *Believe It or Not* panels Billy read in Mister Pennymaker's New York Evening Post that was mailed to the store weekly. A few bold souls don masks of self-righteousness. Even in death the traits of their previous life follow them here. Billy clears his throat and shakes his head. It won't be long before the waxy sanctimonious expressions of these few melt when they near the blazing pits throughout the underworld.

"Charon, what has you disgruntled today?"

Billy's thoughts are distracted as Jeb teases the ferryman.

Luke flashes a quick grin Billy's way.

"Ach, you three back again. That in itself is enough to sour my mood." Charon grabs their coins jerking his head to signal for them to move to the front of the ferry. Billy unsheathes his sword to sit next to Jeb and rests his arms atop the hilt. The three asps twist around his arm and dose.

Luke sits heavily next to him draping his arms along the ferry's siderail.

The chain binding the demon conquests snaps just as they start to sit. Jeb clucks his tongue and shakes his head. "You will be standing for the crossing. Move in closer."

A glistening wet crimson colors the iron cuffs around the conquests' wrists and Billy's eye twitches. He turns his head with a furrowed brow catching Jeb's eye.

Jeb coughs up an imaginary insect. "They all make me sick. Especially that murdering Daryl Lee. After what he did to Mister Hairston…" He stops short and grimaces. "Best to let them get used to what lays ahead of them with eternal repayment for whatever deals they made with the Demon King."

Thinking about the way Daryl Lee shot Mister Hairston in cold blood, Billy raises an eyebrow shrugging. "As if standing on this excuse of a boat is anything like what lays ahead for them."

The conquests' faces fall.

*How could they not know the price of bargaining away their souls?* Billy gives them all a once over but reminds himself of the Demon King's smooth lies. It has taken him two centuries to achieve clarity in this matter, and so he can see how they may have been deceived.

A few of the chained passengers stagger into each other as Charon burst through knocking into them. Those on the periphery desperately grasp onto the siderail to avoid falling overboard.

Charon stops short by Billy. "You. What name would you be goin' by this time 'round?"

He sees the crotchety old demon through the hair hanging over his face. Now that he is finally sitting, it is as if he had never done so before, and to have to move even a bit is torment. Aside from this aching fatigue, he is plagued with frustration to find himself back in Tartarus once again. Another life gone by, and they were not able to defeat the Demon King and win their freedom. What's more, this journey is haunted by the image of a beautiful young woman who he feels he knows but just cannot remember how. Again, as he thinks of her, the swirl of warmth and soft vanilla envelope him. He rubs his arm.

"I asked a question flesh-barer." Spittle sprays from between Charon's sharp black teeth.

"Billy." He responds with a thickened voice.

"Well, you watch what you say 'bout my ship Billy." More spittle. "She has served to carry yar sorry excuse for an existence 'nough times asn't she?"

"Yes, Charon. What was I thinking? It is a fine craft. Very fine." *How true his words are. So many times on this ferry. Our own personal gateway to hell and servitude within the Demon King's protectorate.* "We," Billy looks to both Luke and Jeb, "are grateful for your service."

Luke gives a nod and then jabs Jeb in the side who follows with his head cocked and a flick of a smile.

Charon's chest puffs out a bit. He gives a you-betacha nod of the head and stomps off mumbling under his breath sending more demon conquests cruelly off balance.

Billy shakes his head before resting it on his arm. This will be his last opportunity for peace, and he chooses not to have it disrupted by arguing with the cantankerous Charon. His companions chuckle under their breath, and he looks up at them in disdain whispering, "Jeb, Luke do not aggravate the old demon. He has a miserable existence as ferryman considering he once ruled Tartarus."

"Yes, we know you are right about this. Right, Jeb?" Luke amiably agrees.

Jeb just snickers and reluctantly nods his agreement before shouting at the conquests to straighten back up while jerking on the chain.

Billy notices a small blue feather with a white tip just inside his waist strap, and he draws it up spinning it between his fingers. Never has one presented itself to him in the underworld. Why would one? It is a plain feather though—unlike the ones on Earth that have a delicate ribbon tied to them. An exchange of a blue jay feather between him and his father had been a tradition during his original life in Williamsburg. It was done whenever they were going to be apart from one another for an extended time. Later. After the curse. A blue jay feather with a delicate ribbon tied to its quill would signify the approach of a harvest. The color of the ribbon would hint what laid ahead for him and the Circle of Souls before the end of that life came.

He studies the feather for a moment longer before laying it against the hilt of his sword where he secures it with leather cording. Spying Luke watching him, a flush of heat brings color to his cheeks, and he quickly diverts his eyes without understanding what has triggered this feeling of embarrassment. Perhaps, the tender sentiment he feels with seeing the feather. *But, why?* He bites down hard on his lower lip to keep it at bay.

Raucous screeching from above cuts through the air as large-headed birds with piercing eyes, rapacious beaks, dark wings, and hooked claws start veering towards them. The three human warriors look at one another without alarm, but the remaining occupants squirm with apprehension. Luke and Jeb casually look down the rows of the judged souls laying lots against who is to be taken by the flock.

The creatures drop down, and each grips the shoulders of a judged soul violently flapping its wings tugging viciously. Those near the victims cower like frightened children leaning as far away as they possibly can. The birds shake their chosen targets until the physical body of the person is torn away, trapped by the lethal talons, screaming and kicking. The beasts fly away with their prizes filling the air with victorious caws. Remaining behind are Shades—blank-faced with terror reflecting in their eyes. Transparent images of what once was. The Shades are destined to ride on the barges of the Phlegethon for eternity. Punishment for a life of indifference. A non-existence.

The remaining passengers are reluctant to return to their former positions warily looking up towards the murky sky.

Charon, who has been leaning casually against the tiller, suddenly stands straight taking on the look of demon authority mixed with cruise ship cordiality. "Aye, thar now. Thems just the Strix of Tartarus laying claim on tha Shades. A tasty treat for thar young. Twern't no random act, and tha rest of you lot 'ave nothing else to fear while aboard my ship. Take yer seats and settle down. Tha trip be near done now." Charon settles back to steering the ferry and the boat's occupants reluctantly reclaim their original positions.

An exchange of arm punches occurs between Jeb and Luke. Billy cannot help but reveal a thin smile. Such is the way of existence in Tartarus. The ferry has reached the opposite shore, and the chained demon conquests are led off the vessel by Jeb into the mist that hangs heavy throughout the land. All of the judged souls follow and make their way to the shoreline where they meet with their guides and slowly disappear from view. The newly formed Shades remain sitting listless in their seats. They will be transferred to barges on the Phlegethon.

Charon moves to close the ferry's ramp as the last of the passengers step off. The three asps awaken and sway with their tongues twitching in and out as Billy holds his sword over his shoulder and stands to leave.

"Ahoy thar, scab." Charon growls at him.

Billy stops to look at the old demon.

"Until the next time then?"

Billy nods and starts to move off the ferry.

"You know." Charon reaches up and rubs the back of his scaly neck turning it to noisily release a kink.

Billy stops again to look at Charon.

"Before I was thwarted from my Tartarian throne by the current Demon King I lived where you be headed." Charon growls and points a gnarled finger towards a hill inland from the river.

"Yes, I have been told this. You were a most formidable lord they say."

A prideful nostalgia lights the demon's face. "That I was, and yet this is what I 'ave been reduced to. Memory can be both curse and blessing."

Billy nods in agreement.

"I 'ave found within tha monotony of my current existence a certain advantage transporting both tha doomed and blessed to their next destination. It seems I 'ave more knowledge of tha souls who pass by me now than I ever did as lord and master. Paimon, our current king," his voice snarls with this acknowledgement, "is too busy finding new conquests and adding to his collection of human trinkets to take interest in the humdrum crossings of judged souls. Only I have full understanding of the general make up of

Tartarus' inhabitants."

"Yes, Charon, I can see the advantage with your situation." Billy maintains a stiff cordiality unsure why Charon has now spoken more words to him than in any other time they have crossed paths.

"In all yar crossings, flesh-barer, no despondency has ever emanated from your soul. Thar has been a change to all that with this crossing. You are dragging it behind yarself to be sure, an' it needs to be dealt with before Paimon becomes aware and uses it to his benefit. I canna have that." Charon rubs his chin eyeing Billy.

*Yes, it would seem this conversation is leading to something. But, what?* Billy keeps his cards close.

"I remember up thar on tha hill, behind Paimon's dwelling, thar grows a pomegranate tree."

Billy looks at him curiously, and nods knowing the tree he speaks of.

"It be Persephone's tree. It be said that tha seeded fruit of that tree—when eaten—creates a passage back to tha great Mesu and realms beyond."

Billy comprehends fully what is being said. *The Mesu will give me passage back to Earth. Home. Maybe the woman lingering at the border of my memory.* His eyebrow arches high, and he leans in to listen. The Tartarian mist slowly swirls around affording them a shroud of protection from prying eyes and ears.

"No debt payment, no demon wars to battle, no sacrifice of

self and blood to the whims of the lustful sirens and thirsty lamia." Charon steps closer to Billy. The asps on Billy's arm raise their heads poised to strike, and the ferryman glances their way before peering into Billy's eyes.

*Yes indeed, I want this chance to return to Earth. Now. Do not let it show,* Billy beseeches himself. No demon can be trusted.

"Of course," Charon slides into his finale. "If one were to return to Tartarus after such treachery, the suffering would be great. Perhaps so great that not even the blessin' of a fallen angel, not bathin' in the waters of the mighty Styx, and not a band of tethered comrades would prevent a Death of Death. I would not enjoy seeing you meet a sticky end." He tilts his head giving Billy a lop-sided once over.

"What payment Charon?" *Keep your emotions in check.*

"Perhaps something later, if you survive. For now, just enjoyment for me. Enjoyment watching tha nefarious Demon King lose his bridge to Earth. Resmelda's curse bounds you tightly to tha king giving him tha ability to go to Earth and enrich himself while you are living there. He will be…motivated to get you back. So, you know, it may not be lasting. Not like it would if you could find a way to defeat him. Conquer him." A sharp-tooth grin spreads wide on his face.

Billy gives a curt nod and steps off the ferry into the water. He makes his traditional dive beneath the surface of the Styx always hopeful the water will provide some protection from mortal harm before making his way across the rocky terrain to catch up to Luke. Charon's words echo in his thoughts while he walks. Twice he loses his footing due to this distraction. Once the incline starts the path is less treacherous, and he has an easier go of it. Tufts of sparse vegetation pushing up through the hard ground brush his leg, and he leaves behind a wake in the swirling mist as he walks catching up to Luke. Jeb is already ahead of them leading the conquests to the Demon King's abode.

"What is on your mind?" Luke has been waiting for Billy near a tree with meandering branches and crisp leaves. Scrambling insects are pecked from the bark by featherless birds with brilliant red beaks and beady pink eyes.

He tells Luke what Charon said. "If this is something I decide to risk, I want you and Jeb to consider it as well. This is a great opportunity for all of us. If we left of our own accord, we would not have to endure Paimon's passage ceremony and be forced to drink the water from the Lethe. If we cross on our own accord, our memories will not be tampered with by the Lethe's water. We will remember one another, have strength in this unity during the next life, and perhaps find a way to break the curse."

"Yes, that is a possibility." Luke speaks slowly and almost as though asking a question. He takes a deep breath and exhales slowly. "But I cannot leave here until Sadie returns. She is the love of my life." He pauses and cuts a laugh short. "Well, lives actually. She was able to escape this place for the moment by avoiding the harvest in Fayerdale and has an opportunity to live a full life. I want her to have a long life on Earth. What if we beat him, break the curse, and it is our final life to live? To live completely. We do not know if the other tethered souls will be freed and, if they are, we will not know if we can ever find them. We all need to be together before taking the risk of conquering him. I do not want that without her."

"You are right of course. I was not thinking clearly about your situation. We will stay until Sadie returns and then give it consideration."

"No, you misunderstand me. *I* cannot leave but *you* certainly can. I do not know why, but I think there is something else you are meant to do. Not here—on Earth. If you return to Tartarus after that, we will deal with the Demon King's wrath as we always have in the past."

"If I were to go now, I will have to return later and bring together the remaining circle before we can make a final stand. There will be significant consequences, if I defy the Demon King in such a way—perhaps even a death of death." He pauses forcing himself to suppress a shudder. "I have much to consider."

"Perhaps," Luke says tentatively. "However, I sense the decision is made."

"Perhaps."

The remaining trek is silent until they reach the crest of the hill where their destination lays before them. Jeb is leading the conquests to an entrance at the bowels of the abode while Luke and Billy walk around to a side entrance. The sentry is a pair of twin creatures who are separate beings but who function as one. They are half as tall as Billy, with prominent brows shading dark eyes, Roman noses, and square jaws peppered with a shadow of coarse black hair. Their arms are muscled with a continuance of the dark hair but longer than the hair on their faces and wiry. Each stands stiffly on bowed legs.

"Cercopes, what a pleasure to see you again." Luke bends forward in mock reverence. He lurches forward staggering when Cercopes on the left tilts the handle of its spear ever-so-slightly tripping Luke as he passes.

The pair briskly return to a statue-like stance with set faces.

Luke shoots them a threatening look, and Billy closes his eyes and shakes his head walking past the sentry without a word.

They step into an entryway gleaming in torch light. White walls contrast against a brilliant red floor. In the center of the room candlelight from a crystal candelabrum reflects off a black lacquer table with gold inlay. Surrounding the candelabrum are bowls of fresh fruit, nuts, and other refreshments. Billy's stomach rumbles a request to be filled, but he knows from previous experience that the food is unobtainable. One can reach for, and even grasp the desired item, but once it is lifted from the platter it becomes vaporous and disappears. His mouth waters, but he stands next to Luke ignoring the table and its elusive treasure.

A rectangle of wall opens inward with a whoosh, and a conquest in an ill-fitting butler suit lumbers into the entryway holding his head at a strange forward-tilted angle. He motions for Luke and Billy. They sheath their swords and step through the passageway into a large room. The space is exquisitely decorated from the 1920's era with several collectibles and furniture tastefully arranged.

The boundaries of the curse allow Paimon free passage to Earth only during Billy's lifetimes. Since Paimon's lust for mortal collectibles can only be satisfied periodically by the bridge Billy's humanity creates, he wastes no time in updating his home with décor obtained through trickery, thievery, and the occasional bargain.

A demon with blue-black skin is lounging on a settee. She appears nearly human except for the unusual color of her skin and two small horns protruding from her upper forehead. Her slinky flapper-style evening dress sparkles in the dim light while she lazily fans herself. She eyes them as he and Luke walk across the room towards a lavish desk. Behind the desk is a huge window that spans from ceiling to floor and the entire length of the wall. Paimon is sitting at the desk talking with a lamia, a vampire-like creature, who still has blood at the corner of her mouth from her last meal. Desire's twitch flicks at her lips when Billy and Luke approach, but she follows Paimon's suit and does not overtly acknowledge the two humans. Billy studies a winged creature sitting on a perch near the desk who does show great interest in he and Luke. It stares at them with its red eyes while bobbing its head back and forth. Billy thinks it looks like an albino condor, and he cannot help but feel that they are being sized up for a meal while it croons coarsely rocking back and forth.

Beyond the glass wall is the garden. It is the only place in Tartarus that hints of sunshine. The ground gently slopes away from the dwelling, and at its center grows Persephone's pomegranate tree burdened with fruit. Billy's jaw is set while he studies the tree hearing Charon's words replay in his head.

Bowing and backing away for several feet, the lamia turns and disappears from the room. Paimon sorts through some items on the desk and reaches for a cup holding it up several seconds before looking up and bellowing, "Smyth!"

The butler trudges forward from the back of the room bumping into a pedestal nearly knocking a statue off of it. Recovering the piece, he places it gingerly back on its perch. Paimon rolls his eyes and taps a long cloudy fingernail on the desk. Smyth reaches the desk and stands dull-eyed shifting his weight from foot to foot until Paimon waves the cup emphatically.

"It's empty, Smyth. Why am I waiting?" He snarls like a rabid dog.

Smyth reaches for the cup, and a thick black substance begins soaking into the collar of his shirt.

"Damned cursed wound. It has never healed properly.

Blood everywhere." Paimon jumps up from his desk looking over it at the floor. He is seething. "Resmelda may have slit your throat you blundering idiot, but I will deepen the cut and rid you of that hollow head."

Billy glances down seeing a few dark drops on the elaborate rug. He quickly moves his eyes up as Paimon storms from the room. Smyth gropes at his throat and sulks his way back to his corner of the room.

The pomegranate tree seems to have a spotlight on it drawing Billy's attention once more. There is a flash of the young woman's face that he had woken up thinking about in the Asphodel Meadow, hazel eyes, a soft curl to her auburn hair, and a sad smile. He even catches a light scent of warm vanilla. Then there are several different flashes in rapid succession of her, and he realizes that he knows her outside of Tartarus, and that she is someone important. His pulse explodes against his neck, and a swirl of heat steals his breath away.

Eurynomos, the blue-black demon, remains reclining and now studying her blood red nails. The bird creature is sleeping. Luke is standing next to him, and the drops of Smyth's black blood remain on the carpet. A nerve at the corner of his eye takes on a twitch matching the slow ticking of a clock on the wall that doesn't keep meaningful time since time in the underworld is irrelevant.

Billy blinks focusing on the memory of the girl and remembers her name is Hallie, and he loves her. There is a flash of a kiss, lingering, sweet, and powerful. An inferno ignites inside him even with just the memory of her. Finally, he also remembers she was there at the edge of darkness when Paimon came to Fayerdale to complete the harvest. Billy's throat suddenly constricts, and the next memory is of incredible pain and then nothing. He has no idea what happened to her, but he is certain that she was in Tartarus before he crossed the Styx. He draws his sword holding it up and stares at the blue jay feather. His red and black serpent companions weave their heads also studying the feather.

Hallie had a journey to make, but he can't remember where. If she passed through Tartarus, she would have had to go to the great Mesu to leave the underworld. The Mesu is the only way one can pass to the mundane plain. *How could she have known how to get into Tartarus as a living soul and traverse its territory safely?*

Luke sucks air through his teeth. "How long is he going to have us stand here?"

Billy doesn't reply. Instead he studies the tree in the garden a moment longer.

Luke follows his gaze through the glass wall out into the garden and releases a deep and heavy sigh before speaking again. "I'm sure it will not be too much longer. He is trying to make a point by making us stand here before telling us what our task for this stay is. Wouldn't you imagine?"

Billy still doesn't reply. He walks around the desk, past the sleeping bird and up to the glass wall. He taps it with a fingertip.

Luke pulls his sword from its sheath. "Of course," he says as he surveys the room. None of its inhabitants are giving either human any consideration. "Someone could get his attention somehow and shorten our wait." His muscles tense, and he adjusts the grip on his sword as he continues to watch Billy.

Billy sees all his friend's preparation from the corner of his eye, but he says nothing. For a moment, Luke's grip relaxes. Billy looks back and flashes a penitent smile to his friend. "I have to go, Luke."

"I know."

"Will you explain to Jeb? Apologize for me? I remember now. I remember Hallie. I have to try to find her."

"Yes, of course. I remember her too. Jeb will understand. Hell, he will probably find a way to make the chaos your departure will likely cause entertaining. Do not worry about us. Go."

Billy gives a quick nod and turns to the glass wall drawing back his sword. He grips the hilt, and the blue jay feather brushes against his hand. After a brief look back at Luke he takes his stance feeling the tug of war between his muscles as he stretches back. He swings forward triggering the power of his swing like a firing mechanism in a gun. Bam! The glass wall quivers, and a network of cracks extend outward from the point of impact rapidly shattering into a cascade of shards. Several speckle Billy's arms crimson, and he flinches, but his adrenalin kicks in and he ignores the stinging pain. He wills his legs to step over the line. To step away from the confines of his slavery and towards the hope of freedom no matter how brief. All the while leaving his friends behind. He hesitates.

"Damn, Billy that made a mess." Luke's voice slides with thick sarcasm.

The bird squawks and flies to another part of the room.

Eurynomos runs from the room and collides into a conquest from the scullery that just arrived carrying Paimon's full glass on a tray. The tray and glass crash to the floor, and the conquest stands trembling with eyes bulging.

Billy flinches, and he looks over his shoulder at Luke.

"I am the one who told you to go. You need to go now. I will cover you. It will only be moments before he returns." Luke's muscles twitch and his eyes meet Billy's. "All will be well, my friend."

He steps up to Billy. "Truly. You must be quick now."

Billy's jaw sets, and he gives Luke a nod. They race through the fractured glass wall into the garden with swords at the ready quickly approaching the tree.

Paimon steps through the broken glass wall into the garden moments later and lets out a tremendous roar. Demons of all sorts begin spilling over the garden wall.

"Billy get a piece of the fruit," Luke yells out as they reach the tree.

Billy swings the sword upward cutting fruit from the tree and catches one in his hand. The first swarm of demons is rapidly approaching. "Luke, come with me," he shouts over the bedlam of demon war cries.

"No. Open it and eat the seeds." Luke strikes down the first demon to reach them. "Do it now!"

Billy tears open the fruit and pulls out a cluster of red seeds, pushing them into his mouth. They burst with a bitter sweetness as he bites down. He sees Luke turn taking down two more demons easily. Billy raises his sword fatally striking a keres demon and turns to take down another just as he starts to dissipate. There is a melting sensation and a brutal yank upward. His thoughts spin and suddenly it all stops, and he is standing at the roots of the Mesu.

A searing pain erupts in his chest and panicked concern for Luke's safety weighs heavy on his shoulders. *What have I done?* He paces haphazardly over the roots berating himself for leaving Luke behind. The feather on his sword brushes against his hand, and he stops short. He bites his lip and forces slower more purposeful breaths reminding himself how extremely capable Luke is and, if all else fails, he knows his friend will signal a surrender.

The three asps sway and study him intently as though asking, "Are you quite done now? Then let's get on with it."

He nods and starts the trek over the twisting roots ducking to avoid the fleshy cords hanging down from above. He surveys the area feeling satisfied he is alone and begins looking for the head waters of the five rivers. The glassy Acheron comes into view first, and he strips down kneeling by its edge. Although he has not been in Tartarus long, he feels a need to purge himself of its evil residue before entering the sacred Mesu.

He plunges his head under splashing water over his back and arms. The sharp pain of remorse courses through his body. He pulls his head up flinging it back, and his muscles shudder with a force that could ping a seven on the Richter scale. The droplets on his skin and hair quiver a path back into the river taking his tribulations with them. He is dry and his heart is light for the moment.

A soft glow from the Mesu's entrance welcomes him as he steps inside. The gentle pulsing of the tree's heart matches the wax and wane of the light. Throughout the tree's core nectar collects in crevices and small delicate flowers grow along the path. A portal to his right illuminates with a golden glow, and he steps into it. As he walks, the asps on his arm calm and lay against his flesh turning back into wiry scar tissue. The demon marks fade as do the protective marks. His leather gear transforms into jeans and a white t-shirt and pair of black boots. His hair shortens slightly and is brushed back away from his face with pomade. Only a couple strands hang over his brow. A flutter captures his heart and a sudden weightlessness strikes when the ground drops from under him. There is a rushing plunge downward and then nothing.

# CHAPTER 2
## Ferrum, Epiphany

Rubbing the back of his stiff neck the newcomer steps off the train looking back and forth unsure of which direction to go until a large red metal box with "Cola" written on the front catches his eye. It is sitting next to a service station, and his curiosity pushes him to venture across the road to check it out. He remembers, in Fayerdale, the Pennymaker's used to keep bottled cola in an icebox at their store and suddenly thirst grasps ahold as he stares at the shiny nemesis before him trying to figure out how it works. Vending machines had not found their way to Fayerdale in 1928. Besides, yesterday's memories, and his life as Billy White, are now decades away.

"Hello there young man. Can I help you with something?" A middle-aged man wiping grease from his hands with a shop rag strolls over.

"Yes sir. I was interested in getting a drink."

The man looks at him for a moment, and then his brows jump upward, and his face lights up seeming to realize that the young man doesn't understand the workings of the Vendo V-81 standing before them. He clears his throat. "Well son, you put a dime into that slot right there, the door releases, you open it, and take a bottle out."

The newcomer fumbles at the pockets of his blue jeans finding a wallet in his back pocket, but no coins. He opens the wallet staring down at the edge of a driver's license and slides it up reading: H. William White, brown hair, brown eyes, 5'11", and 165 lbs. He slides it back in place and investigates the billfold finding a five-dollar bill minted 1957 but not a single dime. Shifting his weight, he starts to ask about getting change when the man withdraws a dime from his own pocket and drops it into the slot retrieving an icy cold bottle of cola. He pops the top off with the bottle opener on the door and hands it over.

"Thank you, sir." He takes a long pull off the bottle drinking it about half empty letting the cool refreshment revive him. He holds the bottle out admiring it for the simple pleasure it holds.

"You new in town then?"

"Yes sir." He stretches out his hand. "Will White. It is a pleasure to meet you."

The man shakes his hand firmly. "Cleo Adkins. Welcome to Ferrum, Virginia son."

§

It's now 1958 and Will thinks back on that day, nearly a year ago, realizing that the cola machine was a beacon. Cleo Adkins' amusement with his befuddlement sparked conversation, and he took a liking to Will immediately. He offered both employment and a place to stay in a small studio apartment located off the back of the garage that very day. The job seems to suit Will's needs fine, and the apartment is the right price, no-charge.

Eventually, memories of past lives drifted back. All triggered by small incidences during the day—laughter between friends, hushed discussion about a nearby still operation, the smell of fresh-baked bread, or a gentle breeze with the spicy scent of the woods. The time he spent in the underworld of Tartarus have needed no gentle reminders. Those memories invade his sleep in the form of nightmares often waking him drenched in sweat.

Will looks over at his bed where his Book of Lineages lays. He retrieved it some weeks after arriving along with his other things near the old iron mine even though the town of Fayerdale, where he lived in 1928, no longer exists. When he learned the land was turned into a recreational area called Fairy Stone State Park, he lost his appetite but not his focus. He hitched a ride to the park and dug through the dirt with his bare hands. His stomach maintained a tight knot until his first glimpse of the sheepskin covering the box with the Book of Lineages. He resurrected it from its grave rifling through the pages to see the status of the Circle of Souls.

A lump in his throat was hard to swallow when he saw Sadie's unbroken line. She escaped their previous harvest and is still alive today. It won't be too much longer before their paths will cross. No one survives him twice. She most likely went to Washington, D. C. with her Aunt Tessie, as this was the plan that last night in Fayerdale. He was shocked to see Maybelle's line had also moved forward with a new life as Connie Sealy starting in 1954. Until he retrieved the Book of Lineages, he thought it was just him and Sadie in this life. How had Connie crossed over from the underworld? After all, his own departure was in defiance of the Demon King and without the required ceremony at the Mesu.

It was a few weeks after finding the book that their paths crossed.

§

"Well, hello there." Connie greets him cheerfully when he walks into the Snip 'n Style salon gracelessly bumping into the manicure tray toppling bottles of polish over.

"Oh, I apologize." He sets down the box he has and begins picking the bottles up off the floor.

She pauses from rolling pink plastic curlers onto the head of a freckled-face girl named Beezie who blushes candy apple red at his appearance in the shop. The women under the hair dryers smile discretely enjoying his uneasiness with being in the salon.

The last of the polish is returned to the tray, and he turns back to Connie. "Uh, Mister Adkins sent me over with this package. He said to tell you it was left at the garage by accident."

"Well, that's where my hair supplies have been." She secures the final curler to Beezie's head and walks over to take the box from him. She looks to be in her mid-twenties. He hasn't known her to be this much older than him since their original lives. She has on a pair of black capris and a pink sweater with a pearl pin worn over her heart.

He searches her eyes for a moment but sees no recognition in them. It would make no difference. She would not be an ally anyway. She barely has tolerated him ever since the loss of two souls from the Circle of Souls—one being his cousin, the man she loved.

She waits a moment to see if he is going say something and laughs a little. "I can take that hon. Unless it's heavy, and then you can just set it over there in the back corner."

He snaps back from his thoughts. "I have it."

Every eye in the salon follows him, and the tingling sensation sweeping across his face is foreign. He doesn't like it.

"Well, thanks," she says delaying his escape. "Hey, what's your name any way?"

"Will. It is William White, but you can call me Will."

"Gotcha. Nice to meet you Will. I'm Connie. You tell Cleo I said thanks for sending that on over now."

"Yes, Miss I will." He reaches for the door opening it to a pair of girls heading into the shop that are startled by him. There is a shuffling of positions as he clears the way for them, and then he gratefully wins his freedom from the shop. It was an experience reminiscent of passing through one of the many gates of hell into a new realm. There is a burst of giggles coming from inside. The door shuts with a clang silencing the shop banter and he promises, "I must remember never to cross that threshold again during business hours."

§

Aside from the surprise of Connie's presence in town, there is also the pressed copper piece, a refashioned penny. Will runs his thumb over its embossed surface, He found it one night inside the Book of Lineages with the image of a structure and its name, the Chesapeake Bay Bridge-Tunnel, embossed onto the surface. With some research at the Ferrum College library, he learned the structure was non-existent, but plans were in place to build it in order to replace the ferry system being used to bring vehicles across the Chesapeake Bay at Virginia's Eastern Shore. On the flip side "HSO" and "2018" were etched into the copper.

Will's mind shuffles through these events from the past several months like a juke box selecting the next 45 record to play while he finishes dressing. He puts the pressed penny in his pocket, as he has done every day since finding it and leaves his apartment. It is a workday, but not too many in town are going to work this morning. There is a funeral to attend. Pauline McCaffrey is dead. She was a pillar in town—known, respected, and liked by all. Will only knew her a short time, but he quickly realized that there are not many people he has come across like her. He knew her through the garage. Although her son, Dillon, usually brought her vehicles in for service there was occasion when Missus McCaffrey came into the shop herself. She was somewhere in her fifties and had survived her husband and then a daughter who died as a teenager. Dillon was her youngest child and in his twenties. He worshiped the ground his mother walked on, and Will wonders how he is holding up.

After the church and grave-side service there is to be a picnic at the McCaffrey home. The First Baptist Women's Auxiliary organized it all, and it promises to be worthy of Missus McCaffrey's memory. Nearly all the merchants, including Adkins Garage, decided to close for the morning to honor the memory of this highly respected woman.

Will has on a pair of black trousers with a short-sleeved shirt. He doesn't own a tie, and these are his best clothes, so they will have to do. He smooths the front of his shirt while walking over to the '77 Restaurant to get some breakfast before heading to Mister Adkins' house where he is going to get a ride to First Baptist.

The restaurant is bustling, and he takes a seat at the counter like he has done most mornings for the past year. There are several customers sitting at booths and more at the counter. A few look up and give him a greeting or nod of the head.

The waitress, Sally, comes over and sets a glass of milk in front of him. "Well, morning sugar. You gonna have your usual?"

Her voice is as sweet as the maple syrup they serve for pancakes.

"Yes ma'am, thank you." Will takes a long drink of the ice-cold milk. Sally puts his order in at the kitchen and comes back with the milk pitcher to refill his glass. He thanks her again and reaches over to get a section of newspaper that was left by a previous customer.

There is a picture of a young girl from Patrick County that has been missing for the past few weeks. Her body was recently found and there is a brief account of the circumstances surrounding her disappearance with limited detail concerning the murder. There are no suspects, but there is speculation that it was done by a serial killer. There was another young girl of similar appearance that was killed in a similar manner not too long ago. A single pearl was found at each crime scene. Will studies the picture of the pretty blonde girl. She had been sixteen years old.

The front door of the restaurant opens and closes and one of the customers in a nearby booth hops up from his seat hurrying towards the door. "Azure, I'm glad you came in hera. I'm needing ta talk ta you about my cow. That sista 'o yourn done swore a spell on my Bessie and threatened ta dry up her milk. I dinna think nothin' ov it, but then yesterday we got barely half a what she's normally bin producin'. I need you ta do somethin' bout it dag gonnit." He swipes away a bit of froth that has gathered at the corner of his mouth.

Will watches with interest. Azure Ridge and his sister, Odina, are rumored to practice witchcraft, and there is a lot of concern and superstition generated by this general thinking. Azure's deep velvety voice reassures the man that he will see what he can do, but it is a difficult task, and it will require a dozen brown eggs to reverse a hex that seems to have taken effect so quickly. Will smiles to himself and starts to go back to his newspaper when he notices that Azure is not alone.

A girl about Will's age is standing next to him. She is slender with a fair complexion and auburn hair gently curling to her shoulders. She must feel his eyes on her, and she looks directly at Will. Her hazel eyes are surrounded by thick lashes and hold him captive. His heart forgets to move for a moment. The paper he has been reading falls to the counter, and he turns on his stool to face her straight on. There is a bruise on her forehead, and his brow furrows wondering what happened.

She offers him a smile before walking with Azure to the back dining area, and it feels as though the room has inhaled stealing Will's breath while poking his pulse into over-drive. He suddenly realizes where the pressed penny came from. Sally sets his breakfast of eggs, bacon, grits and biscuits on the counter startling him from his reverie.

"You okay sugar?"

"Oh, yes ma'am thank you." He tries to force his focus on his breakfast, but flashes of the girl are bombarding him. He knows who she is, her name, and where she is from. The HSO on the pressed penny is her, and she was with him in Fayerdale after traveling from the year 2018. She was supposed to go back. *What could have gone wrong?* He runs his fingers through his hair. She obviously traveled forward…just not far enough…another flash of memory, but the image is blurred. He knows that it is from the underworld though. *How could that be?* She was living and human yet not a part of the Circle of Souls. He knows now that she is the reason he defied the Demon King and returned to Earth.

"Will, honey, you sure you're alright? You haven't touched your breakfast."

Blinking, he pulls Sally into focus. "Oh, yes ma'am just a little distracted this morning is all." He takes a bite of his eggs, gives her a smile, and nods. Sally seems satisfied and goes off to check on other customers. Will looks at the clock on the wall. *Still a bit more time before I need to meet Mister and Missus Adkins. Let me see what can be discovered.*

Azure and Hallie are sitting at a table near the far corner of the room. Both look up as Will approaches. Again, his heart revs up and his leg muscles falter with weakness. He commands well-practiced control, and it barely shows. He hopes.

"Will, good morning," Azure says.

For some reason, Abraham Lincoln comes to mind when he looks at Azure. Although Azure's features have a Gypsy influence not found in the president's, the resemblance remains.

Will puts out his hand, and Azure grasps it to give him a friendly shake.

"Good morning Mister Ridge. I am sorry to interrupt." He glances over at Hallie.

"Oh no, no problem young man. Will, this here is Hallie. Hallie, this is Will." He gestures a hand towards each as he speaks their names and reaches for his mug of coffee.

Will extends his hand to Hallie surveying her face for any sign of recognition. She takes his hand pausing for a moment looking at their joined hands and then up to his face. He waits. Nothing.

"It's nice to meet you, Will." That mesmerizing smile flashes again.

"As it is you, Hallie." Their hands reluctantly let go. A spark of warmth moves from his palm up his arm through his scar. He flexes his fingers and straightens them as if the gesture will allow him to grasp a bit more of the splendid feeling.

"Mister Ridge I heard over at the garage that you have been having trouble with that farm tractor you have, and I was wondering if you could use some help with it." Will had been planning a trip to the Ridge's place for this purpose, but now it will give him a chance to find out more about Hallie's situation. He glances over at her again, but she is focused on her oatmeal.

"Well, yes Will that would be mighty helpful."

"Good." Will reigns in what sounds to him like over-enthusiasm by clearing his throat. "Uh, fine." He shifts his weight pulling himself together yet again.

"How about you come by Saturday morning, and we will take a look at 'er. I'm sure Odina will make you some breakfast. I'm going to be picking up a dozen eggs from Abram Mayhew after we're done here."

Will glances down at his feet to hide the flash of a smile. "Yes sir, I will be there." He turns to Hallie. "It was nice to meet you, Hallie."

The sunlight catches the green flecks in her eyes giving them a sparkle. "It was nice meeting you too, Will."

# CHAPTER 3
## Rise

"Will, honey, you come on over here a minute." Missus Adkins is standing on the porch with the kitchen door open calling over to him as he walks into the yard. She has a selection of ties and pulls a gray striped one from the group as Will approaches. "Here you go Will. Cleo has extras that he hasn't worn in a while, and I want you to have this one. Go on in the kitchen to the mirror there and put it on."

"Now, Katie stop bothering the boy with all that. He is fine." Cleo walks away from the mirror after adjusting his own tie.

Will walks over to the mirror while lifting his shirt collar and flipping the tie over his neck. He ties it and turns with his arms out for her inspection.

She gives him a motherly smile and motions him out the door. Will opens the truck passenger door for Missus Adkins, and he climbs into the back. Along the way they pass the narrow tree-sheltered lane leading to the Ridge's place. It takes a steep drop down into a hollow where their log and stone home was built into the side of one of the foothills. The popular rumor is that the back side of the house connects with a deep cave, and that is where most of the witchcraft takes place. Will has a hard time believing Azure and Odina live a dark existence, yet he presses his lips together and shifts his seat in the truck bed while his stomach tightens.

They pick up a few people needing a ride including Drew Mifflin who is renting a room at the Mayhew farm. He works at the shop when Cleo needs extra help. Other days, he is a handy man working at whatever needs to be done for a collection of folks. He is a drifter who came into town shortly before Will. If it hadn't been for Connie Sealy, Drew would have likely moved on. And it is most likely

Drew who is responsible for Connie's amiable disposition in this life—so different from the usually vengeful and spiteful tethered soul that lives within her. In this life she is independent and confident and in love with Drew who is an outgoing and dependable sort of fellow. He reminds Will of his cousin, Daniel, and wonders if Connie has subconsciously connected to the similarity between the two as well.

"Hey Will, how's it going?" Drew sits near Will after greeting the two others sitting as well in the truck bed.

"Good, good. You?"

Drew smiles. "Good." And that is it. It is as if he knows Will's propensity to avoid small talk and respects it.

First Baptist's parking lot is already full, and Mister Adkins lets everyone out before going to park down the road a bit. Will waits with Missus Adkins while the others head into church, and Drew goes to find Connie. Across a field, He sees Azure, Odina, and Hallie walking up towards the church. He watches Hallie intently, and Katie follows his gaze before looking back and smiling at him. Will shifts his weight and clears his throat grateful for Mister Adkins' arrival.

Cleo turns his head over his shoulder. "You coming?"

"Yes, sir." Will pulls his attention from Hallie's approach and jogs to catch up to them.

Cardboard fans are being waved emphatically by those sitting in the pews in an attempt to stir comfort into the summer heat. It's not working and a bead of sweat rolls down between Will's shoulder blades. He stands against the wall across from the door as Mister and Missus Adkins move up the aisle to take the last seats available. From the corner of his eye Will sees Azure's tall frame walk in behind Odina. Hallie is just behind them. They stand along the wall opposite from Will.

A sorrowful tune flows like tears from a lone fiddle while the musician walks up the aisle playing. Dillon McCaffrey follows. His frame is slender, his hair almost white, and his eyes are dark as coal. He has a purple iris in his hand, and he lays it on top of the white casket sitting near the altar before taking his seat in the front pew reserved for the family. The last family member left. Despite the full church, no one would think to sit in that pew alongside the mourning son of Missus Pauline McCaffrey. It is a matter of respect for her.

Pastor Nunley walks in from a door behind the altar and stands at the pulpit until all eyes are on him. He opens the service with song as a small choir and members of a local blue grass band sing a traditional version of *Will the Circle Be Unbroken*. Will looks at Hallie. Her attention is at the front of the church. A tear is slowly rolling down her cheek. The song concludes and the pastor clears his throat.

"A Reading from the Book of Wisdom. The souls of the just are in the hand of God, and no torment shall touch them. They seemed, in the view of the foolish, to be dead; and their passing away was thought an affliction and their going forth from us, utter destruction. But they are in peace." He finishes the reading, words honoring Missus McCaffrey are spoken, and he motions to the musicians once more. They sing *We Are Going Down the Valley*.

Will shifts his weight as images of the vast murky mist and the stark lands of Tartarus appear before his eyes. Scenes from the demon wars and visions of the dead awaiting passage sharpen and dim. He can almost feel the sway of Charon's ferry carrying them across the Stix. Eyes are on him, and he looks across the church first at Hallie, but her attention remains to the front. He shifts his gaze to see the icy blue eyes of Odina Ridge studying him intently. He nods her way, and she returns the acknowledgement ever so slightly. He turns to the front of the church—she does not.

The service ends, and all make way to the graveyard. A final prayer is said and a bagpipe player standing under a tree just beyond the open grave plays *Amazing Grace*. The soulful sound resonates across the graveyard as the coffin is slowly lowered to its resting place. Will looks past the piper where the grave diggers wait to finish their task. Two are sitting on the ground resting against a tree and one is standing with his hands resting on the handle of a shovel. His clothes are a little too well-fitted and pressed to be a gravedigger's though. He has a black fedora on with a small red flower stuck in the band. Amber tinted sunglasses sit on the bridge of his nose, and he grasps one side to lower them slightly looking over the wire frame at Will. A red glint flashes, but it is gone when he raises the glasses back up his nose. He reaches up to lift his hat at Will and turns leaning the shovel against the tree as he walks away. Will's jaw clenches, and the sound of an imaginary clock paces with the beat of his heart.

Mister Adkins pulls out slowly heading back towards town and the McCaffrey home. Hallie and the Ridges are walking along the side of the road. Her hair blows across her face with a gentle breeze, and she reaches up to bring it behind an ear. She sees Will and smiles. He lifts his hand holding it up, and she returns the gesture holding her hand up and steady as though their palms are touching until she is out of site.

A memory of her in the moonlight sliding a strand of hair from in front of her eyes to behind an ear comes into his thoughts. It was in Fayerdale, and it was the same night that she showed him her heart-shaped amulet born from the blood of the Tree of Life as well as the pressed penny he now has in his possession. He closes his eyes trying to remember everything.

The memory of that night renews pangs of emotion. The intensity of the ambiguity he felt then, and even now, constricts his throat with a scorch that spreads down towards his chest like hot lava over the side of a mountain. *People I let get close do not tend to fair well.* Will forces in and out a deep cleansing breath, and he runs his hand through his hair keeping it there to support his head which is beginning to ache.

He cannot believe how quickly enmeshed his existence had become with Hallie in Fayerdale. Her words, '*you* are Liam,' and the bewilderment and sense of relief they brought him then now lighten his mood. The pressed penny was her proof of their connection in a life not yet lived, and it is his proof now of their connection in a life that has already passed. All of the memories from the life in Fayerdale, the harvest, and the afterlife he cheated rush back to him with new meaning. Suddenly, the pressed penny is a token of hope. Hope, that was so foreign to him in the past, now has meaning and familiarity.

The truck comes to a stop pulling him from his thoughts. The McCaffrey house is a large farmhouse that eventually found itself surrounded by the small town, and it sits not too far from the main street shops. Missus Adkins carries a chess pie up the sloping yard to the house while Mister Adkins joins a group of men where an ice cream maker is being cranked near the porch. A warm breeze stirs the stagnant heat while the women from the church auxiliary bustle to finish setting up food. A sheen of sweat at the back of Will's neck finds escape and trickles a path downward. Luckily a large glass container of lemonade sitting on a table in the back yard offers some relief, and he pours a glass downing it with nearly no effort.

Connie and Drew are standing at a tree near the house talking. Connie was close to Missus McCaffrey having styled her hair for quite some time. It is rumored that Missus McCaffrey was the one who helped Connie start her own salon. Will glances up towards the house and sees Dillon leaning against a post on the back porch watching Connie and Drew. He is chewing on a piece of straw and pulls it from his mouth tossing it over the side of the porch. His eyes meet Will's momentarily before he turns and walks into the house.

Will refills his glass pulling another drink from it, but he lowers his cup when he sees Azure's tall frame coming up from the back edge of the property. Just behind him is Odina. Both are dressed very simply in black, but somehow even the conservative mourning clothes have a foreign look. Will half expects a Gypsy wagon to appear over the horizon behind them. Most folks pay no attention to them as they near the gathering; a few nod a greeting to Azure, however, others move to give them a wide berth for passage.

Hallie is walking next to Odina and draws several curious looks that seem to escape her.

Will distractedly fills a second cup of lemonade and walks across the yard toward Hallie. "Hi, I thought you might like some lemonade."

Hallie smiles at him accepting it. "Thank you."

He is entranced watching the ripple along her neck while she drinks. Fine beads of sweat glisten on her skin, and tiny ringlets of her auburn hair hang by her ear.

"Hmm it tastes so good. I needed this." She wipes the back of her hand over her mouth.

Will laughs and hands her his glass. She gladly accepts drinking it too. "I guess I was thirsty."

"So it seems." He takes the empty cup from her. "How about we fill these back up? Maybe get some food?"

A pink hue colors her cheeks as she twists her lips and gives a nod. "I would like that. Let me just tell Odina." Hallie turns to walk over to her, but Odina waves her approval before Hallie has taken more than a step. "Looks like it's okay."

They refill their cups and head over to the food table. Connie and Drew are standing at the end of the line.

"Well, hey there Will. Who's your friend?" Connie smiles broadly. Her arm is looped through Drew's.

"Hi, this is Hallie O'Meara." He turns to Hallie. "This is Connie Sealy and Drew Mifflin."

"Hi, nice to meet you both."

Connie reaches over patting up the bottom of Hallie's hair. "You have great body in your hair. I own the Snip 'n Style salon. You should come by sometime."

"Thanks, I will." Hallie leans in a little to look at the pearl brooch Connie wears. "That brooch is beautiful." There is a pearl in the center with eight smaller pearls circling it and small diamonds bordering the pearls. The setting for the pearls is yellow gold while the diamonds are set in platinum with lacy loops enclosing the setting.

"Drew gave it to me." She gives his arm a squeeze.

Drew pecks her cheek with a kiss and reaches over to shake Will's hand. He turns to Hallie and gives her hand an enthusiastic shake. "Nice to meet you Hallie."

The line moves ahead, and they fill their plates before finding a place in the shade to sit.

"So Hallie," Connie says. "I've not seen you around before. Where are you from?"

"Well, I'm visiting and actually that is kind of a hard question for me to answer."

Connie raises her eyebrows tilting her head to the side and Will sits quietly. He is anxious to hear about how she ended up here as well.

"I'm staying with some family friends, the Ridges. Do you know them?"

"Sure, everyone in town knows the Ridges."

"They have been very kind to me. I apparently had quite a fall sometime during the train ride coming here and hit my head pretty hard." She reaches up to pull her hair back from her forehead showing the healing bump and bruise. "It seems I have some memory loss from it. The first thing I can remember is waking up with Odina tending to me at her cabin."

"Wow, how has that been for you?" Connie leans in to look at the goose egg on Hallie's head.

"Well, it has been a bit frustrating to be honest." Hallie takes a drink of the lemonade. "But, it has also given me a chance to see things with no bias. You know? It's like a clean slate with no prior expectations or preconceptions."

Connie purses her lips nodding and Drew comments. "You've been given a gift."

"A gift?" Two young girls come running up to them—the

younger one asking the question. She is about seven and the other about twelve.

"Well hey there, JT and Sissy! You two are looking very pretty today," Drew says to them, and the others agree.

"Thank you," answers the older of the two. "Momma had me and JT wear our Sunday bests to say good-bye to Missus McCaffrey."

JT turns to Hallie and gives her a hug. "Hi, I'm JT Canaday. Are you Will's girl friend?"

Hallie blushes. "Uh, no we actually just met. He has been nice enough to spend some time with me today and help me feel welcome."

JT sighs and tries to whisper to Hallie, but she is still loud enough for the group to hear. "Well, that's good because Sissy has a terrible crush on him."

The older girl turns a bright red and closes her eyes. She hisses through her teeth, "J—T. Could you *please* be quiet?"

JT's eyes widen, and she furrows her brow. Sissy just rolls her eyes and walks away. JT looks at Hallie and shrugs her shoulders while Will excuses himself reaching to pick a nearby daisy and follow after Sissy.

"Sissy, hey. Wait up a minute." He catches up to her. The young girl's eyes are wet with embarrassment. Will hands her the daisy, and her mouth drops while her cheeks flush.

"I have never been so honored then to become aware of the fact you find me agreeable." His voice has a formality that he has not used in a long time. "So, you can certainly understand my extreme disappointment in knowing that you and I can never be true sweethearts."

She looks from Will to the daisy.

"You know, given our extreme differences in age, and my much lower status in life. Me just a lowly mechanic's assistant, and you destined for so much more."

She smiles and accepts the flower.

He takes her hand and asks, "Perhaps, you would do me the honor of being my friend? Someone like me could greatly benefit from such a connection."

She nods giving him a squeeze around his neck.

JT comes running up to them. "Sissy, Mister McCaffrey said that the ice cream is ready to be scooped out of the maker on the front porch. Wanna go get some?"

Sissy looks at her sister and smiles. "Sure, JT that sounds good." Looking back at Will her smile broadens brightening her eyes. She gives him a wave goodbye.

Will dips his chin towards her and turns walking back to Hallie and the others. Dillon McCaffrey is standing by them talking.

He shakes Dillon's hand. "I am glad that I knew your mother. She will be missed."

"Thank you, Will." Dillon firmly shakes his hand and then puts his hands back in his pockets.

"Dillon, sit with us for a while," Connie coaxes.

"Oh, thank you Connie, but I'm trying to get around to everyone before folks need to head out. I wanted to be sure and come by and thank you for coming to celebrate mother's life. She would have been very pleased with all this."

"Yes," Connie replies. "Especially all the children. She loved being around children."

"Yes, yes she did." Dillon's gaze looks a little distant for a moment before looking back at Connie. "The Canaday girls were particular favorites of hers. You know, that older one could be your twin. She is very much like you."

Connie laughs. "Well, you know they're my Aunt Teechee's girls."

His brow pops up. "No, no I didn't know that." He stands for a moment longer then abruptly refocuses. "Right then. Thank you all again."

They say goodbye to Dillon, and he moves over to a group of

women who are sitting and talking together. They each rise from their chairs to give him a hug.

"Will," Hallie says. "That was really nice what you did for Sissy."

He shrugs. "It was nothing. She is a sweet kid."

Hallie brings a piece of hair behind her ear and smiles at him. Connie and Drew are lost in conversation together, so Will offers a hand to Hallie to help her stand.

"Connie, Drew I need to get back to the garage. Mister Adkins wants to open for the afternoon. It was good to see you both."

"Good to see you Will. Cleo said something about a car needing a brake job and some other repairs that he wanted me to work on for him. I think I'll come check it out tomorrow and maybe get a start on it, so I will probably see you then."

"Okay, sounds good. Connie, see you later."

"Sure thing, honey. Hallie, come by the shop any time."

"Thanks, I will."

Hallie and Will make their way back towards the edge of the yard where Odina and Azure are sitting. "So, you got a pretty nasty bump on your head then." He wants to get her back on the subject.

"Yes, I am thinking it was not one of my most graceful moments."

"It must have been a hard bump for you to have memory loss for this long. How long have you been here now?"

"A week."

"I guess your family is coming to pick you up?"

Hallie looks at him and furrows her brow. "No, I'm staying. I feel fine, and my memory is trying to kick in. I have had some flashes, but nothing I can grab ahold of. Anyway, my aunts are on an overseas trip."

"You remember your aunts?"

"Odina told me. She said that I live with my Aunts Beattie

and Dot. I can picture what they look like, and I have started remembering camping trips with them, but not a whole lot yet."

"Odina knows about your aunts?" He is incredibly confused. If Hallie is here in Ferrum in 1958 by some sort of supernatural accident, how could Odina know her? Know her aunts?

Hallie stops short and jerks her head back squinting at him. "I told you she is a family friend. Why would she not know them?"

"Right, yes, yes of course. It is, uh, just such an incredible turn of events for you. You know, losing your memory on a trip, alone, your family out of the country, and you land here in the tiny town of Ferrum."

Hallie purses her lips, then lifts her brow, and gives a quick shrug. "If you say so. I guess I hadn't picked apart the details." She pauses a moment and shifts her weight grasping ahold of an elbow. "Well, I guess I will be seeing you. Thank you so much for hanging out with me." She starts stepping backwards away from him.

He is worried he has upset her in some way. "You are welcome. It really was my pleasure." He is lost for words.

She crinkles her nose up when she smiles and raises her hand in a parting gesture then turns to head over to Odina who is already preparing to leave. Several others are heading out as well.

He watches Hallie go, and she turns her head back once to look his way.

Will returns to the garage finishing out the afternoon tending the gas pumps and doing a couple oil changes. The heat and work have taken over by the time he flips the sign on the door to show they are closed, and he makes his way back to his room for a shower and dinner. One of the ladies from the auxiliary sent him home with a plate full of fried chicken and sides. After eating what he can, he takes a cola from his refrigerator popping the top off the bottle and heads outside to sit on the old café chair that is on the small cracked concrete slab that serves as a patio by his door. He sits to wait for it to cool down a bit while he drinks the cola.

# CHAPTER 4
# Bombshell

The setting sun burns a brilliant raspberry glow off the mountain top with the last hour of daylight lingering across the small valley. A dog barks off in the distance, and a calico cat is crouched and ready to spring at something hiding in the tall grass across the road from Will's patio. A couple boys with baseball bats and gloves are walking along the road. Their uniforms are dusty and embedded with the orange dirt that is found in Ferrum and the surrounding hills. It has to do with the high iron content in the dirt—hence the town's name which derives from the Latin word for iron.

Will tilts back the bottle of cola finishing it off and leans his head back to rest. It has been a long day, and he is ready for it to be over.

In what seems like a few moments, he hears the sound of hurried footsteps rushing up to him stopping where he is sitting. "Hallie?"

"I-know-who-am." The words escape through her gritted teeth.

He bites his lower lip and nods. "Your memory has returned." His nerves sizzle with anticipation.

"Yes, I got it back. I know where I'm from, where I've been, and what's more who you are." Her hands are fisted, and she paces the patio turning sharply on her heel.

He grips and releases the edge of the café chair. "Hallie, that is good. It should not upset you. How did it happen?"

She stops abruptly folding her arms while she takes stock of him and divulges with a reddened face, "A little bird told me."

He stands and reaches for her trying to calm her, but she pulls away jerking her arm out of his reach glaring at him.

"You were with me almost all day." There is venom in her voice, but her tone changes. Her eyes glisten, and her anger subsides. "How could you not tell me?"

"I…I am sorry. I am so very sorry."

He is unsure what to do. He has never seen her this way. He is accustomed to a calmer more balanced nature where Hallie is concerned. He reaches out to her again gently touching her arm, and this time she doesn't retreat.

She turns to look where he is touching her and back up at him. The tearful anger remains in her eyes and, although her face softens, she looks strange to Will. A chill tingles along his skin. Her hand reaches behind his neck, and she runs her fingers through his hair. His muscles seize. She regards him intently, but her thoughts are a mystery until she pulls him to her bringing his mouth to hers.

His muscles remain stiff, and he shuffles back a step or two, but she is persistent. He cannot keep himself from responding to her advance and pulls her close kissing her deeply. An exciting rush of emotion fills what has been an empty well for him.

She bites at his lip and slides her hands from around his neck downward grabbing his shirt. She jerks it open running her hands down the front of his chest forcefully pushing against him. He staggers and his back strikes the wall. Her mouth moves under his chin and onto his neck. The heat becomes searing, and he flinches. A high-pitch ring fills his ears, and he grabs her by the wrists pushing her back. *What?* Air tries to move into protesting lungs, and he squints trying to clear his vision.

She stares at him from the end of her nose with brilliant green eyes and the skin at her temples and upper cheeks red giving the illusion that her eyes are bleeding. Her hair is wild and full around her face. Blinking slowly, she slides her tongue over her red lush lips.

"Ummmmmm," she whirrs at him.

He straightens his arms putting added distance between them, so he can think more clearly. His breath is now coming in short scatatto bursts with his lungs still refusing to open fully.

A pair of leathery black wings rise up from behind her, and she grins at him.

He lets her go. *This cannot be. A fury.* A guardian of the underworld boundaries. *How can this be?* His mouth opens, but no sound comes out. He tries again to put forth his question to her about how this has happened. Nothing.

A glint of cold steel bursts outward towards him from below her breast. It stops inches away from him, and blood spurts across his chest and face. She makes a raspy gasp looking away from Will and down at the sword just as it pulls back through her disappearing from view. She drops to her knees returning to the Hallie he knows.

His chest ignites with pain and numbness all at the same time. The confusing symptoms spread outward when he kneels down to hold her putting his hand over her wound in vain. The blood flows past his fingers spilling onto the ground in a crimson pool.

She looks up at him with a watery gaze before going limp. Her staring eyes darken. The ground around her begins to shift and pull her down. He clutches her to keep her from being pulled under when he sees the pair of polished shoes just behind where she had stood.

A steady drip of blood smacks at the ground next to one of the shoes. Will's eyes lift to see the tip of a blood-stained sword and, as his eyes rise up the steely blade, he sees a delicate blue jay feather lashed to the hilt of the sword. His own sword. In Paimon's hand.

Red eyes blaze and lips curl upward. He is gloating and, with his free hand, he raises his fedora. He returns the hat to his head and stands statue-like. Waiting.

Will's face contorts wet with tears, and he lunges forward without thinking. Paimon shoots his hand out and upward with a single slender finger raised. Its result is immediate, and Will cannot move. His veins bulge against strained muscles, and his nares flare trying to fill hungry lungs, but he cannot break the invisible grip. The slender pale finger waves back and forth, and Will slumps down in defeat.

Paimon turns his outstretched hand palm up and blows. A puff of blue jay feathers spurts outward fluttering down in front of Will before igniting and turning into ash.

Paimon disappears, and Will looks down as the last ripple of earth comes to rest. All that remains of Hallie is her blood on his hands, face, and chest. He closes his eyes as scorching pain pushes up from his chest to his throat. The dirt resists his fingers trying to dig into it. A primal wail escapes as he raises his head upward letting the agony rip through his body.

Piercing howls from coyote off in the distant hills jolt Will, and he gasps. A dull thud kerplunks as the empty cola bottle falls onto the concrete slab wobbling away. He squints into the darkness beyond the moon's bright glow. Long shadows stretch across the ground without revealing what time it is. His chest wall is pounded by his racing heart and each hyperventilated breath burns his throat and lungs. Sweat rolls down his face, and he looks down at his hands. They are clean. His shirt is buttoned.

He swallows hard and forces himself to slow his breathing. *It was a dream. Or, was it?* He grips his head in his hands trying to pull himself together. *If Paimon saw Hallie at the funeral and recognized her soul from Fayerdale in 1928, it would not take him long to make a connection now. In 1958. Perhaps the dream is a warning.*

Standing, his knees wobble, but a few paces around the patio allow him to collect himself, and he sprints towards the Ridge's cabin cutting through the McCaffrey property. He feels a sudden flutter in his chest, and he stops to look at a lit second floor window briefly wondering how Dillion is doing. Suffering for those left behind in death's wake can be overwhelming. Will's mouth goes dry, and he drops his head grasping the back of his neck with his hands. He has always wished he could have found a way to give his father comfort after the curse had been set during his original life in 1720

Williamsburg. That first harvest stole him from his father without explanation or even a body to mourn over.

He brushes away the cobweb of memories—it has all been replayed in his head more times than he can count. He moves on across the field behind the McCaffrey house and races into the woods where he almost runs into Drew about twenty feet into the trail.

"Will?"

"Yes." Will stops and catches his breath. His brow furrows when he sees Drew who lives on the opposite side of town, but he feels pressed to move on, and does not ask any questions.

"Is everything okay?"

"Not sure. I have to go. Sorry." Will turns to leave slowing the pace.

"Anything I can help with?" Drew calls after him.

"No, I have it. Thanks."

Will doesn't give Drew a second thought. He is grateful for the well-cleared path as the moonlight barely filters through the forest's canopy. The trail takes a steep downward slope, and he rushes into the hollow towards the house.

A miniature spark and flame ignite from the porch of the house, and he stops short of the steps. Odina's face is illuminated as she reaches over to light a lantern sitting on a small table near her rocking chair.

"Will I heard ya coming down offa tha hill like a mule bein' chased by a horde o' bees. What's got ya all fired up boy?" She rocks slowly back and forth. The glow of the lantern light spills out onto the porch and against the front of the house.

"Miss Ridge." The words steal his effort to control his breathing.

"Odina's fine boy."

"Yes ma'am…, Odina." *I did not think this through.*

She steadily rocks waiting for him to provide an explanation.

"Odina, I apologize for calling so late…"

"It be near midnight I'm thinkin'."

"Yes, ma'am. I apologize for calling so extremely late at night…"

"Ya know, boy, ya don't talk much like tha folk from round these parts."

"No ma'am, I am not from around here."

"I'm thinkin' that be what I just said. Maybe ina different way, but same thing none tha less."

Will rolls his shoulders back. His mouth is dryer than the parched ground at the Phlegethon's banks. The rumors surrounding her and Azure begin to dance tauntingly in his thoughts, and he wonders if Odina is stalling for some reason. There is a rustling at the edge of the woods, but he forces himself to focus on the conversation. "Odina, forgive me. I came because I had…"

"Aye, I'm know'n why yar here." She cuts him off keeping her steely blue eyes fixed on him. "I'm thinkin' our conversation will be goin' a might bit better, if ya go on in thar and see for yarself that she's safe."

Will scratches his jaw.

She nods her head towards the cabin door. "By tha big window to tha right. It's tha coolest spot in thar. Go on in and see for yarself. Then ya come on back here for a bit."

He steps onto the porch hesitating as he reaches for the doorknob. She nods at him, and he turns the knob opening the door.

There is a soft glow from an oil lamp and a soft trickle of water underneath the floorboards from the spring where water is drawn. Will glances around the room seeing the large window with moonlight shining through and onto a small cot where Hallie is sleeping. He closes his eyes and breathes his first easy breath since his dream.

The amulet pouch is in her hand. He crouches by the cot, and her eyes flicker open and closed. She turns to her side facing him and mutters, "Liam?"

He lays his hand over hers with the amulet pouch, and a faint glow competes with the lamp and moonlight. Her skin is smooth against the back of his fingers as he glides them along her jaw. "Soon, Hallie, soon."

She smiles. Her breathing is relaxed, and she contently sleeps.

*I have to find a way to help her remember.* He steals a few moments to be close and looks up at the brightly colored scarves that make a valance for the window. Shiny sequins sewn into the fabric sparkle as the fabric billows with the gentle breeze. Hallie is sleeping on an ornately carved bench that is made up into very comfortable-looking bedding. The entire room is decorated with finely crafted wood furnishings and brightly colored fabrics. Crystals of various colors hang down from the lantern above the kitchen table refracting colorful sparkles of light throughout the room. There are potted plants and stacks of books about the room as well. He sees a heavy wooden door towards the back and wonders about the rumored cave behind the house. A chill rises up his neck, and he shrugs it away while turning his attention back to Hallie. He kisses her on the cheek and walks away.

Back on the porch, Odina remains slowly rocking in her chair. A symphony of night sounds surrounds them.

"Thank you Odina." He steps towards the edge of the porch.

"Aye." She nods at him and motions to the floor. "Let us sit a spell."

He obliges taking a seat on the porch. Peepers chirp in harmony with the crickets, and Will sees the cause of the rustling in the woods he had heard earlier—a red fox. It moves into the clearing with stealth towards Odina's hen house.

She turns to Will. "Tell me how ya know tha girl."

He hesitates and reluctantly looks away from the fox. "She was with Azure at the '77 this morning. I met her there."

Odina twists her lips. "Aye, a chance meeting in tha morning, a couple hours of socializing this afternoon, and then yar all fired up a racin' over here in tha middle of tha night ta thank her for a nice day?" She scoffs. "I'm thinkin' that fox's intentions are less obvious then that fib."

He clears his throat avoiding eye contact with her.

Her chair rocks rhythmically as she considers him. Suddenly there is a loud ruckus in the hen house. Will looks in the direction of the noise feeling the need to chase the fox from the hens. He looks back up at Odina. She is undeterred. She glances from Will to the hen house in response to his concern, but only briefly.

A laugh catches in his throat, and he shakes his head weighing the possibilities for deception that sit before him. *I barely know her, so it makes no sense why I feel compelled to tell her the truth.* He rubs his hands on his thighs and looks out into the clearing. Peace is restored. The fox is trotting back into the woods with a hen in its mouth, and a trail of feathers in its wake. Dozens of lighting bugs flicker brief bursts of light while they float in a gentle breeze that also wafts the sweet scent of holly blossoms across the porch. He shifts his weight uncharacteristically deciding to ignore the many years spent guarded and hunted.

"I know her from before coming to Ferrum." He pauses clearing his throat. "There was an accident. She had almost drowned in a pond near where I lived. I revived her. It was uncertain that she would survive, but she was strong. We got to know each other and became close. I care…," he pauses looking up into those icy blue eyes, and his voice breaks as he continues. "I love her. I thought she was lost to me until I saw her today. We have a connection. A bond so to speak that draws us together across time. I am not from here Odina, but neither is she. We are neither from here nor from this time." He pauses and his jaw tightens as he second-guesses talking to her.

Suddenly, a new thought strikes him. A hunch. He lifts his jaw tilting his head to release the strong-hold of his muscles. "Odina, could it be you already know all this. If so, why are you toying with me?"

She does not hesitate and leans far over towards him. "Let it be clear ta ya boy. I do not take ta games. Thar's no toyin' with ya by *me*." She stands abruptly sending her chair into a chaotic sway. Her nostrils flare, and she looks down at him from her nose. She bites down on her lip and sucks in air with a chirp. "I'm a might bit dry. Let me pull us each a glass of water from tha spring." With that she walks into the house leaving Will with his thoughts.

He slowly shakes his head. The lamplight provides a soft glow and, for the first time, Will takes notice of a crystal sitting on the small table next to Odina's now quiet rocker. It is about three inches tall and about half as wide. A clear pale green pyramid shape sits atop a more irregular base that is a milky pink hue. He stares at it for a moment feeling himself calm and his frustrations spill from his mind.

A few moments later, Odina is back with two glasses of water handing one to Will. The glass slides in his hand from the condensation accumulating on its surface. He tightens his grip and takes a long refreshing drink. He thanks her.

She nods before taking her seat and drinks from her glass. After setting the glass on the table, she adjusts the lamplight and sits back to resume her rocking.

Will watches the face of Odina Ridge with her hair pulled back from her wrinkled olive complexion. Earrings stretch her ear lobes while bobbing to and fro with her rocking. Her crystal blue eyes, however, are her most distinct feature with a spark of mischief.

Reaching into a pocket on her apron she withdraws a blue jay feather with a delicate ribbon tied around its thin quill. Color drains from his skin when she leans forward bringing the feather within his reach. The feather blurs as he looks past it to her face. Motioning her her hand, she urges him to accept the feather.

A hint of defeat washes over him, and his shoulders fall. The feather's reminder of his mortality and certain return to the underworld is unsettling, yet he reaches for it then stops just millimeters from her hand before finally accepting it.

He twirls it between his fingers. The blue jay feather signifies an ending, but it also gives promise of a return. *There can be no beginning without an ending.* He remembers Hallie's account of the angel song from Fayerdale. A black thread is tied to it. Experience tells him that it warns of tragedy for those around him. If it is someone outside the circle, he or she will have at least a tie to someone in the Circle of Souls. It is the same color ribbon for the harvest where he lost his cousin and their friend forever.

Yellow, like the one in Fayerdale, would have held promise of a tethered soul surviving him as Sadie had done. He looks at Odina thinking he sees a flicker of pity in her eyes before the hardness quickly returns.

"I do not understand. Why do you have this? What do you know of it?"

She shrugs. "I know nothin' of it. It was sitting on tha table when I went in ta get tha water, and I sensed it was intended for ya. It seems it is."

He swallows thickly and puts the feather in his shirt pocket. Pausing, he realizes the normal anxiety he feels when the feather presents itself is nowhere to be found. His eyes are drawn to the pyramid-shaped crystal.

She lifts it off the table holding it on her palm between them. "Apophylite." She studies the crystal as though it is the first time she has seen it. "It has been handed down through tha generations of my family originally coming from Poona, India. It's mighty powerful on its own accord, but when it's kept close ta one with magical blood its potential is untold."

"What magic does it hold Odina?" *Why is her mention of magic not bothering me?*

"The crystal holds many powers. It helps form connections ta tha spiritual plan. It is a very powerful crystal for deep peaceful stillness and quieting of tha mind for dream recollection. Apophylite calms tha nerves by releasin' suppressed emotions. This crystal relieves mental blockage along with negative thoughts helpin' uncertainties ta be tolerated an possibilities appreciated. But more importantly, it lets a sharin' of tha minds occur—not philosophically but literally. It is this characteristic of tha crystal I'm wantin' ta share with ya Will." She motions him to take it.

Will stares at the crystal. His mouth goes dry again, and he finishes off his water. He starts to reach for the crystal and stops. *Even innocent-appearing objects can have malevolent properties.* Experience from the underworld triggers hesitation. He searches Odina's eyes for any sign of betrayal, but they hold their secrets well. Drawing in a deep breath through his nose, he accepts the crystal. A tingling sensation plays along his hand, but it is just his nerves. Nothing. *What a bobolyne, William, it is just a piece of mineral. Calm yourself.*

He looks back to Odina intending to return the crystal to her. She has sat back in her chair resuming a wax and wane of movement. Will blinks. It seems she is in slow motion with a kaleidoscope frame surrounding her. He leans back against a porch post.

"That thar crystal is a vessel. It contains its own power ta be sure and, at a time of my choosing, it will be tha means that I pass my own magic onta my next o'kin. If ya are obliging, I'd like ta use it ta help tell ya about my beginins as I see 'em. I figure I'm owin' it ta ya because it is a tale of yar own beginins as ya have come ta know life since that first time ya walked on this earth."

*Wait. What is that you say? Did I say that out loud, or am I just thinking it?* The crystal is blunting his usual rise to arm himself. His racing thoughts slow, and the boundaries of his mind begin to blur. It is like falling through a realm passage in the Mesu. He nods his ascension, but she has already begun.

Odina's voice becomes less harsh as she settles into the tone of storyteller. "Yar curse truly has nothin' ta do with ya comin' and agoin' on this here Earth. Ya was meant ta die. Die and be done with. Ya was ta be a one-time portal between tha underworld and ours for tha nefarious Demon King. One time only. Tha part about ya comin' and agoin' be partly my fault. I am ashamed ta admit it, but I was young with little knowledge of tha ways of tha world—tha mundane or celestial. It was then in tha year 1720 that my family had settled just outside tha reach of tha colonist in tha main place of tha Virginia Colony. It was tha seventh summer I had spent there, and it was tha summer I came ta know two Gadji—non-Romany—girls. They was my age with magical blood coursing through their veins unbeknownst ta them or me, and its power—I come ta realize over tha years— surpassed that of my own. We was destined ta be friends. But we were ignorant ta who else would become entrapped within tha threads of fate tying us together that had been spun by tha Sisters of Fate. We were carefree and young and did not give such things any thought.

"I was considered a magical prodigy by my clan given tha circumstances of my birth. Seventh child of seven daughters in tha seventh year of a new century. So, I was not raised like other Romany girls. I was raised ta honor the family as sacred ta be sure, but the usual matrimonial preparations were not part of it. My life was carefree, and I was allowed privileges normally unheard of for a girl—even a boy—my age. My strong will took full advantage of it…"

The kaleidoscope frame begins to shift and swirl, and Odina is regressing back to a young girl. Will finds himself turning the crystal over and over in his hand. His pupils dilate, and he is pulled, physically, into Odina's tale.

# CHAPTER 5
## 1720, Opus

"Odina. Where are ya going?" her mother, Misha, shouts from the door of the vardo. It is the finest wagon in the caravan with plush furnishings and a brightly painted exterior. The camp is set up with the vardos forming an encircled space for social gatherings and group work endeavors. Misha's brilliant steel blue eyes stare sternly at her daughter.

Odina turns on her heel impatiently. "Daj, I told ya already. I am going ta meet up with Beattie and Dot at tha sweets shop. Dat gave me a farthin'."

"You watch yourself in that place, and do not be late coming back."

"I will," Odina calls back as she heads out of the camp into the woods. Her uncle's dogs run behind her nipping at her heels. "Scat ya mongrels before I hex you!"

"Oh, my. Would you really do that to those innocent creatures?"

Odina looks up into the face of the mixed-blood Pamunkey man they call Old Benjamin. He is leading the copper-colored mare that her Uncle Mihai had helped to doctor seven years ago during the first summer they camped here. The two men forged a friendship generally unheard of for a Romany and colonist. It is not unusual for Old Benjamin to visit the camp throughout the summer while they are here, or for Mihai to visit with Old Benjamin at White Plantation. They both are inventors, artificers, and lovers of fine animals. They work on various projects of interest together throughout the summer.

"Uh, Old Benjamin. I dinna see ya." She steps up to pat the mare's neck. "Acacia is lookin' fine. Uncle Mihai will be happy ta see ya and tha mare. He has spoken of ya both during our travels this past year."

Benjamin nods with a smile looking beyond her at the now retreating pack of dogs. He looks back down at her. "You have grown young one, but none-the-less you take care in your travels between here and the capital. It is not always safe."

"Yes sir, I will." She pets Acacia once again and is off. *I hope they don't think I have changed my mind about meeting them.* She frets while she stops at an old holly tree along the way stooping to push away a layer of dirt, and she lets out a yelp as the sharp point of a holly leaf sticks her finger. She pulls the leaf off tossing it aside and continues her task revealing a soft leather pouch with a cross within a heart within a circle pressed into it. Grabbing her treasure, she runs off towards the edge of the woods, across a field, and onto a side street of Williamsburg.

Her eyes dart in all directions as she takes care to avoid all the gadji heeding her mother's warnings of their cruelty towards her kind. She finds the two sisters waiting patiently for her near Bruton's Parish graveyard sitting below a live oak. Their blond hair is a contrast to Odina's own pitch-black curls, and they are dressed in simple cotton dresses with hems that fall just above the ground. Each has on a white smock over her dress that, on closer inspection, shows their attraction to the outdoors and adventures in the fields and woods. Odina rushes up to them, all three look about, and then at each other with a conspirator's grin.

"Did you bring it?" Dot whispers as Beattie looks expectantly.

"Yes, the bujo is here." She lifts the leather pouch.

"The bu—what?" Beattie asks with a furrowed brow.

"Um, medicine bag. For special keepings." Odina finds a satisfactory description. "Did you bring tha spell and twine?"

Dot nods. Her eyes look serious as she taps the pocket of her smock.

"And tha herbs?"

Beattie holds up a plain cloth sack.

Odina surveys their perimeter satisfied to see no colonist near. "Let us go then." She reaches a hand out to both girls leaning back against their weight to help them stand, and the three run off back towards the woods.

A cicada's song with it crescendo-decrescendo whirl cuts through the thick summer heat, as Odina leads the way taking them to a small clearing inside the woods. They must pull their way through the thick shrubbery and briars growing along its periphery. Beattie's smock gets hung up on a barb, and she gives it a yank leaving a small tear in the fabric.

In the center of the clearing sunlight filters down through the trees above, and the floor is covered in a thick layer of leaves and moss. It is a secret place that Odina shared with them shortly after they met.

"What needs to be done first?" Dot asks while Beattie twists herself back and forth letting her arms flay out to the sides. Dot turns and narrows her eyes. "Take care Beattie. You do not want to spill the herbs."

"Beattie." Odina draws her attention and kneels in the center of the clearing letting her brightly colored skirt flare out. "Go and spread tha herbs from tha sack around the edge of tha clearin'. Make sure ya go all tha way round and then come back here ta sit."

Dot kneels down near Odina, and they wait for Beattie who skips around the periphery throwing the flowery herbs up into the air. The herbs drift down leaving a bright border of yellow, purple, white, and pink. Beattie skips over to them stopping quickly when she sees their solemn looks. She smooths out her smock and ceremoniously kneels down completing the small circle.

"Now." Odina tries on the mysterious-sounding voice she often hears her mother and aunts use when they provide a reading for the gadji that secretly visit their camp. "Dot, let us see tha spell, so we can practice up on it before starting."

Dot pulls the parchment and three pieces of red twine from her pocket laying them in the middle of their circle. They practice until they have it memorized.

"Very well then, Dot, lay out a piece of tha twine stretching it straight, but so it lays across tha invisible lines between us like a cross."

Odina turns her bujo end-up and a short decorative piece of iron work falls out. It has a round crystal encased in thin bands of iron that wrap around it with the long ends meeting below the crystal twisting around each other to spiral downward to a sharp point. Sunlight coming down from the center of the clearing hits the crystal sending rays of rainbow colors out and all around them. Beattie and Dot look up with mouths agape.

"We take tha point of the athame and make a cut in each of our palms, and th..."

"What?" Beattie interrupts her with a high-pitched squeal. "Nobody said nothing about bleeding. What is that a-thay—thing anyway?" She fidgets with her smock hem as she looks from Odina to Dot.

"A-THAM-AY," Odina says slowly. "It is tha only way for it ta be done. If we are ta be sisters in tha blood for all eternity, we gotta mix our blood."

Dot reaches over and lays a hand on Beattie's shoulder. "'Tis alright, Beattie. It only hurts for a minute, and then it is done."

Beattie looks at her sister. Her lower lip starts to tremble.

"Do not be a baby." Dot looks Beattie straight in the eye.

A crow lets out a harsh caw from somewhere in the distance. Beattie flinches, but she does not break eye contact with Dot. She tightens her lip to steady it and gives a single nod. She holds out both her palms and looks to Odina.

Odina gently takes ahold of Beattie's hand giving her a quick look in the eye before taking a deep breath and raking the tip of the Athame across Beattie's palm drawing a line that quickly fills in with blood. A single tear falls from Beattie's eye, but she doesn't move away. Odina passes the athame to Dot, and Beattie's other hand is marked in a similar manner. All take a turn until the deed is done. With the final cut made, Odina stabs the athame's point into the soft dirt and through the parchment with the written spell. The crystal handle is smudged with blood but continues to refract the light.

"Okay," Odina says betraying the slightest quiver in her voice. "Now, we join hands and say tha spell." They grasp hands while blood spills down towards their wrists.

All three gaze down at the athame and begin to recite the spell

*With this blood we tether our souls as only sisters' souls are bound*
*With this blood we make a promise to stand together.*
*With this blood we three shall be recreated as one for all time.*

They pause holding on tightly to one another's hands. The crystal in the athame brightens and its scattered rays of light organize into three multicolored beams that shift downward pointing at the joined girls' hands. Their eyes widen. Odina is the first to recover, and she nods for them to complete the spell. They move their hands down slightly, blood slowly drips onto the twine darkening its already red color.

*With this thread our union holds true.*
*With this thread we bind not just hands but hearts.*
*With this thread we shall live as sisters honoring not just self but all.*

The twine rises towards their joined hands wrapping around them while the beams of rainbow lights brighten. Slowly, they raise their hands upward and the light follows them. The flow of dripping blood stops and rises upward disappearing between their hands. Light from the anthame withdraws, the twine slowly unwinds and falls to the ground, and the girls release their hands inspecting their now healed palms. They stroke their healed wounds and look to one another awestruck for a moment.

Odina reaches over and picks up a piece of twine and motions Beattie to put her foot into the circle. Odina ties the string around Beattie's ankle. Dot does the same for Odina, and Beattie for Dot. Just as the last knot is tied, they hear hurried footsteps coming towards them. A pair of doves startled by the noise fly up from the brushy boundary of the clearing settling onto a tree branch above them.

The girls look at each other with ashen faces knowing any semblance suggesting witchcraft, even for a child, could mean punishment as severe as death. The footsteps are right next to the dense border. The girls scramble to hide on the opposite side beneath a particularly full shrub. Just as Beattie's foot pulls out of view a young woman and man make their way into the clearing moving into the patch of sunshine at the center right next to the parchment that Odina has left impaled into the earth.

The woman's foot taps against the athame, and she looks down curiously. "What is it, Daniel?"

He is not easily distracted from her beauty. Her flaxen hair is pulled up in a simple bun behind her head, her skin is flushed from their run through the woods, and her violet eyes sparkle.

"Daniel." She exhales shaking her head with a quick laugh, and she bends down grasping the crystal handle pulling it up out of the ground. A gentle breeze catches the parchment blowing it away before she can reach for it as well. She looks at the athame. "'Tis beautiful, but I wonder how it got here. I thought we were the only ones who know of this place." She starts to put it into her bag and accidently pricks her finger with the tip. "Ow," She gasps jerking her bloodied finger back.

Daniel grasps ahold of her hand putting her finger in his mouth and then kisses her. "Better?"

She looks up at him through thick lashes and breaks into a smile. Reaching up she draws him close by the back of his neck and kisses him. The gesture is ardently returned.

Odina, Beattie, and Dot lay below the shrub quivering yet wide-eyed by the couple's tender embrace and passionate kiss. It is a brief moment though, as there is yet another disturbance in the woods just outside the sheltered clearing. The girls shrink further into the shrub's shelter.

Daniel grasps the young woman's hand in an attempt to get them quickly out of the clearing. They are heading straight for the girls, but do not make it before two men on horseback break through the thicket and intrude on the once quiet space.

The men quickly jump down from their mounts. One grabs Daniel and the other the young woman. Before Daniel can react, he is struck viciously in the stomach. The blow snaps him forward only to be met with an upper cut to the jaw bashing him to his knees. Daniel's head snaps to the side when a third blow to his face knocks him out. The man gives him a severe kick in the side then turns his attention to the young woman.

Her face is streaked with tears, and Odina can see her trembling all over. The brute walks towards her taking his glove off, and he raises his hand slapping her so harshly on the face she is knocked to the ground. His crony is jolted and motions to help her up, but one look from the cruel man causes the second to stand down. Crumpled on the ground, her shoulders shake with her sobs.

Towering over her, he commands, "Look at me." The harsh voice resonates in the clearing. Odina cringes and puts her arms around Beattie and Dot offering and accepting comfort.

The girls watch as the woman pulls her resolve together and raises her eyes up towards her assailant. A welt and bruise have begun to form already where she was struck. Her lower lip trembles, and her eyes avert to look at Daniel who lays unmoving on the ground. Odina can see his chest rise and fall, so she knows that Daniel is only unconscious. A sigh of relief escapes her, and Dot shoots a look her way obviously fearful her sigh had been too loud. Luckily, no one else notices, and they turn their attention back to the commotion in the clearing.

"Look at me," the man commands. "You are not to look his way again. I am your father, and you will not disobey me." The man's voice is full of malice, and she quickly looks back up at him forcing herself to stand up. She straightens and lifts her chin.

"Melinda, God help me not to kill you right now. If you jeopardize my efforts over this past year, even God almighty will be no help to you. You leave here now. Be sure to take the less traveled streets home and stay in the house until your face recovers."

She falters.

"Go, now." He growls and grabs her arm pulling her towards the bordering shrubs. She steals a look at Daniel and, at that moment, she catches Odina's eye seeing the girls for the first time. Her eyes widen, but she recovers and turns disappearing through the thicket into the woods.

The man walks back over to his horse gathering the reins when the other speaks up. "What would you like to do with him Mister Holt?"

Holt looks over at the still unconscious Daniel and sighs. "Nothing for now. He is Harry White's nephew."

The second man twists his hands. "But, sir…" He hesitates.

"It is not a well-known fact. The boy lives with Old Benjamin, White's field manager. I tell you this. If that boy interferes with my plans for forging a profitable relationship with Harry White, I will personally see to it he meets a painful and untimely death." He purses his lips frowning as if a foul smell were in the air. Turning quickly, he mounts his horse. "Leave him. He is still breathing from what I can tell and, when he comes to, he can find his way home." With that Holt cracks a leather crop over the back of his horse causing it to lurch forward and move out of the clearing.

The second man hesitates a moment looking around the clearing. Odina crouches back further under the shrub afraid to breathe. He gives a final look at Daniel and mounts his horse giving it a nudge in the sides moving it out of the clearing as well.

The girls let out a collective sigh of relief and scramble out from under the shrub. Dot tears a strip of fabric from the bottom of her smock and hands it to Beattie. "Go wet this in the stream just over yonder." Beattie looks up at her with mouth agape. "'Tis safe Beattie. They are gone." Dot reassures her with a gentle smile.

Odina and Dot walk over to where Daniel lays kneeling beside him. He has a cut above his left eye and blood is coming from his nose as well. Odina looks across Daniel at Dot. She is worried for the young couple, but she is more worried about the athame. It belongs to her mother, and she has to get it back. It feels as though ants are crawling all over her, so when Beattie returns, and Dot starts the business of cleaning up Daniel's face, she asks Dot if she will be able to help Daniel with just Beattie to assist.

"I need ta go find that Melinda, and get my daj's athame back, or she will peel my flesh from my bones."

Beattie tucks her chin in with eyebrows arched. "It just be an expression, Beattie." Odina reaches over touching her arm, and Beattie relaxes.

"Yes, we will be fine," Dot assures her. "We have seen our mother do healing many times, and Anne Mercer, the mid-wife we have been staying with, has taught us a bit too. Go and get your mother's property but take care. That woman's father is a horrible sort of man."

# CHAPTER 6
## Twist

Odina reaches the back entrance to the Holt household. She knows the house location because Mister Holt had been responsible for the public flogging of one of her cousins two summers ago. Odina's mother made it a point to show Odina the house warning her to never go near it, and now she stands within feet of it. The adrenaline rush that got her to the house is now refueled by fear that grabs at her middle pushing bile to the back of her throat. She looks up at the heavy oak door convincing herself to knock just as the door opens suddenly, and her racing heart nearly screeches to a halt. The nagging bile drops to the pit of her stomach. A young woman Odina recognizes to be Grissell Mercer, the mid-wife's daughter, stands before her.

Both step back from the other, and Grissell is the first to speak. "Odina? What are you doing here?"

Odina's mouth opens, but no sound comes out. Her tongue is like sandpaper inside her mouth. She tries again starting with a croak before she manages to get out understandable words. "I need ta see Melinda Holt. It be pressing business I have with her."

Grissell scoffs, as she starts to step over the threshold to pull the door shut, but she is cut short when Odina pushes against the door keeping it from closing.

"Odina, are you daft girl? Mister Holt will have you skinned alive, if he sees your Gypsy presence in that house. You need to go—now."

Odina pushes harder against the door. "Grissell, I gotta get in thar ta see Miss Melinda. If not, I will be murdered by my own daj ta be sure. But, know this, even though it be my daj doing tha deed, it be ya that was tha cause."

She stares down at her for a moment. Odina knows that

Grissell is a freed slave but holds no additional power than any other dark-skinned woman in the colony. Grissell presses her lips together. "Well, Momma had me bring some soothing herbs over here saying she had a premonition that Miss Melinda was gonna need them. Maybe I can convince the kitchen maid that I remembered that Momma told me specifically to give the herbs to Miss Melinda myself."

Odina breathes a sigh of relief. They step into the house, and Grissell pulls Odina off to the side taking a scullery kitchen maid's skirt off a hook on the wall handing it to Odina. "Put that on over your flashy skirt. I will not get myself flogged for having you in here. We gonna be in big trouble if Mister Holt shows up and sees us."

Odina complies quickly.

Grissell skillfully convinces the kitchen maid who still looks warily at Odina but lets them go. Once at Melinda's door they argue about Odina going in alone. The stand-off ends when Grissell Huffs out a breath and stomps off to sit at the end of the hall.

Odina lightly taps on the door and peers around it when she hears Melinda beckoning her to come in. Melinda is sitting at a dressing table with a fine mirror before her. She sees Odina in the reflection and turns to look at her directly. Odina winces in sympathy at Melinda's bruised and swollen face and walks up to her stopping short of reaching out to touch her face.

Melinda clears her throat. "You were in the clearing in the woods."

Odina nods.

"Tell me. Is my Daniel safe?"

"Yes Miss. My sisters are tending ta him."

A burdened sigh escapes Melinda, and her eyes fill with tears. Odina sets the basket of herbs onto the dressing table and picks up a finely embroidered handkerchief. She hands it to Melinda who flashes a shaky smile and dabs at her eyes.

"Miss Melinda," Odina hesitates. "I…come ta request ya

return my athame."

Melinda drops her hands into her lap and cocks her head to the side. "Your what?"

"Tha crystal-handled knife ya found in tha clearin'. It belongs to my daj, uh my mother, and I have ta get it back ta her."

Melinda studies her, and her eyes graze over the ill-fitting skirt while taking note of Odina's hair, eyes, and olive complexion. "Home? And, where exactly is that? I do not recall ever seeing you in the capital."

Odina squirms realizing she can't lie about this, but the truth might put her in danger. Before she speaks, however, Melinda answers her own question.

"Never mind, you are one of the Gypsies."

"Rom."

"Pardon?"

"Rom. I am Romany."

"And, what does that mean? What is your name, and where are you from?"

"My name is Odina, and it is not where, but from who am I from." Odina stands before her with a straight back. She is proud of her heritage and, even in the threat of potential danger, she will not allow it to be disrespected. Her people may be wanderers, but she comes from an esteemed clan of Romany artisans, magicians, and impresarios.

Melinda bites the inside of her cheek and eyes Odina. She takes her bag from the top of her dressing table and withdraws the athame gingerly. Her dried blood remains at its needle-like tip from where it bit her earlier. "Is this what you are talking about?"

Odina's fingers tingle while she maintains eye contact with Melinda not wishing to reveal how strongly she wants to grab the knife and run away. She senses that the gadji is not going to give it up too easily.

"Yes, that be it." She swallows as though an appetizing meal has been set before her.

"What were you and the two fair-haired girls doing with this in the woods? And, did I hear you call them sisters?" Melinda's voice is not scolding, but it holds an air of authority that Odina doesn't like. Her eye twitches. Still, she is careful to remain respectful knowing she is in a vulnerable position.

Odina squirms unsure if Melinda can be trusted, but she is going to have to give a little in order to get what she wants. She wets her bottom lip. "Yes…, blood sisters."

Melinda nods looking at Odina from the end of her nose. She takes a slow breath in. "And, what were you up to?

Odina twists the scullery maid skirt between her fingers. "We were promising our bond of sisterhood."

"With witchcraft?" Melinda lowers her voice bending closer to Odina as she glances beyond her towards the door.

Odina doesn't want to answer the question but knows that it has been asked to confirm what is already suspected. She blinks her eyes slowly and gives a miniscule nod of her head.

Melinda's eyes shift side to side as she regards Odina's unrevealing face. She bites her lip and sits upright holding the athame up just beyond Odina's grasp. "I want to make a trade."

Odina's heart skips a beat with restrained hope for salvation, and a thin smile comes to her lips. "Tell me more, pretty lady." She hears her father's enticing tone that he uses when bargaining with a customer echo in her ears as she speaks.

"You saw the man in the woods that hurt Daniel."

"And ya as well." Odina glances at Melinda's bruised cheek and swollen eye.

Melinda reaches up touching her face. "Yes, and me, too." She swallows and blinks back a tear. "He is my step-father, and he has been coercing me to entrap a man in order to gain access to the man's wealth."

"Mister White."

Melinda tips her head back and draws her bottom lip in. She nods warily. "While my father and Mister White were on a business trip I often visited the White Plantation per my father's instructions to maintain a tie between our families in his absence." She pauses twirling a ring with a single pearl on her finger for a moment. "Mister White has a pleasant but proud son who was cordial to me during the visits. We did eventually establish a friendship, but a formal one. On one of my visits he introduced me to his 'friend,' Daniel. He explained to me that Daniel had been away staying with his mother's people at the Pamunkey town through the winter, but he recently returned and was staying with the plantation field manager, Old Benjamin."

Odina stands very still. She sees honesty in Melinda's eyes, but knows this is a relatively new quality for this woman of privilege. Something has caused a change in her life.

"I think I fell in love with Daniel the very first time I saw him." She touches her mouth and blushes. "And thankfully, it was the same for him towards me. We began to see more of each other, and he has confided some secrets to me about his family that no one can know."

"Romany's whole existence is secret out of necessity. I would not even reveal this to my new sisters, if you request such secrecy."

Melinda takes ahold of Odina's shoulders. "Yes, secrecy is absolute. Even if a bargain between us for an equitable trade cannot be reached, the secret must be honored."

"Of course, Miss Melinda."

Melinda withdraws her hands and slides them down the front of her bodice landing them in her lap twisting and untwisting her fingers. "Mister White's son, William, and Daniel are the sons of twin brothers married to sisters of mixed Pamunkey and English blood. They are cousins. William's mother died in childbirth with a stillborn daughter and Daniel's parents were killed during a time of unrest between the settlers and natives. He is being raised by the sisters' brother, Old Benjamin. The two cousins are very similar in nature, but Daniel is fairer in complexion and hair color while William carries more of the characteristics of his mother's Pamunkey heritage."

Knowing firsthand what prejudices can be imparted towards unfamiliar people, Romany or not, Odina feels that she knows where Melinda's secret is going.

"The collaboration between settlers and natives in the area has deteriorated again like the time when William was young, and the violent death of his aunt and uncle has left a horrible impression on him. He is a good person Odina, but he lives in fear of his mixed blood being discovered. He fears that his ability to inherit and to be allowed to keep his father's legacy going will be threatened, if his heritage is discovered. He fears this so much so that the entire White family has gone to great lengths to conceal William's true heritage. Even to the extent that Daniel and Old Benjamin conceal their blood ties to the Whites. If William knew that Daniel told me any of this, he would never speak to Daniel again. He does not completely trust me, and he is justified in this sentiment given how I have allowed my step-father to influence me in the past."

"If tha penalties of tellin' this secret are so high, why are ya includin' me in it?

Melinda pauses for a moment and furrows her brow as she considers Odina. "How old are you?"

"I have seen twelve summers."

Melinda clicks her tongue and nods slowly. "I am telling you this because I need your help and helping me means you need to understand the circumstances of my situation."

"Tell me what is needed." Odina sees her desperation and remembers her father telling her there will be no gammon in words spoken out of misery but take caution anyway.

"I need Daniel to be safe. I want him in my life. I want to be his wife—have his children and grow old with him, but my stepfather will never allow this. I know I have to accept it will never be for Daniel and me no matter how painful it is. I can give all of it up, if I know he will be safe. Safe to live his life, find another love, and be happy. I could go forward and do my stepfather's bidding. But, what I know instead is that Daniel will not allow me to be a part of my step-father's plans. He is Mister White's nephew and, not only does he love me, but he holds an obligation to his family. I know that my stepfather will kill him, if he interferes. I feared that it was going to happen today. I never want to get that close to such a tragedy again."

"If Daniel could be made safe, and ya could be with him, would ya defy yar stepfather?"

Melinda looks at her and drops her gaze to her twisting hands. "Yes, of course, but it will never be. My stepfather is determined and too powerful."

"All I want is tha athame back. I am willing ta offer ya two options. Ya may choose one in exchange for it."

Melinda sits back in her chair.

"Tha first is a bindin' spell that would tether yar soul ta Daniel's. This would strengthen yar ethereal existence, give him protection in that yar vitality would support his life force, and his yars. Tha risk with this is that for tha first fortnight after ya consume tha spell's elixir the vitality is neither yars nor his. It is a test and a price for tha gift before the eternal connection becomes fixed. If somethin' happens ta ya—illness, injury, death—it happens ta him and in tha reverse. Only, tha two of ya fight it tagether. Tagether is stronger. Ya would be able ta stay tagether.”

"And, my second option?"

"A dissolution spell that removes his love for ya from his heart forever. He will not love ya and will not be aware of any deception ya hold towards Mister White. It will be as though ya never existed for him."

"And the risk?"

"No risk—only a price."

"And that would be?"

"Yar feelings for him will always remain."

"But, he will be safe?"

Odina nods.

Melinda doesn't give it a second thought. "I want him to be safe and free from heartbreak."

Odina furrows her eyebrows. "Are ya sure that is what ya want? Ya can be with him, if ya choose tha other option."

"I cannot risk his safety even if we have a unified strength. Who is to say my stepfather will not find a way to harm him even if our souls and vitality are linked? My stepfather made it clear today that he will end my life, if I betray him. Daniel cannot be kept safe just with tethering his soul to mine. I want the second option." She stretches out her hand to Odina.

Odina takes the knife and places it in her bujo. She doesn't agree with Melinda's choice, but acknowledges the woman's decision.

"What do we do next?"

"I will spell a potion for ya. Ya both must drink it. It must be in a public place during the full moon, and it must be done with both of ya near each other. When the full moon sits in the sky within the fortnight it will be done."

Melinda's brow knits tightly and she frowns. "I will have to give this some thought as to how to arrange it. How can I get in contact with you?"

"I will send my sisters ta ya in three days. They will not raise suspicion talking with ya, if they are seen."

"Agreed."

Odina turns and leaves the room. She looks down the hall at Grissell who is sitting looking out a window next to her chair. Odina stomps a foot on the floor and motions her to come.

Grissell's head jerks in her direction. She narrows her eyes at Odina and huffs but abides. "Don't get bossy with me. You are a little runt and do not forget it." She takes ahold of Odina's hand.

Odina smiles up at Grissell and follows her out of the house. They barely miss Mister Holt's arrival seeing him riding towards the house when they turn the corner onto a side street.

Odina and Grissell part paths as each go in the direction of their respective homes. Odina kicks at stones, and swats branches fretting the entire way back to the clearing. When she arrives, Daniel and her sisters are gone. All that remains is the bloody scrap of fabric from Dot's smock. Odina picks it up from the ground and looks around biting her lip. She opens her bujo removing the athame looking at its blood-stained tip and the blood-stained cloth and rushes to put both in the bujo and returns home.

§

Will blinks finding himself back in 1958 and sitting before Odina on the porch of her cabin once again. Her hand moves to remove the crystal pyramid from his hand. While his peripheral vision clears the symphony of night sounds returns to his ears. He looks around for a moment expecting to see the three little girls standing before him, but there is nothing beyond the reach of the lantern light.

He runs his fingers through his hair. "I do not understand Odina. If you traded with Melinda to sever her connection with Daniel, how are you responsible for anything related to me?"

"Aye so it would seem. When I went back ta tha clearing I found tha second important ingredient for tha spell that I intended ta conjure."

"Second?"

"Tha first was tha dried blood on tha tip of tha athame. Melinda's blood."

"You didn't cast the severing spell, did you?"

"Tha image of tha love in their faces. Her unselfish sacrifice…it moved me. Even at tha tender age of twelve I understood tha power of that kind of love. And, I believe ya now have an understandin' of it as well."

He stares down at his hands. "Uh, yes I suppose I do."

"I went back ta tha camp avoidin' my mother because I knew she would know I had been up ta mischief—and she did, but that be a story for another time. I set ta tha task of casting a bindin' spell similar ta tha ties of sisterhood Dot and Beattie and I conjured just hours before. I put tha power of tha spell inta a skin of wine and hid it until tha time was right."

"During the full moon."

"Aye, and at a time it would be safe for Melinda ta be seen with Daniel."

He grasps the back of his neck. "I am still not seeing how this has anything to do with me."

"Ya and yar friends had gone ta a public ball—a masquerade that last night of yar original life as ya knew it ta be."

Will furrows his brow with concentration. The night he encountered Paimon has always been fuzzy to him. He is amazed how some details in past lives are remembered precisely while others evade him—especially this one. He focuses his thoughts, and Odina holds the pyramid crystal up on the palm of her hand. They were there. At the Raleigh Tavern—Daniel, Matthew Carter, Elias Russell, and Caleb Blake. All very good friends. It was during publick times for Williamsburg. Both court and legislation were in session, so the city was bustling with people.

He and his friends met at the tavern for a masquerade ball that evening. Elias and the theatrical troupe he belonged to were part of the entertainment providing music and frivolity for the gathering. Even a few performers from Odina's clan were there. He can see the crowded Apollo Room in Raleigh Tavern. He uses his mind's eye to look around smiling as he sees the faces of his friends. Melinda Holt was there, but not a part of their group that night. Grissell Mercer was serving and attending to their table.

His face falls and he swallows against a tightening throat. "The wine, the last toast of the night…, but how?"

For the first time ever, he sees the hard shell of Odina's eyes waiver with a pool of moisture. "It was a mistake. Tha night was comin' ta a close. Melinda had been thar stayin' at the periphery not wishin' for any of her stepfather's acquaintances ta see her anywhere near Daniel, but she was desperate ta get him ta drink of tha wine. She did not know it was a bindin' spell. She did not think it would have an impact on tha rest of ya, so she went ta yar table as though she was comin' up ta greet just you. Her connection ta ya and yar father was well-known. A conversation with ya would not raise suspicion. She offered a toast pourin' tha wine herself inta everyone's glass even handin' a portion ta Grissell insistin' she drink as well."

Will stares at her seeing it come into focus. He stands up and holds onto the porch post watching feathers flutter over the grass. The scene plays out before him. "Yes, I recall it now." His speech drags, as it all hits home, and he drops his head wiping sweat from the back of his neck. "Please, please tell me that my cursed life did not twist and capture those of my closest friends because of a young girl's dabbling in an occult version of match-making. Oh, God, where was your mercy for them?"

He can see them all gathered in a corner of the Apollo Room. The last dance had not yet been played when Melinda approached pouring wine and proposing a toast for the last drink of the night. Grissell stood nervously in a corner while Matthew stood close enough for their arms to touch—their secret love has always been a challenge for them. Elias and Caleb were laughing about something Daniel had said just before he noticed Melinda rounding their table. He looked intently at her as she passed filling their glasses. Melinda avoided eye contact with Daniel who stood next to him.

She skirted to the other side of William, and she held her glass up high saying, "The fault, dear friends, is not in the stars but in ourselves that we are underlings." He remembers her amended toast stolen from Shakespeare's *Julius Caesar,* and how they had all taken pause before she gave them a cheerful laugh shrugging it off and bringing her glass to her lips. She looked over the rim of her glass at Daniel, and he beamed raising his glass and drinking. The rest chuckled and followed suit. She set her glass down and walked away.

Will flinches, as Odina's voice interrupts the memory. "All of ya took drink. Melinda dinna know what she had given ta ya. No one, except one able ta see souls, would of known that difference."

Will looks over his shoulder at her. *Yes, it does get worse.* His skin prickles.

"Tha spell tethered tha souls changing them—giving them a common trait of tha bindin' that only a soul-seer would recognize."

"Paimon."

"Aye."

He shakes his head. "The blood, none of us, except Daniel and Melinda gave a blood offering to the spell. How could it have bonded all of us?"

"Aye, it would seem that way, but it's not how it works. Tha blood is a catalyst. It ties a tighter bond ta those making tha offerin,' but when tha spell is put inta drink and is shared willingly, a bond of some degree is formed by all who partake. Ya and Daniel already shared tha blood of family binding ya and he tha strongest and, through tha spell, ta Melinda, too.

The muscles in his back stiffen and he scoffs. "Well, it has been nearly two-hundred and forty years. I would say it welded a powerful union for all in the Circle of Souls."

"Aye," she muses. "Some blood be more potent than others as is some magic."

Will steps off the porch. He presses his lips together. A cloud bank has moved east, and the moon's glow is once again casting shadows across the grassy field. He cannot find it in himself to be angry with her when he knows who is truly to blame. He speaks as he watches the lightening bugs flash their last flickers of the night—dawn approaches.

"It really is not the spell that doomed us as much as it was me….my…murder…curse…whatever it was. The spell, their blood, may have been the catalyst to bind us, but it was my encounter with Paimon during the time of risk—you said a fortnight of vulnerability after the spell was put in motion. Is this so?"

"Aye."

He nods and looks back over his shoulder towards the front door beyond which Hallie sleeps peacefully. "I am going to go Odina. I have to work in the morning." He runs a hand through his hair turning towards her as he walks backward away from the cabin. "Thank you for…for taking care of Hallie…and for your honesty."

She nods her head and slowly rocks her chair.

Will gives her a final look before turning to leave. He startles nearly bumping into Azure. "Oh, so sorry Mister Ridge."

Azure accepts and continues past Will towards the cabin. A hunting knife hangs from his belt, and he has ahold of a dead fox by its back legs. It flaccidly swings back and forth as Azure walks across the clearing stirring up a few of the scattered feathers.

# CHAPTER 7
## Memory

Will shuts the door to his apartment not bothering to switch on the light. The moon remains bright in the early morning hour illuminating his small room. He pulls off his shirt, switches the alarm on for his clock, and lays down on his bed. Thoughts about Hallie sleeping peacefully at the Ridge's cabin swirl in his mind with Odina's words reverberating in his ears, *"Tha image of tha love in their faces. Her unselfish sacrifice…it moved me. Even at tha tender age of twelve I understood tha power of that kind of love. And, I believe ya now have an understandin' of it as well."* The weight of his eyelids eventually overcome his ability to keep them open. His thoughts quiet, and his worn muscles relax while his aching head spins into a dream immediately, as one often does when deprived of sleep.

§

He, as William, is once again in 1720 walking the familiar road towards White Plantation on the outskirts of the capital. Although he cannot remember over-indulging in the distilled spirits during the ball at Raleigh Tavern, his head is reeling. The last toast of the evening was with wine. Despite not finishing his glass, the effect was potent. Daniel also commented on the power of the drink opting to remain in town to sleep it off fearing retribution from Old Benjamin, who did not approve of heavy drinking. William decided to walk home hoping the night air would help to clear his head. It rained most of the evening, but it had turned to a fine mist by the time he left the tavern. The time he shared with his friends and other good-natured colonists was pleasant, and his spirits are high. Approaching the house, he notices a light in the barn. The door to the outer stall is standing open.

"Damn." Acacia must have broken from her stall again. His head has cleared some, but exhaustion has also quickly set in. None the less, he needs to fetch the mare before she gets into mischief.

When he reaches the stall door he takes a step back. One of his father's guest, a traveling church deacon from up north, is standing in the stall.

"Mister Tasker."

His hair is long and pulled away from his face bound with a leather cord behind the nape of his neck. He is of slender build, almost wiry, with an edge to his demeanor. His shirt has the top buttons undone with a cravat hanging loosely around his neck. Instead of a formal jacket, he is wearing a banyan of bright green silk, and the lace from his shirt sleeves hangs over his hands from under the jacket. His boots are shiny and look expensive for a deacon. *And, why the smoky glass spectacles prior to the sun rising?*

William clears his throat. "Sir, I was not expecting to see you."

"Nor I you." Mister Taker's tone suggests otherwise. "Out for a night of frivolity?"

William clenches fists at his side as the judgmental edge of Mister Tasker's voice scrapes across his nerves. He clears his throat. "Yes sir. What has you out in the barn at this hour?"

"Well, I have only just come actually. I heard a commotion from my room and, catching a view of the backside of a chestnut horse as it raced from this stall, I thought I should come out to investigate." He brings a piece of straw up to mash between his teeth.

Will notices his long thin fingers and the tapered nails that extend beyond them. "Yes sir, that would be my mare. I came in to get her halter and lead rope in order to fetch her back. She is a spirited horse, and I want to prevent her getting into any trouble."

Mister Tasker leans against the stall wall in front of where the halter and lead are hanging. "Quite a gathering at the Raleigh Tavern this evening." His voice is smooth like a purr.

William hesitates for a moment irritated by the man's disregard for the urgency he feels to find the mare and get some sleep. He bites the inside of his cheek feeling a warning from the hair standing at attention on his arms. *There was no mention by me of where I have been.* William shifts his weight. "Yes sir, quite a gathering."

"Time spent with close friends?"

"Some."

"Who exactly?"

Sweat is beading up along his hairline, and his heart pounds, yet he feels compelled to answer. "Well sir, there were my good friends Matthew Carter and Caleb Blake. Miss Melinda Holt as well as Daniel Isaacs, and another friend, Elias Russell. I believe our group was being tended to by Grissell Mercer."

"Awe, yes young Grissell." He lifts his nose into the air as if smelling an appetizing meal. "Matthew must have been gratified to have her services available this evening."

The feel of spiders crawling up his neck cannot be ignored, and William rubs the sensation away gazing down at the stall floor. *What can this stranger know of Matthew and Grissell?* The lead and halter are still blocked by Mister Tasker.

"Daniel Isaacs," starts Mister Taker in a bold tone as he slides his spectacles a little lower on his nose. He moves away from the wall and takes a few steps closer to William. "Yes, Daniel—he is really more 'family' then 'friend' now. Is he not?

Your late Uncle Frederick's son, if I am not mistaken. Interesting that he bares his mother's maiden name. I think it is interesting how two cousins can have similar blood mixing—I mean Native and English blood—yet look so very different. What with Daniel so fair in comparison to your own darker appearance." He takes another step closer to William.

William's blood is pounding in his head as his heart continues to hammer away. *Who is this man?* He clenches his jaw and the headache peaks. The stall's air feels stingy as he tries to fill his lungs.

A thin smile comes to Mister Tasker's face. "Oh, tsk tsk William. Be still. I am merely an observant man making an obvious comment to your circumstance." His words are drawl and contemptuous as he looks over the smoked glass lenses on his nose. He takes another step towards William putting him less than an arm's length away.

William remains silent while fear dances all over his nerves paralyzing a rise to action. He thinks he sees a crimson flash in Mister Tasker's eyes, and he rubs the image from his own eyes.

"'Tis alright William. I do not really desire a response from you. Not now." He reaches out in a flash taking ahold of Williams' wrist. "Pity really that it is not your father I am charged to 'work with' so to speak. There is so much more potential for bargaining there, but I think you will come around eventually."

A buzz resonates and intensifies. William turns his head to the side and lifts his chin trying to tone it down. He hears Mister Tasker say something about a chance for redemption while helping him "unlock potentials." Then an intense searing pain ignites at his wrist and rises slowly with excruciating pain towards his elbow. He sees an army of scorpions plunging into his flesh, but he is unable to repel them. They tear and rip at his skin but fall to the floor scrambling up Mister Tasker's trousers' and over his chest disappearing behind his neck. William's knees buckle, and his vision tunnels. He wants to scream out with the pain, but the sound never leaves his mouth.

Just before he loses consciousness, he hears Mister Tasker purr, "I will be back in a fortnight William—for the harvest. You have until then to put things in order."

The darkness framing his vision suddenly expands and all goes black.

Although the air he breathes in is desert-like, William feels cold, and a sticky wetness surrounds him. A raw searing pain paralyzes his right arm, and he opens an eye taking in the blurred stretch of the stall floor before him. Reflexively, he draws his arm to his chest and sees a red stain quickly spreading across his shirt. The blur before him slowly sharpens. His shirt sleeve is shredded as though an explosion ripped it apart, and the flesh of his arm is savagely torn—some of it burnt and cauterized, but enough is still bleeding steadily. *What weapon had Mister Tasker used to accomplish such destruction? Why?* Nausea churns his stomach, and he retches violently until what little was in is now out.

*I must get to Grissell's for help.* He uses the wall as a brace and slowly stands groping for the lead rope hanging nearby and does his best to create a tourniquet with it. He commands his legs to move. The muscles quiver with the effort, but progress is made, and he eventually makes it to the far side of the east pastern where the Mercer's home is. Acacia is making a feast of the sweet clover that grows there. When the mare sees him, she trots up and then slows to a walk allowing him to use her as a crutch for the remaining distance to the Mercer's front porch.

Grissell's father, Elton Mercer, is a free man of mixed African and English blood who bought his wife and daughter out of slavery for the price of 150 pounds after petitioning the Governor's Council for permission to free his family. Harry White sold him the small parcel of land where Mister Mercer built his home. He works as a carter transporting goods throughout the capital and surrounding areas for the plantation. Grissell's mother, Anne Mercer, skills as a healer and midwife are sought out by all within the capital even before one of the apothecaries is called upon.

William uses the light glowing from the front windows to find his way. The steps might as well be a towering mountain, and his muscles protest every lift and hobble to climb up and cross the porch. He is spent collapsing onto the porch striking the front of the home.

The door opens, and Anne gasps. "Oh, my goodness child what happened to you?" She rolls him over. "William? Is that you? Oh, lordie, boy you've been tore up by something mighty fierce." She bends down to take a closer look at the wounds. "Elton, I need your help!"

They get William into the cabin and lay him on a padded cot that Anne keeps available for whenever someone ill needs closer supervision. She cleans his wounds and tends to him, but there is not much improvement.

The cabin door opens, and a woman walks in. She has strawberry blonde hair that is gathered up behind her head except the small ringlets falling about the fair complexion of her face. She is heavy with child.

Anne is at the stove preparing another pot of hot water to clean bandages. "Sophia, morning darlin'. Has Missus Walters delivered then?"

"Yes, a beautiful baby girl. Both are doing well. Her husband sent over this basket of vegetables to thank you, and they said to tell you they hope that Grissell will be feeling well soon."

"Well that be mighty nice of them. I wish I knew why she fell ill so suddenly. I am just grateful that you was there to stay with the Walters. You have been such a wonder and help these past couple weeks. I do not know what I am gonna do when you leave. If I did not have you with me tonight, I would not been able to tend to my Grissell."

William hears the conversation as though they are speaking from the far end of a tunnel, and he stirs with concern. *Grissell. What could have happened to her?* A searing pain in his arm reminds him of his own plight, and a groan escapes him.

Sophia turns his way while removing her shawl. She tosses it over a chair and skirts around the table to William's side. "What happened?" She looks over at Anne with a furrowed brow, and Will does not need to see her face to know he is in serious trouble.

"It be Mista White's boy. Showed up here about an hour or so ago bloody and confused. I never seen anything like it. Looks like his skin exploded from the inside out. He already lost an awful lot of blood, and I cannot get it to stop. I wanted to have his daddy fetched, but he would not allow it. Seemed like he was worried for his father not wanting him coming out of the house."

William tries to raise up on his elbow. "My father…must stay clear…must…"

Sophia lays her hand on his shoulder gently encouraging him to lay back down. She starts to say something to him and stops short grasping her gravid abdomen. "Whoa, little one." She looks down. "That was quite a flip." She flashes a thin smile and then gently lifts William's arm.

"So much blood." His voice is raspy and weak.

She nods and looks over her shoulder. Anne mouths to her that the dressings have been changed twice. Sophia bites down on her lower lip.

His chest and face glisten in sweat, and his respirations feel shallow and irregular. Sophia checks his pulse at his neck. Her fingers are warm against his clammy skin. "He's nearly in shock."

"That he is." Anne says pulling a batch of clean bandages from a pot of boiling water and starts hanging them to dry. She takes dry ones from the line and carries them over to Sophia.

"This is *Harry* White's son?"

"Right again, Sophia."

She slowly blinks pressing her lips together and starts to unwrap the bandages while singing softly. Her touch is gentle as her hands work efficiently, and her song swirls through the air around William.

"My, that be a sweet and sorrowful tune Sophia." Anne lays the bandages on the cot.

Sophia looks up at her with a wistful smile and nods. "Yes, it is called *Beautiful Boy* by a man named John Lennon. He wrote it for his son. It's been a long time since I thought about his songs." She draws in a breath and exhales barely above a whisper, "He hasn't been born, yet he has already died. The future and my past." She closes her eyes. The lamplight creates a halo of light around her blonde hair.

William looks up at her not understanding what she is talking about, but everything has been wobbling around him. *Perhaps, I misunderstand. Perhaps, I am not where I think I am.* His words sound distant to him when he asks, "Have I arrived in heaven?"

A puff of air escapes her, she smiles, and slowly shakes her head. "Anne, let me tend to him for a while. Why don't you check on Grissell?"

"Thank you, Sophia."

Sophia waits until she is alone with William and reaches into the pocket of her apron withdrawing a piece of smooth amber that is formed in the shape of a heart with a curving point turning back up towards itself. "There will be no crossing over for you tonight young man." She raises a finger to her lips indicating secrecy before humming the sweet lullaby again as she gently lifts William's injured arm supporting it with hers. The amber immediately extinguishes the fire within his flesh as she glides it along his wounds.

His muscles release the tension that has been holding him hostage, and he is finally able to draw in a complete breath of air. His arm relaxes and his hand happens to come to rest against her rounded abdomen. The baby inside her presses outward towards his hand, and both William and Sophia look down curiously for a moment.

"Are you still awake little one? I feel you there inside reaching out to William." She continues to glide the amber along his wounds, and the edges of his flesh begin joining back together. The amber glows gently, but a stronger light is coming up from beneath his hand against her abdomen where there is also the comforting spread of warmth like a drink of hot tea on a cold day. She finishes up with his arm, and the wounds slowly go from bloody to a beefy red scar. Once the amber is lifted from his skin its glow fades, but the light from beneath his hand does not.

He lifts his hand up and stops short. A glimpse of light glows through Sophia's dress in the shape of a tiny hand. He blinks and looks up at Sophia and back down again. The image is gone, but there is a silvery mark in the shape of the tiny hand on his palm.

"A promise for hope I think." Sophia takes hold of the back of a nearby chair to help herself up off the cot so she can fetch a cup of water from a nearby bucket.

William remains transfixed staring at the palm of his hand. The glistening image tingles when he traces it with a finger and flickers brighter below his fingertip. His eyes go from there to his wrist and the now healing wounds that extend to crook of his arm.

Sophia returns sitting back on the cot next to William and

helps him sit up to drink.

"Thank you. Thank you for helping me."

"Tell me what happened." She gently coaxes.

He stares into the cup as though the answer is there waiting to come out. "If you are asking what shredded my arm, I do not know." He runs a hand along the red scars. "Tell me what healed it."

Sophia shrugs a shoulder. "I possess a magical amulet."

He guffaws. "Magical?"

She raises her eyebrows and tilts her head towards his arm.

"Why would you say such a thing given the risk of arrest?"

"Are you going to tell anyone?"

He twists his lips and minutely shakes his head. "No, indeed. No other feats of medical intervention to be credited then?"

She shakes her head.

"Very well then. And, what about the shimmering handprint? What did you call it?"

"A promise for hope."

"Not influenced by the magical amulet?"

"I don't think so. No."

He flexes his fingers and nods his head.

"So, your turn then. Tell me what happened. Before the attack on your arm."

He sighs and pulls his thoughts together and clears his throat. It is so much easier to concentrate now that most of the pain has improved. "There was a man in our barn. He only just came into the colony earlier in the day, and he had been invited by my father to stay the night with us. We spoke for a moment, and then I am not sure what happened. I remember a tremendous light and blackness all at once. Fire and damp coldness. Fear mandating I run and horror commanding I stay. And then, nothing. I blacked out and woke in the stall bleeding and dazed."

"Is that all? Had anything been said to you by this…man?"

William frowns and draws his lips in. "He made inquiry about my evening, and who I spent it with. He spoke about personal things I did not think were known outside my family." He hesitates but decides to provide her with the details of the conversation.

She sighs. "He sounds like the sort of man that is crafty and knows what is needed to be said to manipulate someone. Make one feel unsalvageable, or unwanted. Using fear to control one's actions."

Although she is looking at him, he feels her words have carried her away for a moment.

She bites down on her lip and refocuses on William. "Did he ask anything of you?"

William shakes his head and stops abruptly meeting her eyes. "I remember him saying something about a harvest, and me getting things in order, and him returning within a fortnight."

She looks down at her hands which rest on her lap. "I see. He does want something from you William. That is to be sure. What I want you to know is that this man…did he give you a name?"

"Mister Tasker."

She wets her lips. "This Mister Tasker knows what needs to be said in order to prevent you from questioning your lot. He will cultivate a feeling of unworthiness on your part in order to prey upon you. Just know this William, we all have weaknesses. We are inherently imperfect beings. Here is your first enlightenment for the endeavor that lies ahead of you: Redemption is for all who seek it with honest intent. There is no entanglement too far gone that prevents one from asking for help. Do not let the tribulations that lay ahead for you pull you into the dark side of existence."

William looks up at her drawing his brow together. *What*

*endeavor is she referring to?* Her words are disquieting, but her tone brings comfort, and he simply nods in acknowledgement.

Another ripple moves across Sophia's abdomen, and they both smile. Her eyes lock on his. "The second thing you need to carry with you is that love is the most powerful force there is. When you have it you should cling to it. Not all creatures that exist are able to feel or comprehend its power, and so it is often underestimated." She reaches for his hand gently turning it palm up to show the fading sparkle of the tiny handprint. "The promise of hope. You must hold onto this, as with it comes the ability to love."

Anne comes back into the kitchen. "Praise be. Grissell just broke her fever, and she is doing much better now. I have no idea what happened to her, but I am sho'nuff grateful it is done."

Running around her on each side are two energetic girls with blonde hair. "Momma!" Both cry out in unison running to hug Sophia. When they notice William they stop short, and a scarlet hue lights upon their cheeks.

"Beattie, Dot say hello to William." Sophia strokes each of their heads gently and smiles at William. "These are my daughters, Beatrice and Dominica."

The girls take a short curtsy and say hello.

§

Suddenly the alarm comes to life with its obnoxious ring rattling the clock over the chipped finish of the wooden table by Will's bed. He reaches over to silence it and grudgingly gets up to sit on the side of his bed turning his palm up. Nothing is visible now, but he knows it is there. His first protective mark. It was soon followed by the one covering his heart that Hester, the fallen angel who is also bound to Paimon, gave him. A final one on his shoulder came later and, although there are only three, their powers hold far stronger than the demon marks that outnumber them three to one. The gentle Sophia's face is still present before his eyes, and he ponders the dream that fully brought back his memory from that fateful night.

Sophia's face slowly fades from view, and in its place is Hallie. An image of her with her hair blowing across her face, and her reaching up to pull it behind an ear before holding a hand up to send him a greeting—a connection to hope. A smile lights his face with the thought.

# CHAPTER 8
## Plan

Buddy Holly and the Crickets' *That'll Be The Day* bounces from the radio in the garage on a morning where the heat could be peeled off only to reveal a new layer of more heat. Drew is on his back working on a McCaffrey car—a sleek black two-door coupe with chrome accents and white wall tires. The elder Mister McCaffrey had bought it new in 1953 just before his family moved to Ferrum. He was a successful railroad executive that always longed for quiet small-town life, and he found it when he retired. Unfortunately, he died suddenly less than a year later.

"Will, hand me the nine-sixteenth wrench." Drew reaches a grease-stained hand out from under the car. Will grabs the tool handing it to Drew and leans against the car complaining about the heat.

"Well damn, Will, take those coveralls off. I don't see how you can stand those things in this heat."

"Yes, well that is not going to work."

"Why not?"

"I am not wearing anything under them trying to stay cool."

Drew laughs. "Oh lord, don't let it get out that you're here going regimental like a Scotsman. We'll have every girly girl coming around hitting the pumps for a 'fill up', and none of us would get any work done."

A new heat flushes Will's cheeks. "I cannot afford to get my jeans stained in this place, and it is too hot to keep them, or anything else, on under these things."

Drew rolls out shaking his head and throws a shop towel at Will. "Go get me that lug wrench over there. I gotta get started on these brakes before lunch, if I'm gonna be done in time to take

Connie out for dinner."

Will fetches the tool for Drew and hands it to him when Deputy Hodges pulls up. He gets out of his patrol car walking over to Cleo Adkins who is sitting on a chair out front drinking a cola and taking a break.

"Well, hey there Ted. What brings you out this way?"

Ted shakes Cleo's hand. They had gone to high school together remaining good friends over the years. Ted works over in the Patrick County sheriff's office. He is stocky but not very tall, and he works hard at standing straight in an effort to make up for it.

He looks around before answering and speaks in a low voice, but Will and Drew are close enough to hear. "Sheriff Shively had me come over. Seems a girl's body was found early this morning. Looks like it could be related to the two killings we've had over our way, and he wants me to have a look at the crime scene."

"You don't say." Cleo pulls a cold cola from his cooler and pops the top off the drink before handing it to his friend. "I hate to hear that. You know we haven't had much trouble out this way in years even with the shine stills. Where abouts did this happen?"

"Just up the road here going out towards Ingramville a piece."

"Up there near the Ridge's place?"

"That's right. Not too far from there."

"What a shame. What a shame."

Will looks at Drew who is focused on loosening lug nuts. He glances over at Will and walks over to the toolbox to put the wrench away. "Cleo, I'm going to take an early lunch break over at the Snip 'n Style with Connie."

"Sure. Sure. See you in a bit. Will, you go on and eat now, too."

Will walks out back to his room to make a sandwich and grab some water and takes it outside to sit under a tree near the shop. He thinks about last night and running into Drew near the Ridge's while picking at his nails with a set jaw.

"Hi, Will." A cheery voice pushes his thoughts aside.

"Hallie, hello." He stands, brushes himself off, and pulls the front of his coveralls straight. "What brings you into town?"

"Boredom mostly." She flashes a smile. "I started out taking a walk on the college campus and found myself heading this way. I thought I might get a milk shake at the '77. Do you have any more time for lunch left?"

"Yes, sure." He shoots a look towards the front of the garage where Cleo and Ted are still talking. "I have some time."

"I heard there is a baseball game this evening," Hallie brings up as they walk to the restaurant. "Would you come see it with me?"

"Uh, yes. Sure." He puts his hands in his pockets. "So, you are a baseball fan?"

"Well, can't really remember if I am or not, but it sounds like something fun to do."

"Any memory coming back for you yet?"

"Um, actually, something felt familiar when I was walking on campus just a bit ago." She puffs out a bit of air from her nose shaking her head as her cheeks color. "I can't help but feel like I have met you before. It know that's way out there, but I haven't felt that way about anyone else. Not even Odina and Azure."

He rubs a finger against the pressed penny in his pocket, and his heart spurs into a higher gear. *Is now the right time?* They reach the '77. *No, there is not enough time.* So, he starts into a light banter enjoying her company.

When Will gets back to the garage Deputy Hodges is gone, and Drew is working on the McCaffrey car again. The temperature remains stifling, the work steady, and the music spills from the radio complementing the natural rhythm of the garage activities. Will is grateful when the workday ends.

Katie Adkins pulls up just as they pull the last door shut. "Hello, Will. I made a pot roast for dinner and found I had cooked more than Cleo and I can possibly eat, so I made up a plate for you. She hands him a warm plate covered with a checkered cloth.

"Thank you, ma'am. It sure smells good."

She smiles warmly. "Well, I hope you enjoy it." She turns to Mister Adkins. "Cleo, I heard they had Ted Hodges come over from Patrick County to help look into the death of that poor girl they found this morning over on the other side of town." She rubs her hands together.

"Katie, now what do you know about all that?"

"Well, I had my women's community projects meeting for Saint James today. It was a combined meeting with our sister church, Grace Methodist, over in Patrick Springs and there was some talk."

"What's being said then Katie?"

"Well one of the women was kin to the second girl they found over there. She said she was a delightful girl." Katie's words catch a hitch. She clears her throat. "She said the girl's momma is devastated. She said there were strange cuts on that poor girl, and a pearl was found in her mouth. Now, Cleo, what can that be about? Who would take an innocent life and do such a thing?"

Mister Adkins puts an arm gently around his wife and looks back. "Will, I'll see you on Monday. You have a nice weekend now. Katie, how about we head home and have some of that delicious meal you made?"

She stifles a soft sob and gives him a nod. He pulls her close as they walk over to their car.

Will can hear Mister Adkin's reassuring tone as they walk

away. "Katie, Ted and his department are doing all they can, and now they are collaborating with the boys here in Franklin County. They'll get to the bottom of all of this. I don't want you worrying."

Will thinks about the recent murders and now understands the black ribbon on his feather. Finding the connection between the murders and the Circle of Souls will be harder to figure out.

# CHAPTER 9
## Exposition

The visiting team is from Floyd County and is leading by two runs with a thin but enthusiastic group of spectators cheering for the home team. The pressed penny in Will's pocket seems to weigh heavier, and he is getting ready to say something to Hallie when a foul ball pops towards them. The ball smacks into his hand when he jumps up to keep it from hitting Hallie, and he tosses it to the umpire.

"Whoa, thanks." Hallie exhales heavily. "I can't imagine what would happen, if I got knocked in the head again."

He chuckles while shaking his hand out. "True enough."

The batter for the Ferrum team swings making contact with the ball sending it over the fence. He brings in two other runners putting them ahead by one run. The crowd stands and cheers as they start to leave—it's the bottom of the ninth.

"I hope you enjoyed the game." Will says as they walk down the road towards the Ridges.

"Oh, I did. And thanks to you, I survived it, too." She shakes her head. "I am so glad that we went. The Ridges have been very kind, but it's pretty isolated at their place. It's nice to do something different."

"Yes, their place is secluded." He fidgets with the pressed penny in his pocket, and the tread of his walk suddenly feels awkward and uncertain. *Tell her*, a voice bellows within him.

"Look, there is Dillon McCaffrey sitting on his front porch. Why don't we go on up and see how he is doing?"

"Sure." He lets go of the penny and the imagined feel of gum on the bottom of his shoes snaps free.

"Hello, Dillon." Will greets him.

Dillon jumps a bit and looks up from the book he is

reading. His face melts into a smile. "Will, good to see you. And, Hallie—is that right?"

"Yes." She nods and smiles at him. "What are you reading?"

He lays the book over his knee. "It's called *Immortality, Inc.* by Robert Sheckly. Do you know it?"

"I don't think so. What is it about?"

"Well," Dillon perks up tapping a hand on the cover before getting a serious look on his face. "It's about a process whereby a human's consciousness may be transferred into a brain-dead body. Kind of a possession-type thing." He pauses raising his eyebrows. "Anyway, there are random killings of strangers by people who are dying and in need of a host."

"Kind of a science fiction thriller then. Sounds like something that would be interesting to read."

"Well, if you need reading material, I have quite the collection. I would be more than happy to lend you some books."

"I may take you up on that. Thanks."

"My pleasure." He turns his attention to Will. "I saw today that Mister Adkins has my coupe pulled into the shop. Does that mean he has started working on it?"

"Yes, actually Drew is doing the work."

"Drew?"

"Yes, Drew Mifflin."

"Oh, yes. He does work there with you. He is the fella that Connie Sealy is so smitten with. Is he a qualified mechanic?"

"He has worked at the shop part-time this past year, and Mister Adkins is very happy with him."

"I see. Yes well, if Cleo is pleased, then the coupe must be in good hands." He stares off looking distracted.

Hallie gives Will a sideways glance.

"Well, Dillon it is nice to see you."

"Yes, thank you for stopping to say hello. Hallie, it is very nice to see you again, and please come by sometime to borrow a book."

"Thank you, I will do that. Goodbye."

They turn to leave there's a loud crack, and Hallie stumbles when she steps onto a tread that gives way on the stairs. Will catches her by the arm preventing a fall. "Looks like you have a bit of wood rot on this board Dillon."

Dillon's brow furrows. "Sorry about that. I'll have Mister Gentry, the groundskeeper, take a look at it."

"Goodbye," Hallie calls back over her shoulder.

"Goodbye," Dillon calls after before returning to his reading.

"Dillon seems to be doing okay." She loops a bit of hair behind her ear and presses her lips together. "Do you think he has a crush on Connie?"

Will frowns and furrows his brow "Perhaps," he answers noncommittally.

"No? I guess I don't really know him well enough to tell."

"Not quite sure. I don't know him all that well myself. His comment would suggest it, but he also seems a little off. I am not exactly sure." He shrugs.

Hallie twists her lips. "Well, he has been through a lot recently. I can see that."

The sun sinks lower in the evening sky creating a rosy glow on the horizon that accents the mountain peaks just as they step into the woods. A few lightening bugs are starting to flicker, and the chirps of the night are in the air.

Hallie takes a deep breath inhaling the woodsy scent. "Ummm, my favorite place is outside and in the woods."

Will smiles. "How about the beach?"

She thinks a moment. "Yes, the beach, too."

Do you have any memories about the beach?"

"Water. I have a strong feeling about water—a little nervous trigger with the thought, but not sure what that is about."

They arrive at the Ridges' cabin.

"Do you think we could sit and talk awhile before you go in?" Will asks when they reach the clearing.

"Sure, I'd like that. How about we sit over in the garden?"

They swirl up some feathers from last night's fox raid while walking to the garden. The old tractor that Will is to come help work on tomorrow sits between the hen house and garden. There is a large equipment shed towards the back of the clearing. A fence made of bent willow branches surrounds the garden's burgeoning plants, and a meandering stone path goes through the center. A rustic bench and dozens of chimes, strings of colored glass, and bird houses dangling from tree branches are in the center of the garden. Torch lights are scattered about, and Hallie reaches into a wooden box taking out a match. She strikes it on a stepping stone bringing a flame to the tip in order to light the wicks.

Will looks around. "This is amazing."

"Yes, Azure and Odina have a gift with nature." Hallie gets the last torch lit. "I love this garden."

They sit on the bench and Hallie looks at Will's scarred arm. He holds it out for her to see. "How did it happen?"

He takes a moment before answering trying to decide just what to tell her. He doesn't know the full circumstances of her memory loss, but he knows it has nothing to do with a fall on a train. He takes a breath and reaches into his pocket taking out the pressed penny holding it in his closed hand.

"Hallie, remember telling me earlier today that you felt like you know me from before?"

"Yes." She nods her head and looks down knitting her fingers.

He leans down attempting to make eye contact. "Hallie?"

A flush colors her cheeks while her eyes glide his way. Her eyebrows jump up and she shrugs a shoulder.

"What is it?"

"A dream. I think."

"A dream about remembering me?"

"Maybe. It was you, but not quite you."

He gives a nod of encouragement.

"Well, I had on a black dress with blue flowers, and you had on a blue shirt to match them. Your hair was combed like you are wearing it now, and we were dancing to a slow tune."

He pinches his lips for a moment. "I do not recall a moment like that, but it sounds nice."

She shrugs a shoulder bending her neck into it and flashes a shy smile.

"Hallie, what if it is a memory and not a dream?" He searches her eyes afraid to push too hard.

"I'm confused. Are you saying you do know about it?"

"No, not that moment, but we have met before. I am just not sure how to explain it to you."

"Just tell me." She scoots a little closer to the edge of the bench with imploring eyes.

"There is a lot to tell."

She looks around and shrugs. "I think we have time."

He holds her gaze. "There was a time when you had to tell me about us. You gave me this to show me where you were from." He opens his hand. The pressed penny catches a bit of torchlight.

She looks at him quizzically and down at his hand reaching to pick up the pressed penny and holds it up to the light.

Chesapeake Bay Bridge-Tunnel." She flips it over. "H.S.O. 2018. Hm, that's my initials—Hallie Shawn O'Meara. What do you think the 2018 is?"

"It is the year, Hallie."

"You mean like sixty years from now? Yeah, right." She snorts a laugh but cuts it short when she sees he is serious.

"Yes, sixty year from now, but my first memory of seeing you—knowing you—is from 1928. I think the memory you have of our dance is from the future, and so I do not recall it. Yet."

Her mouth opens and closes. She attempts to speak again. "O…kay…so this pressed penny is mine?"

He nods.

"And, it is from the future, and you and I knew each other before now, but it was thirty years ago?"

"Yes." He waits. He sees her struggling to make sense of it, but she is not falling apart or becoming hysterical like in his dream. Her amulet bag is at the waist of her shorts. He realizes it is Odina's bujo from the memory she shared with him, and he thinly smiles to himself. "Hallie, can you take out the amber heart in your pouch?"

She looks down starting to loosen the straps and stops. "How? How do you know about my amber heart?"

"Because I have seen it before. Because it healed this." He holds up his scarred arm.

She blinks several times biting her lip and finishes loosening the amulet bag from the loop on her shorts to take the heart out, and she holds it up on the palm of her hand.

He looks at her indicating that he wants to take ahold of her hand.

She gives a nod.

Their palms press together, and their fingers entwine.  A soft glow arcs growing in brightness until it envelopes them.

"Whoa," Hallie exclaims and looks up and around. The garden and torch lights become hazy shadows beyond the glow of the amber's light.

The wonder in her eyes pulls a smile across Will's face.

She looks at him, her eyes glisten, and her lip quivers.

He lowers their hands loosening his grip. The arc of light vanishes and slowly the glow fades.

"I'm not from this time." The torchlight glistens in her watery eyes as she looks around. She stands up and Will tenses wondering if his dream about her turning into a fury was a premonition.

Her voice quivers "I was born in 2000 and raised by Beattie and Dot on the Eastern Shore." She runs her hands over the foliage along the perimeter and turns squinting her eyes at him for a moment. Again, his muscles twitch.

"I came to Southwest Virginia the summer of 2018 to work at Fairy Stone State Park and live with our family friend, Joan Shively. That is where I met Liam—William White—you, and my world changed. I remember thinking your life was…is such a mystery, but I learned mine is, too." She over at him. "Thank you. It has been hard not remembering." She hesitates before eliminating the space between them and hugs him.

*There it is. There is that soft vanilla scent and cascading warmth.* He inhales deeply savoring the moment before he holds her back at arm's length. "Hallie, what do you remember about the Demon King? The revenuer from Fayerdale? The man you called Joe from the future?"

She stands back straightening her shoulders. "You mean Paimon? Everything." She looks at the amber piece in her hand before returning it to her bag and takes out the fairy stone. "But we have this now. I found it next to where you had me bury your box." Her hand tremors as she hands the stone to Will. "Did you get your things?"

He cups the side of her face in his hand. "I did. That's how I came across the pressed penny. I am truly sorry that you had to go through all of that. If I had known that was how things would end…with you there…you must have been terrified that night. Please forgive me."

She starts to reply, but nothing comes out. A tear spills from her eye, and he wipes it away.

He withdrawals his hand and looks down. "I am afraid that I cannot offer much comfort for this life either. The blue jay feather is already with me, so time is short."

Hallie pinches her lip. "I know, Will. But, look at the fairy stone. It's very unusual. The Maltese cross is so distinct with a beautiful garnet in the center and look at the surrounding stone edge. It has five points." She traces its borders over the palm of his hand.

A surge of heat flushes his hand and quickly rises up his arm. He clears his throat. "A pentagram."

Her eyes sparkle, and she gives him a crooked smile.

He flushes knowing she is aware of the effect her touch has on him.

She brushes her fingers across the palm of his hand again and picks up the stone to turn it over.

More heat. He blows out a breath almost as if this will extinguish the flame and finds himself lost in her eyes.

She raises an eyebrow and darts her eyes downward. She has to do this twice before he looks back down at the stone.

He glances down briefly, but his eyes are lassoed back. Etched deeply into the back of the stone is another star.

"Two stars."

"Yes," Hallie confirms. "One pentagram and one hexagram. What can it mean?"

"I do not know." He turns the stone over several times. "Both stars have so many different meanings to so many different people. Although, there is always the debate about the Key of

Solomon."

She furrows her brow picking the stone up to re-examine it. "What debate?"

"Well, there are those who argue about it having a connection to a star. Some say five-pointed others six. Maybe it is both."

Hallie's eyes widen. "Key? The *Key* of Solomon? The angel song mentioned a key. Remember? I told you about that. And, Hester asked me, if I found the key when she found me in the iron mine in Fayerdale. It was just before she helped me pass through Tartarus. If she knew I had it, why did she bring me here? Could it have been someone…or something else that brought me here? Maybe there is something here for me to find as well."

"I do not know Hallie, but I do not think *this* is actually the Key of Solomon because that is a ring. A metal ring. And, this is a stone, but perhaps the stars on it suggest a connection to the key. It is something we must give more consideration to as well as something else."

She looks at him curiously.

"There is more that you need to know. It is important. I came here last night. I had a…a bad feeling that something happened to you, and without thinking, came here to check on you."

His hands prickle with sweat, and he rubs them along his pant legs. He is not accustomed to having someone in his life that moves him so deeply, and he feels vulnerable, yet he pushes on. "Odina was on the porch. She let me see you, then she 'set me down fer a spell.'"

Hallie giggles. "That sounds just like something she would say."

The grip on his muscles suddenly releases, and he realizes that there is no need for walls with Hallie. His lungs fill with air, and he pushes on. "She proceeded to tell me about a story from her childhood explaining that she had a hand in the curse that binds me to the Demon King. It was unintentional, but—"

"Wait," Hallie interrupts. "Wait. How can Odina be involved with the curse?"

"Hallie, she was there then, and she is here now."

She shrugs her shoulders shaking her head and gives a nod. "Okay, I believe. I mean why not? It's apparently a supernatural world, and I am just a supernatural girl." The Madonna *Material Girl* reference is lost on him. She nods to him and finally rolls her eyes good-naturedly.

"It's a spin from a song. Your future self as Liam will understand. I forgot that Madonna's debut is a few decades away. I guess I am saying Odina is just another quirky piece to the ever-growing puzzle that lies before us. Taunting us I believe."

"Yes, so it would seem. However, there is a bit more."

"Say what else you need to tell me."

He waivers. "Maybe I should not have brought any of this up just yet."

"What? You have given me a gift. You have brought me back to who I am, and what we have together. Tell me. So long as you stand by me, I can take whatever else you have to say."

"It's about the night of the curse. I have recovered that memory. After the Demon King inflicted the wound on my arm, I went to the house of a healer that lived nearby." He pauses.

She waits.

"When I was there I met two little girls and their mother. The girls' names were Beatrice and Dominica. Beattie and Dot. Do you remember me telling you in Fayerdale I had met them before? We speculated that the amber heart has preserved their lives, or at least slowed their aging. I knew I had seen them in 1720. I just did not remember the circumstances."

"Yes, I remember you saying you knew my aunts from your original life."

He nods quick little jerks of his head raising his hands emphatically. "Hallie, there is much more to it."

She could get no closer to the edge of her seat without falling off the bench.

"I met their mother. Hallie, she looked so much like you. Her name was Sophia."

"But," Hallie's voice fails her. She clears her throat. "My mother's name was Sophia. Beattie and Dot almost never mention her, but there is a book in their office that has a photograph tucked between the pages. Will, she was dressed in modern clothing."

"I know Hallie, but I am telling you she looked so much like you. Plus, she had the amber heart. She used it to heal my arm. And Hallie, she was with child at the time. She was probably about six or seven months along. When she was holding my arm to heal it my hand came to rest against her stomach, and it glowed like ours did just now when we held the amber heart together."

Tears stream from her eyes.

"Hallie when my hand moved from her stomach there was a tiny handprint that glowed through Sophia's dress, and there was a silvery image of it on the palm of my hand. It actually is visible when I am in the underworld. It is a protective mark."

She cuts a sob short and nods wiping the tears from her face. "Yes, I saw it when Hester and I made the passage through Tartarus."

"Sophia said it was a promise of hope."

"And, you must hold onto to hope as with it comes the ability to love." Hallie looks at him and draws her lips inward. "Beattie, the every-optimistic, always says that." She shrugs a shoulder.

"It took me awhile to understand that. It took until I met

you."

"Will, I see it. I do. So much points to the truth of what you are saying. Sophia must have traveled across time just like I have. We both must be travelers of some sort, but I have no memories of any life before the one I have with my aunts. Or, I suppose they are my sisters. That was *me* Sophia was pregnant with? Oh my God. This is crazy." She rubs her arms.

"Yes, crazy, but we will figure it out. I promise."

She nods and dries the last of her tears straightening her back and jutting her chin out. "Yes, I know that we will. For now though, we have to figure out why I came here. Why in Ferrum and in the year 1958? I have no clue. There have been no angel songs to guide me, but now I have my memory back maybe something will come to me." Her eyes widen. "What about Paimon? Will, do we have enough time before he starts the harvest?"

"We are going to do our best, but Hallie I need you to understand that this is not the life that I will defeat him. It has to be in 2018 when the circle is complete. You knew me—will know me—so you have to hold that thought close to you no matter what happens here."

She looks at him. The tears return to her eyes.

"It will be okay. I promise. We are going to get you back home."

"Yes, I can do this. I will be strong."

"You are strong, Hallie."

"What do we do now?"

"We need to try to live as normally as possible while we figure the rest of this out. We know that Odina and Azure know our situation, but no one else."

"How much time do we have?" She clears her throat and swallows with effort.

"We are just going to have faith that there is time enough."
"A promise of hope then?"
"Hope and what it brings."

# CHAPTER 10
# Unearth

Will arrives early Saturday morning to help Azure repair the old tractor while Hallie and Odina go in search of herbs and to check the wild ginseng that Odina plans to harvest later in the year. As they head out, Odina explains to Hallie the process of harvesting the ginseng's valuable roots. She sells it to an Asian healer that comes through Rocky Mount once a year to purchase ingredients.

"He hails from somewhere up in tha north," she explains and stops short as she stoops down. "See here are some. They like ta grow beneath tha big hardwoods in tha shade. They are just forming berries. See here in tha center?"

Hallie sits on a patch of soft moss listening to Odina who shows her other companion plants that often grow with the ginseng. They find blood root and cohosh, and Odina shows her what parts are used. These too can be sold, but she will also keep some for her own remedies.

"Now, see here. This be Solomon's seal." She shows Hallie the small white tubular flowers hanging from the underside of the stem where the leaves zigzag on both sides. "Tha berries will start ta form towards tha end of this month inta early July. All parts of tha plants can be used, but tha root is what I use ta make a tincture that helps with stiff achy joints and muscles. Azure 'preciates it come tha winter months."

"How did it get its name?"

Odina gently harvests leaves from a nearby plant. "Well, if you dig up a root—usually folks do that in tha fall afta tha leaves start ta wilt—tha stems pull away from tha root and leave a circle—like seal. A seal like tha one King Solomon had or was said ta have anyways."

"Will and I were just taking about Solomon's ring yesterday."

"Aye, I'm thinkin' I know about tha legend. Tha king had a seal ring with tha name of God engraved on it. King Solomon used tha ring ta control demons an angels. It was supposed ta be given ta Solomon from heaven above, and it was partly brass and partly iron."

*Iron.* Hallie's attention perks. Gooseflesh prickles to life along her arms.

"It is also said that Solomon was given four jewels from four different angels, and that he set them in tha ring so that he could control tha four elements. Tha legend says that a demon king called Asmodeus once got aholt of tha ring and threw it inta tha sea, and that Solomon was deprived of his power until he found tha ring from inside a fish."

"Do you think it was a ring he wore?" Hallie looks at the delicate white flowers.

"I dunno. Maybe he wore it, or maybe it was just a ring like a circle is a ring."

§

At the Ridges, Will finishes with the tractor and goes back to town to work at the garage last minute. As he is closing up, Katie Adkins comes by to thank him for giving Cleo a chance to take the afternoon off. "Will, why don't you and Hallie come to Sunday service with us at Saint James? After, we are going to Fairy Stone."

"Yes, Ma'am that sounds fine. Thank you." It will be a good distraction, but it will also give him and Hallie time together to try to figure out why she is here and how to get her back home. He lifts the blue jay feather from his shirt pocket, and his skin prickles with thoughts of the harvest hoping there is enough time to assure Hallie's safety.

Sunday morning the Adkins pick Hallie up for the church service where he meets them waiting in the cool shade of the trees behind the church. He smooths out his shirt and straightens his tie when they pull up. Hallie steps out of the car wearing a pale green cotton dress with sandals. She flashes a smile and waves as they walk up.

"That tie looks might nice, Will." Katie pats his chest.

An unfamiliar flush up his neck triggers a boyish grin, and he nods at Missus Adkins before walking over to Hallie offering his hand.

They walk to the front entrance, and Will glances up to the pointed arch of the church roof. Just below it is a round stained glass window with a six-pointed star. He pauses for a moment to look at it giving Hallie a tug while pointing it out to her.

"Will, how nice to see you."

"Yes sir, thank you. Pastor Williams, this is Hallie O'Meara. She is staying with the Ridges for a while."

Pastor Williams shakes Hallie's hand enthusiastically. "Very nice to meet you young lady."

"Thank you, it's nice to meet you, too."

They step into the church as Pastor Williams greets a young couple with a newborn coming in next. The sanctuary is simply decorated. Will's fingers tingle. This is now the second time he has stepped into a church in less than a week. During his original life he attended only the monthly service mandated by law. It's not that he isn't a believer, he just isn't comfortable with the many nuances of organized religion. The pew squeaks as they sit, and he picks up a well-worn hymnal and holds it in his lap. Hallie reaches over taking his hand as though she senses his discomfort. He takes a breath in and focuses on the warmth from her hand.

Will leans towards Hallie's ear to whisper. "Did you see the window below the roof arch?"

"Yes. Will, I feel stronger than ever that I am in 1958 Ferrum for Solomon's key."

The opening hymn is sung and the service proceeds as Pastor Williams reads from Deuteronomy 31:6 "Be strong and of a good courage, fear not, nor be afraid of them." He gives an inspiring sermon on the courageous who persevere despite the presence of fear.

After service, they arrive at Fairy Stone and gather up the picnic items, towels and blankets that Missus Adkins put together. Plans were made at church for Connie and Drew to meet them at the park later.

Hallie looks about as she walks towards the bath houses and beach area. "Wow, so different from 2018."

Will nods. "Yes, and different from 1928. That restaurant is where one of the houses from Fayerdale had stood."

"Yes, I remember that. Well, in 2018 it becomes Fayerdale Hall where the employee reunion was held that I told you about thinking it was a dream. It had a 1950's theme party. That's why you had looked like you but not."

He raises an **eye**brow.

"Kind of a retro celebration, decorations, cars, clothes, you know."

He shrugs into a shoulder.

"Well, you will know. We have a really nice time." She blushes. "I had this great dress, and…oh my God…it got drenched by…" Her mouth drops open. "Oh, my God! Will, Connie is Ivy without the perpetual scowl. How could I have not realized this?"

"I am guessing you are referring to Connie's future life?"

Hallie nods with her mouth slightly agape.

"Yes, this is an unusual life for her. Much happier. If I had not known her from my original life, when she was similar to now, I would not have recognized her either."

"Huh, amazing."

"You know, Sadie is still here too, but I am assuming she is living in or near D.C. where her Aunt Tessie had taken her that last night in Fayerdale. When Sadie comes into town, or we hear of her in some way, we will know that the harvest has begun."

"Sadie." Hallie smiles. "Sadie is my friend, Becky, in the future and Connie is Ivy—I knew she looked familiar—and she was Maybelle from Fayerdale. I should have realized this, but she is just so different here. She is older too. Does that often happen?"

"We can start our lives at any age. There is a ripple in reality that triggers an alteration allowing us to pick up as though we have always been there. In my original life, my true life, I was twenty at the time of the curse. Connie was in her mid-twenties, so it can happen for her to be older during a life."

Hallie nods. "I don't understand why she is here though. When did you first meet her here?"

"She was here when I arrived and had actually been here for a few years. Why?"

"Well, when I traveled through Tartarus from Fayerdale to here, Hester and I ran into her only she was a…what did Hester say she was? I can't remember."

"A fury." Will silently recalls his dream of Hallie turning into and falling before his eyes as a fury. He rubs the back of his neck. "They are guardians of the gateways to the underworld and very fierce warriors."

"Yeah, I know. She and Hester got into it. Hester may be 'the tiny ballerina-type,' but she is tough. The fury was fierce, but the angel kicked butt."

Will laughs. "Kicked butt?"

"Uh, yeah. It's an expression…from the future. She was

victorious."

They spread the tablecloth and Hallie stacks the plates and gets silverware from the basket. "Anyway, Ivy…or I guess she was Maybelle at the time, was knocked out. Hester brought her with us but left her at the roots of the Mesu when she went to show me the way through the tree."

Will hands Hallie items from the basket. "We all crossover from the Mesu. The curse requires a ceremonial crossing with Paimon in order to complete the transition. The tethered souls drink from the Lethe in order to abolish memories—at least for a while. My return to Earth provides the Demon King a portal during the time I am alive. The tethered souls are not directly bound by the curse so they are not tied directly to the Demon King, and he would not be aware for quite a while if Connie crossed over before she should have. Perhaps she awoke while Hester was with you and wandered into the tree. You have to remember that time is irrelevant in the underworld and crossing through the Mesu is kind of the same. You may have entered a path to June 1958, and she came through some time in 1954, or whenever it was that she came here."

"Well, she did have water from the Lethe because Hester gave it to her in order to protect you since she saw me with you." Hallie grasps at her stomach and sits down on the picnic bench with a furrowed brow. "You know Will, how will I ever get back to where I left from? There are too many variables—too many unknowns. In order to travel, I have to cross Tartarus and go through the Mesu, but how will we know where it is going to send me? How did my mother know?"

"Hallie, look at me." Will sits next to her, and she searches his eyes. "Before you came here, I had memories of you from Fayerdale. I knew you when you walked into the '77 that morning with Azure. I am sure that my memory of this life once I am Liam is going to be altered as well. He…I will find a way for you to be summoned back there just as Odina brought you here.”

Hallie's head jolts back and her mouth drops open. She starts to speak but can't say anything because the Adkins walk up.

“Thank you both so much for getting this all set.” Katie looks the table over with a big smile. “Why don't you go get your suits on and head out to the water for a while? We'll wait for Connie and Drew to arrive before we eat.”

“Yes ma'am, that sounds good to me.” Will picks up his and Hallie's bags, and they walk up to the bath house.

As soon as they are away from the Adkins, Hallie asks the question Will was expecting. “What do you mean Odina summoned me here? Is that why I didn't make it back to where I should have been going?”

“Hallie I honestly don't know. I am wondering if you were intended to be here all along. She told me that she had been following signs of some sort that you were to come here but your actual arrival was unknown to her until the night you crossed. The more I think of it the more I wonder if Solomon's lost key is beckoning you. The angel songs for the key in Fayerdale made it seem like you were meant to find the fairy stone there. It has to be that you are meant to find something here. There is a lot of lore surrounding Solomon's key, and we may be able to find out more about it.”

She rubs an arm. “I just feel so frustrated, and scared to be honest, that we have no control over the situation. I just wish that the angel song would come to me.”

“I think we do not understand the situation for now, but we will. We have control over what happens here to a certain extent. We just need more information to try to do the right thing. I know time is short, but we have to go with what we have. Beyond that I just do not know. Let us not wait for some otherworldly confirmation."

She purses her lips and nods. "Okay. We can figure this out, and we will figure the 'beyond here' out too." She looks around and up at the sky taking in a breath. "In the meantime, today is a beautiful day, and I want to spend it just like I am supposed to be here. I am going in that bath house, put on this 1950's 'very hot' suit, swim, feel the sun on my face, and be with you. Just for today—a reprieve. Alright?"

He readily agrees very happy to steal a day, even a moment, to be with her.

"Alright then." She smiles cheerfully and goes into the bath house.

Will turns towards the men's bath house bumping into Connie and Drew.

"Well, hey there Will. Y'all getting changed for a swim then?" Connie asks.

"Hello, yes Hallie just went in the bath house."

She grabs a pair of swim trunks out of her bag handing them to Drew. "Well then I guess she and I will see you two at the beach." She gives them a big grin and turns to go into the bath house.

Drew holds up the trunks giving Will a look. "Hmm, let's hope they come out of there wearing something a little cuter than this." He laughs and walks past Will into the men's bath house.

Will thinks about the strange attire Hallie had on when he found her in Fayerdale. Now, knowing it was her swimsuit, he smiles thinking whatever she walks out of that bath house wearing will be cute.

Will and Drew are changed and back at the picnic table before Hallie and Connie get out of the bath house, but they aren't too far behind. The Adkins have chairs set up in the shade and are visiting with friends.

Connie walks up to Drew giving him a kiss and takes off her cover-up to reveal a black strapless bathing suit.

"Tell me why this is the first time we have come here?" Drew smiles broadly. She just gives him a slap on the shoulder and laughs as they head out to the water.

Hallie's suit is a baby blue one piece. She leans over to Will and says, "You're gonna like the one I wear in 2018 much better."

"Actually, I have seen that one, and it is indeed fine swim attire; however, this one is also very agreeable."

She looks at him for a moment and her eyes widen. "That's right. I forgot that I had my swimsuit on when you found me in Fayerdale. I bet that was a bit of a sensation, huh?"

"Well, actually only Jeb, Sadie, and I saw the suit on you."

"And who removed it?" She teases.

He blushes. "That would be Sadie. Although, it was perplexing to know what to do for you before she arrived. That suit…I did opt just to wrap you in warm blankets."

"Yeah, well lucky for you. Somehow I think Sadie would have had plenty to say had you done things any differently."

A chuckle escapes him. "Undoubtedly."

Hallie laughs with him and then runs into the water plunging forward to swim towards the diving dock. He follows her catching up easily and grabs her by the foot to pull her back moving ahead.

It is a pleasant afternoon. They all enjoy a delicious meal after swimming and sitting afterwards to relax in the sun.

"Hey, there's Dillon McCaffrey over by that tree," Connie comments. "We should go and say hello."

"Uh, you go ahead Connie. I think I will stay here a bit," Drew answers.

"I'll go with you," Hallie speaks up and walks across the

hill with Connie.

Dillon looks up from his book and greets them enthusiastically.

Drew watches them for a moment and stiffens as though an icy chill suddenly blew by. "That guy is an odd bird."

Will looks at Drew and over to Dillon. He has always been a loner, but Will hadn't given Dillon much thought before the past couple weeks.

Drew picks at the blanket watching the trio. "He's got this thing for Connie." He shakes his head and looks back at Will. "I'm not jealous mind you. I know what Connie and I have is real. Hell, I want to marry her. It's just that he…I don't know…he puts me on edge."

Will rubs his chest over his heart feeling as though Drew's discomfort has clutched onto him. He hesitates not understanding why and shrugs a shoulder. "He has been through a lot with his family all dying over the last several years. Perhaps that has something to do with it."

"Perhaps," Drew huffs. "You know that Caddie Coupe I'm working on for him? It has all kinds of mud and muck up in its undercarriage. It looks like someone washed it down pretty good but didn't know to clean underneath. And the brakes—they are shot. *And* I found this intense hunting knife behind the driver's seat. Who does that with a car that cherry? I mean it looks perfect just standing next to it—pristine almost, but when you get up under the hood and carriage, it's a different story." He shakes his head.

Will nods and pinches his lower lip and starts to reply, but Connie and Hallie start to walk back over. Dillon is watching them leave, and his eyes meet Will's. He holds his stare for a moment before returning to reading his book.

"How about another swim?" Hallie unzips her coverup.

He looks up and gives her a smile. "Sure."

The Adkins are ready to head back after a while, and it's decided that Will and Hallie will ride back to town with Connie and Drew, so they can spend more time swimming. Storm clouds, however, quickly roll in, and they all change and start towards the parking lot just as a down pour hits.

"Oh my gosh," Connie shouts. "What was the sense in changing back into our clothes?"

They cover their heads with the towels in vain while running to the car. Everyone jumps in and sits in the car dripping before they enjoy a good laugh and head out.

"Drew just stop at the cut-over for the Ridges. I will walk Hallie home from there."

"You sure? I can go around to their road."

"No, it is okay. The rain has stopped, and it will be quicker for you and Connie to get back to her place."

"Okay then." Drew pulls the car over. They thank them for the ride and start across the field to the path at the wood's edge. The shrubberies at the trail head are wet and Hallie swings a branch back at Will laughing as the water sprinkles on his already damp clothes.

He grabs her at the waist and shakes some higher branches over her head.

"Will," she teases. "You're going to mess up my hair." She pats her already rumpled locks.

"What was I thinking? I am so very sorry." He roughs the top of her head up and takes her hand. She bumps playfully into his side and reaches up to smooth her hair back out as they walk towards the hollow.

"Do you want to stay for supper?" Hallie asks.

"No, it would probably be best if I did not show up unexpected for a meal. I do not want to get on Odina's bad side. Besides, I have all this food in my refrigerator that I need to eat. I think Missus Adkins thinks I need to fatten up." He pats his stomach and laughs.

"Okay then." Hallie shakes her head with a chuckle. "I can try to come into town tomorrow and have lunch with you if you would like."

"That would be very nice."

They approach the edge of the woods and Hallie stops. "How about we say good-bye here?" She takes his other hand and looks up at him.

"I can walk you to the porch."

"No, here is good. I want you to kiss me, and I am thinking here is a better place than there in the open, on the porch, in the open." She smiles innocently at him.

He hesitates, "I know that it has been thirty years since we last shared a kiss…"

"Not quite."

He gives her a sideways look.

"I kissed you in Tartarus. I'm not sure where that fits in the time continuum, but it was after the kiss I believe you are referring to."

He gives a nod and then moves his head side-to-side. "Oh, *that* kiss—I do not remember it. I believe I was not truly conscious at the time, so technically that one does not count. The kiss in Fayerdale, on the other hand, I am very aware of. I am afraid that you were nearly ravished by my momentary loss of control. It forced me to resist temptation in this life."

"Umm, yes." She smiles teasingly moving closer to him. "I do remember the circumstances there, but I am not sure that you can be held solely responsible for all of that."

He steps back slightly but finds himself stopped short by a tree. He clears his throat. "I just do not think it is a good idea." His speaks resolutely.

Her lower lip puckers, and she releases his hands abruptly. "Fine then. If you find me so undesirable that you are able to resist a seriously *good* make-out session, then so be it." She turns away from him to start out towards the clearing. He reaches across her back grabbing her wrist preventing her departure.

She turns her head over her shoulder looking at her wrist and up at him with what seems to be the best angry look she can muster. "Seriously Will, you have insulted me in the worse possible way. I am not sure you fully comprehend the mistake you have made."

He jerks her playfully towards him turning her smoothly as though they are on a dance floor, and now she is the one backed up against the tree. Her breath catches, and he looks at her with eyes full of mischief, and she smirks back at him. He holds her wrist above her head and slides a finger from his other hand over her silky skin tracing the inner line of her wrist down her arm into the bend of her elbow then over towards her shoulder and up her neck taking a moment to caress her hair. It's curled and still damp. He slides a stray curl behind her ear and rests his hand against the side of her face lightly stroking her lower lip with his thumb.

She shivers as he leans in brushing his lips across hers to kiss the corner of her mouth. He kisses down her cheek to her jaw line following it to her ear lobe lingering there. Goosebumps erupt along her skin as he kisses her below and behind her ear moving down her neck gradually increasing the intensity of his contact with her skin. The pulse in her neck quickens. Her breathing becomes irregular. She flushes. Her intoxication is his, and he savors it like the finest wine.

He pulls away from her neck and looks her in the eye raising his eyebrows and says, "Okay…but do not say I did not give fair warning." He speaks as he approaches her mouth giving her several light kisses before pressing firmly against her lips opening his mouth exploring and eagerly tasting her. Bringing her free hand up behind his neck to hold him close, a soft moan rises up from deep inside her.

He releases her wrist sliding his hands down slowly over the sides of her breasts to her waist where he holds onto her, leaning against her, pressing her more tightly against the tree. He kisses and kisses and kisses her giving way to the pleasure while she arches her back moving forward towards him electrifying the moment more intensely.

When he breaks away from the kiss, he lightly leans his forehead against hers breathless, but the pause is brief. The next kiss is slow while he takes his time surrendering to her fully. There is a serious threat of him not preserving the innocence of the moment. The line has truly been crossed further than he intended. *Yes, much too far. Oh, God this is perfection.* Every encounter a human makes with another changes their soul. *Do not forget Paimon.* An exchange of sorts occurs. *He will know.* The pecking thoughts nag at his conscience. *Do not allow our physical relationship to progress further than it had in 2018, or Paimon will see the change in her soul and know she is connected to me.* The love they share gives an intensity to their physical contact that he has never known before she came into his life. *I must regain control.* He reluctantly pulls away.

He inhales deeply forcing himself to relax and release her waist moving his hands to cup her face kissing her gently once more before he whispers, "I love you."

She swallows hard struggling to control her breathing looking at him in wonder. "I love you."

He gives her a quick nod finding himself also somewhat breathless. "Are we good then?" A devilish grin lights his face.

"Uh, yeah. We're better than good."

He shifts his weight leaning his hand against the tree

straightening his arm to put space between them once again.

Hallie smooths her dress taking a deep breath. "That was amazing."

"You are amazing."

Color lights her cheeks and she tucks her chin in. "Uh, well, thank you for a *very* pleasant day." She returns to the tone of their previous light banter. "Lunch tomorrow then?"

He nods and she turns stepping to the side and towards the clearing. Her gait wavers a bit. She looks back at him rolling her eyes and shrugging her shoulders. He chuckles and watches as she moves out of the woods. She raises her hand in a farewell gesture. Raising his hand in return he watches her turn towards the cabin.

He starts to go, but his knees seem to be plagued with the same affliction as Hallie's. He pauses for a moment smiling to himself and waits for his legs to steady before whistling a tune while walking back to town.

# CHAPTER 11
## Revelation

It is a typical Monday with folks coming through town for business. The Snip 'n Style opens at noon on Mondays, and Connie is opening up the shop when Hallie and Will walk by on their way to the '77 Restaurant for lunch.

"Well, hey ya'll." She is sliding her board with weekly specials out in front of the shop.

"Hey Connie," Hallie returns.

"Hello." Will takes the board from her setting it up near the door.

"Thank you, darlin'. You two headed over for some lunch?"

"Yes, Will's on his break."

"Watcha going to do after lunch Hallie?" Connie asks

"Well, probably just head back over to the Ridges. I don't really have too much going on today."

"Perfect. You come on by here after y'all finish lunch, and I will treat you to a manicure."

"Okay, that sounds great. Thanks."

"Alright then, I'll see you in a little while. Have a good lunch."

Will and Hallie turn to leave and nearly bump into two customers walking up to the door.

"Excuse us. Very sorry." Will says as he puts an arm around Hallie swerving to miss the two women.

"No problem sugar." A woman with bleached blonde hair and cat-eyed sunglasses replies with a smile. She turns and lowers her glasses on her nose watching Will and Hallie walk down the road towards the restaurant making a grunt as she pulls her sunglasses off. "God, he flips my switch," she comments in a hushed tone.

Connie rolls her eyes. "Carol Ann you're almost old enough to be his mother for Pete's sake."

"I am not. He's nineteen years old." She indignantly shifts her emerald green blouse and tucks it into her fitted skirt. "*And*, if I look like I could be his momma, then I need to find a different salon to go to missy."

"Okay, okay. You're beautiful and don't look a day over…what would you like the number to be?" Connie chides.

Carol Ann raises her eyebrows and tucks her chin down to look Connie in the eye. "Very funny…and, for today, just old enough NOT to be *his* momma." She laughs folding her sunglasses and pops them into her purse. Carol Ann's flashy appearance looks out of place in the small town of Ferrum, but her cheerful personality is a perfect fit.

"Old enough to be whose momma?" A brunette with a silk scarf on her head walks up to them along with Beezie who is popping gum and twirling her hair.

"Well, hey Linda. Hey Beezie." Connie props a fist on her hip. "Glad y'all could make it to work. Thought you were going to be here to open up for me." She raises her eyebrows looking at the two.

They both look anywhere but at Connie.

"Glad I got here a little early by chance. God forbid Carol Ann and Maude would have to stand out here checking out the passersby while the shop door is locked." Connie fusses good-naturedly as she holds the door open for everyone.

"Maude, honey, go ahead and sit there at the sink, and Beezie will get your hair washed." Connie gestures Maude over to the chair by the sink and turns to Beezie. "Gum out Beezie."

Beezie's eyes roll as she takes the gum out of her mouth

tossing it in the trash. She pulls a pink cape off the shelf and lets it fly behind her as she walks over to the subdued Maude. Beezie leans forward securing the cape around Maude's neck and flips the chair back towards the sink catching Maude by surprise.

"So," Linda starts as she walks over to her station and turns her chair for Carol Ann to sit. "Who's going to tell me who Carol Ann is old enough to be a momma to?"

"Ugh." Connie plops down in the chair at her own station while she waits for Maude's hair to get washed. "Carol Ann was out there drooling over Will White."

"I was not drooling," she says indignantly. "And, as I said, I am *not* old enough to be his momma. Besides I simply commented that he 'flips my switch'." Her voice raises an octave and she flushes slightly.

"Same thing." Connie laughs. "And you know, he is a really nice kid. You shouldn't be talking like that about him."

"It's not like I would do anything about it. Besides my sweet Boyd reaps all the benefits of any lustful thoughts I may incur during the day."

"You know," Beezie comments with the best adult-like tone she can muster. "The good book says that impure thoughts are just as sinful as the actions they inspire."

All the women in the shop turn and look at her—even Maude glances up at her in disbelief. There is a moment of silence before Linda blurts out, "Oh shut up, Beezie!" They all burst out into laughter with Beezie looking affronted as she turns her attention back to massaging the shampoo into Maude's scalp.

"Yes, Beezie, dear," Carol Ann says as she lifts her chin for Linda to bring the cape around her neck in preparation for her root touch-up. "I was here the first day that kid, as Connie calls him, walked into this shop, and I believe your jaw dropped lower than anybody else's."

"Now, Carol Ann, give Beezie some slack," Linda chides. "After all her daddy is Pastor Williams, and she does have standards to keep." She winks adding, "Besides she gives equal time both here and in church. I saw about three shades of red hit her face when he walked into services yesterday holding that pretty little girl's hand."

Beezie opens her mouth to protest and thinks better of it opting instead to reach for the bottle of conditioner squirting some into her hand and starts to massage it into Maude's hair before she realizes she hadn't completely rinsed the shampoo out.

"Beezie, don't give anyone in here a second thought." Connie calls over her shoulder and cuts her eyes at Linda and Carol Ann scolding through gritted teeth. "Don't y'all be upsetting Beezie—she's the first shampoo girl I have been able to keep for this long. Y'all are too mean."

"And, they tip like crap." Beezie says under her breath but loud enough for everyone to hear.

Linda drops her jaw, and they all bust out in laughter again.

"Where is that pretty little thing he has been with from any way?" Carol Ann asks while Linda combs through her hair.

"Um, I think she said something about living over on the Eastern Shore with her aunts." Connie answers. "I guess the Ridges are friends of the family, and she is staying with them."

Carol Ann guffaws. "Oh, come on. There's something else going on there. Odina Ridge keeps company with no one except that brother of hers. They are gypsies. How they ever grabbed a piece of land and settled is a wonder to me."

Connie looks at her for a moment. Even for Carol Ann the words are harsh, and she wonders if she had a run in with Odina in the past. "Well, I know there are a lot of rumors about the Ridges and such, but I think they are harmless. There is no law in keeping to yourself is there?"

"Con artist Connie. That young girl has no business being in that cabin with them." Carol Ann's lip curls up, but she says no more.

Connie is grateful to see Beezie finish up with Maude.

Maude walks over from the shampoo sink with a towel over her head and water dripping onto her cape. She is an anthropology professor at Ferrum College. At twenty-nine years age, she carries a demeanor more fitting fifty-nine years. Her brown-black hair sits shoulder length and is always challenging for Connie, but Maude's complexion and huge Betty Davis eyes do give a certain allure.

"So, Maude, what's it going to be today? A trim?" Connie starts combing through Maude's hair looking at her in the round beveled mirror in front of them.

Maude reaches into her purse tentatively pulling out a piece of folded paper. She opens it and presses it flat against her chest. It is a page from a magazine with a picture of Elizabeth Taylor in a short stylish cut. She hands it to Connie. "I was thinking about going short like Liz wears hers. What do you think?"

Connie takes the page and combs through Maude's hair some more. "I think it is real cute. You sure you want to go that short?"

Maude nods. "Yes, I think it will look nice with my curls."

"Well, how about that?" Connie perks up. She has always thought that Maude did not accentuate her natural attributes well enough, and a short cut would be much easier to manage. "I'd love to Maude. Honey, you aren't going to recognize yourself when we're done today."

Linda sets the bleach for Carol Ann and Connie goes to work snipping away at Maude's hair bringing the new style to life.

"You know," Maude speaks taking Connie a bit by surprise given that Maude rarely says more than what is needed to be said when she is in the shop. "There is often a lot to be said about folklore and stories that are passed on through the generations. The Ridges, for instance, are an interesting pair that have stimulated much speculation bound to become a part of local legend and lore one day."

Connie braces herself and makes no comment hoping not to incite a new tantrum from Carol Ann. She focuses on Maude's hair sending long pieces of hair floating down onto the cape and floor. Maude sits for a while and breaks the silence with another unexpected observation. "That young man, William, *is* beautiful."

Connie looks at her in the mirror thinking the use of the word beautiful to describe a man is odd, but it does seem to fit. "You mean, Will?"

Maude blushes a bit. "Uh yes, Will. It's just an observation really. He's not the only one. I've noticed others with similar traits."

Connie nods at her in the mirror curious about Maude's change in demeanor. "Really? Like who?"

Maude shifts in her seat a bit and looks up in the mirror at Connie. "Uh, well your beaux, for instance."

Connie stops cutting. "Drew?"

"Um, yes." She brings her arms out from under the cape and absent-mindedly brushes her fallen locks from her lap onto the floor. "He, in particular, has some of the very same characteristics as Will actually. Although there is something…well, I can't really put my finger on it." She shrugs pausing and looks up at Connie in the mirror.

Connie returns to cutting Maude's hair. "Huh, well you know I find Drew extremely attractive—especially in a nice fitting pair of dungarees." She laughs in an attempt to keep things light.

"It's not really physically attractive qualities I am speaking of when I say 'beautiful'." Maude's voice is less tentative and more professor-like suddenly. "Although most are drawn in by their physical appearance, which is usually very pleasant as well, it's more the 'feeling' that is generated by being near them that's the true attraction. You know—an ethereal quality. A heaven-on-earth or, occasionally, otherworld-on-earth trait—not all are benevolent." She raises an eyebrow and twists her lip saying this as though Connie is in the know somehow. "It's just that Drew exhumes a similar mood perimeter so to speak as Will. Similar, but not the same."

"Mood perimeter?"

"Like an aura. You know some spiritually sensitive people claim to see a color aura around people or other beings. What I am speaking of is an aura that is felt. No special gift is needed to feel it. It is usually unconsciously received. Although someone who is 'tuned-in' would have a more cognizant awareness of the source."

"Oh yes, of course." Connie has to force herself to return to cutting Maude's hair.

"It's odd how similar their perimeters are. I actually thought they were brothers when Will first came into town, and I met him, but that is highly unlikely given only one offspring is produced. Occasionally, twins will be born, and there is still that shadowed edge on Drew's perimeter. It is perplexing to me." Maude is talking freely until she sees Connie staring at her once again in the mirror.

"Huh." No other words come to mind for Connie. She is dumbfounded thinking she has no idea what Maude is talking about *'one offspring is produced', 'mood perimeters and shadowed edges'. What does that mean?* Connie leans down a little to see if she can smell any alcohol on Maude, but there is nothing. *Who knew that quiet, unassuming Maude even harbored thoughts like these? Is she a closet lunatic?* Her chest seems to cave in and she rubs her temple with the ball of her hand while the scissors remain poised around her finger and thumb.

She finishes the cut and flips her fingers through Maude's hair to get a look at her work. "Well, let's set you under the dryer."

Maude presses her lips. She shifts her glance to look at herself in the mirror reaching up with her hands to lightly finger the ends of her newly shortened hair. She gives the shy smile that Connie is accustomed to and walks over to the dryer where Connie sets the timer and heat control. Maude sits down in the chair and grasps Connie's arm.

"Nephilim, Connie, the prodigy of the earth-bound Watchers from the heavens above. Giants by mythology, but really they are just beings capable of greatness—a hybrid so to speak. Good and Evil. You need to look in the Book of Genesis in your bible. Go to the library and look it up too. You will see." Maude rushes through her explanation before moving her hand from Connie's arm to set it in her lap.

Connie sets the dryer's metallic dome down over Maude's head and steps away. A high-pitched ring muffles her hearing, and her hands are shaking. Beezie is sweeping up Maude's hair from the floor keeping her eyes fixed on her task but Connie senses that her ears have been tuned in.

Carol Ann and Linda too have limited their chatter in order to be privy to what is being said at the next workstation, and both now look at Connie via the mirror, but she acknowledges no one. She walks to the back of the salon to get supplies for her station. Putting her hands on the countertop in the prep room, she steadies herself while her head spins. Images of Drew flash through her mind first slowly then quickly transforming to images of times unknown to her with his face more of a blur then a crisp image. Images of Will that she cannot explain are there too. She holds her hands to her head willing it to stop. Her skin prickles with gooseflesh as her blood runs icy cold.

Beezie walks up to her with the broom and full dustpan. "Excuse me Connie. I just need to dump this in the trash."

Her wired nerves jolt. Clammy sweat coats her brow, and she fumbles for a towel.

"You okay?" Beezie empties the dust pain contents into the trash.

Connie looks over at her struggling to concentrate, the flashing images vanish, but a fearful chill persists. "Uh, sure. I'm fine. I think I need something to eat." She pulls a few dollars from her pocket. "How about you go over to the '77 Restaurant and get me a burger and some fries? You can use the rest to get something for yourself. Make sure you check with the others to see if they want you to bring them anything."

Beezie looks at her with a furrowed brow before nodding. "Okay, sure. I'll be back in a jiffy."

Connie wipes her face and looks up at herself in the tiny mirror on the wall. *Maude is obviously experiencing some sort of breakdown. The new hair. Her bizarre claims. Stand tall Connie.* She straightens her shoulders. *Do NOT fall down the rabbit hole with her.* She stares into the mirror until the last twitch of frayed nerves ceases.

# CHAPTER 12
## Disclosure

Will holds onto Hallie's hand as they continue from the salon towards the '77 Restaurant.

"It's kind of hard for me to get used to the idea of Ivy…I mean Connie being so nice to me." Hallie says out of the blue.

"What do you mean?"

"Well, in 2018 she couldn't stand me. It seemed to have to do with my connection to you somehow, but it wasn't a jealously thing. It was more like she was angry or something. She made working at the park a challenge some days."

"Yes, she is unusually pleasant in this life. I have even thought so, but she is older than usual, independent, and she is in love."

"She hasn't had those things before?"

"No, not in a very long time." Will falters in the shackles of shame that have been his constant companions. "She had love…in our original life and for a couple lives after that."

Hallie squeezes his hand. "What happened?"

"She had an extremely possessive and controlling step-father in our original life. He actually was forging a business partnership with my father in the months before I was cursed."

"Oh, my God—Robert Holt—Connie is Melinda Holt!"

Will looks at her dumb founded. "How do you know that?"

Hallie is shaking her head and looks at Will a moment before his question registers. "The story—the story that my aunts, uh sisters, told me over and over as I was growing up. Robert Holt was conniving to gain control of your father's assets. He was pushing Melinda to marry your father."

"Yes, so I have recently learned from Odina."

They arrive to the '77. Will holds the door open for Hallie. It is crowded but a table in the back dining area is open.

"So weird."

"What is weird, Hallie?" Will looks around to see if there is something he missed.

"Well, this is the same table you and I will sit at in 2018." Hallie looks up on the shelf. "Except for a bit of wear and tear, it is exactly the same." She looks up at the few books that are on the shelf by their table but doesn't seem to see what she is looking for.

"What are you looking for?"

She pokes out her lower lip and then looks over at Will. "*The Martian Chronicles*. It's not here."

"Sorry?"

"Oh, there was this book…" She stops short. "That's right. The bookmark with my birthday for a serial number. It was dated July 4, 1958." She puffs out air from her mouth. "It was a train ticket turned bookmark, but I doubt it has even been bought yet."

He gives a crooked smile. "Surreal isn't it?"

"Yes. It. Is. The book hasn't been put on the shelf yet." She shakes her head.

"Hi, y'all. What can I get you to drink?" The waitress hands them menus. They give her their drink orders and start looking though the menus.

Will clears his throat. "Are you aware from the story you were told by Beattie and Dot about my father's trip with Mister Holt to the Chesapeake Bay and Watt's Island."

"Yes."

"During their absence, Melinda maintained contact with me and visited our plantation fairly often. We actually became friends. On one of these visits she met my cousin, Daniel. They grew very close. Daniel was older than me. He was Melinda's age, and they were well-matched. They complemented one another. Daniel was very much like our Uncle Benjamin in that he honored the traditions of our grandmother's people—the Pamunkey.

"Our uncle was a great man. Benjamin was grounded and patient and unpretentious. He raised Daniel after his parents had been killed. Melinda was also a good person, but she was spirited and used to a lavish lifestyle. Somehow, she gave his life spark, and he gave hers repose. Their love could be felt whenever you were around them." Emotion steals his breath, and he stops for a moment. He is grateful that the waitress returns placing their drinks on the table before taking their food orders. It gives him a moment to compose himself as he takes a drink and collects his thoughts.

He runs his fingers through his hair. "Melinda was rich and spoiled, but she also had been bullied and constrained by her step-father. Her mother died when she was young, and Mister Holt had tremendous influence over her. Daniel, I believe, showed her a different potential for her life. They fell in love that spring when her father was gone. She had changed so much during that time and was happy."

"What happened?" Hallie leans in.

"Well, the ship returned from the Chesapeake. Melinda and Daniel had to be very careful about being seen together. Daniel was educated, but he was considered part of the middling class—not someone who would normally be married to a woman with Melinda's social standing. Mister Holt was a formidable man, even a dangerous man, and Daniel was cautiously working on a way to approach him for permission to court Melinda. He never got the chance though because of the curse. How ironic it is."

"I don't understand. Why ironic?" Hallie's brow furrows. The waitress comes up with their orders and sets a ketchup bottle on the table. "Anything else right now?" She asks cheerfully.

"No, thank you." Will looks up and smiles courteously, and

she moves on to another table.

He takes a bite of his sandwich and a drink trying to swallow past the lump in his throat. "Ironic because, according to Odina, Daniel and Melinda's relationship was what led to the Circle of Souls being tethered to me. It was unintentional, but it has been a bond that has survived for all but two souls for over two hundred years. You see, Daniel also was a tethered soul."

"Was?"

"Yes, he and another—Elias—have since suffered a death of death." He presses his lips in and bites down on them.

Hallie tilts her head and purses her lips.

"In the beginning—because I was so angry and bent on self-destruction—I often did not abide by the Demon King's rules. Mostly I hadn't completely figured them out, but I knew enough to know better than to put the others at risk. I had the Book of Lineages and used it to keep track of the circle—I knew that each soul had at least one gateway relative that would provide an anchor to earth.

"Each soul needs an anchor so to speak to bring them back to Earth from the Mesu except for me, and I serve as Paimon's anchor while I am on Earth. I knew that much—I knew the importance of protecting the gateway relative. I should have heeded Daniel's warning, but I was so caught up in my hate-driven pride. My time in the underworld was brutal. Time has no meaning there, so it could seem endless. We were part of the legions protecting the Tartarian protectorate. Because we maintain our humanity and flesh during our servitude, there is usually a lot of contempt towards us. Humans are envied by most because we hold God's favor above all of his creation. So, I rebelled when I was on Earth. I refused to accept my fate and refused to do the Demon King's bidding. It often put us in some dangerous situations. You have witnessed a glimpse of his brutality during the harvest in

Fayerdale but, trust me, that was nothing." He rubs the back of his neck and pulls a drink from his straw.

"It was October 1781. We were part of the Virginia Militia fighting under George Washington, and we were being led into the final assault against the British who were in Yorktown. We were in the regiment led by Alexander Hamilton. Daniel, Elias, Matthew Carter, and Caleb Blake were there. We kept our original names then, but you would know Matthew and Caleb as Luke and Jeb from Fayerdale. Unfortunately, the two lineage gateways for Daniel and Elias were there as well. They were young boys though and not a part of direct battle. They mostly provided servant duties to the officers, and I thought they would be safe since they remained in the camp away from the front line." He reaches for his drink and looks up at Hallie.

Hallie takes his hand, and he smiles at her through pressed lips then takes a drink. "Daniel had tried to tell me that there was someone in the ranks who," he pauses for a moment thinking, remembering. "Who 'put him on edge' was what he had said to me. I should have looked into it, but I did not, and soon the final advance was ordered and there was no time. It was to be a silent advance—no muskets—bayonets only. Of course, by the end of the advancement Daniel, Elias, Matthew and Caleb helped to make up the total number of nine dead on the American side. The Demon King had their bodies all there at a clearing nearby for the final harvest. Grissell and Melinda were still alive and had been drawn in from Yorktown. The two gateway relatives for Daniel and Elias were lying dead at the center of the clearing. They had suffered wounds from a bayonet. It was then that I saw the very man that Daniel had tried to warn me about. He stood in uniform with a bloody bayonet fixed to his musket.

"Melinda was inconsolable as the Demon King tormented her with Daniel and Elias' demise. She tried to bargain with him to reclaim them. He offered her false hope saying it would all be settled in Tartarus. One-by-one he struck us down saving the foot soldier for last." He bites his lips closing his eyes for a moment before he looks at Hallie with a pained expression. "Or, at least until just before he executed me."

Hallie's face contorts and her voice falters. "What…what happened after that?"

"We woke on the shores of the Styx as always. The means of our transition has not changed since that first awakening after the original harvest in 1720.  Daniel and Elias were with us and, at first, it seemed that the Demon King had granted Melinda her wish. Within no time he walked up to us through the murky haze."

Hallie nods with a shudder.

"The foot soldier from the Battle of Yorktown was with him. It struck me as odd, and I remember feeling alarmed. Even then I knew Paimon's conquests never traveled with him. They are barely above us—the human slaves of Tartarus sit only above the shades in the underworld's cast system. I was not alone in my apprehension because I could see the others become tense as they readied themselves for trouble. We had all transitioned to our underworld appearances which at the time were those of underling warriors and servants to Paimon. We had weapons but no armor aside from our protective marks. The soldier too had transitioned, but he was in full battlement gear. He was huge with long braided hair hanging to the middle of his back, red skin, and a cloven hoof at the end of his left leg. He bore no wings, the same as us, but when he turned you could see he had them at one time—they were severed, and his flesh bore the scars of a crudely stitched repair."

Will looks around. He suddenly appreciates this may not be the best place for this conversation to take place.

Hallie follows his gaze and squeezes his hand. "It's okay, Will. This place is hopping busy, and no one has even glanced our way."

He sees that she is right and wets his bottom lip before continuing. "Well, we realized quickly that he was not a conquest. He only barely resembled the man we thought he was when we were on Earth. The power he wielded in the underworld could be felt all around him. There was a sizzle of electricity surrounding him. You know?"

She nods with eyes wide.

"Paimon's eyes glowed a brilliant red as they stepped up to us. It was evident he was anticipating the moment with enthusiasm. We were told that the soldier's name was Sariel, and that he desired a union with Melinda. He was a great demon warrior and chief, and he had admired Melinda from afar over the past sixty some years both in the underworld and on Earth.

"He…," Will's voice catches. "He had struck a bargain with the Demon King to earn her as a conquest. By killing Daniel's gateway relative, he assured my cousin would no longer have passage to Earth, and now he desired banishment from the underworld for Daniel as well. This would assure no future threat of losing Melinda in either realm. Daniel would have one opportunity to turn the table of doom. The death of Elias' kin was collateral damage, but he would be granted a chance for reprieve alongside Daniel. They were given the 'generous' offer to fight together against the lone Sariel. There was to be a fight to the death of death between the three."

Will drinks from his glass again. It is a struggle between the solace of relief to talk about all of this, and the ever-present nagging shame screaming at him to be silent. He forges on. "We were dumbfounded. None of us had ever seen nor heard of Sariel before. It was unsettling to think of what else could possibly exist beyond the notice of the Circle of Souls that saw us as prey waiting to pick us off one-by-one. I learned a valuable lesson from that day to never trust anyone, and to remain wary at all times. I made up my mind to be stronger and more vigilant. At that point though none of it mattered. We all stepped forward to stand by Daniel and Elias, but one wave of the Demon King's hand, and we were swept away to the periphery where all we could do was bear witness to the slaughter. Sariel was a powerful demon."

"Was?" Hallie leans forward. Her eyes glisten with tears.

"When Daniel fell, just before the ground of Tartarus consumed him, Melinda ran to his side. She was devastated. Sariel stepped up to take her by the arm and claim his prize. He was focused on the object of his desire seeing a final victory after decades of lurking in the shadows of her existence. He had no warning for what was to happen next. Melinda unsheathed Daniel's long knife from his waist strap and, when Sariel laid ahold of her arm, she turned plunging the knife deeply under his breast plate catching him off guard." Will stares at the carbonation in his drink and pinches the bridge of his nose. "His black blood oozed down over Melinda's hand and arm as she held steadfast twisting the knife to assure its deadly effect while watching the light of life leave his yellow eyes. Sariel dropped to his knees, and the ground of the riverbank shifted to pull him under along with Daniel before anyone could react.

"When the Demon King grasped what happened, he scattered us across his dominion sending Melinda to the furies and the rest of us to the legions where we have served in the underworld's protectorate wars ever since. He started forcing the souls to drink from the Lethe before entering the Mesu and dividing us during the passage.

"That was when I became more determined to find a way to work his system, so to speak, and get us all out. But with the influences of the Lethe on the other souls' memories, it has been a difficult task. I have been mostly alone until meeting you. In the beginning we all had memory of past lives, and Daniel was always a voice of reason trying to keep me from going too far beyond the rules. It was too late by the time I learned to appreciate it, but now I have you. I will not make the same mistake twice."

"Will, I am so sorry."

"It was my own doing. My fault. All that rage and fury that I let cloud my judgment and dictate my actions really made no difference in our situation. At the end of the day, or the end of a life, I—well we all—remained enslaved. Trapped. It took me the loss of two good people to realize that we choose how we face our lives—and deaths. Even when the end is very clear, the manner in which we go about life leading towards that end is *our* choice—it is the prime envy of all creatures towards the human race. Our free will. Even with the curse, and Paimon's never-ending manipulations attempting to control us, we still maintain our free will. I had not used it wisely up to that day. I do not want you to misunderstand me, and I want to be honest with you about who I am Hallie. I am not saying I have become a pacifist. I will not back down. I believe that there are things worthy of rage and battle— you just cannot let others dictate what inspires a fight for you."

"I know who you are Will without any words from you. I know who you are about to be too, and it's the same person. You have always been the same person and whether you are inspired to kindness, love, passion, joy, light, dark, sorrow, indifference, hatred, or mischievousness I will always—always love you."

He reaches across the table taking both her hands wanting to say something, but he is suddenly too overwhelmed. Too grateful. His voice is gravely, and he can barely speak above a whisper when he finally pulls himself together. "And, I you."

She shrugs her head into a shoulder and flashes him her brilliant smile then straightens up in her seat. "We're done eating. How about we go outside for some fresh air?"

"That sounds wonderful."

When they go to the register at the counter to pay, Beezie is sitting on one of the stools waiting for her lunch order. She has a fresh stick of gum in her mouth that she is popping loudly much to the annoyance of the man sitting next to her who is eating a plate of pulled pork and coleslaw.

She turns on her stool to face them. "Well, hey Will!"

"Hello, Beezie." He answers as he reaches into his back pocket for his wallet. A waitress at the register greets him and takes his bill. She rings it up making small talk as she goes about getting his change together.

Beezie looks at Hallie for a moment making several pops of her gum. "Hello, I'm Beezie Williams. I saw you at church yesterday at Saint James."

"Oh, yes. I went to service with the Adkins and Will. I'm Hallie O'Meara. It's nice to meet you."

"Same here." Beezie sits with her elbows propped against the counter behind her. "Hallie." She says the name like she is trying it on for size. "That's kind of different, but I think I like it."

"Thanks. I was named after my father, Halbrook."

"Huh, a girl being named after her daddy." Beezie thinks on this a moment. "Well my real name is Debbie. So, I would always draw a bee—you know, bumble bees—with my name. Deb-*bie*.  Bumble-*bee*. I'd been doing it that way since I first learned how to write my name. Not sure how it started but folks just started calling me Beezie, and it stuck. I dunno, but I like it anyway."

"Yes." Hallie nods. "I like it too. It's unique."

Will finishes at the register as a waitress brings Beezie's bag to her. She hops down from the stool. "Well, gotta take this to Connie."

"Are you going over to the Snip 'n Style?" Hallie asks.

"Sure am. I work there during the summer and weekends and stuff."

"Well, I'm going there too. Connie is going to do my nails for me."

"No kidding? Well, how about we walk together then?" Beezie gives her a smile and then broadens it looking at Will.

He puts his wallet into his back pocket saying nothing, and steps forward opening the door for them.

Beezie talks incessantly as they make their way to the Snip 'n Style asking Hallie about what it is like staying with the Ferrum Witch and interjecting comments about people they pass and tidbits of information about the different shops and houses in town. Hallie mostly nods and answers questions. Will says nothing and is grateful when they arrive at the Snip 'n Style.
The bell jingles when Beezie opens the door to the Snip 'n Style. She leans against it waiting for Hallie.

"Um, I'll be there in a minute."

Beezie shrugs. "Okey dokey." And walks in letting the door shut behind her.

Hallie looks up at Will smiling with a furrowed brow. "Sorry. I had no idea she was…so…energenic…and…loquacious."

He laughs. "No, it is fine. She is not so bad."

"So, are you working until closing today?"

"No, actually Drew is finishing up Dillon McCaffrey's car this afternoon, and he said he would get the shop closed up, so I am done at three."

"Well, did you finish up that stockpile of food in your refrigerator yesterday?"

"Actually, I came home with this incredible appetite."

"Hmm, wonder where that came from." She pokes him in the side.

"No idea." He grabs her hand and holds onto it.

"So, I spoke to Odina before I walked into town today and asked if you could have supper with us tonight, and she said yes. Would you like to come over?"

"I am always up for spending time with you. What time?"

"Why don't you just come over after you're done with work?"

"Alright, but I will have to shower and change before I head over. I can be there by four I think."

Hallie smiles and steps up on her toes kissing him before she turns and goes into the salon.

# CHAPTER 13
## Espial

Hallie comes running across the clearing to meet Will when he steps out of the woods into the hollow. "Will, I met the most unusual woman today at the Snip 'N Style."

He puts his arm around her. "Who?" He goes to walk towards the cabin, but Hallie pulls him towards the garden.

"I need to tell you about her. Let's go to the garden to talk."

"Do we have time before supper?"

"Yes, I just checked the chicken for Odina, and it has about thirty minutes left to cook."

They go to the back of the garden and sit on the bench. "Will, have you ever met Maude Cavander?"

"The college professor?"

Hallie nods.

"Yes. Not too long after I came into town, I did some temp work for the college moving furniture. I met her then. She teaches history or something like that."

"She teaches Anthropology." Hallie slides to the edge of the bench. "She was in the shop finishing up a haircut and manicure just before Connie did my nails." Hallie holds up her hands showing Will her pink nails.

"Very nice." He kisses her hands.

She flashes a smile. "Anyway, I only got to talk to Doctor Cavander just enough to be introduced. She did seem to have an interest in Odina and Azure, but Connie seemed a bit in a hurry to get her checked out. I guess so she could get my manicure started before her next customer. While I was sitting waiting for my nails to dry Beezie sat by me to talk."

Will's eyebrows arch upward.

"Well, actually it wasn't too bad because she caught me up on the salon gossip."

Will smirks with a do-I-really-want-to-hear-it? look.

"Will." Hallie pushes against him. "Just listen to what I have to say before you judge. Beezie said that Doctor Cavander was in a peculiar mood today and was very talkative. Beezie did not hear all that was said—just bits and pieces. She heard Doctor Cavander say something to Connie about Nephilim and Watchers. Beezie thought it was just crazy talk, but I remember reading about them in an old book of angel lore that Dot has back home."

Will shrugs his shoulders. "I am with Beezie. What are they?"

Hallie readjusts her seat. She purses her lips and furrows her brow. "Oh, well maybe it is just folklore, but they are also mentioned in the Bible. I thought for sure it could mean something—that you would know of them. You know, because of your contact with demons and angels and what not."

"Hallie, tell me what *you* know about them. Just because I cross between realms does not mean that I am aware of all beings that exist. Creation is too complex for someone as paltry as me to know all possibilities."

"Will…don't say that."

He raises his eyebrows and prods her to on.

"So, there is a book that Dot has that is very old and hand-scribed. Actually, it's similar to your Book of Lineages in that it has a family-tree-type drawing on the back pages. I don't really remember too much about that part of the book, but the front section has these beautiful ink drawings of angels and humans, masculine angels, beautiful women, and children. There are handwritten entries that call them Grigori, and some of the passages call them Angelic Watchers. It seems they came down from the heavens and ended up remaining on Earth. It says that many of the Watchers grew bored with life on Earth and became more demon-like corrupting humans. One of the passages even says it was this turnover in the Watchers and their prodigy—they are called Nephilim—that moved God to flood the Earth during the time of Noah to rid mankind of their influence."

Will listens to her intently. The late afternoon sun plays off of her hair giving a halo effect. He smiles thinking that the only angel on Earth he knows is her.

Hallie pauses for a moment. "Will, are you listening?" She raises her eyebrows and tips her head looking directly into his eyes.

He blinks and nods as a smile flickers across his face.

"Well, I don't know about the accuracy of the flood's purpose because further into the book there are passages talking about Watchers throughout history, after Noah's time, both good and evil."

Will leans back on the bench. "There could be something to it Hallie. Aside from it having a supernatural basis, what does it have to do with us? Directly, I mean."

Hallie looks at him intently. She swallows hard. "Beezie said that Doctor Cavander suggested that you and Drew are Nephilim." She blurts it out and waits with a furrowed brow.

He guffaws. "What does Maude Cavander even know of Drew and me?  I think *I* would know if there was Grigori blood running through my veins. She might have some sort of connection to the supernatural and sees something odd in me, but Drew? I don't know Hallie. I am not sure that beauty parlor conversation is the best source for valid information."

Hallie shrugs. "I know, Will. It sounds crazy, but even if the Grigori lore is just fantasy, she has seen *something* in you."

"And Drew. Hallie, come on."

"How do you know there's not something about Drew that

is unique?  Unique like you?"

He stops and looks at her a moment. He starts to rebuff her but hesitates. "I guess I cannot, but I do not know that about anyone else either—at least anyone outside you, me, Connie, and Sadie for the moment, and I guess Odina too.  The five of us are the only ones I can be certain of. But honestly Hallie, descendants of Watchers? Hester would have said something to me. I would know."

"Maybe."

He shakes his head and rolls his eyes.

"Connie is drawn to Drew. Why?"

"I do not know, but I am not willing to bet on it being an angelic heritage."

Hallie sits for a moment. "Okay, but I still want to go talk to Doctor Cavander. I want to see what she can tell us about Solomon's key, and her interest in you will most likely be the foot in the door that we need. Between this and what Odina told me when we were collecting herbs. It just convinces me that I am here to find Solomon's key. It has to be the reason."

"Right then, we will go see Maude Cavander." Will agrees.

She stops short and looks at him. "No argument?"

"With her background in anthropology I think you are right. She can tell us about the key and, if it takes a little bait to get to her, we should use it. I am willing to lure her with my Nephilim charm. When do you want to go?" He straightens his back and adjusts his collar.

Hallie rolls her eyes. "Soon. Do you have any time off this week?"

"I am off all day on Wednesday."

"Okay, I'll see what I can find out about her schedule, and we can make a 'chance' meeting with her."

"Agreed."

# CHAPTER 14
# Glimpse

Hallie is walking and so deep in thought about finding out about Maude Cavander's schedule and Nephilim that she is startled when the black Cadillac pulls alongside matching her pace. The sun glints off its polished finish, and she flashes back momentarily to Joe's, an earthly name used by the Demon King, car on the bridge-tunnel. Her stomach knots tighter than a sailor's rigging, and she imagines a strange glint in the driver's eyes before she realizes it is Dillon McCaffrey.

He has said something to her that she missed, and she forces herself to refocus on the black languid eyes. "Dillon." Hallie blinks. "I'm sorry. My mind is somewhere far away."

"Yes. I am often guilty of that myself. I just thought I would offer you a ride. How about it?"

"Oh." Hallie looks beyond him at the empty passenger seat of the pristine automobile. A prickle of frosty caution sprinkles along the back of her neck. "Um, I'm just walking to campus. It's really not all that far."

"Yes." He is friendly and his words smooth. "I thought, however, you would enjoy a bit of a scenic drive first. I can show you some of the countryside." Hallie starts to speak, but he pushes on before she can object. "Nothing too long. It really is a beautiful area, and I will drop you off in front of the very building you plan to visit on campus afterward. How about it?"

An image of a fly struggling in the sticky threads of a web crosses her mind and, uncharacteristically, she ignores the alarm pulsing in her chest. "Yes, sure. That will be nice."

"Wonderful." He leans over opening the passenger door as Hallie walks around. She climbs in glancing around the car's interior. Although it is much more luxurious, it makes her think of her classic Mustang, and she longs to be able to drive it once again.

"I just got my car back from Adkins' Garage and wanted to give it a test run. How much time do you have?"

"Oh, I dunno. I'm not on a schedule, but I would like to go to the college library before lunch."

"Ah, yes." Dillon focuses on the road as he speaks. "You have a propensity for books. Are you still interested in borrowing a book or two from my collection?"

"Yes, that would be nice."

"Very well. Once you have finished your task on campus come to my house. If I am not home Missus Mitchell, my housekeeper, will let you in. You can make yourself at home and make your selection."

"Thank you, I will." Hallie looks out the window at the lush beautiful mountain ridges. She traces their rise and fall on the horizon with her eyes thinking about the ups and downs of her life over the last few months. She could have never guessed what her first solo trip from the Eastern Shore to the Blue Ridge had in store for her.

"I thought I would take a loop up over the mountain and then back down Shooting Creek. It is a nice drive and will take less than an hour. Will that do?"

Hallie pulls her eyes away from the view and nods. They don't engage in much conversation. Dillon occasionally points out something of interest, but he mostly allows Hallie to enjoy the views. It is a clear day, and once they climb to a higher altitude the views are magical stretching across three to four mountain ridges before melting into the wispy blue horizon. Steep pastures are etched with trails cut by cows habitually following the same patterned routes to and from favorite grazing areas. A cow and her calf walk along one of the precarious paths of a steep rise and

Hallie is amazed at how sure-footed the otherwise large and awkward-looking animals are.

They turn onto Shooting Creek and begin the steep tortuous drive down the side of the mountain. Trees grow close to the roadway and, on portions of the drive, the upper branches of trees meet creating a tunnel over the hardtop. The effect is immediate with a refreshing drop in the temperature. Darkened hollows where the twisted bends of the creek weave back and forth through the forest hold their secrets well except for where the occasional patch of sunshine makes its way to the floor of the woods brightening a patch of ferns or an interesting rock formation. The hum of the Cadillac Coupe, the gentle sway as Dillon negotiates the curves, and the cool air lull Hallie into a quiet and tranquil state.

The car slows and comes to a stop pulling Hallie's attention away from the woodland scenery. An old green pick-up truck is stopped ahead of them, and it makes her think about Liam's truck exploding pangs of longing inside her. This quickly changes to concern, however, when she sees the sheriff department vehicles parked along the roadway just beyond the truck. A deputy is talking to the driver of the pick-up and checking the man's identification. Hallie glances over at Dillon whose gaze is fixed towards the front of the car. He has the look of unperturbed boredom.

In the woods, several officers in different uniforms are walking through the trees where a man with a pair of dogs walks ahead of them. Hallie gasps and raises a shaky hand to her mouth when she sees a white sheet lying crumpled on the ground near them. She looks more intently at the area as the car begins to slowly roll forward.

"Good morning officer." Dillon's slightly formal but friendly voice sounds distant while she watches the pair of dogs going through the underbrush.

"Morning sir. Driver's license please." Hallie recognizes the man's voice and turns leaning down to look through the window at him.

"Officer Simms?"

He looks down through the window at Hallie, and she sees recognition on his face, but she can see that he is not sure how he knows her.

"Hallie O'Meara, sir. We met at Fairy Stone last weekend. I was there with the Adkins."

A smile cracks across the official look of his face. "Yes, Hallie, of course. You were with the group of young people that Cleo and Katie had out last Sunday. I believe it was Connie and the two boys Cleo has working for him, Will and Drew. Isn't that right?"

"Yes, sir." Hallie answers him

He nods his head thoughtfully and looks from Hallie to Dillon. "What brings you out this way this morning Mister," he looks down at Dillon's license, "McCaffrey?"

"Oh, well." Dillon seems caught off guard that the conversation now includes him. "I am just taking Hallie for a short drive showing her some of the sites in the area since she is a visitor to the county."

Officer Simms glances over at Hallie looking for an affirmation of this and seems satisfied with no words from her. He hands Dillon's identification back to him. Dillon tucks it into his wallet and glances through the passenger side window beyond Hallie asking, "Is everything alright officer?"

The deputy glances over at the woods, the body, and the search then he looks down at Dillon and studies him a moment. "No sir, not at the moment." With that he steps away from the Cadillac and waves them on.

Dillon moves the car forward slowly. Hallie looks back

through the rearview window. She sees Officer Simms look at the Cadillac and write in a note pad. There is a battered rusty red car stopped a little further down the mountain coming from the opposite direction. A deputy is standing by the driver's window. Both the driver and deputy pause to watch the Cadillac while Dillon drives it forward. Hallie looks at the interior once again and the shiny black hood beyond the windshield gaining an appreciation for how exquisite, and very out-of-place, the car she sits in is.

The Cadillac accelerates when they pass the last car pulled over on the roadside. It is black with "CORONER" written in gold lettering on the driver's door. Hallie wills herself to breath in and out grateful that Dillon makes no attempt for conversation, and relief washes over her when they pull onto the Ferrum College campus. Will is walking along the roadside.

"Uh, Dillon you can drop me off here, if you don't mind."

He lifts his foot off the accelerator and pulls off to the side of the road. "Not at all."

Will shades his eyes with a hand squinting towards them.

"Now be sure to come by the house later today. I will leave instructions with Missus Mitchell to show you my library, and to allow you to take whatever you like."

Hallie looks at him avoiding his eyes before opening the door. "Okay, I will. Thank you for the ride."

He nods graciously, and she steps out shutting the door behind her. She watches the car disappear down the road before walking towards Will.

"Hallie?" He rushes up to her. His ears percuss with the pulsations from his pounding heart. "Is that Dillon McCaffrey? I thought you said you were coming to campus before lunch. The garage was slow, so Mister Adkins let me leave, and I overheard talk about another girl being murdered. You were nowhere to be found." He pauses for a moment to take a breath attempting to lose the edge in his voice. "I was…worried." He is not successful.

"Will, I'm sorry. If I knew you were coming, I would have never…"

"What were you doing with Dillon McCaffrey?" He is failing miserably at tempering his anger, but it is fueled by his apprehension.

"Oh, well he…" Hallie stops short looking at Will. "Are you angry with me? Because if you are, you need to explain why." Her tone matches his, and it snaps him back in focus.

He flexes his fingers and shifts his weight taking a deep breath. "No, I'm sorry. I was worried—just as I said." He takes another deep breath in through his nose holding it a moment and then exhales slowly closing his eyes. He opens them looking her in the eye. "Hallie, there is not any jealousy, any possessiveness, any command in what I need to say to you." *Tread lightly.*

She looks at him biting the inside of her lower lip.

"Please don't go anywhere alone. Don't go off alone with anyone. Not Dillon McCaffrey, not Drew, not anyone."

She stands for a moment releasing the bite on her lip. "I do understand what you are saying, Will." She holds her hand up gesturing towards the road in the direction that Dillon drove towards. "You know, I wasn't comfortable getting into that car, but I did. I never do that…never! And Will, we drove by where I think the murder happened. It looks like it is still being investigated. I saw a body under a sheet. There were dogs and men from Patrick, Henry and Franklin Counties there. The coroner's car was there." Her voice catches, and she rubs her arms to calm a shudder. "It all looked so…newly discovered. I don't understand how you heard about it."

"I overheard a conversation where they were looking for a few people to help out with a search near Shooting Creek. I didn't need to hear more to know what it was about. I immediately went to find you."

Her eyes drift downward. "Listen, Will…it was strange. On the drive we passed it all." Her eyes moisten and she locks them on his. "You know, it didn't have any effect on him…Dillon, I mean. He had a cool disinterest and, even though he asked the officer if something was wrong, the tone in his voice was off."

Will takes her hand.

"I thought maybe he sensed it had upset me and decided not to make it worse, but I don't know Will."

"Something else to figure out?"

"Maybe. Sounds to me though that you may have some of it already figured out." She leans into him, and he slides his arms around her embracing her warmly.

"Hallie, when we were at Fairy Stone Drew said that Dillon put him on edge."
Hallie looks up at him, and her eyes widen. "Same thing Daniel said about the foot soldier."

"Yes."

"Oh my God, Will. Do you really think there is anything there? I mean I just was alone with the man."

"I don't know Hallie, but it came to me last night when I was thinking about our conversation at the '77. I honestly don't know about Drew either."

"Why? What happened?"

"Nothing really, just little things. The night the Franklin County girl was killed was the night I came to the Ridges' to check on you, and I ran into Drew. It was just odd to see him out that way at that time of night. He stays at the Mayhew's which is much further out of town. Then Connie came by the garage this morning and said that Drew was supposed to take her out last night but never showed up. She wanted to see if any of us had heard from him."

Hallie frowns and shakes her head.

"The time is getting close Hallie. I can feel it. Paimon made his presence known, the blue jay feather presented itself, the killings have gotten closer to Ferrum, and now they are happening more often."

"We need to not waste time then. Can you come with me to the library?"

"Yes, of course."

"Okay, good then. We'll do this now instead of waiting until your day off tomorrow."

They walk across the campus mall towards the library. The air ripples in front of them creating a magical summer shimmer. Hallie points it out to Will. "I wish I could step through it like a veil and be back where I started." She tells him about the day they came to campus with David and Becky, and about the raw beat from the street band, the banter of the Jack Tale Players, and the slow sweet tune that they danced to under the trees on the plywood dance floor. The joyous noise of that day is yet to come, and now they walk through a serene quiet that is a contrast to how Will feels inside. He holds the library door open for Hallie, and the step inside where a different kind of quiet swallows them.

There is a young man at the circulation desk reading a magazine with an earpiece from a transistor radio in his left ear. He is bopping his head to a concealed beat.

Hallie whispers, "Excuse me."

The young man glances up and abruptly pulls the earpiece out by the wire, and they can now hear the miniaturized beat escaping the tiny hole from the center of white plastic. He blushes and reaches over to lower the volume.

"Hi, can I help you?" He is polite with a welcoming smile. The badge on his shirt tells them his name is Joel.

"Hi, yes. We are looking for books about anthropology and folklore. Does the library carry anything like that?"

He walks around the counter indicating to follow him. "Do you have a specific title in mind?"

"No, not really." Hallie answers him.

"Well let's look in the topics card catalog and see what we might have." He stops in front of a trio of wood cabinets. Each with a set of tiny drawers organized alphabetically. He pulls open a drawer in the upper left corner. The cards inside have worn edges and a smudged line down the centers from years of fingertips perusing the contents of the drawer. Joel scans the contents until he finds what he is looking for.

"Here we are." He pushes back the cards to show the first listing for anthropology. "The library holds two texts. One of them is just a discussion of the discipline really. This one though talks about anthropological similarities between primitive and modern cultures. What exactly are you looking for?"

"Well, we're looking for information on folklore and symbolism in various cultures."

"Oh, I don't think you are going to find that here. There might be a small mention of it in this book if you are interested in checking."

"We were really hoping to find something more in-depth than that." She sighs. "We need the information for…a project."

"Well, you could always see what Doctor Cavander has in her private collection." He shrugs as he starts to walk back towards the circulation desk talking as he goes. "She is working this summer, so she is keeping office hours. I'm sure she would be glad to meet with you."

"Really?"

"I don't see why not. You can ask her yourself. She's over there in the back side of the library where the lounging chairs are.

She comes in every day at lunch to read the newspapers."

Hallie glances towards the back side of the library, at Will, and then back at Joel. "Really?"

Joel nods at her like it is no mystery and makes his way back around to the other side of the circulation desk.

Hallie whispers, "Is it really going to be this easy?"

Will shrugs whispering back, "Is it supposed to be difficult?"

She pushes into his side, and he puts his arm around her pulling her close as she tries to stifle a laugh. He puts a finger to his lips holding onto her as they make their way past the stacks. The temperature in the library is cool but there still is a slight musty smell in the air. They turn a corner and see the back of Maude's head at the couch. She is holding a paper up in front of her flipping through the pages.

Will lets go of Hallie and makes a dramatic sweep with his arm directing her towards Maude. She rolls her eyes at him as he falls in step behind her.

Maude's head perks up before they reach her, and she folds the paper setting it on her lap. She turns her head in anticipation giving a smile looking first at Hallie before drifting her gaze towards Will to extend the greeting.

"Hello, Doctor Cavander. We are sorry for disturbing you, but we were wondering if we could set up a time to come see you to discuss some questions we have."

"Hallie, Will, hello. A time to meet? Yes, of course. What would it be concerning?"

Hallie glances back at Will, and he steps forward. "We actually need to speak you about Solomon's key."

Maude blinks for a moment and Will quickly adds, "And, to discuss Nephilim."

She nods. "Yes, of course." She sets the paper aside

standing up facing them and glances down at her watch. "I have a meeting in thirty minutes, and then I am going to a conference in Roanoke for a few days. Perhaps when I return?"

Will's fingers twitch with urgency; however, he thinks pushing her to meet sooner might not go well. "Yes ma'am, we would greatly appreciate it. When is a good time for us to come by your office?"

"Friday, about four o'clock should be good. It's a holiday, but I'll be here for a bit."

They say good-bye and make their way back through the stacks. Will stops short putting his arm out to prevent Hallie from stepping forward. He moves back towards the wall finding the handle to a door and opens it keeping Hallie behind him backing into a small closet.

Through the door louvers they see Paimon standing with his back to them by the circulation desk. He is talking with Joel, but he raises his head alerting as though his attention is suddenly pulled in another direction.

Will whispers, "Take out the amulet."

Hallie takes it out and they hold hands entwining their fingers around the amulet. A gentle glow gives their hands a translucent appearance, and it spread beyond their hands out into the closet space. It forms a thin wall between them and the door. Will and Hallie raise their hands upward and the luminescent shield extends from ceiling to floor. Paimon relaxes and continues his conversation with Joel.

Hallie's hand grows moist with perspiration and her breaths quicken to a staccato pace. Paimon eventually walks from circulation desk towards them, and she holds her breath. Every nerve Will has stands at attention. Paimon's eyes are covered with a pair of purple tinted glasses, and he passes without taking notice of the closet door and is soon out of view. The library door opens and gently closes.

Hallie's pupils are dilated. Neither of them dares to speak. They keep their hands together while the stagnant closet air makes it hard to breath. Will's blood is rushing through his veins, and the close proximity to Hallie is building heat that causes his muscles to tense. He does not dare open the door until enough time has passed to assure Paimon is well gone.

Her hand touches his chest and slides up towards his shoulder. She trembles as she slides it behind his neck. He looks down seeing more than a need for comfort. He pulls her closer, and she rises up on her toes pressing her velvety lips against his neck under his chin. He closes his eyes while the effect of her kiss swells through his body. She moves up to his mouth kissing him first tentatively and then desperately. The close encounter creates a need to assure themselves that they can find safety in each other's arms.

Hallie pulls away from Will, their hands remain joined with the glow from the amulet intensifying with their kiss. Sweat glistens over her cheeks and Will brushes back a few strands of hair that cling to the side of her face. He bends down kissing her, tasting the salty sweetness of her hot skin and mouth. The stifling conditions of the closed space, and the stress from their near encounter with Paimon has his skin tingling and his desire simmering with a craving for her that he cannot restrain. He melts into her and a soft amorous moan rises from deep within him, but he exhales it forcing himself to pull away from her.

"Will, take me back to your apartment. Please." She begs him with a breathless whisper.

He searches her eyes. The fear has not left them, and he knows he cannot do what she asks no matter how much he wants to. He cannot risk the essence of her soul being changed creating a potential for the Demon King to see their connection.

"Hallie, there is nothing I want more." He loosens his grip on her hand and the amulet to hold her face between his hands while gently caressing her skin. Her lip quivers. Despite voicing the desire that burns within, his tone expresses the restraint he fights to maintain. He sees the look of rejection overshadow her fear and feels her ever so slightly withdrawal from him. He pulls her back kissing her slowly, deeply, and then nibbles her lip lightly moving to her neck sliding his hands down to her shoulders.

His voice cracks with emotion. "Nothing more than you, Hallie. I promise you that, but not now. Not with me—it's Liam you fell in love with, and it's Liam you should be with. I am so sorry that I am giving you mixed messages here. This happened suddenly and without warning, and I was caught off guard. We have to keep you safe. You are the one who is going to see this through to the end."

She starts to avert her gaze from him, and he fears that there is guilt clouding over her eyes. He gently holds her face keeping her focused on him. "Hallie, being with you would be beautiful and right in itself no matter where life takes us in the future, but we are not dealing just with those issues right now. At this moment, Paimon has no idea who you are and that affords you some safety…"

She opens her mouth to contradict him, but he forges on. "Hallie, trust me. You are a pure soul. There are attractions a pure soul has to a demon, but Paimon usually will not try to tamper with one unless there is strong motivation. I do not want to be that motivation where you are concerned. We have to delay his discovery of you for as long as possible."

A tear forms finding its way over her lower lashes onto her cheek. It glistens in the slowly fading glow of the amulet. His chest tightens threatening to squeeze his heart to a standstill.

"You and Liam are one in the same, as was Billy, and I am

sure William was." Her whisper is draped in sadness. "It's all so…"

They are startled when the closet door opens suddenly letting cool air rush in. They pull apart seeing Joel, broom in hand, standing with wide eyes and a sudden coloring of his cheeks. He is dumbfounded, and it is Will who speaks first as he takes Hallie's hand stepping out of the closet and around Joel with her in tow.

"Hey, Joel."

Joel doesn't have a chance to reply before they pass through the doors of the library. Will takes a quick survey of the mall assuring there is no sign of Paimon. There is a gentle breeze and the temperature below the trees on the campus mall is cooler drying the moisture from their skin. They look at each other and laugh.

Will is relieved to see her relax again. "I know I have said this before, but my future self is going to figure out what needs to be done to defeat Paimon. Trust me Hallie *this* is going to happen. It just has to be safe. It has to be forever. I cannot give that to you right now."

She raises an eyebrow and licks her lips. Slowly.

A quiver lights across the back of his neck and he rubs it away. "You know," Will leans down to catch her eye and attempts a steady voice. "I once read that abstinence is the world's most potent aphrodisiac."

Hallie folds her arms saying nothing for a moment and then laughs. "Thank you, Will.  Thank you for…your strength and sense of humor. When the time comes, we are going to need an entire week to work through all that tension I think."

"I will look forward to it then." He pulls in a breath letting it out slowly knowing how right she is.

# CHAPTER 15
# Ascertain

"Hello, Mister Adkins."

"Will, Hallie, hello." Mister Adkins flashes a broad smile. "Will, what are you doing here? I thought you had some things to get done over at the college." He replaces the gas nozzle on the pump and takes payment from his customer.

"Yes, sir we just left from there. I was wondering if I could use the office phone and, if you have seen Drew today."

"Sure, sure you go on in and use the phone. Drew got in not too long after you left this morning. He said he had a bit of a rough night last night. He's around the back of the garage repairing a tire for Lottie Perdue."

Will thanks him, and he and Hallie walk over to the garage office.

Hallie wrinkles her nose. "Who do you need to call?"

"Well, I am not sure what Paimon was doing on campus, but I know it was not innocent. Regardless, it is now the second time I have seen him. I do not think we can wait until Friday to talk to Maude Cavander. I am going to offer to drive her to her conference."

"Drive to Roanoke?"

"Yes, or wherever she needs to go."

"I want to go too."

"Yes, of course. We both need to talk to her." Will opens the office door for Hallie.

The aroma of motor oil and coffee surrounds them when they walk in. A round metal clock with an advertisement for Signal Oil lets him know it is twelve-thirty. *Wonder what time Maude is leaving.*

"There's a racecar driver from Ferrum?" Hallie asks while looking at several framed newspaper articles on the wall. "The Ferrum Flash?"

"Yes, his race car, the number '77, is also the name of his restaurant."

"Oh, wow. Now that I think about it, I remember David—uh, that would be the future Luke—saying something about the restaurant being named after a race car."

"Yes, well Mister Adkins is a big fan." Will dials the operator and asks to be connected to the Ferrum College main line then waits to get transferred to Maude Cavander's office while Hallie reads through the articles on the wall.

"Doctor Cavander?"

"Speaking."

"Yes ma'am, this is Will White. I am wondering if we could be of some service to one another."

"Oh hello, Will. What do you have in mind?"

"Hallie and I need to speak with you sooner than Friday, and I thought we could drive you to your conference this afternoon in order to have some time to talk."

"Well, the college was to provide a car, but I suppose I could cancel that, if you have an urgent need to speak with me today. Could you be at my office in Beckam Hall in about three hours?"

"Yes ma'am. We will get there by three o'clock to be sure we leave on time." He looks over at Hallie to be sure this was good for her, and she nods to him.

"Yes, ma'am we can definitely do that."

"Okay, I will see you both then."

"Thank you. We appreciate your willingness to talk to us." He hangs up and looks over at Hallie as they walk out. "Okay, it is set. Now, we just need to get a car."

She stops short and laughs. "Details, details."

"Get your call made?" Mister Adkins asks, as he walks towards the office.

"Yes sir, thank you." Will says.

"Good then." He steps past them opening the office door turning back towards them with a somber look. "Will, uh, I'm not sure if you heard or not, but another girl was found dead this morning."

"Yes sir, we heard."

"The girl was the daughter of a friend of Katie's from over at Woolwine, and I told her that I would go with her to her friend's home tomorrow. Can you open the shop for me in the morning? I should be back later in the morning, and you can have the afternoon off."

"Yes sir, of course, if there is anything else I can do please let me know."

"Me too Mister Adkins," Hallie adds.

He nods at them and steps into the office.

"I guess the word has gotten out," Will says.

They walk around back to find Drew. A strange surge of uncertainty bubbles up from somewhere in Will's chest. *Where is that coming from?* He swallows hard and presses his lips together.

Drew is bent over with a tire he is repairing in a half barrel of water.

Will clears his throat as he and Hallie walk up. "Hello, Drew."

Drew looks back at them. "Will, I thought Mister Adkins said that you had business to attend to today."

"Yes, it is just about finished." Will lets go of Hallie's hand and walks in front of Drew.

"Drew, is everything okay with you?"

"Yeah, everything is okay."

Will swipes his chin with his knuckles and gives a nod.

"What?" Drew straightens with a tight jaw.

Will glances back at Hallie. She shifts her weight and swings her arms around in front of herself. "Uh, I'm going to walk down to the '77 and get some ice cream. Y'all want anything?"

Drew's expression softens. "No, I'm good. Thanks Hallie."

She looks towards Will, and he smiles at her shaking his head "No, but thank you."

Drew turns his attention to the tire he was working on. "What's on your mind Will? I'm assuming it is not my general state of health you're asking about."

"Drew, tell me why Dillon McCaffrey 'puts you on edge'. I have thought about what you said at the lake, and I am…curious."

"Well, you know what they say about curiosity." Drew's voice has a hint of bitterness.

"I believe that is in reference to cats."

"Perhaps." Drew threads a tar worm through the plugging tool. He lifts the tire from the half barrel of water and pushes the plug into the hole. "What do you want me to say? It's just a feeling about him. I can't explain it. He makes me edgy." Drew rolls the tire and lets it lean against the building then takes a shop rag from his back pocket and wipes his hands.

Will draws in a breath. There is something about Drew that he likes—feels connected to. *Just say it.* "Another girl was found dead this morning."

"Yeah, I heard about that."

"Connie was here earlier this morning looking for you when we opened."

"Yeah…I know…I went by her place before I came in today."

Will rubs the back of his neck.

"What are you asking here, Will? You wanting to know

about Dillon McCaffrey or me?"

"Connie said you no-showed for a date last night."

"Yeah."

"I ran into you in the woods the night that girl from Franklin County was killed. It was less than a half mile from where they found her body."

Drew makes a sucking sound with his teeth. "Oh, okay I'm seeing where this is going now. You accusing me of something? You some kind of P.I. or something, Will?"

Will's back snaps straight. "I am just asking. You said you found a hunting knife in Dillon's car, and that the car looked like it was driven in some rough terrain."

"Yeah, I did, and it was."

"Okay, so I learned an ill-fated lesson a long time ago about ignoring instincts."

"Really? You have an instinct churning inside of you needing validation, Will?"

"I need to know, if you know anything about the murders." Will squeezes his eyes shut pinching the bridge of his nose. *Damn. What am I saying?* He draws in a breath.

Drew laughs. "Man, you are a piece of work. First of all, if I did, do you believe I would say so to you? I mean you are accusing me of being responsible, right?"

Will starts to answer but Drew holds up his hand. "They were rhetorical questions." He steps closer to Will. "Here's one I want you to answer. What do you think of me? I mean we have known each other for…awhile."

Will answers him without hesitation. "I like you. I respect you."

"Why the questions, Will? Tell me what is going on." Drew is inches from Will red-faced and eyes narrowed.

Will takes a step back. "I have no foundation for thinking

that Dillon McCaffrey has something to do with the murders except your comment about him putting you on edge and…his car's condition…the knife. Anyone could be responsible for those deaths at this point, but I cannot ignore your observations. I have had some…discomfort with him as well. I…have some discomfort…with you, too…just not the same kind. I need to clarify. I am trying to be honest here."

"Honesty." He scoffs. "Is that what you are expressing? I mean while you make it sound like I am on the 'A' list of suspects." He looks up shaking his head clenching his fists.

Will studies the dust on his shoes but pushes himself to go on. "Yes, well I have noticed that all the victims so far look like Connie. I would think nothing of it, but seeing you that night near the Ridges, and knowing you could not be found last night gives only a natural inclination to consider it. I do not believe it, but I had to ask."

Drew relaxes a bit but remains standing directly in front of Will. "Fair enough. The first night I met Azure in the woods to help him set some snares for a fox that was getting into their hen house. Last night…I don't have an alibi."

Will's face flushes as a sweaty heat rushes up the back of his neck. The image of Azure walking back through the clearing with a dead fox the night he had been at his and Odina's cabin comes into view.

Drew continues. "I finished Dillon's car yesterday, and Mister Adkins asked me to drive it over to his place for him. We closed up for the night, and I took the car over. I parked it in the garage and went to take the keys up to the house. Dillon wasn't there but Missus Mitchell was just leaving and took the keys from me saying she'd let Dillon know the car was in the garage. I headed out to take the path back towards the Mayhew's, and I guess I slipped or something and struck my head on a rock." He rubs the back of his head. "I have a hell of a welt. Anyway, I woke up in the woods not knowing what time it was, but it was too late to go to Connie's. I went to my room at the Mayhew's and fell asleep. I woke late, so I didn't get to work on time."

Will knows that Drew's account of last night would not hold up in a court of law, no witnesses, nothing credible to support it; however, he believes him. He nods at Drew communicating this trust. "What about Dillon?"

"I don't know. The guy is strange, but that doesn't make him a murderer—hell, a serial killer at that. There's some real psychopathy with that." Drew sounds as though he is trying to convince himself as much as Will.

"So, you think I am way off on this?"

"No, I didn't say that either. His fascination with Connie is creepy, and I heard that all the girls have had a pearl in their mouths."

"Yes."

Drew looks over towards the Snip 'n Style and back at Will. "Well Connie has this thing about pearls. You know, how something so beautiful starts from a simple grain of sand—an irritation made beautiful." He cuts a laugh short shaking his head as his cheeks flush. "She thinks they are romantic. A Cinderella kind of thing. Anyway, it's why I got her that brooch that she wears—you know, with the pearls. I bought it from Missus McCaffrey. And, what's more Missus McCaffrey always liked Connie. She helped her get her business going, and she gave Connie a pair of pearl earrings telling her she wanted her to have them to go with the brooch. Connie was deeply touched by the gift. Dillon *has* to know all this."

"Drew, we need to go talk to Sheriff Shively."

"Not we, just me."

Will gives him a sideways look.

"Trust me Will. When something like these murders is going on the public is scared, and law enforcement is frustrated. Anyone could be guilty, and some guy coming to them about half-cocked theories is going to be a suspect until proven otherwise. You don't need to be a part of it. You and I have not been here long enough to be seen as much more than drifters who have pulled off onto the side of the road for a while." He puts his hand on Will's shoulder. "I already had it in mind to go see Sheriff Shively. I figure he's gonna be pretty busy today, so I'll wait."

Will studies Drew for a moment. "Okay then."

Drew rolls the tire back around to the front of the garage to fill it with air. Will follows finding Hallie sitting on a crate talking to Beezie who is putting air in a bicycle tire. He sends a smile Hallie's way, and greets Beezie asking her if he can help.

"That's okay, I am done already. See y'all."

They say their goodbyes to Beezie and Drew and head around the back of the station.

"How did it go?"

Will's lip twitches downward. "Fine."

"Is it okay for me to be around Drew then?"

Will laughs. "Yes probably, but not until they have caught the person doing all this. I just would rather not take any chances."

"Well, you're not going to like this idea then."

He waits for her to continue.

"I want to go up to Dillon McCaffrey's. He invited me to check out his library and borrow a couple books. It might be a good way for me to get a look around."

"Yes, you are right. Not a good idea."

"Well, now is the perfect time because he isn't home. His housekeeper is expecting me, and she is going to let me in."

"He only *said* he is not going to be there. You don't know that for sure."

"Well…you could come."

He gives this some thought and reluctantly agrees. He wants to stop by the Snip 'n Style first and see if Connie will let him borrow her car to drive Maude to Roanoke.

They cross over the railway tracks towards the salon, and Will is relieved to see that it is quiet in the shop. Linda is styling an elderly woman's hair and greets Will and Hallie when they come in. Connie is sitting at her station reading a fashion magazine.

She looks up to see who Linda is talking to. Will thinks he sees a flash of an old acquaintance, very old, on Connie's face when she meets his eye, but he can't be sure. Her demeanor gives no tell, and she is friendly enough.

"Will, Hallie, what are you two up to today?"

"Actually, we need to make a trip to Roanoke this afternoon, and I was wondering if you would be willing to loan me your car. I will be sure to fill the tank before I return it."

Connie stands up and pulls her purse out of a cabinet at her station getting her keys for him. "You most definitely can borrow my car. It will finally let me do something to thank you for all those times you have been there to help Drew fix things up around here." She hands him the keys. The key ring has a trinket hanging off it that is an intricate piece of wrought iron twisting around a piece of crystal.

*Just like Odina's anthame without the sharp point.* Will hesitates before he takes it.

"Interesting piece isn't it?" She reaches over and taps it making it swing back and forth to catch the sunlight sending beams of refracted light off in different directions. "I ran across it at a curiosity shop and couldn't resist it. It called to me from across time." She looks directly at Will, and he stares back unblinking.

"Across time?" Hallie questions Connie while transfixed by the beams of light coming from the ball missing the moment between Will and Connie. She glances up at Connie.

Connie breaks her stare away from Will and looks over at Hallie rolling her eyes. "What am I saying? I meant from across the *room* of course. It was just hanging there on the display rack, and I saw it the moment I walked in. I thought it would make a nice trinket for my key chain. It is surprisingly light-weight."

Will puts the keys with the sparkling crystal bobble into his pocket and thanks Connie assuring her he will return her car this evening. A prickle of heat flickers at the palm of his hand, and he runs it through his hair.

A boy hands Hallie and Will a flier along the way to the McCaffrey house about the upcoming Fourth of July celebration. There is to be a carnival, picnic, music and fireworks.

"I have lost total track of time." Hallie looks at the flier. "I can't believe that July Fourth is just a few days away. Maybe we could go?"

"Sorry. Go?" He releases his grip on Connie's key ring inside his pocket.

She shows him the flier.

"Sure, looks like it will be fun." *If Paimon's sickle hasn't swung by then.*

# CHAPTER 16
## Sense

Will stands with Hallie on the front porch of the McCaffrey house waiting for someone to answer Hallie's knock. "It is about two o'clock. We do not have too much time."

"Okay, just a quick look-see, *if* we can get anyone to come to the door."

The doorbell is not working, rust clings to the decorative metallic trim. She knocks again and, at that moment, the door swings open startling Hallie. An elderly woman stands on the other side of the threshold. She gives them a smile looking from Hallie to Will.

"Missus Mitchell?" Hallie's voice pitches up.

"Yes."

"I'm Hallie O'Meara. Dillon said that I could come by and look through his library."

"Oh, yes dear." She looks towards Will pursing her lips. "He did not say anything about a young man being with you."

"Uh, this is Will White. He works over at Adkins' Garage right here in town."

Missus Mitchell nods politely but doesn't budge from her spot at the doorway.

"Well, he was going to wait for me on the porch, if that's alright."

Will shoots a look at Hallie. She keeps focused on Missus Mitchell. He shifts his weight side to side. Missus Mitchell steps aside, and Hallie slips cross the threshold before Will can object. He resists an urge to grab Hallie's arm and prevent her from stepping into the house despite the uneasy feeling that cascades over him.

Hallie turns back to look at him. "It'll be okay." The door shuts.

Will spins around on his foot sucking air through his teeth. *What is she thinking? What am I thinking?* He paces the porch leaning over the side rail looking back towards the garage. Its door is open, and he cannot see the coupe. Dillon isn't home, Will knows this, but his muscles twitch like a prize fighter stepping into the ring. He walks to the other end of the porch glancing through a window and sees Hallie. She is standing in a room across the hall from the front living room area looking up at the books on a shelf before turning to look at something on a table in the room.

He turns away from the window and sits on a rocking chair unable to decide if it is anger or apprehension that dictates his mood. Dillon isn't home. He knows that he can get to her in moments, if needed. But these thoughts do not appease him—there is something else that is raising an alarm for him. Something Hallie does not seem to be aware of, or she would not have gone into that house.

The recent near encounter with Paimon has him on edge, and that could explain his uneasiness but *no*. He sighs in frustration looking up at the porch ceiling and pauses looking at it more closely. There are signs of decay with a dark ooze of mildew creeping out of the corners along the borders of the ceiling towards the center where the light blue paint is wrinkling and starting to chip. The edges of the corrosion seem to be migrating across the porch as though the house's decline is evolving before his eyes.

He has not been to the McCaffrey house often but, when he did visit, it has always been pristine—like the Cadillac coupe and yard landscaping. Even as recently as Missus McCaffrey's funeral, the house had been in excellent shape. The only exception was the tread on the steps the other day. He looks down at the floorboards of the porch, the trim around the windows, the porch railing, and siding on the house, even the chair he is sitting in—all are showing the creeping progression of an almost sinister decay. He springs up from the chair knowing now this insidious decay is the source of his uneasiness. It is one and the same as the suffocating rot in the underworld that wraps itself around a target slowly draining the victim's vitality. He breathes in snapping the constriction around his chest and looks in the window. No Hallie.

He swears under his breath just as the door opens and Hallie steps out. She has a book in one hand holding it up to him with a smile, and she pulls the door closed behind her. He thinks he sees a shadow of darkness lurch after her from the door as she steps away, and he quickly eliminates the distance between them. The shadow dissipates like grains of sand falling downward through the cracks between the porch boards.

"What were you thinking Hallie? What was I thinking? I cannot believe you walked into that house alone." His jaw muscles clamp tight. "We should have had a plan before we even came here."

"I'm sorry Will, but I needed to get in there and take a look around." They make their way down the steps to walk over to Connie's to pick up her car. "I told Missus Mitchell I had to use the bathroom, so I was able to go upstairs too." Her eyes widen and spark a twinkle.

Will says nothing brooding.

She stops short raising a hand up and flicking it to the side. "Will, you were right there on the porch. I could have screamed, and you would have been there in a minute. Give it a rest—I am not helpless." She quickens her pace, and he lets her get a little ahead of him before he shakes his head giving up and catches back up to her.

"Hey," he shouts at her a little louder than he intends.

She stops short looking at him, eyebrows raised, lips

pursed, and ready for a fight.

He lowers his voice, but his tone is raw. "You do not know what we are up against here. I am worried, angry too, but mostly worried."

"Will, Dillon was not home. We don't know if he is involved with the killings. If we are going to find out, his house is a good place to start."

"Hallie," he hesitates a moment.

"What, Will?" Her attitude seethes over a sharp edge.

"I think there is more to it. I think Dillon is involved in something, maybe the killings, but there is definitely something else. Something bigger than Dillon is involved here. There is a familiarity to it. An evil familiarity. If we had not gone to the house, we would not have been warned, so I do appreciate the value of the venture. I just…am not sure that it is worth something happening to you."

She looks at him and exhales through her nose and draws her lower lip in pressing down on it with her teeth.

His anger dissipates like vinegar in water. It is replaced with an urgency to secure Hallie's safety and find a way to get her back to where she belongs.

"I'm sorry, Will. I didn't know. I didn't get a sense of danger when I was in the house."

"No, I know you didn't. I am sorry as well."

She reaches up and kisses him and hugs him. "I am sorry I left you out on the porch to sit and worry, but she wasn't going to let us in. He wasn't home, and we needed to take advantage of it."

"I know, you are right."

"Do you want to know what I found out?"

"Of course."

They continue on their way.

"Well," she hesitates. "Not too much really."

He laughs and shakes his head. "What book did you borrow?"

She holds it up. "It's called *The Red Kite Clue*. I haven't read it yet, so I thought this would be a good one to borrow. Dot is a big fan of the author. He was a Free Mason you know." Hallie looks at him expectantly.

Will just looks back not registering anything from the comment.

"Oh, right—that was a conversation we had in 2018. I think I'm losing track of things a bit. You were taking care of a horse at Fairy Stone and told me about your uncle being a Free Mason and how Acacia got her name."

"Acacia? The horse my uncle gave me?"

"Well, not exactly. A horse *like* the one your uncle gave you. You said they looked and acted a lot alike."

"I have a horse in 2018?"

"She's not yours really. The day I arrived there was some sort of accident at the park. She fell down a ravine and was injured. You cared for her and got her healthy. You were amazing, and she connected with you." Hallie pauses smiling. She clears her throat and continues. "She's being kept at the park until a home can be found."

"I don't understand. Why? What about the horse's owner?"

Hallie shrugs. "There was no owner that anyone knew of."

He considers this for a moment. "Is the park a more open place than it is now?"

"No, if anything, it's more secure. But still, it's not Fort Knox. Why?"

"It just seems odd that a horse would show up in a state park with no owner to be found." He shrugs it off and looks over at the book. "So, you found a novel to read."

"Yes, I did." She laughs and the sparkle in her eyes and the wrinkle in her nose have a tranquilizing effect on him. "There also was a flask on a table with pearls in it."

"Pearls?"

"Yes, pearls. That might just be coincidental though. I mean why would he leave something like that out in the open, if he were using them in a psychopathic killing binge?"

"I do not know." Will shrugs. "But I do not think people would call them psychopaths, if they commanded rationale thinking."

"True," she says somberly.

They walk quietly the rest of the way until they reach Connie's car and get in. Will cannot seem to get comfortable in the seat.

She tilts her head in curiosity.

"I am afraid that I have provoked a force that would have been better off left alone. I defied the Demon King. I laid destruction against his home, I stole the forbidden fruit from Persephone's tree, I struck down a demon guard outside the lines of battle, and I crossed through the Mesu without ceremonial passage."

"I see," she replies and strokes her chin. "That all sounds very bad. Is it considered a bad thing in a world of demons and malevolence too?"

He cuts a laugh off in his throat and nods. "It is when you are human and the slave of the Demon King."

"Why did you do all that?"

"You. I needed to find you. I did not understand what I was doing. I barely remembered you at the time—I just reacted. Just a glimpse of a memory of you was that powerful."

Her cheeks color, and she reaches over taking his hand. "Well, who knows what might have happened if you didn't do what you did. I mean this has to be a life you had before. Don't you think? Only the *you* in 2018 knows for sure, but I went to Fayerdale and you were there. I went to Fairy Stone, and you were there. I am thinking that that you had to have been here already—not because of what happened in the underworld. The only difference was timing and means, right? And, now of course, my presence. You just adjusted the course of this life, or for that matter, I did by traveling and ending up here."

He steers the car towards the college. "Perhaps." He squeezes Hallie's hand. "Let us see what insight Doctor Cavander has to offer. I am just hoping my actions did not open some sort of doorway between here and Tartarus."

# CHAPTER 17
## Discern

The door to Maude Cavander's office is slightly ajar creaking in when Will knocks. Hallie steps past him poking her head around the door.

"Doctor Cavander?"

Hallie turns toward Will shrugging her shoulders stepping sideways into the small but extremely tidy space. There are items set on top of a bookcase, and a piece of crystal catches Will's eye. He picks it up feeling the same lull he felt on the porch at the Ridges. Light from the window twinkles through it, and he notices a tear-drop shape of something amber-colored at its core near the base of the pyramid.

"Quite a nice piece of crystal isn't it?" Maude walks into the office with a suitcase in hand.

"Doctor Cavander." Will sets the crystal back on top of the bookcase. "Yes ma'am, it is very nice. I actually have seen it before."

"Odina must have shared it with you." Maude sets her suitcase down and walks around to the other side of her desk to straighten papers sorting them into the slots of her letter holder. "She just gave it to me today. She was my appointment after I saw you in the library. I was surprised when she contacted me the other day. Odina Ridge is not known to have much interest in people. However, it seems that she and I are related. I am her niece in a long line of Romany heritage from what she tells me."

Will looks at Hallie. The news is certainly astounding.

"I know." Maude looks at them both and sounds as though she is still convincing herself. "Interesting that I have dedicated my whole career to anthropology and the history of people across the globe, but I never really knew much about my own lineage. Apparently, Azure Ridge has been searching for the lost daughter of one of his brothers, and it turns out to be me." She adjusts the waist of her skirt.

"That truly is amazing. How does it feel to have family all of a sudden?" Hallie asks.

"The news is still new so to speak, and I need to give it some thought—perhaps do a little research myself. Odina also gave me the documents that Azure used to find me, so I'll start with them. She wanted me to have the crystal. She was adamant about that, so I took it for now until I can get everything confirmed. She was very kind to trust it to me. I've been invited for dinner on Sunday, and I think I will go." She finishes sorting her papers and turns her attention away from the desk searching through the rest of her office.

Will looks over to Hallie. "Doctor Cavander can we help you find something?"

"Yes, thank you. I am looking for a letter from one of the members of the board of trustees. I am supposed to meet a woman at the train station in Roanoke on Friday before I return to Ferrum from the conference. She is supposed to give a civil rights speech at the college on Monday, but I can't remember the time I am supposed to meet her. My mind seems to be a flutter. I'm afraid my meeting with Odina put me out of sorts a bit." Maude looks on top of a file cabinet and goes through more papers.

Will and Hallie start to look carefully through her papers on her desk.

"It's on college letterhead like this," she holds up a sheet of paper. "And it is hand-written. I only just received it, so I can't imagine that I have lost it."

A piece of paper on the floor near Maude's desk catches Will's eye. He crouches down and picks it up. The letter is written in a thin ornate hand familiar to him. His heart floods with dread, and it pumps a scourge through his body making his breathing rapid and shallow.

# Ferrum College

*Dear Dr. Cavander,*

*The Ferrum College Board of Trustees has sponsored a speaker for a civil rights presentation to be given at the college on Monday, July seventh. We understand you will be attending the American Anthropological Association's southern regional conference this week in Roanoke. We request that you meet our speaker, Miss Sadie Hairston, at the train station in Roanoke on July 4th at 12:00 noon and accompany her back to campus. We have arranged for transportation for you from Roanoke to Ferrum.*

*Additionally, we have some activities planned for the weekend in honor of the Fourth of July holiday and Miss Hairston's arrival that you are invited to attend. If you have any questions concerning this matter, please contact me.*

*Joseph Tasker*
*Ferrum College Board of Trustees*

Will glances at Maude who is focused on the papers on top of her filing cabinet. He steps closer to Hallie showing her the letter. Her color drains, and Will has no comfort to offer her. The letter only affirms what he already knows to be inevitable.

"Doctor Cavander I believe I have found the letter you are looking for."

"Yes, this is it. Thank you Will." Maude reads it over and looks up at the pair. "I am very proud to know that the school is making strides to address some of the more controversial social issues we are dealing with. I believe Miss Hairston is going to speak about efforts in the District of Columbia to desegregate the schools there. She is a lawyer in the District and a respected member of the NAACP.

"Despite the Brown decision, Virginia's senator, Harry F. Byrd, has worked hard to thwart integration in our public schools. It is hard to believe that so many have supported his Massive Resistance Movement. So much energy dedicated to prejudice and intolerance. A theme in one form or another all too often found throughout civilizations across history. I wonder if it will ever be conquered." She takes a manila folder from a box in a storage cabinet and carefully lays the letter inside before sliding it into her satchel.

"Doctor Cavander, I hope you don't mind me asking, but when did you receive that letter?" Will asks.

"Joel from the library gave it to me before I left to meet with Odina today. Apparently, this Joseph Tasker was unsure of my office location, and he left the letter at the circulation desk for me." She secures her satchel and lifts her suitcase. "Are you ready to go?"

"Yes ma'am," Will answers. He hesitates. "Doctor Cavander perhaps you should take the crystal Odina gave you on your trip."

She looks from Will to the crystal and blinks with recollection. "Yes, of course. She did suggest that I keep it with me at all times. She never said why, but I sensed it was important to her." Maude places it in her satchel. "So, where are you parked?"

"In the lot just outside the building." Will steps forward reaching a hand out to take Maude's suitcase.

Her brow creases the canopy of a blank look before her cheeks flush. "Oh, yes. Of course, thank you very much Will." She surrenders the suitcase to him.

Will closes the door behind them instinctively looking up and down the hallway wary of Paimon's potential presence. A light above them flickers, and their footsteps echo off the walls as they make their way outside. They settle into the car with Hallie in the center of the front seat. He pulls the car onto the road, and they sit in silence for a few moments until they turn onto the main road towards Rocky Mount.

Saint James Church is not too far ahead of them on the right, and Hallie asks about it. "Doctor Cavander, I couldn't help but notice the six-pointed star on the window above the door at Saint James. It seems odd to me that it is on a Christian church. I have always thought it was a Jewish symbol."

Maude glances up at the window as they pass. "Yes, the star," her voice trails off, and she turns giving Hallie her full attention. "It actually has symbolic significance in many cultures and traditions."

She studies Hallie.

Hallie fidgets glancing over at Will and adjusts her seat just as Maude speaks.

"In Christianity, just as the faith has many denominations, the views of the star vary greatly. Overall, I would say I have often seen Christian interpretation to be that the six-pointed star is viewed as the Creator's Star. Its six points stand for the six days of creation and also represent the six attributes of God: power, wisdom, majesty, love, mercy and justice. I am thinking from our conversation in the library *your* primary interest lies in the legend of Solomon's ring since it is rumored the hexagram star is found within it."

Hallie opens her mouth to speak but Maude goes on. "When I met with Odina today she told me that there is a task that is yours to complete, and that I will have a role in this endeavor. It's still not very clear to me just what it may be, but most worthwhile ventures require discovery in some form, and I am up for the challenge."

She smiles and motions a hand from Hallie to Will. "There is something here with you both that speaks to me—compels me to help. So, which version and what part of the legend has piqued your attention?"

Hallie glances over at Will, but he is keeping focused on the road. He is intent on listening to the conversation, but he does not want to hinder it feeling that Hallie is handling things well.

She bends her head into her shoulder and looks back at Maude. "Well, the aspect of its use as a key I suppose." Maude glances passed Hallie towards Will, and she too looks through the windshield at the road ahead as she speaks. "Its use as a key?"

"Um hum."

Maude tugs at her sweater and smooths it. She bites her lip and turns to Hallie. "Well, there are ancient prophetic writings in angelic lore about its use as a key. It is not common knowledge, and those who knew of the writings rarely spoke of them and now…well, now no one speaks of them at all."

Hallie frowns and snaps her head back. "Why?"

Maude swallows and clears her throat. "Let me back up a bit first before we get to that. It's written in the angelic lore that the key's potential is much greater than what legend from other sources claim. Well-known versions of the key's lore claim that it allowed Solomon to command angels and demons. However, angelic lore suggests that Solomon's key is also part of what is called the Trinity Amulet. It's foretold that if the key is united with two other components, it holds a potential power beyond our comprehension. It is suggested that the Trinity Amulet holds power that can end things as we known them to be."

"Total destruction?"

"No." Maude looks out the car door window. "Just *different*. 'Different from what we know it to be' is how the writings translate." She looks back at Hallie. "It is speculated that the Trinity Amulet opens a gateway for angels to enter the mundane plane freely and conceivably rid the world of demons. Perhaps though…the angels would want something in return. The amulet's purpose all depends on the source of the amulet's power." Her voice trails off and her pupils vacillate as she turns and studies Hallie's face.

"Well, where does the power truly lie?"

Maude sighs. "It all lies within the third component of the Trinity Amulet. There are two keys and then the third component. A human being. The nature. Tendencies. The make-up of that third component will determine the outcome. The focus and the force."

"And, this human could be anyone?"

Maude nods. "Anyone the keys choose. Although, it was written that the human needs to be pure of heart yet know the dark influences of the underworld. So, how many humans that includes cannot be too many."

"Why would that be necessary?"

Maude raises a shoulder. "Perhaps, a testimony of worthiness. Translation of prophetic writings can be challenging, and this particular part was very challenging."

Will shifts in his seat. His knuckles are white with his grip on the steering wheel, and he tries to ignore the prickle of sweat on his brow. *This cannot be.* He chews the inside of his cheek. The prickle wins, and he swipes a hand across his face glancing at Hallie. Her skin pales slightly, but she draws in a breath and flashes a tentative smile at him.

Maude looks back at the road. "It is written that the keys come from heaven and, if engaged, they form an encoded bond between the two and the human beholder's DNA creating the Trinity Amulet."

"An encoded bond?"

"Yes."

"Keys that require a code to work?"

Maude gives this consideration and raises her eyebrows. "Yes, that is an interesting way to think of it. A *genetic* code actually."

It is as though Paimon's scorpions are dancing over Will's nerves, and he can stand it no longer. "But, what—" he almost shouts. He twists his neck releasing some tension and starts again. "But, what of the person? What happens to the person?"

Maude turns her head meeting Will's fretful face and searches his eyes. She draws in a breath and exhales her answer. "I am sorry, Will, but I do not know. I just do not know."

"More challenges with the translation I suppose." He declares over gritted teeth.

"Yes, Will, in many ways this was so." Maude fires back. She clears her throat and continues with a lighter tone. "No worries though. It is thought that the union of the amulet's components is highly unlikely."

His eyebrows furrow. "I do not understand. Why is that?"

"Although you would think something within heaven would be hard to obtain, that is not so for many beings, and the keys have crossed into the mundane plain before. Hence Solomon having his ring for quite some time. The writings, however, suggest that the keys will be or were stolen making their location unknown to all but the thief."

"Stolen?" Hallie's voice springs up.

Maude presses her lips together and nods. "Yes, but that's not the only barrier for the creation of the Trinity Amulet."

Hallie cocks her head to the side. "What more could there be?"

Will feels like he is off in the distance hearing the conversation being carried by the wind. Maude has Hallie entranced with what she is saying, and Will is having trouble concentrating on his driving.

"It is predicted in the writings that not only will the keys be stolen, but they will be placed in a time-lock so to speak. Hidden in time." Her shoulders twitch up. "At least that is what is thought to be the correct interpretation and, if true, this one act seems to have made the keys safe."

"How?"

"Well, there has been no indication of them crossing into the mundane plain since King Solomon had his ring."

Will sucks air through his teeth. "Truly, Doctor Cavender? I mean, how would anyone know? These are ancient. Prophetic writings. Have there been updates in the translation? Do you truly know anything beyond what these writings had to say?" He pinches his lips and shakes his head.

Hallie lays a hand on his leg raising her eyebrows at him.

"Yes. Yes, there is more beyond what is in the writings." Maude's words fire back with lost restraint. "Danger." She stops and smooths her sweater with her hands. She turns looking at Hallie. "It is dangerous. Not just with the formation of the amulet but even with the knowledge of it. And, perhaps I don't know

every facet of the keys' destiny, but I do know about the danger."
Her voice catches, and she scratches at the collar of her sweater.

Will sighs. "Doctor Cavander I apologize. I do not mean to
lose patience. Please tell us what you know." He looks to Hallie.
"It is…vital…that we know as much as possible, and we truly
appreciate your time and what you have to offer us."

Her shoulders relax and her face softens. She rests her
hands in her lap. "Well, most of what I know about the more
guarded information was told to me by…a colleague… a man I
worked with and admired deeply." She pauses momentarily but
quickly adds, "Let me give you the background information first. It
will lend…better understanding for you about my…anxiety and
why no one speaks of any of this any longer. I think we have
time."

"At least an hour drive to Roanoke," Will concedes, and he
surrenders to this tangent hoping it will bring them more
information.

"About ten or eleven years ago a Bedouin shepherd
wandered into a cave and came across several clay jars that
contained ancient scrolls, the Dead Sea Scrolls included, but others
as well. It was quite a discovery. Naturally, there was a lot of
controversy over the legitimacy of the discovery and what it meant
in terms of modern teachings. The final scrolls were discovered
only about two years ago.

"Seven years ago, I was a graduate student working with an
expert in Aramaic language and historical documents, Doctor Eban
Maven." She blushes slightly and feathers her fingers across her
mouth. "He was a brilliant and energetic man, and he was invited
to go to Jerusalem to be part of a special team to examine an odd
collection of writings from angelic lore that was found with the
other scrolls. He was to do carbon dating and other evaluations.
The writings had been part of the original discovery along with the

Dead Sea scrolls, but not much detail had been given to him before the trip. It was very secretive. He needed an assistant for the trip and was permitted to choose one."

"You were chosen to go with him?" Hallie's voice peaks a half octave.

"Well, not exactly." She sighs laughing mostly to herself. "I was certainly the most qualified of the four graduate students who worked with him at the time, but I was the only woman in the group."

"Oh." Hallie sighs. "He chose a man over you."

"Not him really. I believe had it been solely up to him he would have chosen me. The expedition was to the Middle East for the evaluation of extremely important religious documents, and women were not permitted to participate in such things." She pauses and sighs heavily before continuing. "Even today this is so."

Hallie wrinkles her forehead, and her eyebrows flit upward. "But you did go didn't you?"

Will finds his muscles are relaxing, and he chuckles at Hallie's mischievous tone.

"Yes." Maude lowers her voice as though they could be overheard. "The student he chose became ill the night before the trip. I happened to run across him at the library and provided him assistance. He looked awful, and I knew he was not going to be able to travel any time soon. When I was helping him back to his room I noticed something. He and I, aside from the length of our hair, truly favored each other. He was a small man and our height and weight were close. He had an olive complexion like me, and it got me thinking."

"Oh my, did you?" Hallie shifts her seat turning towards Maude.

Maude nods. "I convinced him that I was the best candidate

of the remaining graduate students. He gave me his passport, his clothes, and his luggage. I was going to become him for the duration of the expedition. It was agreed that if I was caught, I would be solely responsible, and he would claim both sabotage and theft. If not, he received all the credit for my work."

Will looks over at Maude amazed. He reminds himself that until you know someone, you do not really know them. And, he worries what they still do not know about Maude Cavender.

Her head shakes almost imperceptibly. "It was a dangerous undertaking. Such an impersonation in the Middle East carries a high penalty. Not to mention what would happen to my career in anthropology. It would have been over before it even started. Of course, I had to avoid Eban, uh, Doctor Maven until we were far enough underway, so it would not be practical for him to send me back. He was the only one in the group that would have known I was not the graduate student he planned to bring to Jerusalem. Oh, when he discovered me—you see I didn't think about the berthing arrangements on the ship. Doctor Maven and his companion were berthed together."

She tilts her head down pressing her lips against her bent fingers and swallows a chuckle. She sits upright smoothing out her sweater looking over to Hallie. "Well, the point is that I was there." She breathes in sighing and bending her head towards a shoulder. "I was a part of this great discovery and exploration. The angelic lore I am talking about was never released to the public. At the time I didn't understand why, but I never questioned it either. I clung to a faith that these scholarly men had reasons for what was done. Everything about the expedition had me awe-struck."

"Huh, Doctor Cavander, who would have known?" Hallie speaks without thinking, but she voices Will's very thoughts. She quickly recovers. "I mean…you here in the very small town of Ferrum working as a college professor, yet you are holding all this…adventure…inside you."

"Yes, well," Maude's normal tentative tone returns. "Peel an onion, and you'll find many layers." She offers a weak smile. "What you need to know though is that sometimes 'what you know' can be very dangerous. Some people even go so far as to hide from the truth saying once you know it, there's no giving it back. I myself did not used to agree with this thinking, but for many years now I have wished I *didn't* know what I know. Remember, *you* want to know this information. I worry for your…safety." Maude's persona dissolves.

"Hallie, reach into Doctor Cavander's satchel and give her Odina's crystal to hold."

She does what he asks gently taking ahold of Maude's hand placing the crystal onto her open palm.

Maude closes her fingers over the crystal and takes some deep breaths. Her shoulders lift, and she turns her head springing her chin upward. A thin smile creases her face.

"The only reason I am speaking of this now is because of Odina. Her words only reaffirm what I have been suspecting, sensing deep inside, for a while now—I must have some other purpose for being here. Odina said that she was relieved to find me because you—the both of you—need help, and it was for me to get it done." She flashes a smile and returns her focus to the curving road ahead wringing her hands. They are approaching Windy Gap and the Roanoke County line.

"Every man on that expedition is dead." Her voice catches and she draws in a sorrowful breath. "It took several years but, one-by-one, they were hunted down and murdered. Even the unfortunate graduate student whose identity I borrowed is dead. I am convinced that I still live because it was unknown that I was even there—whoever killed all of them thought I was the graduate student Eban selected to go. After all, it was his name and identification I used. I had cut my hair, wore his clothes, and interacted as little as possible with everyone except Eban. They all just thought I was extremely introverted. No one knew my true identity."

Hallie glances at Will. He wonders if Maude's anonymity will be enough to protect her now that she has become involved with Hallie and him.

"My Eban died when his car was forced off the road. They said it was suspicious, but proof could not be found to confirm any foul play. I didn't need any proof. I knew it was not accidental. The coroner gave me Eban's personal belongings when I went to identify his body. There was a beautiful engagement ring in a small black velvet box. We were to go out that night for dinner and dancing. We were very happy."

"Doctor Cavender, I'm so sorry."

"Yes ma'am, I am sorry for your loss as well."

Her eyes moisten. "It was such a shock at first. I began to doubt my suspicions of his death being intentional until I got word about others in the expedition group dying under similar circumstances. There were six people in that group including me…well, seven counting the other graduate student. I am the last living soul. I assumed a life of obscurity in order to avoid discovery. So, truly Hallie, Ferrum is the perfect place for me. The last of the men was killed two years ago. It may be all over, but it may be that I just haven't been found. I guess I will never know for sure. You have to understand I am only discussing this with you now because Odina has convinced me your need is urgent and you are both trustworthy." She clears her throat. "And, I believe her."

Silence swallows the car. Will cannot shake the feeling that there is so much more to this. A wariness that he normally feels in Tartarus, and even when he was sitting on Dillon McCaffrey's porch, is trickling over him. He wonders if Paimon is connected in any way. There is nothing more the Demon King would want than to collect those souls and find out about the power of the Trinity Amulet. Perhaps, to find a way to manipulate the amulet's angelic powers to benefit demons instead. Will is pulled from his reverie when he hears Maude's voice resonating once again with strength and resolve.

"I found myself drawn to the secret writings that the small expedition group had been called upon to study and translate. Eban would review his discoveries from the day with me every night, but he was only given access to a portion of the scrolls. It was the same for each member of the team as far as I knew. This way no single person knew all the information. After Eban's death, however, I found additional notes he made. It seemed that he obtained more information about the scrolls after we had left the Middle East. I have since burned his notes out of fear of discovery."

Will's hopes plunge, conversely, Hallie presses on. "You remember them though."

Maude glances at her with a crooked smile. "Of course, I do."

"What more do we need to know, Doctor Cavander?"

"Well, in terms of Solomon's key, you need to know that Solomon was a wise king, and was favored by God, but he was thought to fall under the influence of corruption. Some say that the corruption was from Solomon's pagan wives, but the writings say that it was the key's potential power and connection to the Trinity Amulet. Solomon must have pondered if he could possibly be the human component. This makes sense, however, there is no record indicating he ever came upon the other key.

"So, the first thing you need to know is that possession of an object capable of unlocking such power also holds a potential for great influence over one's life. The character of the person who possesses it will eventually come to light. Solomon was a man of great fortitude and wisdom. He was able to resist the temptation and avoid wasting a lifetime seeking a nebulous treasure."

"Do you think the writings are correct? Solomon never found the other key?" Hallie asks.

"Yes. I do." She sighs. "The keys cannot be found by the human component. They must present themselves. There is no other way. Solomon had to have figured this out. They were originally a gift from God and will always remain a heavenly legacy. Beyond our grasp, if we demand it. Yet always within our reach, if we go the distance."

"So, neither key has presented itself to anyone in the mundane plain since Solomon's time?"

Maude looks at Hallie, opens her mouth to speak, pauses and starts again. "No. The theft, if the writings are correct, seems to have kept this from happening. They may not even have been brought to the mundane plain. And, even if they had been taken here, what human can unlock time? Their thief is or was quite clever and strongly motivated to keep the keys well hidden."

Hallie grasps her amulet bag and looks at Will, but she speaks to Maude. "Doctor Cavander…if I showed you…"

Will shoots a look at Hallie suddenly feeling the car is suffocating despite its opened windows. He cuts Hallie off. "Doctor Cavender, what does the other key look like?"

"Hm?" Maude looks over at Will.

"The other key."

"Oh, yes. Raphael's key. He is the archangel of healing, and he used the key to cross the mundane plane providing healing and peace where it was needed most, and then the key would bring him back to heaven. The only other way an angel, since the time of the Watchers, can cross the mundane plain is to fall. After that, there is no return to heaven."

He looks past Hallie towards Maude. "Are there any descriptions of Raphael's key?"

"Yes, just one…" She looks out the window. They have arrived.

Maude bites her lip. "I would like to take you and Hallie to supper. Let me get my bag up to my room and get checked into the conference. I will be just a little while. You can park the car and wait for me here. We can finish our conversation before you head back to Ferrum. Do you have time?"

Will glances at Hallie, and she nods. "Yes, thank you."

# CHAPTER 18
# Seeing

Will and Hallie wait for Maude on the grassy slope near the hotel entrance. Hallie rests on bent elbows with her head flexed back enjoying the late afternoon sun on her face.

They sit for a while in silence before Will speaks up. "How about Doctor Cavander? Quite amazing."

Hallie agrees.

"Hallie." Will stops short.

"Hm?"

He clears his throat. "You fully understand everything she was saying do you not?"

"I do."

"Why do you not show any…alarm over it?"

"She told us about a prophesy. A prediction of what may be."

He cuts a growl of frustration off. "You are living it. For God sake, Hallie, you are…"

"Stop Will." She cuts him off and sits up. "We. We are living it. And, because of the 'we' I am choosing not to allow the fear to swallow me. We asked her because we need to know. What she has told us is a prophesy not an absolute. *The keys will set free more than the two*. Remember? The angel song made a prediction too."

He bites down on the inside of his lower lip and gives a curt nod and looks at her through the hair hanging over his eyes. "Yes, the keys. There was no mention of this Trinity Amulet that has every likelihood of…" He stops unable to bring himself to give it credence with his words.

Hallie reaches over and lays her hand softly against his

face. "That point was not lost to me, Will." She sighs. "Tell me why you didn't want me to show her the fairy stone."

"I do not know. A feeling. I think it best we learn as much as she has to offer without divulging what we know or have."

Hallie flashes a smile. "Old habits die hard I suppose."

"Yes, so it would seem."

"Okay, that makes sense, but then we need to move on and not let it create a burden. Let it pass"

He takes her hand and kisses her palm. Her words trigger a memory and he looks down to study the blades of grass.

"What is it Will?"

"You know, when I was about twelve my Uncle Benjamin told me a story about Solomon's ring. It was not a supernatural story. It was more like a folk tale."

"Tell me." She settles back on her elbows, and he cannot help but smile.

"My uncle was a fascinating man and extremely wise. He had many stories to tell." Will laughs shaking his head.

"Tell me the story he told you." Hallie prods.

"In order to tell it properly you would need to know why he told me the story to begin with and, unfortunately, it was meant to be a lesson for me. I am not proud of how I was then.

"Really? How were you?"

He sighs. "Very prideful, arrogant, and…frightened…all the time." His cheeks burn, and he diverts his gaze away from Hallie.

"Fear of what, Will?"

"Discovery." He looks back at Hallie with misty eyes. She squeezes his hand and gives him a flicker of a smile.

"Anyway, that particular day I had been especially…what would they call it now…bratty and obnoxious…yes, I think that fits. I believe even Daniel had his fill of me. He and I had a run-in earlier with a vestryman. We were in town performing an errand for my father, and we were sporting." He smiles thinking back on it all. "It was a sunny summer day—hot but with a gentle breeze just like today." He feels a tug as he is pulled back hearing the banter between the two of them.

§

"What a dandy prat you are William." Daniel pushes against his cousin. The day is glorious and the two want to get back home quickly for an afternoon of fishing.

"Stop it Daniel." William scowls at his cousin. Daniel is three years older, but only an inch or so taller.

"Oh, come now William," Daniel taunts. "How trifling can you be? Who cares what an old codger like Hammond Gilford has to say? He is a frustrated church vestryman with no power beyond his small rabble of parishioners. Put his words behind you. We have delivered your father's documents and let us be off to College Creek. Perhaps Old Benjamin will come and cook the catch along the bank. We shall make a feast of it." He prods William eyeing him with expectation.

William's scowl melts into a smile, and he nods. Daniel pushes him backwards onto the ground just as he runs off dodging a gaggle of women. They cackled with high-pitched declarations as they scatter. William recovers and runs after the culprit scattering the group once again. Easily catching up, he runs side-by-side with Daniel towards Old Benjamin's cabin. They are almost to their destination when the two slow their pace to a walk.

After a few minutes Daniel asks, "Tell me William, were you offended by Mister Gilford's words because they were disrespectful of the Original People, our mothers' people? Or, were you fearful because he targeted *you* claiming you to be a 'wild Indian running about'—even though he is ignorant of who you truly are?"

William looks at his cousin. His veil of pride is transparent to Daniel's eyes, and it makes him feel vulnerable. William's facial expression betrays his wounded spirit, and he fights to swallow past the sharp-edged lump that suddenly becomes lodged in his throat. "I barely knew my mother. She died along with my stillborn sister who I never knew either."

Daniel stops walking, cutting William off and, very uncharacteristically, grabs him roughly by the arm. "You knew her parents, my own mother—her sister—and you know her brother, Old Benjamin. It does not matter what face you wear for the rest of the world to see. What you know and feel to be right on the inside does not have to be lost to you in order to preserve and inherit your father's holdings. Your father does not want that for you. No one does."

William cannot find room in his heart for his cousin's words. He does not want to challenge his beliefs or sense of security by giving the stinging words consideration, so he stands vexed and silent. Daniel is resolute, holding onto his arm, watching him for a moment before his face softens. He loosens his grip from William's arm and smooths the sleeve of his shirt. William avoids looking at him.

"'Tis okay little cousin. I know how it is for you, but you will be a man soon, and you need to learn that there are no material solutions for one's spiritual problems. A day will come when you realize that words spoken and actions taken to make something look right even when you know…you know *here*… it to be wrong," Daniel pokes William in the chest and holds his hand there as he continues, "are words that are shallow, and actions that are soon evanescent. They will not sustain you. They will leave you empty with a hole here in your heart. I know, little cousin, that there is more to you than that. I look forward to the day when all of you stands before me."

Daniel resumes his walk back home and William falls in step behind him. They remain silent for the remainder of the walk. Daniel's stride slowly lightens, and he picks up a tune to whistle. William remains sullen and troubled.

They reach the cabin and go to fetch rods, a basket of worms they dug earlier in the day, and a sack of food. Benjamin is there and is easily convinced to go with them and, in a matter of minutes, the trio head out to the bank of College Creek where their favorite fishing spot awaits them. They walk to a place where the creek widens, and the deep water runs calmly. There is a downed tree lying below the water's surface where fish gather, and a large flat stone sits on the land's edge easily accommodating three people. They prepare their rods putting worms on the hooks. William is still feeling grumpy about his run-in with Mister Gilford, and Daniel's troublesome words echo in his ears.

Benjamin notices William's irritation and looks up a couple times from the task of preparing his rod before he pauses to watch William struggle with his own rod while mumbling expletives under his breath. Benjamin glances over at Daniel who is finished and walking to sit on the flat stone.

"What troubles you William?"

William shrugs a shoulder reluctantly looking up at his uncle. "I am sorry sir. I do not mean to be ill-tempered."

Benjamin raises his eyebrows. "Yes, indeed, but what has you so?"

William concedes defeat with a heavy sigh. "Twas Mister Gilford, sir. He made comment about Daniel and me. I took offense."

"And Mister Gilford's words are those you value?"

William snaps his chin up. "No sir. They hold no value to me at all."

"Then be done with them William."

"Yes, sir.  Daniel gave the same counsel."

"And?"

"I am giving it much effort sir, but I cannot seem to let it go."

Benjamin puts a gentle hand on William's shoulder. "Come and sit by the creek, so I can cast my line before Daniel catches the first fish." He winks. "I want to share something with you, and you can finish your task of preparing your rod there on the stone while you listen."

"Yes sir." William walks alongside his uncle and takes a seat next to him on the large stone. Its warmth from the afternoon sun penetrates his britches and radiates against his legs. Daniel sits on Benjamin's opposite side focused on his fishing line patiently waiting for a bite.

Benjamin expertly casts his line out into the water. Drawing a breath in, he comments, "I enjoy times like this. It is important to appreciate them and express gratitude when we are blessed by such pleasure for nothing lasts forever."

The boys look at him each knowing that a story is at hand. William's fishing line is finally set, and he casts it out settling in to hear Benjamin's voice bring the tale alive.

"There once was a great king named Solomon. He became king at a very young age, but despite this he was very wise. He asked the Creator for the gift of wisdom, and it was bestowed upon him because the Creator appreciated his desire to serve the people well. As king, Solomon had many guards in his palace, and the captain of his guards was named Benaiah. The king relied on Benaiah for all things and, as a result, Benaiah was very prideful. He made sure to let all those around him know how much the great king relied on him whenever anything needed to be done, and how important he was to the king. He bragged so much that soon people began to whisper, 'he's just a bit too proud.'

"However, Benaiah was truthful. The king did depend on him for all matters. King Solomon knew that if he asked Benaiah to get something done, the task would get done. Yet, one day the king decided that Benaiah needed a lesson in humility because his pride had gotten too much. So, the king summoned Benaiah and gave him an impossible mission to fulfill."

"Impossible in order to humble Benaiah, Old Benjamin?"

"Yes, William. King Solomon declared, 'You are my most faithful servant.' Benaiah readily agreed and was aglow with arrogance. His chest stuck out. The king folded his arms leaning back and continued, 'I have heard rumors of a wonderful magical ring that has a unique power. It is told that when a sad man gazes upon it he becomes happy, but when a happy man gazes upon it he becomes sad. Find this ring and bring it to me within six months' time.'

"So Benaiah set out to find this magical ring. He traveled nearly the entire six months and was yet to find it. He had looked in all the places where such a fantastical ring would be found. He went to see everyone who had anything to do with jewelry."

"Everywhere Old Benjamin?"

"Oh yes, William. He went to every gold and silver smith he could find, and everywhere he went he would tell the people that he had a most important order from the king himself. He told them that he needed a magical ring that could make a happy man sad and a sad man happy. Unfortunately, no one had ever heard of such a ring. Benaiah was very disheartened. Still, he knew if King Solomon said that such a ring existed, it existed, and he had to find it. He kept his mission his priority no matter how badly things seemed to be going for him."

Both boys were fixed on their uncle's animated face, as he brought the story to life. Benjamin checked his fishing line and continued with his tale. "Benaiah eventually became very tired. He still had no ring to present to Solomon, and he began to think that he was going to fail. He was about to give up when, on the final day of his mission, he spotted a shop that sold junk. An old man was sitting out front and Benaiah approached the man describing the object of his search. The old man grinned and invited him into the shop.

"The man pulled a boxful of baubles from a shelf, and he took a plain ring from the box. It was plated with brass and had an iron core. He engraved some words on it and gave it to Benaiah who read the inscription and nodded with a smile. He emptied his bag of gold onto a table in the shop thanking the man and headed back to the palace."

"So, Benaiah was happy then, Old Benjamin?"

"Indeed, William, he was. And, the night he returned everyone in King Solomon's court was gathered around. Now, King Solomon was relishing the thought of having this chance to humble Benaiah in front of everyone. He wanted to teach Benaiah a lesson when he admitted he had sent him out on a journey to find a ring that did not exist. He thought this one thing would certainly humble Benaiah, so he would no longer be so arrogant.

"Well, you can imagine King Solomon grinning as he sat on his throne expecting an unsuccessful—and humbled—Benaiah. So when Benaiah strode in and handed him the ring, the king was quite shocked. Inspecting it, he read the inscription and let out a melancholy sigh. He no longer felt the anticipated joy in teaching Benaiah a lesson. What's more he realized that all he had achieved would someday be nothing and others would eventually come and replace him. He became very very sad.

"As the king looked again at the ring, he realized that it was exactly the ring he had told Benaiah to find for him. It was a ring that would make a sad man happy because it tells him that his situation will change. And, it was a ring that would make a happy man sad because it predicts that his situation also will change.

"King Solomon looked at his hand and removed all of his valuable rings giving them to Benaiah saying, 'Here, from now on these are yours.' He slipped on the ring from the junk shop. 'It was I who needed a lesson in humility,' he said. 'This ring has reminded me that wealth and power are fleeting things and I, King Solomon, with all my riches and all my wisdom am just like everyone else—flesh and blood. A servant of our Creator and my fellow man.'"

Benjamin takes a deep breath and works his fishing line a bit.

William glances out towards the water where Benjamin's line is cast thinking perhaps a fish has distracted his uncle from the story, but the line remains undisturbed and the water still. He shifts in his seat. "Old Benjamin, what compelled the king to think this? Did the ring truly have magical powers?"

Benjamin smiles. "Well, that depends on what you call magic. If 'tis something that nudges one to a different way of thinking, then perhaps that old junk ring truly was magical. Tales of it over the years have boasted great powers are granted to its beholder."

"What gave it so much power Old Benjamin?"

"Well, for King Solomon 'twas *insight*. You see, young William, that junk store merchant had engraved upon the ring, 'This too shall pass'."

Daniel smiles to himself.

William nods as though he understands, but his brow is furrowed. "But what of the powers the tales boast of?"

"Well," Benjamin answers. "For a wise man, like King Solomon, the words alone were powerful enough. He understood and acted. Perhaps, however, for another it would need to be different. Perhaps, a grander magical or miraculous scheme would need to be conjured in order to make the true simplicity of it believable." At that moment a fish strikes Benjamin's line, and he pulls back standing up to bring in his catch.

Daniel leans towards William. "Do not worry, little cousin, your hubble-bubble thinking shall pass. You just need to find that King Solomon fellow's ring and make it so." He pushes against William's shoulder knocking him off-balance. Daniel lets out a hearty laugh and William scowls at him.

§

Will sighs at the memory.

Hallie looks at him grinning. "A very telling tale I would say."

"Yes, in many ways to be sure."

She sits up giving him a gentle kiss. Maude walks up behind them clearing her throat.

Will clears his throat and stands offering a hand to Hallie. "Doctor Cavander…are you ready then?"

"Yes, I am. I thought that we could walk on over to Church Street and grab a bite at the Texas Tavern. How would that be?"

"Sounds just fine."*

# CHAPTER 19
## Recognition

Maude turns to talk with Hallie and Will as they progress through the city. "It is written, as I have said, that Raphael is the high angel of healing for Earth. There was a time when he visited often using his key. He had a deep appreciation for the Earth and our kind. The description of his key was vague, but Eban thought it would be something from here—Earth—Something natural, lasting, like a stone. Most likely with religious symbolism engraved or formed in it somehow, and a precious gem. The gem stores its energy. And, it would have to have a shape that allows it to bond with Solomon's key. Circular maybe. A star is a possibility."

"I see." Will bites the inside of his cheek and turns his head as though he has just swallowed something sour. "Doctor Cavender."

"Yes, Will?"

"What about demon lore?"

She stops and color drains from her face. "Why do ask about that?" She continues without waiting. "Demons do not provide insights to their world. You should…" She turns and starts walking at a quicker pace smoothing her sweater and adjusting her hair.

Will starts to speak, but Maude flies a hand up. "No. I don't want to know your motivations for this conversation. Odina said to help. Help and get it done. That is what I am doing."

Hallie raises her eyebrows and shrugs at Will. She speeds up to close the few paces between them and Doctor Cavander. Will shakes his head and catches up as well.

"Maybe just one more question Doctor Cavander. If you

don't mind." Hallie looks over at Maude with a dipped chin and gentle smile.

Maude wets her lips and gives her head a nod.

"I don't understand how it all works. Do the keys just bond? Does the person do something? How does it work?"

"That's something I can't tell you. Once the Trinity Amulet generates there will be no need for questions because all will be known. How it gets to that point, I don't know. In the hands of a person, the result will be one thing, but if it were to fall into the hands of…a demon, the result will be quite different."

Hallie stops short. "How? How could that happen?"

"Influence, possession, some other devious means. It's possible."

Hallie presses her lips together and raises her eyebrows offering a short, "huh."

"I hope that I have not muddied the waters too much for you, but rather given you the next step of your journey. More needs to be learned. The point is only you can decide the direction—for whatever reason you are embarking on this…journey."

Maude becomes increasingly more distracted and anxious looking back behind them a couple times and almost walks past the Texas Tavern. She stops and waves her hand as though she is swatting a fly and continues. "I do need to speak to you both about one other thing."

Will opens the door, and they all walk in. There are ten or so stools at a counter. The tavern is nearly empty, but the smell of French fries and chili permeates the room so strongly there is no doubt they'd just missed the lunch crowd. Two customers, railroad workers, sit on stools near the door. While a man in a white t-shirt leans against a cooler behind the counter. He walks up to the threesome after they take seats at the far end of the counter.

"Hello, folks. Whadaya have?" He takes their orders and turns his head towards the grill area. "Three bowls and one with a slab."

Within minutes three hot bowls of delicious food is set before them. The door opens, and an old woman in ragged clothes steps in standing tentatively at the door. The man behind the counter pauses from his work to see who walked in. The woman looks at him from under the brim of her hat. He presses his lips together and tilts his head towards an empty stool a seat away from Will.

Her faded cotton dress is wearing thin at the edges, and the finely woven straw hat on her head has tattered silk flowers arranged off the back with a frayed brim. Her large sack is burdened with a heavy load that seems to collapse with relief when she sits it on the floor near her stool.

"Hello there, Jerry." Her smile is warm while her eyes reflect sadness deep inside.

"Hello, Missus Mason. How about a nice bowl of chili with a slab of cheese on it?"

"Oh, yes. That would be lovely."

Jerry turns to get the woman's order placed and he pours her a glass of cold water setting it on the counter in front of the stool where she stands. He turns taking money from his tip jar to pay for her meal.

Although Will is focused on his meal, he can feel Missus Mason's eyes on him, and he adjusts his seat and takes a drink. She catches her breath, and her wispy glance draws his attention. He offers a thin smile intending to re-engage his meal, but he is unable to look away. She studies him with her languid eyes, and he can see a spark of life start to light up in them. Her gaze averts to the horrendous scar on his arm, but he does not feel the need to conceal it like usual. She walks over and reaches out to touch his arm.

Her cool fingers gently grasp his wrist, and the grit from the harsh homeless life she lives can be seen under her nails. Once a woman of status now lost to the world by a gradual unhinging of her mind. Will can see all of this as her eyes willingly reveal her soul and, for the first time, he knows what a soul-seer like her and others like her, capture in a glance.

"A compatriot of the suffering I see," she says to him as her head wobbles.

He sees her yellowed and aged teeth when she leans in to speak to him like an accomplice. The smell of alcohol wafts towards him.

She steals a look towards Hallie, and Will sees that she now knows the essence of Hallie's soul as well. A nervous edge begins to scrape through his veins, and his thoughts vibrate on a course of uncertainty.

Missus Mason's eyes focus back on his, and she smiles reassuringly at him releasing an intoxicating rush of endorphins. "Take ease boy. 'Tis merely a meeting by chance of compatriots, as I have already said. You have given an old woman renewed hope, so let her bring the same to you." Her grasp on his wrist loosens and she opens her hand sliding her palm down over his.

The small handprint from Sophia's unborn child is visible as it glistens icy silver on his palm. A soothing calm melts over his wired nerves, yet he slowly clenches his fist withdrawing from Missus Mason's hand. His eyes rise to fix on her gaze. Her lower lids droop under gray eyes that seem to sparkle now. There is a flash of happier times before the deep wrinkles and steady tremor of her head and hands took hold.

She taps the countertop. "All suffering comes to an end young man. Yours—and mine. I thank you for this reminder. I wonder what forces have come into play to make things right for you—to bestow mercy for all those lives and dives into darkness before now."

Will stares at her trance-like. Never before has he crossed paths on Earth with someone like her.

She leans back in and whispers to his ear. "I must tell you that you have a vessel in your midst."

Will's muscles seize and he starts to turn to look beside him, but Missus Mason grasps ahold of his wrist. His gaze ricochets towards her eyes, and they flash a reflection of Maude eating her chili. His breath catches and Missus Mason loosens her grip giving his hand a gentle pat.

"It sits empty for now and she knows not herself. Today, all is well. Maybe never. Maybe soon. Take caution." Missus Mason fixes on a crack in the counter near Will's hand as she whispers to him.

His fingers tingle and he works them in and out, but he does not move his hand away from Missus Mason. He swells with gratitude for crossing paths with her and for the caution he has taken today where Maude is concerned reminding himself once again that you do not know someone until you know them. He is pulled back from his thoughts by the sound of Jerry's voice.

"Missus Mason, your chili is at your seat. Let these folks be now."

She blinks giving Will a last knowing look and turns to take her seat. Jerry shrugs an apology. Will glances down at his palm. The mark is gone.

The reprieve that the meal seems to have given Maude's recent surge of anxiety is short-lived. She pays the bill and stands to leave. Will drinks the last of his coke and stands taking Hallie's hand.

As they walk by, Hallie lays money next to Missus Mason who is bent over and focused on her bowl of chili. Her scuffed shoes are propped on the footrest of her stool, and her tremulous hand precariously moves chili on a spoon to her mouth. Will turns back as he opens the door for Maude and Hallie and sees Missus Mason's sidelong glance towards them and her crooked smile.

They aren't three steps from the door when Maude exclaims. "She's a seer." She stammers, "Uh, I didn't mean to just blurt that out. I apologize. She caught me off-guard."

Will looks at her unwilling to admit that Missus Mason had the same effect on him. He waits for Maude to continue hoping she did not hear Missus Mason's declaration that Maude is a vessel—a potential host to demons and angels alike.

"I am a seer of sorts," she awkwardly declares tugging the cuffs of her sweater sleeves straight. "It's not something one talks about much. Only since meeting with Odina and spending this brief time with the two of you, am I beginning to come to an understanding after a long time of confusion and...I guess... fear...can I say it to you."

They continue to walk, and Will remains silent. He is pleased that Maude has so freely opened up to him and Hallie. Odina is deserving of his gratitude for this he realizes. However, he will not reciprocate. Silence truly is golden when one's words can potentially put an adversary in a position of advantage. Empty vessel or not, it unnerves him that she too is aware of Missus Mason's unearthly talent let alone that she is holding some sort of speculation about his own.

"Uh, let me explain. I have always known that I had this...this ability to...not *see*—not like what just happened—more like *feel* the essence of one's soul. It was a curiosity for me, and I did research it quite a bit which led me to a variety of cultural interpretations of such things. I believe that research influenced my career choice." She hesitates and twists her lips while smoothing her sweater yet again. "I have this knack for feeling the essence of one's soul. It is partly what has kept me safe I believe these last several years. And our conversation today, affirms to me that I need to tell you what your aura reveals." She looks at Will.

He gives a shrug of his shoulder neither committing to nor shunning her perspective.

"Your energy ring—uh, that's what I call what I feel from people—feels different from others. I have only met one other, a museum curator in Jerusalem. Curiously, in the small town of Ferrum, there are two of you."

She begins to fidget again looking around, and Will grows impatient. "Doctor Cavander, I need for you to say what you have to say." He stops, and again she looks about them nodding her head for them to move on. Will sighs and complies.

"You are a descendant of a Watcher."

He chuckles shaking his head. "You think I am Nephilim?"

"Not a *child* of a Watcher, perhaps grandchild, maybe great-grandchild."

Hallie remains silent.

"That's ridiculous." Will speaks more harshly then he intends, and it takes him by surprise. A familiar fear creeps up his spine. Discovery. Someone seeing a characteristic that makes him different and, perhaps, a threat to others. Surely, Maude's speculation is outlandish. He lets out a burdened sigh. "Doctor Cavander, I just do not believe that can be so. The Nephilim were supposedly washed from the Earth during the great flood. They were supposed to be giants of men. They were supposed to be evil. Ma'am I am neither that old, that large and, despite my incursions through the darkness, I hope not to be evil."

"No, no indeed not. None of those things. I am so sorry. Of course, that is the general understanding. The writings, the very ones that tell of the Trinity Amulet, say otherwise though."

He looks at her. A flicker of hope. He waits.

"Throughout time Watchers have lived among us claiming their free will, but not falling from grace, not demonizing themselves. There have only been a few. The writings indicate that this trend would continue through the centuries but, of course, only one knowing what to see or, as in my case, feel, can know for sure. First in Jerusalem and now again in Virginia."

"I have never felt different from others. I have never been seen as different by others."

"Ah, but I think you probably have been seen differently by at least a few through the course of your existence. However, because you do not feel any differently about yourself, the advantage they have seen in your uniqueness is lost to you allowing them to exploit what you feel no ownership of."

"What advantages are there to be the descendant of a Watcher?"

"No doubt many," Maude answers. She has once again relaxed losing her twitchy anxiety. "However, I believe for *you* it has made you capable of knowing the darkness of the underworld and survive it. It gives you great potential but, in your case, a partnership is needed to realize the complete potential."

Maude looks at Hallie and smiles. "It does not take the skill of a seer to understand the pureness of heart that resides inside you."

Will's mind races and his throat tightens as he realizes what Maude is saying, and how much Odina must have told her. Hallie still does not seem to pull the pieces together yet.

"What are you saying Doctor Cavander?"

"A sacred union bringing together the human aspect, uh person well people in your case, of the Trinity Amulet, if the keys were to summon you."

*She is putting together the pieces.* An unforeseen force constricts around his chest. He forces a breath in. *Or, maybe she just speculates.*

"To what end?" Hallie looks over at him as comprehension washes over her.

"I don't know," Maude answers. "Perhaps wrongs righted. Likely, more than we are capable of comprehending. Only the force behind the amulet knows for sure, and only the keys choose who and when."

"A sacred union?" Hallie asks.

Maude looks at her raising her eyebrows. "Yes."

They arrive at the hotel and stop for a moment before Maude speaks up. "Perhaps we should give all this time. Think it through and plan to meet again to talk about it more in hopes of finding perspective. I will be back on Friday, and I am to have supper at the Ridges on Sunday. We can talk then."

Will nods and Hallie agrees. They say their good-byes and turn to leave.

Will hesitates a moment turning back. "Doctor Cavander, please keep Odina's crystal with you at all times."

She smiles at him lifting it from her purse.

Hallie's voice is breathy when she exclaims, "Oh, my God. Will, there is more to this then we could have even imagined."

He pulls her closer as they walk. "Yes, so it would seem, and I am afraid there is no turning back." Maude's words about Nephilim crowd his mind, and he realizes that he did not ask her about the second soul she found in Ferrum that is…like him. Hallie reminds him what Beezie told her about Maude's hair salon visit—it has to be Drew. Connie will know.

# CHAPTER 20
# Yielding

A storm is brewing on the other side of the mountain when Will drops Hallie off at the Ridges'. He plans with her to meet tomorrow and kisses her before she gets out of the car. The electric current of her touch still courses through his veins as he drives away. He doesn't want to leave her but forces himself to drive back to town leaving Connie's car near her apartment. She isn't home, and he is good with that. He doesn't want to talk "Nephilim" with her tonight.

Sleep beckons, but his mind races. Despite all there is to think over from the day's events, the harvest certainly looming, and the other dangers threatening them, he cannot pull his thoughts away from the soft curl of Hallie's hair, and how it comes to rest against her shoulders and along the smooth inward curve of her neck. Her chin, her full lips, her ivory skin lightly freckled by the sun, and her ever changing hazel eyes—all this preoccupies his thoughts as he walks to his small apartment. These thoughts over-rule any attempt to contemplate solutions for the challenges that lay ahead. He decides a shower and a night's sleep will help to clear his head and give him focus.

Lightning flashes across the sky flickering shadows around Will as he slides his key into the lock opening his apartment door. His hair is blown by the brisk wind, and he can see dust from the road swirling in a mini tornado skirting across his porch. He steps inside and shuts the door behind him cutting the wind short. The light flickers on when he swipes the switch by the door. A carton of milk in the refrigerator offers refreshment, and he takes a long drink before he puts it back in and shuts the door. Lightning flashes again, and the lights in his room waver.

While the shower quickly fills the tiny bathroom with steam he undresses. The hot water is the only reliable feature of the studio apartment, and tonight he is especially grateful letting it wash away the tension in his muscles. Booming rumbles from the storm grow louder announcing the storm is at the door. The lights sputter again, and he looks up anticipating the inevitable outage, but it isn't going to be this time. Will turns to reach for the soap when a static-charged image flashes before his eyes. He jerks his head up towards the bulb on the ceiling but it's no different.

Flash. There is an image of Hallie, desperate, tearful, and then…relieved. She is looking up at him, and he feels the heat of her body while he holds her close. There is a gentle rain falling on her face, and she urgently reaches up kissing him. Static…and the image is gone. He turns and looks behind. The shower water runs steadily. The steam wafts up from the floor. He stands mechanically washing. *Where is that image coming from?* Flash. It's like a television station with poor reception.

His hands reach out to hold her face. He kisses her cheek gently. She trembles. A door opens and someone stumbles past them bumping his shoulder. He turns to watch the man walk away. His attire is colonial. It is dark but the view comes into focus—the pebbled road and the hitched horses. It's the back entrance to the Raleigh Tavern in Williamsburg. *How is this possible?* Flash and the image is gone. He searches his memory. There is nothing else like it.

Will finishes his shower turning off the water and grabbing a towel from the rack on the wall. He wipes the steamy haze from the mirror and pours some tooth powder on his palm to brush his teeth. Hallie's reflection appears in the mirror—she is standing behind him with her auburn hair in ringlets cascading down around her face from under a bonnet. He turns around but she isn't there. Looking back at the mirror, his nerves twitch, she is not there. He empties his mouth of the froth and tugs the string on the bulb overhead.

A bright flash ignites the window by his bed and seconds later the booming thunder sounds. The lights flicker in protest and finally give out. He collapses on the bed watching the sky light up in intervals listening to the rumbles and booms following each burst of light—some make the windowpanes rattle. Large drops of rain begin to bounce off the window, and he reaches up pushing the window out feeling a few of the wet drops as they splash against the sill. A cool breeze pushes aside the stagnant air while the clock on the nightstand ticks away the seconds. The unrelenting storm lights up red through his closed eyelids.

There is an absence of sound, the air is still, and the humidity dissipates. Even the rain drops he knows to be pounding the window cannot be heard. His eyes snap open. The electricity is still out, and the darkness prevails only interrupted by the flickering lightening from the storm. He waits for the boom, but it doesn't show up, and he thinks he catches sight of Hallie standing in the far corner of the room. He sits upright in surprise straining his eyes, but she is not there.

A second series of flashes, however, show her again. Closer. Approaching. She is wearing a man's white shirt with a ruffled neckline and cuffs. A monogram below the left shoulder of the shirt displays fancy needlework. "HWW" in gray silk thread. It goes dark again, and the image disappears.

Another succession of flashes lights the sky, and Hallie is standing next to his bed. The fine linen shirt is all that she is wearing. Its hem hangs to just above her knees, and the sleeve beyond her fingertips draws back on her arm as she points towards his nightstand. Her image disappears again in the darkness. He looks where she pointed and remembers the candle he has there. With a pounding heart thumping steadily against his chest wall, he scavenges the nightstand drawer searching for a book of matches. Success. A spark finally takes hold after several strikes igniting the tip releasing a sulfurous smell but no sound. The candle sputters before the wick takes the flame. Its sphere of light pushes away the darkness. Now, with the soft steady glow she is fully visible to him. She gives a mischievous smile, and she sits on the bed facing him.

His skin ignites when she touches his face, runs her fingers over his lips and slides them downward over his neck, his chest, his abdomen…. There is no sound when he gasps in a breath charged with the excitement her touch induces. Although, he seems to be momentarily deaf, his other senses are intensified. A warm vanilla scent floats in the air, and he raises his hand up behind her neck grasping gently at her hair as he pulls her towards him. He kisses her full of desire and unconcealed passion. There are no thoughts of the Demon King cluttering his mind or concern for tainting Hallie's soul. At some level of consciousness, he questions the reality of this moment even though the physical response of every cell in his body is undeniably real. The scale has been tipped and there is no holding back.

She leans back away from him sitting up straight. Grasping the bottom edge of the shirt, she pulls it up and over her head. Her hair falls back down over her shoulders as the shirt lifts, and she casually tosses it aside onto the floor. The candlelight flickers and reflects off her soft curls and hazel eyes. He is frozen entranced by the sight of her. She takes his hand and places it over her breast. Her skin is warm and silky smooth, and she shivers with his touch, but there is a steadiness to her hand she too touches him lightly caressing his skin, encouraging him, enticing him. There is a certainty with her kisses. She commands his full attention. *This* Hallie knows him and his body. She knows him like a practiced lover. There is no nervous hesitancy as there was when they were in the woods both in Fayerdale and here in Ferrum.

He feels no obligation for restraint and turns laying her back on his bed. He looks at her overwhelmed by her beauty and the love he feels not just for her, but from her. She is here, in some form, with him. He has neither the will power nor the desire to resist her. The rush of his fiery blood pulses and pounds within him, and he runs his hand up along the outside of her thigh grasping her at her hip and pulling her towards him. He feels her surrounding him, charging his passion. She arches her back and synchronizes her rolling swell of desire with his. A silent groan vibrates upward from deep inside him as he responds taking the lead, their aching need for one another escalating. He kisses her neck but seeks her mouth with urgency relishing in the immediate satisfaction he feels when he reaches her lips. He kisses her deeply and hungrily. They are lost in one another, and ardently embrace the moment with sweet surrender. The ecstasy carries them steadily higher when suddenly the pinnacle is before them exploding with immense gratification. The intensity of the moment melts and a satisfied exhaustion overcomes them.

A thin sheen of sweat glistens off of Will's skin mollifying the heat within. His breathing slows, and he looks at Hallie smiling as he tucks a stray curl of her hair behind her ear. He lowers his head and kisses her. "I love you, Hallie." He feels the words vibrate across his lips but the silence prevails.

She blinks slowly as a satisfied smile lights up her face, and he sees her reply. "I love you, Liam."

He blinks and looks at her taken back for a moment, but quickly recovers, he will soon *be* Liam. Her words, and perhaps the reason she is here tonight, give him confirmation that he will survive the Demon King's wrath and what lays ahead for him in Tartarus. There is hope that not only will he survive, but he will be with her in the future. His chest lightens with relief.

Will lays back resting next to her shoulder-to-shoulder. She reaches her hand up and he grasps ahold of her hand momentarily before she moves tracing her fingertips down and along the tentacles of his scar. Her touch is soothing, and he closes his eyes for a moment allowing the calm she induces to wash over him. When he opens his eyes he sees a metallic glitter in the candlelight. An intricately carved band of silver circles her ring finger. She turns her head towards him smiling, and takes his left hand holding it up to reveal a band of black showing equal craftsmanship resting on his finger as well. They are his parent's rings. His father had kept them in a box in his bed chamber all those years after Will's mother died until one day they just disappeared. *How are these here?*

Her face is now relaxed with sleepy contentment. She closes her eyes, and a slow rhythmic rise and fall of her chest can be seen from below the thin sheet. He reaches out to touch her left hand and the ring just as a rush of air blows in from the window, rain pounds audibly against the glass, wetness splashes at him from the sill, and a thunderclap rattles the room.

The candle flame wavers and goes out, and Hallie is gone. The bed where she had been lying feels warm when he runs his hands over the sheet. *How extraordinary.* He has lived through so many impossibilities already, and he convinces himself that what just happened was genuine at some level of consciousness or realm of existence. *It had to be real.* The ring on his finger is gone, but in its place is an intricately scrolled protective mark spilling over from the base of his finger to his knuckle and hand. It glistens back at him much like the candle's flame had illuminated Hallie.

He dreams when sleep overcomes him about each of his protective marks. The first mark is the tiny handprint on his palm. The next, the triskele that lays over his heart was a gift from Hester prior to the first demon war he fought in. It has shielded his heart protecting him from a death of death more times than he can count. And there is the mark over his left shoulder which was given to him by Daniel before he fought and was struck down by the demon, Sariel. Daniel knew it would be the last time they saw each other, and he walked over touching William's left shoulder. Will can still feel the icy-hot sensation that Daniel's touch had induced.

In his sleep he sees Daniel's gift that guards his non-dominant side keeping him strong and at the ready all the way around. It is a tribal symbol of ram horns butting up against each other signifying strength and humility. A ram will fight fiercely against an adversary, but it also submits humbly to slaughter. It was Daniel's way of telling him to fight hard, yet to remember to be humble.

The storm wanes and the thunder dwindles to distant reverberations while raindrops become a gentle pattering against the window rippling the small puddles that have already formed on the sill. Humidity is replaced by a cool breeze and the sounds of night—chirps and rustles—outside of his window take over once again. The transformation and its symphony go on without his notice, as he lays sleeping contently in his bed.

# CHAPTER 21
## Hint

It is relatively cool for a July morning with crisp air and a clear sky complements of the previous night's storm. Last night replays in Will's mind as he walks to the bathroom. He distractedly grabs the can of tooth powder from the medicine cabinet and shuts the door pausing for a moment seeing a mirror image of the triskele on his chest. A chill colder than the hand of the Demon King himself grabs his neck. He stares into the mirror and turns seeing the ram horns reflect back at him. The small handprint— there too. He hesitates raising his left hand finding the newest protective mark. *This is not good. Not good at all.*

Leaning on the sink, he waits. Nothing. He frantically surveys his face, his back, his chest. Still nothing, and his lungs fill with a wash of relief. *No demon marks.* The demon marks are much darker and larger than the protective marks. Still, even the finely intricate protective marks will be visible if someone looks. He busies himself with washing his face, combing his hair, and pulling on his coveralls—the sleeves are short but still cover Daniel's mark on his upper arm. The last of the milk in the fridge goes down quickly and he tosses the carton into the trash.

No one has gotten to the garage yet, and he flips on the lights and the radio before walking into the office looking at the work list for the morning. There are a few vehicles that were dropped off before closing yesterday. Mostly simple servicing that he can go ahead and get started on before Drew and Mister Adkins arrive.

Boyd Hopkins dropped his wife's car off yesterday for an oil change. Will grabs the keys. It's a cherry red Corvette with black leather interior and white wall tires. The Hopkins' and

McCaffrey's by far have some of the finest vehicles in town—probably the county. He runs his hand along the driver's side door admiring the finish before getting in. With a turn of the ignition a soft rumble ensues, and he sits closing his eye for a moment before pulling the car into the garage.

While Will works grease partially obscures the etched glitter on his hand, and he runs his thumb across the mark smearing more of the slick blackness to conceal it. Flipping over his right hand he does the same for the tiny handprint. It should hide them well enough while he works.

He presses his lips together while he replaces the Corvette's oil filter, and his mind eventually wanders past last night's dream resurrecting memories from Fayerdale before everything was changed by Hallie's arrival. He thinks about the beautiful landscape, his dog Holmes, and for some reason Mister Elkins and his wood carvings. The finest stick Will remembers Mister Elkins had carved was the one the old man gave to Doc Hutchinson, the family physician who lived in Fayerdale. Will was with the doctor when Mister Elkins brought the stick to him.

§

The memory washes over Will—he went by Billy then and was on his knees hammering down some loose floorboards in the front room of the doctor's office when Mister Elkins walked in carrying the intricately carved walking stick.

"Howdy do Billy, is Doc Hutchison in?"

"Yes sir, Mister Elkins, he is in the back room. I will go fetch him for you."

Doc walks in alongside Billy. His crooked neck cane taps the floor as he goes. "You feeling alright Isaac?"

Mister Elkins lowers his head and shifts his weight. "Uh, oh yes sar Doc Hutchison. Yes, sar I'ma jes fine."

The doctor relaxes and waits for Mister Elkins to state his

business.

"I wanted ta bring you this here gift thankin' you for taking such good care of my grand boy."

The doctor's eyes light up, and he leans his old cane against the desk to accept the walking stick. Slowly running his fingers over the intricate carving, he admires the craftmanship. "This is mighty fine, mighty fine indeed Isaac. But it is too fine for an old country doc like me. Much too fine to be sure."

"Oh, no sar doc. Ita be just right. Yes sar. And even with this here gift, I will always be beholding to you. That boy is all I got left of his momma afta she was kilt by that thar Spanish flu that hit the mountains. She was my only child, and my missus and me would have never survived her death without that boy ta keep us agoin'. No, sar I'ma might bit grateful for tha care and concern you give ta all tha folks round these parts—no matta who they be. You a good man doc."

Doc Hutchison's cheeks flush. "Well then Isaac, I accept your gift most humbly. Now, let's take a seat here while you tell me more about this extraordinary walking stick."

"Uh yes sar, be more than glad ta."

The doctor and Mister Elkins take seats near the bay window in a couple of the chairs that Doc Hutchison keeps in the front room for patients waiting to be seen. Billy starts cleaning up, but the doctor tells him to take a break and to sit and hear Isaac's 'story of the stick'.

Mister Elkins clears his throat and takes the stick from the doctor holding it up. "Well, tha first thang you need ta know is this here stick presented itself to me when I was walkin' a trail thinkin' on how I could thank you for what you done for my grand boy. It's important knownin' it was a gift from tha tree because it means tha spirit of tha tree still lives within tha wood. What's more it's a stem of flying rowan."

Billy's brow furrows.

The doctor sees his confusion. "It is an epiphyte."

Billy nods in understanding, but now Mister Elkins is confused.

"I was just explaining to the boy that it came from a rowan that had grown from the trunk of another type tree. You know, with the seeds from the rowan's berries that are carried by birds after eating them. It is quite amazing how the seeds are 'planted' so to speak by the bird's droppings that land in a fork or hole of a tree where leaves have accumulated".

Mister Elkins nods and continues his account of the walking stick's creation. "Yes sar, and most fortunate too. Tha wood from a flying rowan is even more special than if tha tree was ta grow up from tha ground like usual. This here walking stick was a branch growing up outta tha base of a huge old cedar tree that is up on tha ridge near Otis Hairston's place."

Billy's brow pops up. "Yes, I know that tree. It truly is an odd-looking tree."

"That's right." Mister Elkins nods. "Tha two trees have very different types of wood. I ain't never seen it before—I mean tha two different types a wood a growin' *inta* one anotha. If you look closely thar near at tha shaft of the walking stick, you can see where tha two different types of wood grew together. Tha rowan is tha primary wood but thar at tha handle part is cedar wood that done grew up into tha rowan. You gotta turn it upside down ta see it betta. That be most unusual ta find a piece like this. Tha tree was most generous." He runs his weathered hands along the spot where the wood grain changes. A precise replica of the cedar's tiny prickly needle leaves is carved into the wood. They gracefully hang downward towards the point of union with the rowan where tiny carved oval leaves and clusters of berries start.

"I was a walkin' by tha tree like I done a hundred times

before an this branch caught onta me an snapped off near tha trunk of that old cedar. I knowed the meaning of it right then, and I thanked tha tree sincerely. When I looked at that broken stick it appeared in my mind's eye just how you see it here. Tha staff, the tree branches, an tha twisting snake rising upwards. The snake is just like tha one that inspired that Greek healer fellow." He tilts his head and bites his lip.

"Asclepius?" Doc offers.

Mister Elkins slaps a hand on his thigh. "That be tha one. I saw tha snake's image, and I knew that it was meant for me ta carve it for Doc Hutchison."

§

Will blinks and sees the stick today as though it was in front of him right now—the snake in perfect detail rising towards the handle. A loop of the snake's body coming from the side of the staff just below the handle where there is a small hole. The center opening with a triangular appearance to it which had meant nothing to Billy at the time, but it suddenly has meaning to Will— it forms the downward triangle of the six-pointed star. When he forces his memory's vision further he can see the triangle's upward counterpart carved into the edges of the loop's inner circle. He wonders what Mister Elkins knew of the symbol, and he focuses back to the memory and the old man's voice.

§

"Them old timey Greek folks worshipped ol' Asclepius like a god." He turns to Billy to explain further. "He was a doctoring fella just like tha doc here helping people. Ana he angered tha great god of the Greeks." Isaac hesitates darting a look towards Doc.

"Zeus." Doc Hutchison fills in for him.

"Thata be right. Zeus got angry with Asclepius when he cured a fella from death. Ole Zeus thought that only tha gods should be immortal ana he thought, 'if Asclepius has this power what would be next?' So, Zeus struck him down with a lightning bolt. Now Asclepius was tha son of Apollo." He stops and grins at Doc. "Ana, when his pa heard what happened ta him Apollo asked Zeus ta send his son ta tha heavens. Zeus did but as one of tha great constellations in the sky." Again, Isaac hesitates a moment.

"Ophiuchus." The doctor smiles visibly impressed by Isaac's knowledge of Greek mythology. Doc Hutchison lifts the walking stick from Isaac's lap. He explains the significance of the design to Billy. "There were temples of healing called Asclepion where sick people slept believing that they would be healed if they stayed in the temples. They were tended to by priests who were trained in the secret art of healing. The Aesculapian snakes," he hands the stick to Billy for him to see the snake more closely, "roamed the temples freely."

Billy jerks his head back and shoots his eyebrows upward.

Doc waves off his look of surprise. "The snakes are non-venomous, harmless."

Billy nods his head. "This is a mighty fine walking stick you have carved Mister Elkins." He hands the stick back to Doc Hutchison who now focuses on the ferrule of the stick.

Mister Elkins speaks up. "I had Otis Hairston fashion me that copper cap for tha tip thar. 'Course now it be turning black with time but ita protect tha stick from wear and tear on these here hills. Tha metal is nice an thick an fixed on thar real good."

"Yes, indeed Isaac. It is finely crafted all the way around. I thank you."

"Yes sar, I best be on my way. The Pettigrew boys are due back in bout twenty minutes or so from Philpott way, ana I'll be needing ta help them unload Mister Pennymaker's shipment from tha train. Rumor be a revenuer is coming ta town ana folks are…preparing. Lots of orders come in through tha general store tryin ta get stocked up I suppose before he starts a pokin' round."

"Well, then Isaac you best be off. Billy and I are pretty much done for the day, so he can head out with you. I'm sure his old hound is over at the depot waiting."

When they walk back towards the depot Mister Elkins whispers to Billy, "Somethin' bad has come this way. I finished tha walkin' stick jest in time."

"Sorry?"

"Ita keep tha doctor safe an anyone else who mighta be in need of its magic. Tha wood from a flying rowan is most powerful, and tha cedar that grew up into it is a most fortunate thang. You know tha Tree of Life is a cedar."

"Yes, actually I do."

Isaac nods. "You are a smart young man. Unusually so. Ima guessin' you will understand tha importance of what Ima gonna tell you. Maybe not now but later."

Billy looks at him but says nothing.

"King Solomon built his great temple using cedar and stone. Tha wood has tha power ta protect and preserve, it makes light in tha darkness, ana it clears negative forces from a place before works are ta be done."

"Works?"

Isaac nods. They are almost to the depot. Holmes, Billy's blood hound, is laying on the back platform and raises his head watching them approach.

"Magical works. Of course, that cedar in tha walkin' stick is really just a bonus. The rowan comes from the astral dimension, and its many doorways. It is tha world tree—some folks call it tha Mesu."

Billy looks at him wondering how this seemingly uncomplicated man knows about all of this. Billy knows his face betrays his thoughts when Mister Elkins smiles patting his arm before forging ahead.

"It gives passage ta tha mundane world—tha one where we is right now. It is where tha Three Fates dispense tha lot of men and test their free will."

They arrive at the depot and Mister Elkins rushes through his explanation holding onto Billy's arm, but Billy would not have walked away from Mister Elkins, if the depot was ablaze.

"Tha rowan has many names. Some call it mountain ash, but no matter what it's called its power is tha same. It is tha enemy of all evil witchery and protects one from being carried away against his will. Course for a demon tha effects are much different. It immobilizes tha fiend keeping it from crossing over ta tha other worlds—giving neither life nor death. It is tha demon version of being a human Shade in tha underworld." His eyes hold tight to Billy's.

Billy stares back unblinking while ignoring a line of sweat rolling down the side of his face. Holmes walks up nudging his hand, and Mister Elkins turns to look at Holmes. He reaches over to rub the dog's head. The train pulls in, and he bids Billy good-bye. Before he leaves, however, he leans closer to Billy, "You hold on ta what I've said. Ita serve you well one day young man." He turns and walks towards the platform.

The train's brakes protest as it slows to a stop. There is a great puff of black smoke, and the engine makes its last objection before suddenly giving up coming to a stop. Luke waves to Billy from the engine and Billy nods his head. He walks towards the holding pond where he is due to meet Jeb Curry about some business involving the Wilsons, one of the moonshine and bootlegging families in the area.

§

It amazes Will to think that not too long after that encounter, Billy would rescue Hallie from the very same pond and nothing would be the same again.

He tries to leave the memory as he looks around and realizes he is finished with the oil change. He brushes off his coveralls before getting into the car. Turning to look out the back window, he sees Drew standing in the middle of the bay door. He's looking at Will, and Will hesitates before putting the car in reverse. Drew steps away walking into the office. A prickly sensation erupts over Will's hands.

# CHAPTER 22
## Divulge

**W**ill walks into the office wiping grease from his hand without thinking about the concealed marks. "Hey, you okay? I thought you were going to be in early today."

Drew glances up from the work schedule. "Yeah, well I got a late start. Was that the Hopkins' car?"

"Yes, all done."

Drew marks it from the list. "Okay, that gray pick-up is next on the list. It's just an oil change too, so you can take it."

The phone rings, and Drew picks it up. "Adkins' Garage. Yes, we can take care of it for you. When to do you want to drop it off? Okay, I will write it in on the schedule." He hangs up the phone.

Will sees Drews eyes light on his hand and he puts it in a pocket missing the first attempt.

"Dillon McCaffrey wants to bring his Chevy in for maintenance."

*Maybe he didn't see it.* Will clears his throat. "That old Fleetline he has?"

"Yea."

Will fidgets. "So, when is he bringing it in?"

"Sometime tomorrow morning. He said he was going out of town for the holiday, so no rush in getting it done. He will pick it up first of the week sometime."

"Holiday?"

"July Fourth."

Will nods. "Right, right. Hallie said something about going to the town picnic. Apparently, there is going to be a carnival too. Are you and Connie going to go?"

Drew shrugs. "Maybe." His jaw tightens, and he makes a note on the schedule about the McCaffrey car before tossing the pencil onto the desk.

The bell for the full-service pump rings. It's Connie. Will filled her car up before dropping it off yesterday, so he knows she doesn't need fuel. She sits in her car looking straight ahead. He glances over at Drew unsure if he should tend the gas pump. Drew turns taking the keys for the gray truck and walks towards the door. "She's not here to see me. I'll take care of the pick-up."

Will watches Drew walk away and turns again to look out towards the gas pumps. Connie remains focused on her windshield or whatever view is beyond it. He walks to the driver's side of her car. Her knuckles are white on the steering wheel, and her eyes are on Drew watching him walk across the lot.

"Connie, you okay?"

She flinches at the sound of his voice. Her eyes are red from lack of sleep, he presumes, and perhaps tears. "I will be," she answers him tersely. "Can you come by my shop later today? I have a shelf that I need to get up."

"Uh." Will glances over towards Drew who is now starting the truck. "Sure. I'd be glad to. I can come over at lunch time."

"It might take a little longer than that."

"Okay, sure. No problem. I am actually off work after this morning and do not have to be anywhere until late this afternoon."

She blinks her eyes slowly. "Fine. Thank you." She drives off.

"Huh." He goes to pinch his lip unsure what to think about Connie catching site of the new protective mark. He self-consciously rubs it before walking over to Drew who is already under the gray pick-up draining the oil. Will leans a hand on the truck and talks to the lower half of Drew's legs. "Drew, is everything okay?"

There is no response from below the truck for a moment, but Drew stops what he is doing. "Will, are you really asking me that again?"

Will hesitates picking at the cuff of his coverall sleeve. *Why am I skirting around the issue? Drew is right.* For some reason Will does not feel his usual confident self. He cannot explain it, but he feels like a fledgling. He scuffs his shoe on the floor. "Yes, I did just ask that, but I guess it is moot."

Drew rolls out from under the truck. "Moot? Have you even considered attempting to speak like a teenager?" Before he can reply Drew shakes his head and slides back under the truck. "Never mind. You always were a dandy prat."

Will gets ready to raise an objection when he stops short at Drew's insult. "What did you call me?"

"William, am I to believe that you have suddenly lost your hearing? Or has ignorance settled between those ears of yours and it's comprehension you lack?"

There is something familiar in the sarcasm that laces Drew's words. Will feels a sudden angst overshadowed by hesitant hopefulness. He walks away from the truck only to turn on his heel to walk back. "Drew." His voice cracks. He clears his throat and restarts. "Drew slide out."

"Look Will, Mister Adkins does expect us to work while he is paying us. I have no time, and no desire really, to discuss my issues with Connie, or your general lack of perspicacity."

"What?" Will feels like a mouse being unmercifully toyed with.

Drew laughs as he continues to work on the truck. "Lack of perceptiveness, astuteness, cleverness, and general intelligence. I believe that defines the word, and you well enough."

Will's frustration grows just as Drew wheels the creeper

out from under the truck. He wipes the grease from his hands with a shop cloth he has laying on his chest and holds his hand up for Will to pull him up. Will hesitates before extending his hand. Drew stands holding on tightly staring at him directly in the eye. He turns his hand forcing Will's to be knuckle up. "Why do you have a protective mark of commitment on your left hand? What have you been up to little cousin?"

Will blinks while an emotional storm blusters within him. Both hold a firm grip on the other's hand standing tight-jawed and tense. There is a vaguely perceptible ripple in the air, and the veneer of anonymity vaporizes between them. Drew looks no different, but Will sees him for who he really is. Not just a waylaid drifter but his cousin. Emotion glistens in both young men's eyes.

"Daniel?" Anarchy assaults Will's breathing.

His cousin nods his head and brings a finger up to his lips motioning behind Will.

Mister Adkins walks around the corner and stops short seeing the two of them with fists clasped and seemingly poised for a fight.

"Is everything alright boys?"

Will and Drew release their grip. Drew is the first to recover. "Yes, sir.  Everything is just fine."

Mister Adkins nods and walks into the office where the phone is ringing. The door shuts behind him.

Will's stands firm over an earthquake of revelation.

Drew clears his throat. "Look, we'll talk but we're going to have to work while we talk. Mister Adkins does not need to be made suspicious of anything."

"You suffered a death of death. I saw it. I caused it."

Daniel points under the truck's hood grabbing a case of oil and the filters from the top of a toolbox. Will commands his legs to walk to the truck.

"First of all, that was not your fault. Sariel was bound to have me out of the way. He wanted Melinda and was delusional enough to think that my absence alone would solve his problem. It was certain to happen. You are not to blame."

"How are you here?"

"Here in Ferrum? Or, here at all?"

"Both, but I guess the 'here at all' part first."

"Go under the truck and make sure I got the plug tight on the oil pan before I get this new oil going in."

Will nods laying on the creeper rolling under the truck. Drew loosens the oil filter.

"There is no death of death, Will. At least not the way we thought. The best way I can explain is that there is, in a way, a conservation of energy throughout the universe."

"You mean like the theory, Galileo-type stuff?" Will rolls back out and stands.

"Yes, Galileo-type stuff I guess, but there is much more to it than the limits set by our thinking in the mundane plane."

"So, 'energy,' or a being's existence can change its location within the universe—across worlds—it can even change its form, but it cannot be destroyed."

"Right. There is what there is. Nothing, since God's original foray, is created or destroyed. What's out there though is so vast there are infinite possibilities."

Will scratches his chin when his face flushes. "Where have you been? How could you let me, Melinda—uh, Connie—*all* of us go on thinking you were lost forever? And, what of Elias?" Will feels sickness churn his stomach, and he grabs the front of Drew's shirt knocking him off balance.

Mister Adkins looks up through the office door window. Will forces himself to relax lowering his hands.

Drew snorts a dismissive laugh. "Cousin you may surpass

me in height, but I promise I will give you a run for your money, if you challenge my strength."

Will glances towards the shop's office door. Mister Adkins is focused back on his phone conversation. Will considers Drew for a moment and sighs imploringly. "What of Elias?"

Drew lowers his chin to his chest and his shoulders fall limp. "I did not know for the longest time, but I began to hear whispers of him. I regained hope that he too had somehow survived in a realm where we might eventually re-unite."

Impatience and confusion hijack Will's thoughts. He is elated that his cousin lives, yet angry thinking he has been betrayed, and feverishly concerned for their friend who had always been a little vulnerable. "Drew. What. Of. Elias?"

Drew breaks his gaze from Will and pulls a hand down his face wrapping his grasp around the back of his neck. "He is in the bowels of a barge of Shades."

"What?" Will turns abruptly away from Drew. The great flaming river of Phlegethon is where the barges of the Shades travel throughout the underworld of Tartarus. Will walks out of the garage and then pivoting back and rushes towards Drew stopping within inches of him. Venom spurs his words. "You knew this and did nothing? The vilest existence for any being and Elias still…whole…still…himself…and you did nothing?"

"Hey!" Drew reacts and his muscles tense with forced restraint. "I only just learned of his fate. I was working on a plan when I ended up here and everything was fuzzy until recently. He…he is on a barge, but he is not a Shade. Do not condemn me cousin. You of all people have no right to serve as my judge and jury."

Chagrinned, Will refuses to let this conversation to become about him. "How is it you are *here*? Tell me Drew."

Drew's chest heaves with effort. "Sariel. I had somehow

been bonded to him when Melinda stabbed him. We traveled across the lands of more worlds than I ever knew existed. We fought more battles then I knew there was blood to feed. And through it all, Sariel was driven by a desire to find a way to return to obtain revenge and claim Melinda."

Will swallows back the feeling of sickness churning from his stomach to his throat. He knows without anything more said that if Daniel is here so is the demon he is bonded to. Sariel had been the Demon King's greatest ally. *What is to happen to us all if both these forces unite once again? How will I keep Hallie safe?*

"Where is he Drew?"

Drew shifts his weight. "Let me worry with that. When he crossed over through the Mesu he became disoriented. He doesn't know who he is himself. Not yet anyway."

"He came through the Mesu? Did he drink from the Lethe?"

Drew shakes his head. "No. You never do either, yet there is still some confusion for a while, right?"

Will nods. "And you. How is it you are so clear of thought? For how long have you had your memory?"

A spark comes to Drew's eyes and spreads across his face. His muscles relax. "Will, I found the waters of the Mnemosyne."

Will looks at him as Drew's words take effect. "Where?"

"Within the Mesu. There is a tiny pool just beyond the entrance of the tree. Its sparkling waters caught my eye when I ran in trying to seek out Sariel. When I stepped up to where the waters pool and looked down into them the memories from my past were swirling deep within the water despite no movement of the water itself. I could see my memories. Crisp. Clear. They were slowly rising to the surface of the water towards me, and I knew then what it was. I put my hand in. Not a ripple came across the water as I lifted it to my mouth and drank."

The storm inside Will throws a pair of lightning bolts at his heart—one each of concern and admiration. "But we had always been warned never to touch or take of anything from within the tree. We were warned of the dangers." He searches Drew's eyes.

Drew stands with his head cocked allowing Will's words to resonate a moment. "Will, who gave that warning?"

Will searches for answers within his cousin's patient eyes who stands as though waiting for a young pupil to grasp ahold of a new concept.

"The Demon King," Will utters and understanding alights followed by frustration. "We all could have benefitted, if only we had the courage to take a chance."

"Fear, uncertainty, doubt little cousin. These are most powerful weapons for those skilled in the wielding of them."

Will nods. He relaxes and joy overpowers the anger and fear. "No more."

Drew reaches out grasping Will's left shoulder. "This is the time for the warrior ram; however, there will be one more submission to the slaughter that is necessary."

Will nods with understanding. They must return to Tartarus for the others and Elias. The full circle must be brought together for the final defeat of the Demon King.

"What of Sariel? Do you know where he is?"

"Here in Ferrum."

"Who?" Will hesitates a moment until understanding brings this awareness to light as well. "Never mind, I know."

"I only suspect. I'll know for sure soon."

"You are right. I know you are. You need to know that Joe Tasker, the Demon King, is here."

"Has he seen you?"

Will nods. "He knows I'm here, so it won't be long. I am beginning to sense the end."

"Listen to me Will. Sariel won't seek him out. If he gets his revenge, it will break the Circle of Souls and give Sariel power over us. The Demon King is not going to let that happen."

"Let us hope not. We need to find a way to defeat Sariel here on Earth where he is his weakest."

"Will, have you not heard what I have said? There is no destruction. For demons, and even angels, there is no hope of renewal by the grace of God like there is for humans. Do you understand? They remain the same. Death is not enough for Sariel. He will always be as he is, and he will find a way back to us."

"There has to be a way. Listen, there is someone who can help." He hesitates a moment considering Drew's reaction before he continues.

"Who?"

"Odina Ridge."

Drew snorts and shakes his head with disbelief. When he sees Will's steadfast stance he stops short. "So, the rumors are true. How could you suggest we seek counsel with a witch? Was it not the scheming and devious actions of such a creature that befell the original curse upon us all to begin with? What are you thinking?"

"I know. I know this, but there is more to them then we have known. We have been closed-minded because of our lot and the limited view we have taken as a result. Not all are sewn from the same cloth."

Drew's brow furrows deeply, and he looks over towards the office door. "We will discuss this later."

Mister Adkins has finished up his phone call and is heading their way. "Hello boys. I need to ask you both again if everything is okay. It is looking pretty intense over here."

Will forces himself to relax. "Oh, yes sir. We just have this ongoing debate over stock car drivers, and it can get pretty heated."

"Well, there's no arguing that Paul Radford, our own local driver of the number '77 car, is one of the best."

"Yes sir, that is just what I was telling Drew, but he seems to favor Curtis Turner from over the mountain in Floyd County."

"Well, Curtis is a mighty fine driver." He looks over to Drew. "But son, if you're going to be living here in Ferrum, it's the Ferrum Flash you need to be standing behind."

Drew smirks at Will. "Yes sir, I will certainly give it some thought. An alliance with loyalty can be a hard thing to change though, sir." He cuts another look towards Will.

Mister Adkins smiles. "I respect that son, and a little healthy debate can't cause any harm, so long as you boys keep it all in perspective."

Both acquiesce with an actor's skill.

"Well, it looks like you boys have gotten a good start to the morning. This pick-up finished?"

"Yes sir."

"Good. Will why don't you drive it out and get that old blue Ford in here?" He tosses Will a set of keys. Will catches them and starts to walk towards the driver's side of the gray pick up. Mister Adkins turns to face Drew. "Son, I need to know if you are in any trouble. I just got off the phone with Sheriff Shively, and he was asking an awful lot of questions about you."

Will gets in the truck hesitating to turn the ignition as he catches a glance from Drew. He can hear the start of his reply. "Uh, no sir. My time is pretty much occupied by work and Connie. I don't have much opportunity for getting into any trouble."

Will starts the engine and pulls the truck out. He knows Drew had planned to go to the Sheriff's office yesterday with concerns about Dillon McCaffrey, and wonders if something happened when Drew was there. Will decides that he is going to see what he can find out from Connie. He's going to have to risk triggering her memories, if he is to put to rest any concerns he may have for his cousin.

# CHAPTER 23
## Sparked

"Hey, Will!" Beezie pops her gum as she bounces out the door of the hair salon. "Watcha doing here? I thought you hated coming in here."

"Hey, Beezie." Will steps aside to let her by and shrugs. "It's just usually a bit crowded and noisy."

"Uh-huh." She smiles at him. "Well there's none of that today. Connie cancelled all the appointments we had on the book. I've been cleaning up the place, but I'm done. My dad and I are going to get things ready for the town picnic and carnival on Friday. You and Hallie going?"

"Yes, I think so. We will be there for a while at least."

"Well you gotta stay for the fireworks. Daddy said that there's gonna be some new fella that specializes in Chinese fireworks out of Martinsville doing the display this year. It's supposed to be a real kick."

"Yes, well we will definitely have to stay for that."

She gives him a quick smile, a pop of her gum, and a wave goodbye. He lifts a hand to say goodbye and steps into the shop. The sticky sweet smell of hair products in the air plucks his nose. Just past the chrome hair dryers Connie is sitting at a table with nail polish bottles, jars of cotton and creams, and what looks like instruments of torture. She is sipping on a cola and holding her hand out looking at her nails. Her face doesn't show any of the anger that dominated her mood earlier in the day.

"Hello, Connie."

He walks past her and sits on the arm of a chair at the hair wash station. A salon cape had been left draped over it causing Will to slide, and he adjusts his seat gracelessly to pull the cape out from under him. Heat rises up his neck. The lights are off except a small lamp near Connie, and it's a little darker in the back of the salon where the rays of sunshine from the front windows don't quite reach.

She looks up at him. "Will, thanks for coming over." She looks calm. Her eyes are clear and her hand steady.

*Perhaps, she was just tired this morning.* "No problem. Are you doing okay?"

Her lower lip puckers out, and she shrugs her shoulders giving a non-committal response. She takes another sip of her cola and fans her nails.

"Where is the shelf you need hung?"

She stands up and points towards a darkened doorway just beyond the wash station area. "It's leaning against the back wall of the prep room. I left everything you will need next to it. There's a pull string for the light just inside the door. I'll be up front, if you need anything."

"Right."

She gives him a nod and walks away.

Will lights up the prep room with a yank on its bare bulb's string. A blue chalk line shows where Connie wants the shelf hung, so he gets to work looking over the supplies she has laid out for him. A travel brochure catches his eye. It's stuck between the pages of a black leather-bound book, and he lifts the book from the table opening it to look at the brochure. *Guide Map and General Information for Visitors, An Official Leaflet Issued by Colonial Williamsburg, Restored by John D. Rockefeller, Jr.* Will recognizes the image of the governor's mansion on the cover. He looks over his shoulder towards the front of the store and can see the back of Connie's head bent down reviewing receipts by the register.

He starts to set the brochure back where it was but takes a second look at the book. It isn't just a book. It is a Bible. The brochure is between the pages of the story of Noah in the book of Genesis in a very old King James Version.

"What's this?" Chapter six, line four is marked with a star. *There were Giants in the earth in those daies: and also after that, when the sonnes of God came in unto the daughters of men, and they bare children to them; the same became mightie men, which were of old, men of renowme.* He puts the travel brochure back into the bible. The pages leaf closed, a faded ink signature is inside the front cover, *Melinda Holt.*

She keeps a hold box, like he does, to preserve items of importance from lives lived on Earth, and he wonders when enough of her memory had returned for her to recall its existence and where to retrieve it.

His thoughts drift to his father, his gentle nature, intellect, and generosity. He had a sense of fairness and respect towards all men, and his tolerance towards a prideful and head-strong son was unmatched. He also was a tremendous success as a businessman and as a human being. He was a great *man* not an angelic watcher. Will cannot understand what part of his genetics evoked proclamations of Nephilim status by Maude, the stranger in the diner, and now Connie. The scriptures speak as though the watchers were masculine, yet he briefly considers his mother as a genetic explanation. And then he remembers that Maude had also inferred a similar heritage for Drew. Any blood tie to a Watcher could not be solely from one of his own parents.

He grabs a hand drill making starter holes in the wall. Using a screwdriver, he sets the brackets. He thinks about his cousin while he works. Their mothers were sisters and their fathers had been twins. He smiles when he thinks of their maternal grandfather. He was a colonist turned native who loved the Pamunkey that he lived with and, in the end, he left behind his English heritage traveling west with them when relations between the colonist and natives deteriorated.

Will thinks about his own fears that he had during his life in Williamsburg. He sacrificed the opportunity to learn the ways of his mother's people in order to preserve a life that he thought would offer him security and an enviable position in the colony but, without warning, everything was gone. It is funny how things work out. Without the loss of that life, and its replacement with the cursed lives that followed, he would have been a lost soul. Not much more than a Shade, and he ironically feels blessed. He will find a way to honor his mother's father and her people. He knew his maternal grandfather was a great man, even a giant among men, but he was not the source of the Watcher bloodline.

Will fixes the shelf to the brackets and checks it with a level. He wonders if his father was aware of his angelic heritage. It had to have been Will's paternal grandfather. Will never knew him. The story was that his grandfather was an adventurer who rarely was home. The twin brothers, Harry and Frederick, had been raised primarily by their mother. Will decides that, if the Nephilim story is true, it has to be from his paternal blood line.

He picks up the tools and puts them in a toolbox that Connie has in the small prep room. He sweeps up the dust from the floor and wipes off the countertop. Taking a look around, he is satisfied, and he gives the string for the light a tug and walks towards the front of the shop.

Connie has just finished with the receipts. She closes her book and puts it away when Will walks up behind her.

"Connie, I am finished."

She continues with what she is doing as though she hasn't heard him.

"Connie, I have got the shelf up."

Still no response as she continues to tidy up the register area.

He closes his eyes drawing in a breath and heavily exhales it. "*Melinda*, I have finished hanging the shelf."

She pauses cocking her head and hits the cash register button pulling two dollars from the drawer. She turns and tucks the bills into his shirt pocket.

"Such efficiency William. It took you no time at all."

"Payment is not necessary."

"Don't be silly. You can use it tomorrow at the carnival to show Hallie a good time. I want you to take it."

He bites the inside of his cheek and thanks her with a nod of his head. There is a brief moment of uncomfortable silence before he shifts his weight and speaks. "I noticed your bible in the back room."

She tilts her head back and looks at him by the end of her nose. Her expression is stern, and he catches a flash of the anger he had seen this morning light up in her eyes. "Did you?" She pauses only briefly and continues not waiting for his affirmation. "So, William." She speaks as though it takes great effort. "How long have you known?"

"Known what?" He is truly perplexed by the question. There is so much going on right now. She could have meant anything—her identity, his, Drew's, the possibility of him and Drew being descendants of a Watcher, and even Hallie. He does not intend to be irksome in anyway, but she doesn't see it that way.

"Who-I-am. Why does it always have to be this way William?"

"If I tried to explain to you, to any of you, before your memories come back you would think I was crazy. Do not condemn me for that Melinda."

"Yes, yes what am I thinking? Let's not lay any false blame upon your shoulders. You have plenty of valid guilt to weigh you down." Her eyes fill with emotion.

Will runs his fingers through his hair forcing himself to be calm, as he struggles with the truth of her accusation while trying to maintain a composed and level tone when he speaks. "Melinda much is different in this life. Things are changing, *have* changed. Please, I know how you feel about me."

"Do you?"

"Yes, I do. I cannot change what has happened, but I will make it right."

She scoffs.

"Please, can I have a word? It is very important."

She twists her lips turning her head away from him, giving a quick nod.

He swallows hard and pulls in a breath. It was like a tug-of-war with the air. "When did your memory come back?"

She turns her head back eyeing him. "You said *you* wanted a word. Am I to participate as well?"

His jaw tightens. Melinda is back in full force, and Connie is nowhere to be found. They never could exchange more than hostile words with one another after Daniel had been lost.

She rolls her eyes answering his question without need for prodding. "Bits and pieces for a few days—ever since one of my customers made some unusual proclamations."

"Maude."

Curiosity flashes in her eyes. "Yes."

"And when did it all come together?"

"About three hours ago. I had just seen Dillon McCaffrey. He gave me the Williamsburg brochure. I'm sure you saw it in my bible. I thought it would be a nice tou…"

"Dillon? Why were you with him?" He cuts her off, and his words come out harsher than he intends, but it terrifies him to think she was with Dillon alone.

Her eyes narrow, and she puts her hands on her hips. He

knows he struck a chord and silently admonishes himself.

"What is it to you William? You and Drew…" She trails off for a moment and then fires off at him, "How could you let me get involved with Drew? That is something you could have taken care of but didn't. How could you let me fall in love? All this time, all those lives since…since I lost Daniel, and not once did such a thing happen. You know that nothing like that can end well for any of us. How could you let me go through that again, and cause Drew pain when I have some tragic unexplained death?"

He starts to speak, but she isn't finished yet. "No, it cannot end well, and you are soon to learn this. What is this relationship you have with Hallie? How can you lead her on when you know you have nothing to offer her?"

Again, he starts to speak, but she charges forward. "What is going on? You *never* let anyone that close to you. You said things are different this time. Is it her?"

He stands for a moment unsure if she is going to let him speak, and she flicks her hands outward raising her eyebrows impatiently waiting for him to speak. He chooses his words carefully not wanting to entice her anger any further.

"Yes, it is different this time, but I am not sure why. At first, I thought it was because we were not supposed to be here. You and I that is. I crossed through the Mesu without ceremony, and without Paimon's consent. You did the same. Do you have any of your underworld memories back yet? Do you know how you got here?"

She rolls her eyes and shrugs shaking her head. "I have no idea. My last memory in Tartarus was…" She stops short. He waits her out, and her eyes widen. "Hallie was there kneeling over you, and all of a sudden Hester came at me. Damn. We fought and she cold-cocked me and, well, *that* is the last thing I recall. Who knew Hester could pack a punch like that?" She rubs her chin almost smiling. "Who or what is Hallie? How could she have been there on the banks of the Styx? She was alive. She was flesh and blood the same as us. How can that be?"

"I am not completely sure. I think it may be part of her genetic makeup. She's…different… She is one of Sophia's daughters."

"Sophia?"

"Yes, do you remember the woman who was staying for a short time with Grissell Mercer's family? She helped Grissell's mother, Anne, with healing and birthing children. She had her two young daughters with her, and she was pregnant with her third daughter. It was during the time the curse had been set."

Her face lights and she nods. "Yes, she came to attend Elias when he had been beaten so badly by those ruffians from my father's warehouse." The bridge of her nose wrinkles and her eyes narrow. "How can that be William? Sophia lived two hundred and forty years ago. And, how would you know she had a third *daughter*? You were dead before she delivered."

"I just know. Sophia tended my wounds the night the curse was cast. While she was caring for me my hand came to rest against her stomach. The baby inside her reached out towards my palm." He holds up his hand.

She grasps ahold of his hand to look at the mark. "Why can I see this here?"

He shrugs. "Melinda, Sophia was a traveler. Hallie is her third daughter, and she inherited the gene."

"A traveler? Like the trekkers from heaven's forth realm? Humans tied to a physical existence are not capable of such things."

"I have no idea how it works, but I am telling you Sophia did not seem to be a woman from colonial times. Hallie was in Fayerdale in 1928. She traveled there from the year 2018, and now she is here." He finds himself rushing through his explanation worrying that she is not going to let him finish—not believe him, and he desperately needs her to believe him. He pauses for a moment taking a breath before he continues almost pleadingly. "With all we have seen, been subjected to, you have to believe that there is infinitely more to creation then we can possibly be aware of. You have to believe this, Melinda."

She stands with her arms folded leaning against the counter.

"Hallie was in Fayerdale, she is here, and she knew us in the year 2018—or, will know us."

Understanding cuts through her agitation. "She will know us? So, if what you are saying is true, we move on from this life? We survive the Demon King's wrath?"

He nods relieved that she is taking interest. "It seems we do. I am not sure how well, but it cannot be too badly because Hallie recognizes us both." A laugh shoots up from his chest, but he cuts it short. "Look, I do not know how Hallie 'fits' into everything, but I know that I believe in her and…I love her."

She smirks. "Good. Because nothing but tragedy can result from you loving anyone, and you are due." She scrubs a hand over her face as soon as she says it and bows her head shaking it slowly. "I'm sorry William, despite my vow of hatred towards you, I do not wish that on anyone."

"Melinda."

She looks back up at him.

"I am deeply ashamed. I am sorry that I did not remain vigilant, that I did not prevent Sariel's treachery, and I am sorry for all these years of pain you have suffered. For the suffering I caused Daniel and Elias. We are going to make it right." He pauses for a moment considering the impact of what he has to say, "I need to tell you something. Something I just found out."

She purses her lips raising her eyebrows. She folds her arms again and cocks her head to the side.

"Drew is Daniel."

She snorts with disbelief. "What? William, you are daft. Daniel is gone forever."

He slowly shakes his head.

"How?"

He can see realization hitting her in bits and pieces. Tears come to her eyes, and she heads towards the door, but he stops her.

She looks up at him. "I have to go find him. I have been so horrible to him knowing something wasn't right about me even though I hadn't known what. Then today, I realized that I was sensing the end. The harvest is near. I had to spare him the tragic loss of the woman he loves. Make him hate me, so it wouldn't be as hard on him." She tries to pull her arm free from Will's grasp. "Let me go, William."

"Just give me a few more moments. There is more."

She looks at him with face reddened and a glistening of sweat above her lip, but she sighs and acquiesces.

"Drew can give you the details, but he has been bound to Sariel all this time. He has traversed universal plains and crossed realms with the demon. Everywhere except Earth where the boundary between demons and humans is a little more complex. Drew said there is no death of death. All energy—even a life force—is preserved in some manner. He somehow maintained his form but was bound to Sariel while Elias has been in the bowels of one of the barges of Shades. Drew spent every moment he could trying to find a way back to you and, strangely enough, the one who separated you gave him the means to find you. He followed Sariel across the Mesu."

She looks at him. Her mouth drops and tears well in her eyes. "But that's not possible. A demon cannot cross without a human conquest. Not even the Demon King can cross without you."

"Daniel said Sariel crossed with you and then he followed Sariel."

Her breathing catches like a fast pitch hit her in the chest, and he sees the fear percolating.

"William, could I have become a conquest without my knowledge? I made no bargain. I have not accepted any terms." She twists her hands and the tears begin to spill onto her cheeks.

"You could not be his conquest, or you would have found yourself at his beck and call."

"What if he hasn't beckoned or called? Perhaps my freedom—or at least the piece of it not consumed by Paimon—is a farce." She rubs her upper arms.

"From what Daniel said they had run across you by accident. They saw you at the Mesu."

She frowns and her brow furrows. "I remember fighting Hester, as I have already said…I remember the skin on the back of my legs being raw and my shoulder aching. I remember opening my eyes and seeing the roots and hanging coils of the Mesu. I remember its calming pulse beckoning me to enter up into its trunk, but I couldn't walk. It was as though I floated to it, and it was beautiful. It was like a dream."

"Daniel said Sariel carried you into the tree."

She frowns. "I can't remember, but there couldn't have been a ceremony. He defiled the tree."

"Maybe he somehow possessed you for the moment to move through the tree."

At first her face relaxes, but Will sees the calm supplanted by fear as her eyes widen.

"William what of Elias? You said he was on a barge of Shades?"

Will nods.

"We've got to get him out of there."

"We will. I told you I promise to make all this right, but we cannot help Elias until we return to Tartarus and, Melinda, we need to accomplish a few tasks here. We have to act quickly."

She looks at him quizzically.

"Drew thinks that Dillon McCaffrey is the vessel for Sariel."

The color drains from her face.

Will continues. "It makes sense. He would not want to risk triggering a memory for you by taking his usual human form. I do not know that he would be cloaked as Daniel has been. Only possession can shroud a demon."

She hugs her arms around herself. "My God, I just spent an hour with him. I had driven out to Philpott to sit and think, and he was there. I thought it was a bit odd at first, but Dillon is a loner, and I figured he wanted to have some solitude as well. The past month has been a bit difficult for him—so I thought." She shakes her head.

"He was sitting near the water's edge reading one of those science fiction books that he always has. I sat near him, and we talked. He told me he was planning to go to Williamsburg and see the Fourth of July celebration there. I believe he said that he was leaving out of Ferrum on the train later today or tomorrow. That's when he gave me the brochure."

She shudders and then grasps her chin feathering her fingers down her neck. She stops short catching site of his hand. "Why do you have a protective mark on your left ring finger?" She lifts his shirt sleeve. "And why are your other marks visible here?"

"I cannot explain the mark, or why it and all the rest are visible."

She nods her head, and she bites in her lower lip giving him consideration before she speaks. "The harvest is close."

"I know."

"I won't lose Daniel—Drew—again."

"You will not, Melinda."

She nods as her tears are renewed. "Call me Connie."

He laughs, and he reaches to hold the door open for her. They walk to the garage pausing when they come to Will's apartment door. Connie shrugs and gives him a smile. She pinches pink into her cheeks, smooths her hair and her shirt, and she walks around the corner of the building to find Drew.

# CHAPTER 24
## Combustion

Will cuts across the McCaffrey place on his way to the Ridges'. He has the strange sensation of being watched and looks up at the house. The decay he had seen the other day has progressed. The windows are hazy and dark. The shrubbery thin and brown.

"Hey there, Will." A friendly voice calls out.

Will startles and turns his back to the house to see Mister Gentry, the grounds keeper, standing before him.

"Mister Gentry, good day sir."

Mister Gentry laughs leaning on his broom. "Good *day*. Will, there's times when I wonder where you come from boy. Good day." He shakes his head and laughs again.

Will gives him an awkward smile. "Yes sir." There is a brief silence. "Mister Gentry, I was just noticing the mold and such on the McCaffrey house."

Mister Gentry looks agape. "What are you talking about Will? That house is pristine." Miter Gentry looks up at the house and his chest expands. "Me and my boy just gave the clapboards a good washing this past weekend and the gardens have never looked better. Missus McCaffrey would have loved it."

Will turns back towards the house seeing it just as Mister Gentry described his view of the house and grounds. Will clears his throat. "Uh, yes I see that. I must have been mistaken. Perhaps a shadow or something came across giving the impression of decay."

Mister Gentry's offense melts, and he gives Will's shoulder a pat. "Perhaps, boy."

"Mister Gentry, did you drop your handkerchief?" Will bends over to pick up the gray and blue plaid cloth lying on the ground in front of them. He intentionally uses his left hand to pick it up making sure the protective mark on his hand is fully visible.

Mister Gentry reaches into his front pants pocket and comes out empty-handed. "Well, sure enough. It must have dropped from my pocket. Thank you." He makes no indication that he sees the mark accepting the handkerchief from Will.

Will bids him goodbye. He is used to the unexpected, the hidden truths, the emotional burns, and the need to bare the undesirable. He is used to the never-ending fear and the courage required to continue living on the edge, but he will never get used to the thin line between absolute evil and the fragile human world that is his home. The thought of Sariel's simmering evil in this place full of beauty and genuinely kind people sickens him. Sariel has to be contained in a realm somewhere out of reach.

Despite his focus on the problem at hand, he has not seen a way to the solution. He reaches the other side of the woods and steps into the clearing. Hallie is across the field on her knees tending Odina's garden. The sight of her pushes away any remnants of Sariel from his mind.

"Well, hey there." She stands up wiping the dirt from the knees of her jeans.

"Hello." His heart swells and he inhales a chest full of sweet air. Without thought he closes the space between them taking her in his arms kissing her. He moves his hands to the back of her neck where her skin is moist from the hot sun. Her natural warm vanilla scent is accentuated by the spicy smell of nature, and her sweet velvet lips soothe the pain of his aching and troubled soul. In her arms there is no ticking of the clock and no solid ground to stand upon. He breaks away from their kiss, and the sunshine glistens in her eyes before she closes them with a smile of contentment.

"Ummm, it's so good to see you." She opens her eyes

looking at him.

He smiles and gives her a hug. "So, it looks like you have had a productive morning."

"I like it out here. It makes me feel as though Beattie and Dot are close by. How was your morning?"

"Very interesting actually. Melinda has awakened."

Hallie's jaw drops. "Really?"

"Yes, but I think it is alright." He smiles hopefully. "There is more."

She tilts her head drawing her eyebrows together.

"My cousin Daniel is alive. Drew—Drew is actually Daniel."

Hallie starts to speak and stops. She hugs Will. "How?"

He fills her in on Drew pausing for a moment and hesitantly goes on. "There's still more."

"Wow, really?"

"Yes." He takes a breath and lets it out slowly. "He traveled through the Mesu with Sariel, and we have to find a way to conquer Sariel and keep him fixed in a realm that will keep him contained. For the moment, this is more important than finding a way to break the curse."

"Us conquer a demon." She trembles and rubs her arms. "Do you know why he's here?"

"It has to be Melinda, uh Connie."

She nods and stops suddenly. "Does all this mean Elias is alive as well?

"Yes, we think so, but he is trapped in Tartarus in the bowels of one of the barges of Shades."

Hallie shudders even more at the thought of a living soul being trapped on one of the scorched barges, and then she remembers the eye with the split eyebrow. She pales and grasps onto Will. "Does Elias have a scar across one of his eyebrows?"

Will's forehead wrinkles. "Yes, actually he does."

"I saw the barges. I was on two of them with Hester when we crossed the Phlegethon. He was there below the deck. Hester convinced me it was not possible for someone living to be on a barge. We were in such a hurry. I was exhausted and heart broken. My God, how could I have doubted what I saw?" She describes the barge for Will.

He tries to soothe her knowing the fear and confusion she must have been feeling at the time.

Her eyes fill with tears. "They are horrifying." She drops her head. "I cannot believe I could have helped him and didn't."

Will lifts her chin tenderly with his fingers. "Hallie, I will find the barge by your description. The horror of the barges is just one of many reasons why we have to prevent any of the underworld from seeping into the mundane plane. First, we must stop Sariel from conquering Melinda thus pulling power from the circle and much worse—possibly gaining passageway to the human world. He is of a different sort than the Demon King believe it or not. He is ruthless beyond imagination."

"Didn't you tell me once that Paimon would not allow that to happen?"

"Yes, but given the recent circumstances, I do not want to rely on that assumption. Sariel was one of his greatest allies and, right now, Connie and I are not. I am not sure how our crossing over in the way it happened has impacted Paimon. Our time on Earth is generally his opportunity to scavenge and collect trinkets, treasures, and conquests. It strengthens his power and grip over all those in Tartarus. If he has been able to satisfy his lust for such things, it may appease him. But without knowing for sure, we cannot take any chances."

"So, what do we need to do?"

"That is the question of the moment. I do not know. I am

not even sure where to look for the answer."

"Perhaps Drew or Connie will know."

"Perhaps. After they have had some time to catch-up with one another, we will go see them."

"Do you think that will be any time soon?"

He smiles and shrugs. "Not likely." He brings Hallie's hand up to kiss.

Her eyes pop wide and her chin drops. She holds on and brings his hand down to look at it more closely. She takes his right hand and flips it palm up staring down at the image. Her eyes rise up to meet his. "Will, what does this mean?  Has this ever happened before?"

He stares down at his hands as well. "No, it has not happened before, and I do not quite understand it now. It cannot be Sariel's presence because he has been on Earth before. Even then the protective marks did not present themselves. But maybe it is because he is a known threat this time. I am not completely sure."

"They weren't there yesterday."

He hesitates a moment feeling flush while a nervous tension stings his hands.

"Will, what is it?"

"A dream. At least I think it was a dream." He holds her hand and walks over to the shade of Azure's equipment shed. They sit down leaning against it.

"You were there in my apartment last night. The storm hit and the electricity went out. I was in bed and, with the flashes of lightening, I could see images of you approaching me until you were there next to my bed."

She smiles devilishly at him. "And?"

"Everything was very distorted. I could hear nothing. Not the storm. Not the ticking of my alarm clock. Not anything. I lit a candle, and when I turned back you were there. You had on one of my shirts that I wore…a long time ago. At least you had it on for a moment."

She leans her head back. "Oh, I see. No need to say more. Although, you may show me if you'd like." She teases and kisses him.

"I would like to very much. Soon. But…"

"Yes, I know 'demon-soul-seeing-vision' endangering me. Why do you think you had the dream?"

"I am not convinced it was just a dream. It was too real."

"How real?"

"Very very real, Hallie."

"So unfair, Will."

"You know, you called me Liam just before you disappeared."

Hallie sits for a moment. "Curious that I would be wearing one of your shirts from long ago but call you Liam. Just how long ago would you say?"

"It was one of my shirts from Williamsburg. From my original life."

"Huh, yet I called you Liam."

"Yes."

"You believe this vision, and not Sariel's presence, is the reason you now have the protective marks."

"Yes. You think it was a vision and not a dream?"

"Yes, I do." Her eyes become misty. "Beattie and Dot speak very little about my mother, but occasionally something slips out. Now that I know what I know, I understand their hesitancy to talk much about her. I remember a conversation between them that I wasn't supposed to hear. We were camping. I had laid down to rest, and they thought I was sleeping. Beattie thought that she had seen something near the edge of the fire's light, but it was just a rock. You know what I mean?"

Will nods. "You see something at the periphery of your vision that you think is one thing but, when you look again, it is something else."

"Yes. Well, she said that it reminded her of Sophia and her imaginings. Beattie's voice sounded sad—which is really unusual for her. Sophia apparently saw visions of occurrences she could not explain. When the imaginings happened all sound was lost. I remember feeling a chill run up my spine while I listened to them talk. Beattie and Dot spoke of them with a reverence though. It was so bizarre. Of course, I had no idea at the time that Sophia was my mother. I hadn't learned my mother's name, in reference to her being my mother, until much later."

"Do you think what I experienced last night was something like Sophia's imaginings?"

"Yes, I do."

"Hm, well it is something to ponder. Did you ever find out what the significance of Sophia's imaginings was?"

She scrunches her lips together smiling apologetically. "No, but I'd never heard of such a thing before. It's odd that you experienced the same type thing. Do you think Sophia was sending you some sort of message? You know, like the angel songs?"

He flushes a little. "Uh, no. I do not think your mother would have sent me that message. I think it had more to do with our conversation with Maude."

"Huh." Hallie picks at one of her fingernails.

They sit in silence for a while. Will leans his head against the side of the shed. His mind races with Maude's words about a sacred union, his parents' rings, and the protective mark on his hand. Despite the signs leading towards a union, he doesn't think it is the safest path for Hallie.

Hallie breaks the silence. "I had an interesting night, too."

He turns his head towards her admiring the green sparkle in

her eyes. "Tell me about it."

"At first I thought that an angel song was floating in the air because I could hear the sing-song chiming in the wind." She inhales deeply. "The angel song sounds like a woman's voice, but a metallic chime keeps a human quality from really coming through. You know what I mean?"

"I think so."

"Anyway, I was definitely dreaming because I was all over the place. The chiming intensified, and suddenly I was walking in the woods along a path. I looked up towards the canopy of tree branches and leaves and saw dozens of wind chimes dangling in the wind. They were like the one's Mister Hairston hung in the woods near his house in Fayerdale—only there were more than could be counted. Their sound was immense and haunting. The wind must have slowed because the chiming became softer and softer until there was just a twinkling of sound. As I came to the edge of the woods, I could see Joan's house. Remember? I told you about her in Fayerdale."

He nods.

"Only it was Sadie's house, too. The garage where you have a room is actually the home that Mister Hairston had built for his family. Joan and her husband converted it to a garage when they built their house. In the dream though it looked just as it did when the Hairstons lived there. I stepped out of the woods and started walking across the clearing. Suddenly there was this loud galloping, and I looked up to see you on Acacia. You came by and leaned over grabbing me and hoisting me behind you. Then, just like that, you were gone, and it was just me riding Acacia. The ride felt like this bobbing up-and-down motion and, although the appearance of the countryside was changing, it felt like I was just riding her around in circles.

"Suddenly, my mother was just ahead, but when I got close

it wasn't her at all. It was a pole with hooks and hoops of gold and silver on them. I leaned over and grabbed one and, when I opened my hand to look down at it, it was a souvenir key chain from Fairy Stone State Park. It had a fairy stone dangling from a ring. I remember thinking that I wished the key to my Mustang had been on it." She shrugs and laughs. "I guess I really miss my car."

He smiles listening to her enjoying the animation of her voice, and the way that her eyes light up when she speaks about certain things.

"Then instantly, I was no longer riding Acacia. I could see her grazing in the grass far off in the misty distance, and you were back at my side again. We turned to walk away, and Doctor Hutchison was there with Mister Elkins from Fayerdale. They were looking at and talking about Doc's walking cane. Remember the really neat carved cane he had with the spiraling snake?"

"I do," he says. "It was a gift from Mister Elkins actually."

Hallie raises her eyebrows. "Hm, that explains why Mister Elkins was there. Maybe my subconscious does know what it's all about after all. They greeted us, and we stood with them while they talked, but I have no idea what was being said. I was distracted because I kept hearing this circus music tune in the wind blowing just above our heads. The rest of you seemed to be completely unaware of it. I did hear Mister Elkins saying something to you about remembering the story of the wood." She shrugs. "It was weird because suddenly Doc and Mister Elkins were gone, but you were still holding Doc's walking stick. The mist from the distant field where Acacia was grazing began to swirl towards us wrapping around our feet and legs. It started to rise higher and all of a sudden it was cotton candy. A puff of it sitting atop a paper cone was presented to me in front of my face obstructing my view until I reached up and grasped ahold.

"When I took ahold of the cotton candy the mist was gone

and, in the clear air, I could see the sun sitting low in the sky giving the fluffy clouds a pink glow. You were gone, but in your place was Dillon McCaffrey."

Will tenses.

Hallie doesn't seem to notice. "The walking stick was lying on the ground, but it had broken apart where the wood changes colors. It think it was cedar blended with something else."

"Rowan."

She nods and raises her eyebrows. "I remember feeling so awful that it lay there broken. Dillon graciously bent down to pick it up grabbing the two pieces and, as he went to hand them to me his finger was stabbed by a splinter from the rowan portion of the stick. He suddenly froze just as he was reaching out to me. It was weird. I looked down at his hand, and I could see it slowing turning the color of the wood with the pattern of knots and rings progressing up his arm. Even though he hadn't transformed completely, he was petrified. Except his eyes moved wildly about until they stopped and focused intently on me." She shudders.

"I stepped away and turned my back to him just as his transformation into the knotty wood began to rise towards his chin. I can't believe that I didn't try to help him. I simply turned away to watch Acacia grazing contently. The next thing I knew I was astride her again bobbing across the field, and my hair was flying wildly behind me. Without warning she stumbled, and we cascaded down through a ravine. I felt weightless as I slowly lifted off her back, and we raced downward side by side. Right before we hit the ground I woke up." She shrugs. "So weird."

His jaw slackens. He cannot believe that she dreamt the solution to their problem. Just like 'that' the answer is theirs, and now they have to find the means to achieve it. From the corner of his eye he sees Azure standing near them by the front of the shed. *How long has he been there?* Will stands and helps Hallie up, and they walk over to Azure greeting him.

"Will. Good to see you. You and Hallie follow me."

He leads them into the equipment shed where they walk past rakes, shovels, hoes. But the objects around them become more foreign and numerous the further they walk into the shed. They eventually have to turn sideways to squeeze between the now towering piles. Light filters down from sky lights illuminating a small but open space with a barrel in the center. On top sits a mason jar with clear fluid in it.

Azure picks up the jar and opens it. The metal rim turning against the glass with a gravely rasp is the only sound in the shed. Azure takes a drink before handing it to Will and slides the heavy barrel off to the side. Straightening he motions Will to take a drink.

There is a gritty feel to the jar's rim as Will drinks. It's moonshine with a burning heat that ignites a pathway to his stomach. He wipes his mouth with the back of his hand, and Azure smiles taking the jar from him handing it to Hallie. She looks to Will, and he gives her a nod. Although, he is not clear about what he is giving his approval for. The warmth of the drink permeates the far reaches of his skin, and his vision sharpens with crystalline rainbows highlighting the objects that sit about them. On the floor where the barrel had been, a round door baring an iron pull appears.

Azure grabs the iron pull. The hinges croaky screams echo around them. Pulling something from his pocket he drops it into the hole. A soft golden glow rises up towards them illuminating a set of steps spiraling downward, and he starts to make his way down.

Hallie shoots a look at Will and takes a step back. Their hesitation is prodded into action as Azure's hand pounds on the top step, and he motions them into the hole.

At first, it seems like it could have been anyone's

basement. The floor is dirt, the walls stone, there are a dozen or so lanterns flickering light throughout the space, and a musty smell plucks their noses like pepper or an onion would. One of the walls is lined with shelves that are crowded with an assortment of storage containers neatly labeled. The opposite wall also holds shelves from floor to ceiling that are packed with ancient-looking books. In front of where Will stands is a simple work bench made of heavy wood that is empty. To the left of it is a table with an assortment of items. There are glass containers sitting on stands. Some have crooked necks while others look like flasks from a chemistry lab. There are bowls precariously stacked high, a mortar and pestle, and a crock burgeoning with an assortment of tools.

Azure takes down a jar and carries it over to the work bench where he pours part of its contents into a bowl on an ornate tripod and then crushes a piece of something else from the shelf adding it as well. The last ingredient is a syrupy-looking liquid. He points at the lantern on the workbench intensifying its glow until a small flaming ball rises up from it. Azure directs the fireball to rest between the legs of the tripod. He twitches his fingers in an upward motion, and it enlarges flickering up the sides of the bowl.

"Alright then. Sorry to let you just stand there, but *that*," he nods his head towards the now simmering solution softly gurgling in the bowl, "will take some time before it is ready, and I wanted to get it started. So…"

Will holds onto Hallie's hand and looks behind at the stairs. The hair on the nape of his neck raises and, turning back to Azure, he yells, "What is all this? What is going on?"

Azure raises his chin and squares his shoulders.

All of a sudden, the slightly awkward man whose pants are always a little too short no longer looks so awkward. He is in his element, confident, and a little too smooth for Will's comfort. Will curses himself for getting too comfortable with the Ridges and not finding a better place for Hallie to stay once Odina had revealed who she really is… then Maude…and now Azure. Perhaps this is where the snare springs trapping Hallie and him.

Azure smothers a chortle raising his hands in a surrendering gesture. "Will, it is alright. There is no deception here. I thought after your talk with Odina the other night you would not need any preparation to understand what I do." His voice is soothing taking a tone that one would use to calm a cornered feral creature. "I am an artificer like Odina's Uncle Mihai and your own Uncle Benjamin. It is one of the disciplines of alchemy."

Will stares at him, opens his mouth to speak, closes it, and shakes his head. "What are you talking about? *My* Uncle? And Odina's Uncle Mihai?"

"Will look around you. Have you not seen these things before?"

Will reluctantly releases Hallie's hand, and she gives him a quick smile. He steps closer to the shelves of jars noticing that there are four columns of shelves. At the center top of each is a carved sign—flora, fauna, material, and esoteria. A flash of memory from Old Benjamin's root cellar comes into focus. The tension in his muscles lessens while he walks about looking at various objects in the room. He pauses in front of a small wooden box. The craftsmanship is familiar to Will, and he looks underneath to see Old Benjamin's mark burned into the wood.

"It was a gift from your uncle to Mihai. They were great friends, if you recall. The box has been passed down through the generations of my family to each of Odina's companions."

Will looks at him and tilts his head towards a shoulder.

"As you know, Odina has lived a very long time. She is actually my aunt if you were to trace our lineage back over time. A child of ice blue eyes has been born each generation, and it is this gift that determines companionship for my dear aunt. The explanation to outsiders of the companion's relationship to her varies with time. Now that I am nearly as old as she appears to be, the status of sibling fits. When I was younger she was my grandmother and, of course, we relocate as needed. It has been the same for her for many years. In some ways I pity her—she has suffered the loss of many she has grown to love over time. It has, I believe, made her the recluse she is today.

"It seems, however, that her travail is nearly over, as her journey is drawing to a close. I am the last companion as far as we can tell from the signs, and she has passed on the crystal that holds the blood from the Tree of Life. We have been here for a while waiting for the traveler's child to arrive. I almost thought we were wrong until a vision led to us summoning the angel, Hester, who then guided the child to us." He glances towards Hallie giving her a reverent nod of acknowledgement.

Will sets Old Benjamin's box back down and walks over towards Hallie.

She takes his hand, and she speaks for the first time, "Azure, I don't understand. You said you're an artificer. Not a witch?"

"Let me explain. Witches are innately magical. An artificer, or alchemist, acquires skills through careful preparation that help to recognize the magical potential inherent in certain rare materials and harness those properties to his or her own advantage."

"Alchemy? Like trying to make gold from…anything? Or finding the elixir of life?"

"That is a popular belief." He motions towards his wall of jars. "The entire universe is divine in origin, and the Creator's wish is for all that comprise it to achieve perfection. I simply seek ways to speed that process up in order to elevate something like a flora, fauna, material, or esoteria to reach its highest level of perfection."

Hallie's eyebrows arch up and she shrugs into her shoulder. "So, why are we here?"

"It seems the night was favorable for insight, for I too had a vision last night. A shadow is being cast by one who poses a threat to those close to you. I was waiting for Will's arrival today to discuss this with you both. When I came out I heard your recount of your own vision last night, and I knew that together we have everything needed to accomplish the task."

"You have a stake made of rowan?" Will asks surprised.

"No, but it grows in these parts. The trick is procuring it from a tree that is willing to make a gift not only of the wood but also a bit of its dryad—its spirit."

"I know where this can be found, and the rowan is a flying rowan."

Azure's eyes widen. "This is very fortunate. The potential omnessence of such wood is more than enough magic for what needs to be accomplished. What type tree does it grow from?"

"A cedar."

"The Tree of Life." Azure looks as though he might kick his heels up any moment.

Hallie is confused, and Will explains what a flying rowan is and its significance.

"Doc Hutchison's walking stick was made from the same flying rowan I am speaking of. It is capable of trapping the essence of demons."

She pales pulling in her lips nodding. "So, tell me now what this is." She points to the simmering concoction.

"Everything living has a spirit, Hallie. Trees have a wisdom that can only be achieved from remaining in one place for a very long time. Human society cannot exist without them, yet we seldom offer them gratitude. This," he gestures towards the concoction which is now quivering with glistening and rippling waves that expand and contract, "is a gift of thanks." He goes on to explain the process of asking a tree for its gift of not just wood but part of its dryad, and the custom of thanking the tree for its gift. He explains that the concoction is highly coveted by trees because it enhances their longevity.

Azure dons a pair of gloves and tips the bowl letting the concoction pour into a flask. The glistening liquid spills downward twisting like a rope with a tuft of light blue smoke floating upward just as he flips the cap over the top. He clicks the latch in place and tucks it into a pocket.

"So, we go to the tree to ask for its help," Will says.

"Yes, we all must go, so the tree knows our thoughts and intentions. Trees, like white witches, wish to preserve the balance of creation and, often to our vexation, dark forces have a role in the balance. The tree must decide at what cost its gift will be upon the equilibrium of this world. An imbalance in one realm may cause worlds to collide and that would be cataclysmic."

Maude's words echo in Will's head. She spoke of changes beyond comprehension if the  Trinity Amulet' components were united. Can they survive either task let alone both? Will hopes that the trust he is extending to Odina and now Azure, and even Maude, is well-laid. Never before has he gone so far outside the Circle of Souls for help and, never before has the flame of hope inside him burned so brightly. He longs for it to be enough to light this unchartered path that lay before them.

"Okay, when can we go?" Will asks.

"Now," Azure answers. "We just need to pick up Drew and Connie. You will need as much life-force on your side as possible. Although the origin of any demon is human, it is a tormented soul that became demonized, and now that this Sariel has crossed realms it is accumulating power. The tree will need to know what lives this demon threatens."

Will nods. "Right, we can go by and pick them up on the way."

# CHAPTER 25
# Reedy

They climb the foot trail towards the Hairston's old place to the clearing on the mountain where the flying rowan grows. The spot on the trail where there is loose gravel—the same spot where Hallie had slipped and nearly fell into the ravine back in 1928 is right in front of them.

"Careful." Will teases.

She cuts her eyes at him bumping his shoulder with hers and gives him a conspirator's smile as color rises to her cheeks. He puts his arm around her and kisses the top of her head. They reach the ridge just before the Hairston's house making their way down the gentle slope. The air is silent except for the sound of the woods approaching evening time. All of the beautiful wind chimes that had hung here in 1928 are long gone.

At the edge of the woods, Hallie pauses and gasps quietly exclaiming, "Zephyr and Olivia."

Will looks in the direction of Hallie's gaze. There are two little girls near the house squatting with their backs to the wood's edge. They are playing a game of some sort. "It can't be Hallie. They have long since grown up."

"What's the hold up?" Drew asks, and Hallie points towards the two little girls.

"It's Sissy and JT." Connie walks past them towards the house making her way across the clearing to her cousins.

"Connie!" The two girls look over their shoulders and spring to their feet running to meet her. They collide trapping her with hugs. Sissy steps back from Connie blushing when she realizes Will is there.

"What are y'all doing here?" Connie asks with her hands

on her hips, but at that moment Missus Canaday comes from around the corner of the house. "Aunt Teechee. I was just asking the girls what y'all are doing here."

Teechee makes her way over to them. Her hair is covered with a bandana and she brushes some dust from her shirt. "Well, hey darlin'. Don't you know? Your Uncle Wade went and bought this place. He got a good buy and is thinking he'll use it for a hunting cabin. The land is beautiful. If the house wasn't so small, I could live here full time." She twists her lips stepping back when she sees Azure Ridge with them but still greets them all cordially before turning to Hallie. "I don't believe I've met you before sugar."

"Oh yes ma'am. I'm Hallie O'Meara. I'm visiting for a while and staying with Odina and Azure."

Teechee's eyebrows rise. "Well it's real nice to meet you." She turns to Azure. "How nice of you to open your doors to this sweet girl."

Will pinches his lower lip knowing Teechee wants to know more by the way she is leaning towards them.

Azure gives her a bow of the head but offers no more, and Teechee's face betrays only the slightest fluster before she quickly recovers turning back to Connie. "So, what are *y'all* doing here?"

Connie doesn't skip a beat. "Well, me and Drew invited Will and Hallie for a hike, and Azure came along to chaperone his house guest."

Teechee gives a nod of approval. "Well, I'm glad that me and Wade aren't the only ones who hold on to what some would call old-fashioned values. I hope y'all have a good time. It's such a beautiful evening."

They talk a few minutes more while Sissy stands by her mother, and JT plays running in-and-out between all of them giggling and carrying on. They say their good-byes heading towards the trail by the willow. Uncle Wade is behind the house, and he nods a greeting in their direction.

A gentle breeze shifts the willow's hanging branches as they approach it, and a pair of birds spring into flight from above as the group approaches the tree. Hallie touches the trunk and looks up towards the top of the tree.

"I love this tree. It reminds me of the Mesu."

Will looks up through the branches and agrees.

"Back in…or I guess soon in 2018." She laughs and shrugs. "There is a man, Mister Wood, who carves walking sticks like the one Mister Elkins made for Doc Hutchison. Liam and I met him at a festival the college was having, and he told us about the wood from a willow. He said that willows are good for healing. Do you think the willow could enhance the power of what you plan to craft Azure?"

Azure steps up to the tree's trunk laying his hands on it. His eyes are closed and his face serene. "It sees you are a child of the ocean and connects with you. Willows are water-loving trees." He turns to look at Hallie. "Walk around the trunk as you rest your hand against the bark and ask the tree if it has anything to offer our cause. It already knows what we desire."

Hallie complies, but she also reaches into her leather pouch taking out the amber heart and fairy stone. She holds them both in hand as she caresses the tree making her way around its trunk. Will steals a look back towards the house, but Wade and Teechee have left with the girls leaving them alone.

Hallie's fingers lightly bump over the bark of the tree. She comes back around to Will's side of the tree and holds her hand out towards him. He grasps ahold and the amber's glow ignites expanding out towards the tree's perimeter. The others watch in awe. The circle of light encompasses the tree, and it becomes perfectly still and perfectly quiet within the glowing dome.

The warmth from Hallie's skin slowly infiltrates Will's scar penetrating deeply into his arm, his shoulder, his chest, his heart. Seeing her hand rests against the tree, he realizes that the source of warmth is not just from Hallie, but from the tree as well. There is a gentle pulsatile glow that illuminates her hand.

Suddenly a curl of a bright yellow plume floats down towards Hallie, and she catches it on the palm of her hand.

Azure speaks up, "That is your gift, Hallie. Its flowers normally bloom in April and May. This part of its dryad holds new life—a new beginning."

Hallie looks up through the branches of the tree and back down at the delicate flower. She gently strokes its silky plume and looks over at Azure with concern. "A gift. Azure I have no gift to offer in return."

"Aye, but you have already given it. You shared the essence from the Tree of Life. Most willow trees have but a short life. This one will be here for many decades to come thanks to you and Will."

Hallie smiles and opens her pouch gently placing the willow's flower inside along with her amulet and the fairy stone. They all step onto the trail heading up to where the flying rowan grows.

"Azure."

He turns his head and looks at Hallie.

"The gift from the willow is a life."

"Yes, it is."

"Dillon McCaffrey," she hesitates. "I didn't know him before…before his possession by Sariel, but could the willow flower be used to save him? I mean after Sariel is subdued and confined."

He thinks for a moment before answering. "I am not well-versed in demonology, but my guess is that Dillon McCaffrey is no longer a part of this world—just his body. A demon as powerful as Sariel conquers. Even though he does not possess and occupy for long. He still destroys whatever life force there is in the vessel."

Hallie nods, and she glances at Will with her lips pressed together in a slight grimace.

"It will be alright Hallie. I have much experience with such creatures as does Drew. We will not enter into this the naïve men we were the first time Sariel challenged us."

"And, you have me." Connie speaks up. "After all, it was my thrust of the knife that did him in last time."

Will nods. "Absolutely. I did not mean to overlook you. As a matter of fact, we need to all be prepared. It could be you, Drew, or I who will need to drive the final blow."

"Given Sariel's hunger for Connie, I don't think that is such a good idea little cousin." Drew stiffens.

"I am just saying Drew that we should be prepared."

"It's not going to go down that way, Will." A twitch flickers at the corner of his eye.

"Hey, calm down," Connie demands. "I and I alone will decide what actions I take. Both of you be done with this strife."

Tension spills over as a tight-lipped Drew looks from Connie to him. Will focuses on the trail ahead understanding Drew's concern. Figuring out a way to assure Hallie is not around when they confront Sariel occupies his thoughts until he feels Hallie tense.

"Azure, there is the tree." Will points. Growing alongside a steep incline of a hill, its odd appearance makes the tree stick out among the others. The cedar tree's gnarled roots cascade down the hillside before disappearing below the rocky soil. The trunk is split about three feet up and its branches stretch out commanding space that is at a premium in the forest beyond the clearing. A few of the branches hang low with their spikey leaves growing off a network of tiny and twisting branches.

The far side of the tree had been struck by lightning many years ago creating a crevice in the trunk where the rowan seed came to rest. Its roots twist down through those of the cedar and its upper branches mingle with its companion. The rowan's flowers are faded and berries that will peak in another month or so take their place. It is majestic, and Will wonders how he could not have been more impressed with it when he saw it during his life in Fayerdale.

Azure walks through the shadows cast down by the setting sun while an evening breeze carries the spicy scent of nature towards them. "Amazing." his voice resonates with a sense of wonder. "The magic of this place drenches the ground and permeates everything around this tree. Why have I not been aware of this before? Amazing."

When he walks back towards them he is beaming. It's the most animated Will has ever seen him.
"The air is reverberating with the tree's crystal clear and high-pitched vibrations. This is one of creation's *thin* places. It is a place where astral and mundane planes are barely separated. I must sit giving the tree my full attention to hear what it has to say before communicating our request. It may take a little while."

"What can we do?" Drew asks.

"Sit and enjoy this wondrous place." He turns to Will handing him the flask of the concoction he made. Will's brow wrinkles, and Azure answers him. "I will let you know when it is time to bring it to the tree."

"Right." Will turns to Hallie, "You okay?"

"It's a little difficult being here." She looks up through the branches of the tree where she sought refuge the night of the harvest. "But, I'm alright." A white lie is pulled through the veil of dark sadness that shades her mood. He can feel it and puts his arm around her.

She leans into his warmth. A single tear spills over her lower lashes.

They sit this way for a while. The sun drops behind the mountains, and the rosy light of evening keeps a steady glow.

Azure crosses the clearing. He glances at Will, and then focuses on Hallie. "The gift is for you to take."

Hallie's brow furrows. "Me?"

"Yes, I will show you the place on the tree."

"O…kay." She raises her eyebrows.

"Hallie, place your hand here." He indicates a spot on the tree just above where the rowan's trunk takes hold, and where its roots twist downward towards the earth.
She nods stepping up to the tree placing her hand against the bark.

Azure steps back indicating to Will, Connie, and Drew that they should do the same.
Hallie turns to look at Will with her eyes glowing and wide.

From the corner of his eye Will sees a snake twisting up from between the gnarled roots towards Hallie. He tenses stepping forward, but Azure puts a hand up to stop him.

Will looks at him while a surge of heat swells inside him. "What is this?  What are you doing?" Tension crackles around him, and Drew and Connie shift to stand by Will's side if needed.

But a serene expression remains on Hallie, her hand still pressed against the smooth bark of the tree.

"It is alright, Will. The serpent will show her which branch is ours." Azure reassures him.

Will remains at the ready turning from Azure to watch Hallie. The snake has climbed up the tree's gnarled roots, making its way up the trunk next to her arm. It slides between her arm and the coarse tree bark swinging back around her wrist pausing for a moment to look at her. Its tongue twitches outward. Hallie shows no fear, and it continues its climb towards a smooth and leafless branch.

It twists up and around the branch flicking its tail beckoning Hallie. She slides her hand up the trunk towards the snake. Just before her hand reaches the tail, the snake twists back on itself pulling its coils quickly around the branch, and its full length arches upward. Its head looks huge to Will, and his muscles instinctively react hurling him towards Hallie. The snake's head flings upward before plunging down striking the branch just above Hallie's grasp snapping the branch off. The snake bounces to the forest floor stunned for a moment, but it glides away quickly blending in with the fallen leaves and ground cover.

Will grasps Hallie's hand turning it over to assure there is no bite. His skin tingles with the penetrating warmth from her hand and a shimmering of light radiates along the periphery of his hands.

"Will, did you hear it? Did you feel the vibrations?"

A stricture in his throat traps his voice for the moment, and he just shakes his head. His heart pounds, and his chest burns with the air he forces in and out of his lungs. He finally clears his throat.

"No, I did not. Did you not see the snake?" *How can she be so calm?*

"Yes, the tree said it would sever the branch that will be the most help to us. How fantastical, Will." She looks up through the branches of the tree. "I had no idea. The tree remembers the night of the last harvest, your bravery, my fear, and Paimon's evil intentions. All of it—Mister Hairston, Daryl Lee, Jeb—she shared this memory with me like one would feel an emotion. She wishes us to succeed not just with Sariel but with Paimon as well, and she asks us to return one day to share our stories with her."

He clears his throat again. "Of course, we will return." *I hope this is a promise I can keep.* A burdened sigh escapes him.

Hallie smiles and catches site of the tree branch on the ground. "Will, Azure's elixir—pour it over the area where the tree sacrificed her branch."

Will takes the flask from his pocket and opens it. Silvery blue wisps of mist rise up. He pours the silky liquid over the area where the branch was snapped. It doesn't drip to the ground but, rather, soaks into the wood flowing inward where the raw wood is exposed from the severed branch as though there is a siphon drawing the elixir in.  The tree heals and forms bark as though there never was a break in the wood. He rubs his hand over the area and feels a vibration of gratitude and blessing for successful endeavors.

An unexpected emotional swell explodes within him. For the first time, he gains an appreciation for his father's and Old Benjamin's connection to the crops they planted, cared for, harvested, and regularly raised thanks for. He becomes acutely aware of the spirit of this living wonder, and the absolute arrogance of his disregard for it and those like it over his many lives. The prickly heat of shame crawls over him as his conscience becomes enlightened, and he sends up an apology to his father and uncle placing his hand back on the tree to give it thanks for the gift and insight it shared today.

# CHAPTER 26
## Hubbub

Thursday, July third is a busy day. Carol Ann Hopkins arrives just in time at her mother-in-law's home to fetch the large picnic basket off the top shelf in the pantry. Her flashy appearance is a stark contrast to the faded woodwork, linens, and general surroundings of the farmhouse. Missus Hopkins stands patiently waiting for her daughter-in-law to get the basket down from the shelf. With her pale green dress and downy white hair she blends in with the kitchen décor. Although others cluck their tongues and question Boyd's choice in this young woman for his bride, Missus Hopkins secretly enjoys her energy and knows she is good for her son in every way. She smiles as Carol Ann hands her the basket and starts talking full throttle about deviled eggs and apple pie.

Neither woman notices Beezie as she zooms by on her bicycle taking a short-cut through the old widow's back yard. She has just left her father who she helped decorate the church with patriotic banners. Beezie is late. She is supposed to be meeting up with Linda at the salon for a manicure. Tyler Hambrick from her biology class is going to the picnic tomorrow, and she wants to look her best.

Her bike feels hard to pedal, and she looks down at the front wheel. The tire is flattening again. It just was filled two days ago. "Ugh!" The frustration escapes in a drawn-out hiss.

Luckily, Adkins' Garage is right across the street, and she hops off the bicycle walking it the short distance. "Okay, one more fill up tire and then I am gonna get you fixed. Dag, I hope Linda waits for me."

Beezie hits the kick stand with her foot and reaches to flip the lever. Nothing. She flips the lever the other way. Nothing.

"Ugh!" she exclaims, stamping her feet until a small dust cloud forms around her knees.

A hand reaches from behind and over her shoulder towards the pump. It flips the lever once successfully bringing the pump to life. A gasp escapes her, and she turns looking at her distorted image reflecting back at her from Dillon McCaffrey's aviator sunglasses. He has a leather satchel and paperback book in hand and, despite his relatively normal appearance, he looks…different to her somehow. A shiver raises the hair on her arms despite the frustration-inspired sweat that clings to her skin.

"Uh, thank you Mister McCaffrey." The whirring wail of the air pump forces her to shout. She stands awkwardly watching herself in his glasses wondering if he is going to say anything. He just gives her a nod and turns to walk towards the garage office. Beezie starts to turn to pick up the air pump hose when she sees a piece of paper spin towards the ground.

"Mister McCaffrey. I think you dropped something." He doesn't hear her over the racket. Beezie rolls her eyes walking away from the pump to pick up the paper. "Mister McCaffrey!" She shouts finally getting his attention. He stops abruptly turning back towards her.

She hesitates for a moment thinking that he looks angry. Perhaps she sounded rude when she yelled for him. The shiver returns creeping up her spine, but she shakes it off. Looking at the paper she realizes it is a train ticket—Ferrum to Danville. Pale thin fingers come into view as they delicately grasp a corner of the ticket, and she looks up to see Dillon's face only a few inches from her own. He raises his eyebrows, and she feels a tug on the ticket as it slips through her fingers. Her crooked likeness is there in his sunglasses, and she jumps back with surprise when her reflection is briefly replaced with a glint of yellow eyes. Dillon hesitates and then gives her a nod of the head and a quick smile before turning on his heel starting again for the garage office.

Beezie grabs the hose up off the ground and hurriedly pumps her tire full. She flips the lever off restoring quiet; although, the sound of her pounding heart echoes in her head. Hopping on her bike she pushes forward on the pedals feeling a sense of relief when she turns the corner leaving the station behind her.

The door to the garage office closes as Dillon McCaffrey leaves walking towards the '77 Restaurant. Mister Adkins watches him for a moment before hanging the car keys on the work board and goes about the task of locking up the garage. When the building is secured he walks over to his truck. Dillon's car is parked next to it.

He inspects the Chevy peering into its windows. Nothing seems out of place, and he shrugs while walking over to his truck climbing in and starting it up. The pocket watch that he keeps on the dash shows that he is right on time. Katie is over at Saint James working with her community projects group and the reverend to set up for tomorrow's Fourth of July celebration charity luncheon and fund-raiser.

He heads over to the church pausing for a moment before turning onto the road when he sees something odd with the McCaffrey house. For a moment, he thinks it looks as though one of the window shutters is askew. Along the house front, the siding is stained with mold and marred by peeling paint. The porch trim work appears to be rotting away. A pinch to the bridge of his nose and second look shows the home is in its typical pristine condition. He takes a breath turning the wheel of his truck hard to the right towards Saint James and the one person that always helps life make sense. The calm begins washing over him when he approaches the church seeing Katie with the other women.

The serene feeling most likely would have taken hold had

he not run into Ted Hodges in the church parking lot. The Patrick County deputy is there to pick up his wife, Rebekah, who had come over with the women from Grace Methodist to lend a hand to their sister organization. The preparations are running a little behind and Deputy Hodges is leaning against the hood of his patrol car patiently waiting. Cleo walks up shaking his hand.

"How's it going over at the garage? Drew still putting in some hours there?"

Cleo shifts his weight scuffing his boot in the dirt looking at his long-time friend. "Oh, sure sure. He and Will help keep the place going for me these days. I'm not sure what I would do without them."

Deputy Hodges nods and says nothing more on the topic. They engage in casual conversation for the next several minutes until the women finish and say their goodbyes.

"How did it go then?" Ted asks.

Rebekah's cheeks are flushed with the day's activities. The work was a good distraction for her. Her heart has been heavy with the horrific crimes against young women in the area. Although, her husband makes a conscious effort to shelter her from the harsh realities of his work; the burdens he carries with him during the current Pearl Murders case, as his office is calling it, seem to weigh heavy on him. She pulls herself back to the moment answering him. "Oh, very well. It was a lovely day."

He nods his acknowledgement keeping his eyes on the road.

She hesitates a moment and asks, "So Ted, how was work today?"

He looks at her and smiles knowingly yet keeps his answer vague. "Fine, just fine Becca."

"And the case?"

He holds a breath and lets it escape slowly through his

nose. "Becca, I can't talk about specifics with you, but today was a good day. We've gone from no clue about the perpetrator to a pretty strong lead. There are two people of interest that we're looking into and maybe a murder weapon, but that's all I can say right now. Okay?"

She bites her lower lip, her eyes are moist, but she displays a smile and nods.

They stop at the railroad crossing while the train from Ferrum to Danville pulls out. It gains momentum as it crosses in front of them. They bump over the tracks once the train passes, and Rebekah sees two young girls with blond hair running down the street towards the '77 Restaurant. Her heart takes a panicked leap that she cannot explain.

"Sissy! Wait up!"

"Well, hurry up, JT. Don't you want to get some ice cream? And look." Sissy points up towards the roadway. "The carnival trucks are coming in. We can go watch them set up."

JT speeds up seeing the colorful trucks pass by. The flat beds have rides of all sorts and, she can't believe it, a carousel is on the back of one of the trucks. While rushing to catch up to her sister, she bumps into a tall, slender man. Her eyes glance up from his shiny shoes, past the pressed suit towards amber-tinted glasses where a magnet seems to lock her in place. He lowers his glasses down his nose at her with a smile creasing his face until Sissy reaches around him jerking JT's arm to pull her away. The feel of spiders dancing on her arms is brushed away by JT as she and Sissy race down the sidewalk.

He slides his glasses back up his nose with a bored sigh and continues on his way towards the college. Final preparations are to be made, and the well-furnished office he procured is cool and quiet. It has been a profitable crossing-over, despite its unexpected start, and he is pleased even though he will never express a sentiment of satisfaction to anyone. He starts whistling Hester's beckoning tune wondering where she is. His patience is wearing thin with her disregard for the tune she is obligated to respond to. It is something that will have to be dealt with. He pauses looking about to see if she has come, but the sole answer he receives is the high-pitched shrill from the afternoon train as it leaves Ferrum behind.

A steam whistle blows in the distance causing Hester to jump a little when it sounds. Her nerves are on edge as unmistakable echoes of the Demon King's beckoning reverberates around her. She knows this time on Earth for the Circle of Souls, a stolen time for the few who claimed it, is drawing to a close, and with them Sadie will be taken as well. She miraculously survived the harvest in Fayerdale, but no one survives twice.

Hester is under no circumstances a guardian angel, but she does her best to assure Sadie and her gateway relatives, Zephyr and Olivia, remain safe. Her heart has been burdened since the loss of Daniel and Elias, and she works hard to assure the remaining souls invariably have a pathway back. William will be returning to Tartarus soon, and Paimon's wrath will be harsh. This harvest will not be pleasant, and she worries for Sadie who still has no recollection of whom she actually is. She is a mature woman, a successful educator, lawyer, and advocate for the civil rights movement. The psychological trauma of a harvest could be enough to tilt the balance of her soul from human to demon, and Hester is determined to spare her the danger of eternal damnation.

Hester knows she already crossed a line when she helped Sophia's youngest child move forward in time. It will be a daunting challenge to keep this a secret from Paimon. She wonders how Hallie is doing and thinks about the Romany woman and man that summoned her to help Hallie. There is a certain familiarity about the woman, but Hester cannot determine why. The only other humans alive that are capable of summoning her are Hallie's sisters and, of course, Resmelda who lays trapped in a grave far from here. Hester shudders involuntarily forcing herself to focus on her task at hand. She looks up at the street sign to get her bearings. Turning off V Street, she steps onto 7th and walks towards Howard University where Sadie is preparing for her trip to Ferrum.

Sadie has her bag with her but feels compelled to stop by her office before heading out to the train station. The Old Dominion heads out of Washington into Richmond where the connecting train won't depart until early Friday morning transporting her along the Virginian Railway to Roanoke. The ticking clock in her office nudges her to hurry while she retrieves her trinket box. It holds mementos that she accumulated over the years. Some are from generations before her, and she wants to leave the box for Zephyr to hold in safe keeping. A treasured photograph of a boy she loved dearly back when she was a girl living in the now forgotten town of Fayerdale brings a tear to her eye. She sets it in the box and leaves a note for Zephyr unable to rationalize any of her urgent actions. The sensation of spiders crawling up her arms brings a chill to her spine and she quickly swipes it away rushing out of the office.

At the train station, she pushes through its hustle and bustle to find a seat and settle in for the lengthy trip. Her hands quiver while she arranges her bag and satchel of papers, and she grasps ahold of the arm rests drawing in a breath. Doubt about her decision to make this trip permeates her thoughts. One of the college's trustees, Joseph Tasker, was most persistent when he telephoned her with the invitation. It, however, was her friend and mentor Thurgood Marshall who finally convinced her of the importance of her trip.

He told her Virginia is wrought with the Massive

Resistance Movement that has been working hard to stall desegregation. He felt that, being from Southwest Virginia, her words of support for their cause may hold more meaning. Sadie is not so certain, and anxiety about the trip weighs heavy churning its sour turmoil in her stomach. She dreads the wait before her train connection in Richmond, and the long travel out to Roanoke on a train that she knows will be segregated with little comfort in the car she will be riding in. Trying to force all these thoughts away, she smooths the front of her blouse leaning her head back to rest.

A pretty young woman captures her attention. Sadie feels she has seen her before but cannot place where. The woman's olive skin is like porcelain, her form like a ballerina, and her almond-shaped eyes darkly reflect sorrow and wisdom beyond her years. The woman offers her a smile which Sadie returns just before closing her eyes hoping to find rest. The train's whistle belches out a shrill call startling her for a moment, but she ultimately finds a fitful sleep. Her dreams hold vivid images from her childhood and friends long gone.

Maude sits up suddenly. She dozed off in her hotel room after a long and full morning of lectures and presentations by the various speakers from the American Anthropologic Society. The plan for a brief break before the afternoon sessions was foiled when she unexpectedly fell asleep. The clock on the nightstand shows it is five o'clock—she missed the afternoon sessions. Maude looks around the hotel room out of breath attempting to steady her nerves. Reaching up she loosens the buttons of her blouse and dabs at the beads of sweat along her neck with an unsteady hand. Reaching for the glass of water on her bedside stand, she bumps it spilling some before managing to grasp it and get it to her mouth. The bed she is sitting on is solid, but only moments before she had been falling down a deep and seemingly endless tunnel.

It was a terrifying dream, but she closes her eyes to sort

through its details. There was a round lavishly decorated room with gleaming white walls and a deep red floor. In the center, a gold inlay black lacquer table was burdened with all sorts of food and drink. Parched, she took a goblet of wine, but when she brought it to her lips the wine swirled like it was being pulled down into a drain before disappearing. The same result when she attempted eating a cluster of luscious grapes. They vaporized and disappeared when she brought them to her lips. She heard the quiet giggling of identical voices and turned to see the sound was coming from a pair of strange creatures that looked like twins standing and acting as one being.

There was a whoosh, and she spun around to see that within the wall there was a door. She passed by the twin sentries to enter the second room. Just inside, an awkward-looking man with greasy yellowish hair in an ill-fitting butler's suit stood fidgeting with his collar that was damp with black sticky goo. Bitter bile percolated up the back of her throat, and she slid past him moving towards a second man who was stylishly dressed and standing at the far end of the room. A tight-lipped smile stretched across his face. A reluctant smile flashed on her face in return, and she found herself moving towards him.

In her hands were the secret translations from the hidden scrolls Eban and his team had worked on. Sweat beaded over her skin. Why did she have the scrolls? Why was she bringing them here? She looked around. To her left was a strange-looking woman with bluish-black skin lounging on a settee looking thoroughly bored. Her head turned from the woman and towards her right where the room was darkened. Her eyes adjusted, and that is when she saw them. Will, Hallie, Connie, Drew and a few other young people she did not recognize. They were grotesquely broken and bound and should have been dead but as she continued walking by them Will's head slowly lifted, and his tormented eyes briefly looked up at her before he closed them letting his head fall forward. She jerked her head away to look at the man at the end of the room. A massive window was behind him, and she gasped seeing her reflection in the glass. Her eyes, a glowing yellow, stared back at her.

That's when the sick rose back into her throat triggering a cough that woke her from the nightmare, and now here she sits on the edge of a comfortable bed centered in a very comfortable room. Sipping water offers no relief from the burning in her throat.

A rainbow shimmers over the bed linens, and Maude looks up to find the source is Odina's crystal refracting the evening sunlight that is cascading into the room. She sets down the water and walks over to the crystal lifting it up regarding it intently. A wash of tranquility courses through her. Her lungs open like sails catching a gust of wind on the open sea, and she holds her breath a moment consuming the oxygen and clearing her head before exhaling the haunting fear that has gathered as a foul-tasting tightness in her throat. If she wasn't supposed to meet and escort the speaker from Howard University tomorrow, she would return home tonight.

# CHAPTER 27
## Bequest

"It is done." Azure kneels near the fire and rolls out a piece of supple leather while Drew gathers more wood to brighten the flame. Odina remains sitting in her chair, but the rest curiously walk over. They stand staring down at three pieces of ornately carved wood.

Will bends down to grasp one, but Azure grasps ahold of him. "Not yet, Will."

Hallie's brow furrows. "They look like something…to sew with. Spindles…well spindles with a twist…scissors I think…and a measuring rod…peculiar. Deadly looking, but I think I was expecting something more like a stake. You know…vampire stuff."

"I believe these will more than suffice." Each spindle has a different intricately carved appearance, but all with thread incorporated in the design. Azure looks at each of them. "Let us sit quietly and hear the tale of the rowan."

Azure takes a seat facing Odina. They look at each other coming to a silent but collective agreement as they each take a seat as well.

"It is asserted that witches have influence o'er those things which possess spirits of thar own: people, beasts, nature and a few revered objects or places, but with a conjurer like Azure…"

"Alchemist or, more precisely, artificer Odina." Azure interjects.

Her pause is brief as she eyes Azure before returning to her explanation. "Artificer then—tha power is surely drawn from a less blatant energy then tha spirits that are tha life force within God's creation. This obscure energy is all around us an tha alchemist knows how ta claim it drawing power ta help what exists be closer ta tha perfect form tha Creator intended.

"Someone like Azure knows tha power, tha magic, which lives in all objects an knows how ta unravel it an then control it. So it was with tha cedar's Rowan. Only tha power of this branch is so great three weapons are given. Tha forms they have taken show tha bequest has bin influenced by tha three Sisters of Fate. Each of tha weapons will reclaim and unwind tha thread of life belongin' ta tha demon that threatens you. It is important for you ta understand each weapon's purpose."

She tosses a sandy mix towards the fire, and the flames swirl up wavering into the images she speaks about. Each time dissipating and then sparking back up to allow them a look at the next image.

"Clotho, tha youngest of tha sisters, is responsible for spinnin' tha thread of mortal life, and hers is tha first spindle ta be thrust. It is tha simplest in form with tha most evident presence of twine in its design as it flows along its lethal end. Lachesis is tha second of tha Fates. She is tha measurer of tha thread woven by Clotho's spindle deciding how much time for life is ta be allowed. She measures tha thread of life with her rod. Hers is ta be thrust next and it is tha spindle with tha marked and measured handle. Atropos is tha oldest of tha Fates, an she chooses tha mechanism of death ta end life by cuttin' tha thread. Hers will finish tha task and is tha spindle with tha twin blades lookin' like a pair of scissors opened wide with tha threads fashioned by Clotho and measured by Lachesis wrapping its center handle and extending outward ta its twin razor-sharp tips."

Will stares at the fire. An icy spread along his spine jabs at him when the rotating fiery image of Atropos seems to static and flash a menacing look his way. He rubs his eye, and it has vanished. None of the others seem to have perceived it.

Odina continues. "A demon is tha creation of a tortured human soul. It is an alteration of humanity whose thread of life is perverted—shrivelin' up and forgotten—usually forever. Tha result is a bein' only capable of evil deeds and self-gratification. Tha purer tha soul tha more powerful tha demon."

The image of the sisters fades and an image of Sariel in full battle gear appears. Hallie inhales sharply, and Will grasps her hand. The fire transforms back to the ordinary. And, Odina glances over at the spindles.

"These will reclaim tha humanity that was torn from tha demon tying it back ta its thread of life. A grain of salt is imbedded in each weapon's tip rendering a most potent antidote for tha poisonous situation that caused tha twistin' of tha soul. This will bring him back to his vulnerable human form once more, and the rowan wood will anchor tha demon keepin' it from crossing realms and keepin' all of those in your Circle of Souls safe. Tha first two spindles," she points to the two single-tipped weapons, "will fall tha demon. Both must pierce deeply into its flesh. Tha third must then be thrust up under tha ribs ta tha great vessels of tha body spilling its blood. Then, a blood offering by tha one claimed by tha third spindle must be offered off its second spike." She points to Atropos' weapon with its twin blades.

They sit silent for a moment before Drew speaks up. "How much blood from the third spindle's chosen one is in the offering Odina?"

"It must flow down tha spindle joining that of tha demon's and continue ta flow until a spark draws a flame. It should be able ta be accomplished without loss of life."

"Assuming the demon doesn't cause 'loss of life' first." He chuckles but cuts it short when Connie glares at him.

"Okay then." Will stands and walks towards the spindle bending to pick up the double edged one. It spins away from him.

"The *spindles* must choose," Azure speaks to all of them.

"And, how does that happen?" Connie asks.

"You come sit by the leather and hold your dominant hand out. The rest will take care of itself."

Connie and Drew stand up and Hallie follows.

"No, not you Hallie." Will takes her hand to sit back down on the blanket.

Will, Drew, and Connie take a seat each holding a hand over the spindles and wait. The two single-tipped spindles quiver a moment and shoot up crossing paths. Lachesis' spindle slaps into Connie's hand and Clotho's to Will's. They all continue to sit and wait, but Atropos' spindle does not move. Hallie sighs getting up from the blanket and sits next to Will. He looks at her, and she looks him in the eye as she holds out her right hand. The spindle does not hesitate as it slaps up into Hallie's palm. She looks at her hand and her eyes pop wide.

Will shouts at Azure, "What is the meaning of this? Hallie is not a warrior!"

Azure answers him with a hint of disdain. "It means the spindle chose Hallie and not Drew. We do not know the reason."

"Yes, I can see that." Will growls and stands pacing with short stiff steps stirring a turmoil of emotion. "She isn't going to be involved with this."

Azure leans down rolling up the leather. "It has been decided. There is nothing to be done."

"Drew, take the spindle from Hallie."

Drew reaches towards the spindle but it pulls back away from him.

"Hallie," Will speaks to her gently. "Let Drew take the spindle."

"Will, I didn't do that. The spindle…it pulled away."

Will's agitation grows. A burning sensation scratches over

his skin as though Paimon's scorpions are ripping him raw.

"If you want to protect her then claim her for your own." Azure's frustration with the situation grows as well. "I don't want Hallie involved any more than you do. I…" He stops short biting his cheek and turns away.

Will glares at him. His mouth opens and closes it—he doesn't know what to say.

Odina, however, does. "No!" She stands pointing her finger at Azure. "*That* is not ta happen. Not now. It is ta be a *sacred* union—that's tha only way. This, this demon must be dealt with, and it will be. Thar is a higher purpose here." She points to Will and Hallie, but her eyes do not leave Azure.

Her face burns with fury, and she closes her eyes taking a deep breath. When her eyes open, calm is restored. Her voice sounds weary. "Tha three of them are capable of handlin' it. If tha situation had been foreseen, it could have been dealt with, but we are beyond that now—what is *is*. Thar is no needing ta endanger Hallie by tha true threat which is tha Demon King. Will already knows this. Do *not* cloud his thinking."

Will looks from Odina to Azure. "Azure?"

Azure speaks despite Odina's censoring look. He turns from Odina rubbing the back of his neck and speaks with a raspy edge. "*This* demon, Sariel, cannot touch you Will without consequences. You are bound to the Demon King. All others must not take from the king unless they are willing to wage war. It is probably why you have survived so long despite the perils of the underworld existence you have endured. The others in your circle do not have this protection, and that is why the lineages must be maintained on Earth. If you want to keep Hallie safe, you must claim her for your own. Bring her into the circle bound to you."

Will's grimaces as he looks at Azure unsure what he is declaring.

"Consummate your relationship—commit to one another—and she will be bound to you and, by proxy, the Demon King."

Will jerks his head. "No. That is not going to happen. Odina is right. Paimon will not have her soul."

"Will." Drew stands by him, and Connie goes to Hallie. "We will figure something out. We will not allow anything to happen to Hallie."

"Will." Connie speaks up. "Sariel will be subdued by the two spindles you and I possess before Hallie will even need to be near him."

He pulls his fingers through his hair. It is as though he has trudged across a dozen underworld battlefields and his shoulders sag with a great weight. "And, she strikes the final blow letting flow…her own blood until a flame ignites. Despite the potential physical danger to Hallie, can you imagine how such an act will affect her emotionally? She is not like us." He is feeling like a trapped animal ready to gnaw off a limb to escape this horrific ordeal. He looks at the spindle in his hand. He is done with this discussion. "It is getting late. Hallie and I need to talk. Odina, if I may, I would like to stay tonight. I will sleep out here by the fire."

Odina nods her assent and stands. She walks to the cabin. Azure follows her. Will turns to Connie and Drew. "I guess we will see each other tomorrow?"

"No," Drew answers. "Connie and I will stay out here with you. We should all stay together from here on out."

"Thank you. I am going to walk Hallie up to the cabin and speak with her for a moment."

"Sure, sure we'll get some more blankets to make it more comfortable out here."

Will nods and stretches his hand out towards Hallie. She grasps ahold, and they walk up towards the porch and set their spindles down. He leads her around to the side of the cabin embracing her.

His frayed nerves lay quiet just being near her. He kisses her, and she responds to him sending shock waves deep to his core. She draws back hesitating, "Will, how distracted are you going to be, if you are worried about me?"

"We will figure something out tomorrow Hallie. It is not going to be an issue."

"Yes, yes, it is. I am scared, but I know this is how it has to be. The magic needs to remain powerful. We cannot risk weakening it by trying to do things differently. There has to be a reason for it. You will be at risk unless you keep your mind focused, so you are going to have to come to terms with this. That is…unless you want to take Azure's suggestion." She pushes against him playfully.

He gives her a smirk and takes her by surprise when he pulls her close again kissing her. He looks into her eyes. "I can't imagine ever seeing you…not for the first time, the last time, and all the times in between without loving you. It will always be. My love will follow you wherever you go. I just…" He pauses. Hallie's eyes fill with tears, and a melancholy look comes over her face.

"Hallie, what is it?"

"*My Love Will Follow You Wherever You Go.*" She draws her lips in biting down on them with a smile and faraway look.

He searches her eyes.

She shrugs. "That is the name of the first song we danced to. It was here in Ferrum at the college during the outdoor arts festival I told you about."

"I look forward to that day. I hope Liam is deserving of you—the kind of person who can share happiness like that with you always."

She leans her head against his chest, and they stand that

way for a while. "Hallie, there just is something not right about all this. I was there. I felt that tree's soul and its connection with you. I cannot believe it would make this…this choice. And I saw something in the fire…" He stops and sighs with effort feeling as though the breath is taken under water.

"Saw what?"

"Nothing. It was nothing." This emotional turmoil is of no use, and he finds practicality his best weapon for the moment. He brushes away the thought of the fiery Atropos's menacing look. "Dillon has gone out of town and will not be back until Sunday. We have time to devise a plan. His car will be at the garage. Perhaps we could plan an ambush of some sort. It can be worked out."

She looks up at him reaching her hand up to the side of his face pulling his thoughts away from his worry, and he leans his face into her hand.

"Will, it's going to be alright. Whatever it takes. We will get through this."

He looks at her feeling his heart hammering inside his chest. Her beauty comes from within, and she makes him a better person. She is his cooling waters. The reason his heart beats. He looks up towards the stars feeling the clear night air against his skin and looks back down with the soft light from the moon illuminating her face as she watches him with expectation. He forces himself to focus on the challenge presented by the demons that stand before them instead of those within him.

"Despite my concern for Sariel, we have the makings of a plan. The demon has been conquered before. You are a strong person Hallie, and I must not underestimate you. I am confident that success will be ours, and then we can focus on the true matter at hand. The Demon King is a much greater threat, and we do not even need to conquer him—just keep him away from you. Once the harvest happens you will be safe."

She gives a single nod downward and searches the ground avoiding his gaze.

"Hey."

She doesn't look up. He bends down to catch her eye, and she gives him a smile although her eyes are spilling over with emotion. He wipes them dry and kisses her tenderly.

"The four of us will go to the celebration tomorrow. Dillon will be out of town. It will give us a day to think things over and relax. Sometimes my best ideas come when I am not focusing on anything at all."

She gives him a reluctant smile. "I know we will figure it out—just no more talk about you leaving. I know it's going to happen I just..." She looks at him with quiet alarm. Her head cocks to the side.

"What is it Hallie?"

"Do you hear that?"

Will stands motionless. He hears a choir of crickets, he hears Connie giggle off in the distance, and he hears Odina's admonishing words to Azure somewhere inside the cabin. He looks at Hallie, and she raises a finger to her lips. And then, there it is. A delicate chiming sound in the distance but approaching quickly.

The chiming becomes a roar swirling around them. Their hair and clothing whip and ripple in the squall and then it stops, and the chiming moves away stopping about five feet from them. An electric current of swaying and sharp spiking lights dances with brilliant colors. It hovers for a few minutes and, as quickly as it came, it is gone.

He looks at Hallie expectantly. Her chest heaves with excitement, and she pries her eyes from the spot where the dancing light had been. Her face is glowing as though she just returned from a run through the woods.

"The angel song." She exhales a quivering breath and lets go a laugh of amazement. "I can't believe it." She takes a couple of steps away from him and turns back reaching for his hand pulling him as she rushes towards the porch pushing open and through the cabin doorway.

Odina and Azure are sitting at the table and look up startled. Hallie races over pulling a piece of paper towards her and starts writing feverishly with a pencil. She snatches the paper and flies back to Will at the door's threshold. Stepping out into the clearing with him where the moonlight is, she reads it.

*Once again, the threat draws near. Stolen lives will be reclaimed while a lineage is at risk by retribution ill begot. This is the moment for saving one of the line lost but not forgot.*
*Take care the time is here.*

*Upon the back of trusted steed, a legend bore is a power gained that one must claim, and one must heed. The one ahead will go behind. Liberation is found in memories newly made haunting body, soul, and mind.*

Will looks at the words on the paper. "I am not quite certain I understand—except the first line of course. Maybe the next couple have to do with Daniel's return as Drew, and hopefully the one to be saved is Elias."

Hallie looks at it. "I don't think it's Elias. It says, 'one of the line,' and that means a relative to someone in the circle. Right? There is no mention of the key. The others were about the keys." She starts re-reading the song.

"The *legend* it refers to must be the key. Solomon's story is very much legend. Look at all the variations of its story." Will points to the line and then rubs his chin.

She nods. "And a legend on a map is also called a key. I

think you're right."

Will watches her reading and re-reading the song.

"Hey." She nudges him and folds the paper loosening her amulet pouch to tuck it inside. "We should get some sleep."

He agrees and escorts her to the porch where they pick up their spindles and step up to the cabin door. He stops in front of the door holding her close for a moment before he kisses her goodnight and turns to join Connie and Drew.

They have prepared him a comfortable sleeping spot and are sitting on a cushion of blankets waiting to wish him a good night before they lay down to sleep. Drew holds Connie close, and they fall off to sleep quickly. Will, however, lays awake for quite a while before sleep claims him. Twice he wakes up thinking he heard something in the nearby woods before drifting back to sleep with visions of yellow eyes watching them from just inside the wood's edge.

# CHAPTER 28
## Event

The next morning, they help with a few chores around the Ridge's before heading out to town about mid-day. Hallie goes to Will's apartment, and they plan for Connie and Drew to pick them up in about an hour.

Will walks from the bathroom drying his hair with just a pair of jeans on seeing Hallie sitting on the edge of his bed leafing through the Book of Lineages. She turns the pages stopping at Sadie's line where Zephyr's and Olivia's names bare the symbol of the pathway kinship for her line, a curved line with a straight line running down it and dot above it. She tenderly runs her fingers over Sadie's name written in blue and looks over her previous lives back to the original.

"Grissell Mercer," she reads out loud.

She looks up flashing a smile at Will and turns the pages until she finds Luke Pettigrew. Unlike Sadie's line, Luke's shows an end in 1928—his pathway kin, Elijah, has a curved line with a straight line down it and dot below it. Again, she works back through the lives finding the names in blue until she reaches the original life and sees that Luke's original name was *Matthew Carter*.

"Were Matthew and Grissell in love?"

Will nods. "Yes, they have always been."

Hallie wets her lips and nods. She flips the pages and finds a line for the original life of *Caleb Blake*. His lineage bares the symbol of a serpent. She follows it down to the last life, 1928 Jeb Curry.

"A serpent for someone afraid of snakes seems odd."

"Yes, so it would seem." Will agrees.

Hallie furrows her brow and flips the page again seeing the name *Elias Russell*. It bears a symbol of two crescents intersecting with one up and one down. The line ends in 1781.

Another turn of the page brings her to the beginning of the lineage for *Melinda Holt*. Her symbol is a plume. On the next page she finds *Daniel (White) Isaacs*. It looks like his pathway kin bares a talon symbol. A fresh line leads to Drew written in for 1958. His name stands alone.

"There's no kinship pathway for Drew."

"No, not yet. I am hoping soon though."

Hallie starts to close the ledger when she notices the back few pages of the book are stuck together by ink that mustn't have dried before it was closed and takes a moment to work them apart. The first page is an intricate drawing of a pair of large wings coming up from the back of an angel who is prostrate on the ground. His face is buried under his arms that are folded over his head. Although the angel's face is not visible, agony and despair emanate from him.

On the opposite page there is a collection of names scattered over the page in all directions. She turns the ledger reading Semjaza, Kokabiel, Armaros, Raziel and many others. Ezekiel has a tic mark by it. Next to that name is Hester.

She holds the book up towards Will. "Angels?"

"What's that?" Will lays a folded quilt on the kitchen table and stops short when he sees Hallie looking at him. Her cheeks flush, and she drops her head down running a hand up and around the back of her neck.

She looks back up. "Uh, nothing. I was just looking at the lineages and saw the drawing of the angel and all the names you've written down."

He reaches for a shirt hanging over the back of a chair by

the table and tosses it over his shoulder. "It is not just an angel. It is a watcher. That image came to me after we spent time with Maude, and after the conversation I had with the homeless woman, Missus Mason. I wanted to get it down. I am unsure about the names. Some I have heard when I was in the underworld. Others I think I have heard in my dreams. I don't know what motivated me to put it all in the book, but I want to be sure that I have it all. You know—for later."

She clamps her lips together and nods as she secures the leather cord around the ledger.

He picks up a can of pomade and hesitates. "Hallie, are you okay?"

She holds her hand up. "Um, you better stay there. Keep a bit of distance."

He cocks his head. "What?"

"It's just that…uh…seeing you…seeing you like *that* with your hair uncombed, your jeans…uh…your shirt off.  It reminds me of when we first met, and…well, you need to stay over there on that side of the room."

She lays the book back down on the nightstand and runs her hands down over her shorts resting them on her knees before she dares to look back up at him giving him a smile that tells him more than her words.

He feels the flush of, first, embarrassment and then desire as he sees her cheeks color brighter. She is beautiful. He fumbles the can of pomade but catches it before it clatters back onto the table. "Right, give me a moment to put my shirt on and comb my hair, and we can wait outside for Drew and Connie."

Hallie gets up walking a bit not really looking at anything in particular until she comes up to the kitchen table where Will's spindle is laying. She reaches over to grasp it, and it twitches ninety degrees swinging its handle away from her. She laughs to herself shaking her head.

"I suppose we should keep them with us." Will is standing by the bathroom door watching. "Did you bring yours?"

She nods opening a satchel Odina gave her. She sighs. "What?"

Hallie shrugs. "This satchel reminds me of the 'gypsy' tent—we called it that—me, Beattie, and Dot have. We used it for outdoor celebrations, and it was fun looking up through its brightly colored patches of fabric all sewn together creating that magical space. This is lined with the same material. I miss Beattie and Dot. I just want to hug them and hear their laughter."

Will lays his spindle next to hers in the satchel, and Hallie looks down at the weapons. "I guess those days of innocence spent with Beattie and Dot are long gone."

He presses his lips together not knowing what to say and rests a hand on her shoulder. "Maybe we should wrap them in something. They are extremely sharp and may tear through your satchel."

He gets the piece of cabretta that Hallie had wrapped around his box of memories and the ledger before burying it in Fayerdale.

"You know, I always wondered how this endured all those years over and over again underground protecting my things. Well, not just enduring because it looks and feels the same as the day my Uncle Benjamin gave it to me. Now that I know about my uncle's connection to not just Azure's ancestors but his trade as well," Will gives a short laugh, "I am sure he did something to make the sheep skin perpetual. It was not too long after he had given me this that I started the book of lineages. I wrote in all the details from each soul's original life that I was privy to. The next morning I wrapped the book in the cabretta and buried it with a few mementos. The first time I dug it all up I was shocked that the ledger updated itself and remained unaged. I gratefully never have trouble locating it either."

Hallie moves her hand across the leather to touch his. He lifts her hand to his mouth kissing it gently.

Will places his spindle on the leather and Hallie does the same. He wraps them and places them back in her satchel.

"How about a cola while we wait for Drew and Connie?" He asks.

"Sure, I'd like that."

He grabs two bottles from the refrigerator and pops off the tops. "Shall we wait outside?"

"Yes."

He hesitates. "Hallie, you go on. I'll be right out."

"Sure." She takes the quilt and closes the door behind her.

Will walks over to his bed and reaches under it pulling out a small wooden box. He sets it on the bed and gathers the items from his nightstand pausing to look at a few of the pictures before he sets them in the box. Lastly, he puts the leather ledger in. Closing the box, he lays a blue jay feather on top with a note addressed to Azure knowing he can preserve the box if needed even without Uncle Benjamin's cabretta. He takes a look around the room before stepping outside.

# CHAPTER 29
## Alary

Maude stands on the platform waiting for the train from Richmond to pull in. A high-pitched blast from a whistle makes her jump, and she turns looking down the tracks.

A man standing near her explains, "That's just Old Gabriel, the railroad's east end shop's whistle, announcing lunch break for the workers. It blows every day. Workday or not."

She gives him a smile and shortly afterward hears the actual train whistle in the distance. Its brakes squeal bringing it to a gradual stop and, soon, the passengers disembark. Sadie Hairston is one of the last to step off the train.

Maude steps forward. "Miss Hairston?"

"Yes." Sadie is dressed in a dark straight skirt with a matching jacket and pillbox hat. She grips a satchel and has a small bag in her other hand.

"Welcome, I am Maude Cavander. It's nice to meet you." She gives Sadie a warm smile.

"Nice to meet you as well Miss Cavander."

"Uh, it's actually Doctor Cavander, but I want you to call me Maude."

"Then you must call me Sadie."

"Wonderful. So, Sadie I thought you might be hungry when you arrived, and I got us something to eat. I uh," Maude hesitates a moment, "wasn't sure where we might be able to be served, uh, here in Roanoke you know, so I got carry out."

Sadie smiles and nods her head. "Thank you. A picnic sounds lovely."

They walk to the car the college arranged for the ride home.

"I was expecting a driver with the car, but I never could find him. Just the keys in the ignition."

"Oh, we can manage." Sadie opens her car door.

Maude smooths the front of her blouse. "Yes, I believe so."

They sit in the front seat with the doors open using the space between them to set the food. Chatting easily, common ground is found—each deciding she likes the other. Once they finish their meal, they head out continuing to talk sharing a few laughs. Sadie has just finished telling Maude about a huge embarrassment she suffered at one of Howard University's major fundraisers when a lumber truck comes from nowhere. Maude sees it from the corner of her eye as it approaches the passenger side of the car.

The truck driver has his foot hard on the brake. The acrid smell of burnt rubber rises into the air as the truck's brakes lock and the tires skid along the asphalt. Sadie hears the squeal and sees the look of terror on Maude's face, but she doesn't even get her head turned to look before the massive truck slams into them. The side of the car crumples inward with a sickening sound. The windshield crystalizes, and the side windows blow out with shattered glass flying everywhere. Sadie dies instantly. Her body slams into Maude just as everything goes black for Maude. The papers Sadie had prepared for her presentation fly from her brief case and out the side window shooting upward until they peak and drift downward towards the pavement.

The driver of the truck is stunned. A glaring light flashed across his windshield obstructing his view of the traffic light. He never saw the red light or the black sedan crossing his path. By the time he realized they were on a collision course, he had had no time to react. He walks around his truck towards the wreckage. People start gathering, sirens sound from a distance, but he is not sure that much can be done. He looks back at his truck. His load has shifted, and rough-hewn logs are littered across the intersection.

Above the chaos on the rooftop of the Wood's Brothers Coffee Company on Campbell Avenue is the H & C Coffee neon sign—a huge teapot pouring coffee that is lit even in the middle of the day. It fills the air at the rooftop with its gentle hum and crackles. At the base of the sign, near the roof's edge, stands Hester. A flash of bright sunlight reflects from her and downward towards the lumber truck's windshield. She lowers her hand tossing a jagged piece of mirrored glass onto the roof and takes a shaky breath in. Sadie is dead—spared the torment of what promises to be a gruesome harvest. Hopefully, her death will defray the damage to the others. Hester regrets involving the college professor, but it could not be avoided.

The Demon King must remain in the dark about Sadie's death for as long as possible and the professor would have been a direct source of the news had the event occurred differently. She managed to save the car's driver the same fate when she found him waiting by the hotel for Maude. Hester sang a tune of confusion into his ear causing him to forget why he was in Roanoke. He wandered away catching a bus out of town convinced he needed to go to Lynchburg where his mother lives. She is grateful this man's soul is no longer in her hands, but one more good deed in the company of so few cannot tilt the scale of her judgment favorably.

Backing away from the edge, she kneels down on the hot roof top and slowly bends forward until her head nearly touches the graveled surface that has already embedded its sharp-edged grit into her knees and elbows. Pain slivers through her as her tattered wings shoot up from between her shoulder blades incapacitating her a moment. She gathers her strength before she springs up and off the roof. Cutting through the hot July air, she swerves downward towards the wreckage just as Maude's bloodied and limp body is being pulled away from the driver's side of the car. There will be no passenger found by the officials attending the accident. Sadie, body and soul, is already lying on the bank of the Styx. Hester circles the wreckage once, and then heads south finally heeding the beckoning song that has tormented her for the past few days.

# CHAPTER 30
## Novelty

Connie parks her car along the roadside near the college, and they walk up to the field towards the celebration. People have come in from neighboring counties to attend, and an electric feeling of excitement is in the air. Carnival music and shouts from barkers can be heard amongst the crowd of people at the rides and various games of skill and chance. The foursome make their way around the carnival attractions. A few people who know them, mostly Connie, give a wave or stop to talk for a moment.

Sissy and JT run up to them with cotton candy in hand and marvel dancing in their eyes. The encounter is brief, and they quickly head off to catch a ride on the carousel. It is majestic and brightly painted, and it completely looks out-of-place on the grassy field of the small country town.

"Oh, Will, I definitely want to ride on the carousel. It is my absolute favorite ride." Hallie's eyes light up as she watches the girls find the end of the line. There are magnificent horses on the carousel, but it also has a giraffe, fierce cat, wolf, antelope, and even a hippogriff along with other mystical creatures. Parts of the ride are fixed and motionless on the platform including a small wooden ship reminiscent of an Old English barge for river crossings, but most of the creatures hypnotically rise and fall as they pass by. The tunes coming from the ride's band organ are foreign-sounding with a pied-piper's attraction.

The entire ride is being maintained by twin little people—brothers with brawny arms covered with leathery skin and wiry hair. One collects tickets while the other escorts and assists the young patrons to a creature for the ride. Their coordinated management of the ride goes on without a spoken word between them. Their coarse exterior is in contrast to the playful and mischievous air that quietly emanates from the two. Hallie is as fascinated by them as much as by the lavish ride.

Chuckling, Will grasps ahold of her arm just as she looks to be taking a mesmerized step away and towards the spinning ride. She swings her head around with a glassy-eyed look.

"If I promise you can come back to take a carousel ride, can we go and find a spot for this?" He holds up the quilt.

"Sorry." She blushes. "That's got to be the most fantastic carousel I have ever seen. I wonder how it ended up here in this small country carnival—all the other rides pale in comparison."

He presses his lips thin raising his eyebrows. "Who knows where these carnivals find their attractions or even the people that work them."

"Well, their carousel is quite a find." She looks back at the ride as they walk away.

They make their way around the crowd of people while following Connie and Drew towards the field beyond the carnival grounds. Dozens of blankets and picnic items are scattered about. There is a spot near the edge where they lay out their blankets before walking across the road to Saint James to buy supper plates of pulled pork, slaw, corn bread, and fried apple pies. Missus Adkins is there and pours each of them a tall cup of sweet tea chatting with them clearly pleased to see Will with Hallie.

Behind her Mister Adkins is talking with Ted Hodges. Connie and Drew are pre-occupied with juggling plates heavy with food, tall drinks, and each other as they walk away towards the spot where the blankets are. Mister Adkins' conversation with the deputy pauses for a moment, and he offers Will a nod of his head. Will returns a greeting noticing the deputy watching Connie and Drew intently. His gaze shifts catching Will's eye for a moment before he casually returns to his conversation with Cleo.

Once they return to the quilt Will realizes that hunger and fatigue have grabbed ahold of his insides. And, after heartily eating, he lays back in deep appreciation of the radiant sky with billowy clouds over head and the refreshing shade from neighboring trees. Closing his eyes, he listens to Hallie, Drew, and Connie's chitchat and laughter. Somewhere in the distance a group of musicians begin to play blue grass. Portions of more remote conversations and laughter filter through the air circulating in swirls around Will turning into a steady hum helping him to forget his worries.

He dozes for quite a while until he is startled by the sound of rhythmically stomping feet and whooping cheers from Connie. Looking around, he sees Hallie sitting on the edge of the quilt next to Connie, and they are watching a group of people flat footing on some plywood that has been laid on the ground. A lively tune keeps the group going including Sissy and JT dancing at the edge of the crowd both grinning broadly full of energy. When the music stops the two girls run off to their next adventure.

"Hey." Hallie slides close to him. "You must have been tired."

He nods. "I think all that good food did me in, but I am rested now. How about that carousel ride?"

"That would be fun." Hallie beams and turns to Connie. "Do you want to go over to the carnival midway with us?"

"Oh, no thanks. I need to go over and visit with my Aunt Teechee a bit, but maybe we'll head over there after that."

"Okay, we'll see you later then."

Hallie and Will walk over to the noise and commotion of the carnival. They are side-tracked by a game that they play until most of Will's coins are gone.

Hallie dramatically fans herself with her newly won paper fan teasing Will with it. They walk laughing and accidently bump into a woman with a huge display of pink cotton candy. She carries it with one hand as the candy fluff teeters to a height nearly twice her size. Recovering nimbly, she looks past them at the game booth and eyes them.

"Your money is better spent on some refreshment. How about some cotton candy for you and this sweet girl you have here?"

Feeling more guilty about nearly knocking her over then hungry, Will hands her a coin and accepts the confection on a paper cone from her. It is already dripping near the bottom with the summer heat, and he gets the stickiness on his hand. Hallie pulls a piece off the cone folding it into a manageable size and pops it into her mouth.

"Ummmm," she teases him. He rolls eyes and hands the treat off to the next young boy that passes by.

Will brings his hand to his mouth and pulls the sugary goo from his skin. His face wrinkles, and he grimaces.

Hallie laughs at his reaction, "Have you never had cotton candy?"

"No, and it is much too sweet."

She puts her arm through his. "How about taking me for a carousel ride before someone else sidetracks us?"

"Right."

They pass a photographer set up below a shade tree making portraits for a nominal fee. The sign promises the photograph will be developed and available at the pharmacy next week. There is a line of people at the edge of the tree's shade waiting for a turn to have their picture taken to commemorate the day. Hallie glances back as they are walking by to see Sissy accepting a small flag from the photographer and nodding her head as the woman gives her instructions for how she wants her to sit in front of the tree and pose. It is a sweet moment.

Organ music from the carousel floats in the air towards them and Hallie turns towards it giving Will a brilliant smile. Picking up the pace, she pulls Will closer to the ride. An unusually cold breeze sweeps past them, and Will tenses looking up at the treetops but sees nothing.

Hester sits perched in a tall tree near the field by the midway just out of view. She presses her hands over her ears blocking the Demon King's beckoning tune until it stops. A sigh of relief escapes her. Her proximity to him makes the call almost deafening. It torments her ears but, despite the pain, she wanted to see if she could find Hallie., and she is pleased to see Hallie looking happy and relaxed, at least for now.

When Hester arrived from Roanoke, she noticed the celebration below circling it sensing William's presence. She knew Hallie would be close by, if she was still here, but Hester had not expected to see Melinda and Daniel as well. Melinda must have crossed through the Mesu, and that was why she had not found her after returning from Hallie's passage through the great tree. Daniel, however, was to have been lost in the death of death, and Hester has no explanation for his presence although she is over-joyed. She now sits on the tree limb giving this all thought.

Her wings open, and she raises her face towards the heavens in meditation grateful for the warmth of the sun on her face. Her skin is radiant. Only the tattered wings betray her true station in life. Despite her status as one who has fallen, she maintains her angelic distinction and the gifts she was empowered with by her mentors, Raphael and Sandalphon. She does not know how Daniel is here, but she knows she has to assure his ability to return to Earth. She looks into the crowd and chooses a gateway kinship for the once lost soul.

There in the line for the carousel she sees a young sandy-haired boy and bestows the mark of Daniel's lineage upon him with the blow of a kiss thus changing his heritage forever. He will merely have to be acknowledged by William to set the path. Her part is accomplished.

Eyes are on her. Looking far off into the distance beyond the crowded field, past the roadway, and onto the college campus she sees the Demon King. He is there on the third floor of a building standing at a window with his red eyes on her. A poisonous smile creases his face, and he turns away letting the curtain fall back into place. She stares at the window for a moment. He can no longer be ignored, and she will have to go to him. An involuntary shudder is evoked as she stands to take leave of her perch. Suddenly, a second wave of evil strikes her, but it comes from a different direction.

She looks over her shoulder downward seeing a man walking under the cover of the woods. His hair is blond and his build slender. She feels confused. *What man would radiate such a feeling?* He looks up into the canopy of the trees and fixes his stare at her. Her heart forgets to beat realizing he can see her. He removes his sunglasses and brilliant yellow eyes are fixed on her. *Sariel!* She postures to take off towards the demon realizing he must have found a way to overcome the death of death and crossed over with Daniel or Melinda. She has to send him back.

Before she can move the searing pain from the Demon King's beckoning tune hits her hard. She tries to cover her ears, but it is no use this time. He knows she is near now and can direct the song precisely at her. Sariel has already returned to his trek. Her ears bleed with the painful vibration, and she knows she has to give up on Sariel and go to her master.

# CHAPTER 31
## Hurtling

The process for obtaining a ride on the carousel is slow and tedious. Once the ticket is handed to the gate keeper his twin brother walks the patron to the platform. They only allow one ticket holder at a time in. There is no mad rush towards a coveted horse or other carousel creature, as Hallie was accustomed to during her childhood.

Hallie looks down at the sandy-haired boy standing in front of her, and nudges Will nodding towards the boy. Will looks down at him and sees a birth mark behind his ear in the shape of a talon. Will's chest lightens, and he puts a hand on the boy's shoulder who turns to look up at him.

"Quite a long wait. Is it not?"

"Yes sir, but my friend Cory said it is the best ride here, so I'm waiting it out. Besides, I'm almost to the gate now."

"Yes, I have heard the same thing—it is worth the wait." Will speaks with him easily.

"Aren't you a little big for this ride mister?"

"Oh," Hallie speaks up. "He's here because I want to ride it."

"Yeah, my older sister wanted to ride, but granny said she needed her to get our supper set up. Too bad for her though. It looks like a fun ride even for a nearly grown-up girl."

"Are you from here?" Will asks.

"No, I stay with my granny up over the mountain in Floyd. We're just down for the day."

"Oh, I see. Well my name is Will White, and this is Hallie

O'Meara."

"Nice ta meetcha. I'm Tucker Mifflin."

"Mifflin?" Will keeps the conversation light. "I know a man named Drew Mifflin. Are you kin?"

Tucker takes a minute to give it some thought. "I'm pretty sure my daddy had a younger brother that went by that name. Don't know for sure. Like I said, I'm living with my granny."

Will nods. "Tucker, it was nice to talk with you." Will extends his hand and Tucker takes it giving him a shake with a novel look of maturity on his face seemingly pleased to be treated as an equal. He gives Hallie a smile and turns when the gate keeper pokes his shoulder with a stick.

"Well, it's my turn. See you on the ride."

Hallie looks at Will with a broad smile. "Can you believe that?"

"Quite remarkable actually." He looks back around and up in the surrounding trees again.

"Do you need to do anything about it?" Hallie asks drawing his attention away from the sky.

"Just acknowledge him." Will glances over at the ride's gatekeeper who is standing statue-like appearing to be uninterested in their conversation.

"We'll have to tell Drew and Connie. Connie will be so relieved to know that there is hope for the future."

Will starts to speak when the gatekeeper opens the gate. Hallie hands him the ticket and Will steps forward.

"Only one at a time. No seat for you any way."

Will looks down at the man. His facial features are coarse with a dark shadow of whiskers on his face. "What are you talking about? There are at least a half dozen more seats open. Besides I am going to just stand on the platform next to her." He points towards Hallie who is being led towards the back of the carousel by the gatekeeper's twin. She looks at Will raising her eyebrows expecting him to be next to her. He waves her to go on, and she shrugs apologetically.

The gatekeeper barks at Will. "The seat chooses, and none want you *and* there is no standing on the ride. Go stand over there and wait." He pushes open a gate to the side that puts Will outside the decorative rail fence. Will huffs shaking his head but does what he is told. The man smirks with satisfaction and shuts the gate.

Will studies him for several minutes. Not a muscle moves or flinches. He rests his hands on the stick that he poked Tucker with while he waits for his brother to reappear. Hallie is coming around from the back of the platform following the attendant. She shrugs and rolls her eyes towards Will.

"This one yours." The man with Hallie stops next to a chestnut-colored horse that is life-sized and magnificently carved and decorated. It's an Indian pony with war paint. A feather hangs from its forelock and only a blanket covers its back. Its head points up with its eyes looking towards the canvas above.

"Thank you." Hallie exhales her gratitude as she looks at the horse from head to tail.

He grunts an acknowledgement and steps towards the inner circle of the ride to retrieve a box for her to use to mount the horse. Hallie looks at the carved horse and the detail of the work. *It looks just like...*

"Here. You use this to get up." He sets the crate on the platform by the horse.

Hallie looks from the carved horse to the man. "Tell me about this horse. It is really very beautiful."

He sighs. "It is the lead creature for the ride—the biggest, most ornate, sits on the outside ring. You are the fortunate rider it chooses. It is a star-gazer." He points to its head. "It looks up towards the sky and stars."

Hallie looks up and notices that the constellations are glistening on the canvas above and she gasps looking along the length of the canvas for as far as she can see. "It's so…so real looking." She looks at the constellation above the carved horse. "Ophiuchus." Sparkling lights represent the stars and a pastel drawing depicts the image.

The man eyes her. "That's right."

Hallie swallows looking down at the man whose expression is unchanged. She collects herself running her hand over the carved horse's neck noticing that the mane is not painted but made with beautifully finished natural wood of varying colors and grains.

The man sees her take notice. "A piece of art most would say. The mane's depth and detail are from different types of inlayed wood—most from the Acacia tree."

Hallie pales. "Thank you, thanks for giving me this seat on the ride."

He remains stoic. "I don't choose. The creature chooses its rider. You the first of the day."

Hallie mounts the horse and she frowns. "What do you mean the creature chooses?" She looks down, but he is gone. Her heart skips a beat and she looks around trying to find where Will is standing. From the corner of her eye she thinks she sees a woman in colonial attire standing next to the platform and looks again realizing it is a huge carving of a fish standing on its tail with its mouth open facing the carousel.

"What is that?" She wonders out loud.

Tucker is sitting on a magnificent cat just in front of her, and he turns his head back. "That's the prize fish."

She tilts her head and curls up the corner of her mouth.

"You know. It holds the 'brass ring'. You gotta try to grab it when it appears in the fish's mouth."

"Oh, gotcha."

"Most carousels give a free ride for it, but this one lets you keep the ring..."

Hallie stares at the fish not hearing anything else Caleb is saying. She feels a burning fire like the lapping waves of the Phlegethon and then a calming coolness like the sheltering boundaries of the Mesu. She knows what she needs to do. The ride lurches forward, and in an instant it takes motion. She feels like her horse is in a full gallop and passes Will twice before she sees him. She gives a wave, and he smiles returning the gesture.

*Such a feeling of freedom, but with a purpose. Focus Hallie.* Tucker turns back once to give her a wave. She smiles at him giving a nod of her head, but she concentrates on the task at hand resolute to see it through.

Hallie watches the fish's mouth as she passes waiting for the ring to show itself wondering if it will—half fearful that it won't and, then again, half fearful that it will. Everything suddenly feels dreamlike as the sound of her own heartbeat overpowers the sound of the band organ that is pumping out music from the center of the ride. She imagines she can hear the beats of the horse's hooves on the carousel platform and its respirations synchronizing with the fast-moving gait. The view on the periphery of the ride becomes a blurred kaleidoscope of color. Only the feel of the carved horse below her and the waiting fish with its opened mouth and teasing eyes are clearly present in her perception.

Will stands with a forced patience outside the ride. He cannot tell from the look on Hallie's face whether she is enjoying the ride or not. It is circling at a dizzying pace, and she has a very determined look. The rest of the carousel riders seem to be enjoying themselves immensely, and he notices that Tucker must be in some imaginary world leaning forward on the sleek black cat he is astride pointing a finger ahead as though he is leading a charge through some exciting engagement of battle. Will looks at each rider noticing that all are self-absorbed in some unique fantasy of their own design.

He briefly envies them until his attention is drawn to a scuttle near the gate. An older boy is exchanging angry words with the gatekeeper and is losing the argument. The gatekeeper swings open the side gate. The boy stands his ground for a moment before kicking at the dirt flinging some onto the gatekeeper's boot and irately turning to leave. The gatekeeper slides his stick in front of the boy tripping him and quickly withdraws it. The boy falls forward picking himself up dusting off his jeans greatly chagrinned as he walks away from the ride. The gatekeeper displays a fleeting sneer and turns to resume his sentinel stance.

Will studies him not wanting to believe what he is thinking. He looks back towards the ride which is still spinning ridiculously fast and sees the gatekeeper's twin next to the ride's controls standing exactly like his brother. His image flickers between the speeding carousel creatures. Will looks from one to the other. A piece of paper blows in front of the gate keeper, and he bends to pick it up and throw it in the trash barrel next to the gate. Will looks at the silk screening on the man's shirt. The faded and cracked writing, *Cercopes Amusements & Other Interests*, across his back sparks an electric current through Will. Cercopes, the mischievous twin guards at Paimon's palace in Tartarus.

*The brothers of one mind and action who share one name.* It is all he can do to restrain from yelling out his thoughts and act on his sudden realized fear. Will's throat clamps tight, and his heart pounds out-of-control. He looks around, but there is no sign of Paimon. Everything looks…normal. He looks back at the ride edging along the fence trying to improve his vantage. Hallie passes by looking carefree and happy now. Behind her is the miniature barge and there is a young boy standing in it with a long stick pretending to move the boat ahead. Two younger children are sitting in the barge enjoying the ride and fighting over a large gold coin. *Charon's ferry!* He looks at the remainder of the creatures on the carousel. Most hold no memory for him, but a few do…like Hallie's horse. He darts a glance over at the gatekeeper who remains steady at his post and back at the carousel. The ride slows, but Will's nerves sizzle with panic until he sees Hallie walking around the carousel towards him.

They find a spot away from the busy midway and on the outskirts of the picnic area. Will takes a breath to steady himself and puts his arms around Hallie. He has experienced many horrific things in his existence but imagining her getting lost amongst the creatures of Tartarus catches him off guard. He doesn't like how he is feeling. First the McCaffrey house with its putrid rot and now…this…although he has no idea what 'this' is. He worries that his stolen life has opened some sort of portal between realms.

He surveys Hallie. "Are you alright?"

She nods. Her cheeks are flushed, and she is exuberant with pure joy. "Will, it was magical. The ride picked up speed and it…it felt like the horse I was on was at a full gallop. Will—the horse is a replica of…"

"Acacia."

"Yes! I can't believe it…Will are *you* alright?" She blinks several times.

He nods and encourages her to finish telling him about the ride.

"Just like the angel song said…the legend would be yielded, no bore, on trusted steed. I knew it was going to happen. I just knew it. There was this…this fish. Tucker told me about the brass ring, and I knew at that moment exactly what needed to be done. I reached as far as I could willing it to be mine. I thought that I had missed because I didn't feel it land in my hand, but when I looked down at my palm there it was. I can't believe it Will. We've got the second key."

He forces a steady hand and lifts the key from her palm. Its outer ring is smooth and made of brass. Its inner portion opens into a pentagram and is made of iron. He turns it over, and there is a clasp imbedded in the outer ring with a hexagram embossed on it; the clasp can be flipped inward towards one of the points of the pentagram. The Hebrew word הוהי is engraved in the metal of the clasp's arm.

"What is it Will?"

"Yahweh, the unspeakable name of God. Look, it is only visible when the clasp is opened to sit within the point of the pentagram." He exhales. It is crafted like nothing else Will has ever seen. He feels unworthy to be holding it and hands it back to Hallie. "What next?" He searches her eyes

Hallie looks at the key and unties her amulet pouch from the loop on her shorts. She opens it taking out Raphael's key and lays it next to Solomon's key. The Maltese cross with garnet center is in its natural state, and its bordering edge forms a pentagram. Hallie turns it until the two pieces match up. She picks up the fairy stone and turns it over. The hexagram star on the back looks like it will align perfectly with the clasp on Solomon's key.

She and Will simultaneously draw a breath in, and Hallie puts the keys back into her amulet pouch alongside her amber heart, the penny, and the willow's flower. She shrugs. "I don't know what's next. Somehow, it doesn't feel like it is our choice to make. At least not now."

"Right, then we wait and see." There is a sudden release of his muscles that he did not realized were locked up.

She looks up at Will, and he hugs her not wanting to let go when Connie runs up to them. Her chest heaves with effort, and she holds her sides trying to find her voice.

# CHAPTER 32
## Misreckoning

"Connie, what's happened?"

Connie straightens. "It's Drew...Ted Hodges and Sheriff Shively...they came up to us with uniformed officers and arrested him."

"What?" Hallie gasps looking from Connie to Will.

"Did they say anything at all Connie?"

"They said they were arresting him in connection with the Pearl Murders. They found a hunting knife near the murder scene by Shooting Creek, and it had Drew's fingerprints on it. They have been waiting for the fingerprint results to come back." A tear spills onto her cheek and she quickly wipes it away. "Will, it's not true. How could this be?"

Will's mind races. Drew had gone to the Sheriff's office to talk to them about Dillon. *What could have gone on during that meeting? How could they have a murder weapon with Drew's fingerprints?* He reaches out his hand hesitating a moment before resting it on her arm. "We will find out what is going on. It has to be a mistake. We will leave now and go to the sheriff's office."

Connie's tears are now streaming as she explains what happened. "People near us overheard what was going on. They immediately were in an uproar ready to believe that Drew was the killer. There was a man there who was kin to the first girl killed and...oh, God. He made threats to Drew. Will, he's not going to be safe. These murders have been so horrible, and people have been so terrified. I'm afraid someone is going to take the law into their own hands."

Hallie puts her arms around Connie letting her cry.

"Connie," Hallie whispers to her. "We should go. We should see what we can find out. Okay?"

"Yes, Hallie is right. So long as he is in custody, he is safe." Will forces confidence in his voice.

They start to make their way back to Connie's car when Teechee runs up to them.

"We can't find the girls!" Her voice screeches with near hysteria. "My God. What if that murdering lunatic has ahold of them?"

Someone walking by overhears. "Maybe they're just off playing. I heard they just arrested that fellow a few minutes ago."

Teechee takes pause for a minute swallowing a breath. "What are you talking about? My girls have been gone for over an hour. They went to get their pictures taken, and they never came back. Who was arrested?"

"Uh, think he was that drifter that has been working for Cleo Adkins. What's his name? Stew?"

Teechee pales. "Drew Mifflin?"

"Yeah, yeah that's it."

Teechee turns to Connie suddenly aware of her niece's tear-stained face. "What's this about Connie?"

"Aunt Teechee you know Drew isn't capable of anything like that." Connie's voice catches with a sob.

"I don't know how much I know about that boy. He's only been in town no more than a year or two."

"Aunt Teechee you know it isn't true. He has been with me all day today. He has nothing to do with JT and Sissy missing. He loves them as much as I do."

Teechee pauses giving Connie's words some thought. "He left just after Hallie and Will went to go on that ride. He was gone quite a bit, Connie. Do you know where he was?"

Connie's color goes ashen. "He went to get me a lemonade.

You saw him come back with it."

Teechee shakes her head too distraught for reasoning.

Will tries to remain calm in a situation getting quickly out of control. Several other people are now gathering around, and he can hear mumblings about what is happening and Drew's name churning in the mix of concern and worry.

"Missus Canaday has anyone begun to look for the girls?" He asks.

She turns to look at Will processing his question. "Yes, yes Wade and his brother have contacted the police and gotten a few people together. They are searching the carnival area."

"Missus Canaday." Hallie is hesitant to speak. "Will and I saw Sissy getting her picture taken over by the shade tree about an hour ago when we were heading over to the carousel. Maybe someone over there saw where she went. We could go and ask."

Teechee nods her head slowly.

"Teechee." A kind woman from the gathering crowd comes up putting an arm around her. "Honey, why don't we let the folks around here do the looking, and you and I go on over to Saint James where it's cool. Any news comes up they can fetch you."

Teechee complies walking with her across the street.

Hallie, Will, and Connie watch her go and turn to look at one another.

"We need to find the girls." Connie dries her tears. "Drew will be safe for now."

"Yes." Will says. "We need to check with the photographer to see if anyone noticed where Sissy and JT may have gone."

They make their way over to the big shade tree at the other side of the midway and speak with the photographer. She remembers Sissy and explains to them that she has a log of pictures taken including frame numbers, names, phone numbers and the time the photos were taken. Retrieving her book, she finds the page where she recorded Sissy's information.

Hallie looks at the page. "Sissy's real name is Priscilla?"

Connie nods. "Um-hm. It looks like she was here at four-thirty."

"What is JT's full name?" Hallie asks as all the color drains from her face.

Connie looks at her. "Why Hallie? What's their names got to do with anything?"

"Joan. Her name is Joan isn't it?" Hallie reaches up rubbing her arms. She closes her eyes and shakes her head.

"Hallie, what is wrong?" Will reaches out to her.

"Will, we have got to find them." Hallie's eyes brim with tears, and she turns to the photographer. "Did you see which direction she went?"

"I think she said something about going to meet her sister to see a fairy ring somewhere near the far back side of the picnic area by the woods."

"Right," Connie says. "They were talking about the fairy ring that they saw when they first got here. They kept talking about running the circle to hear the fairies."

"Yes," Hallie exclaims. They say you run around a fairy circle nine times, and the fairies dance and sing for you. I remember trying that when I was a kid."

"We need to go now." Connie starts out. Hallie and Will follow not too far behind her.

"Will," Hallie whispers to him. "We have to hurry. JT is Joan, the friend I was staying with in the year 2018. She never talks much about it, but her sister, Priscilla, was murdered. There is a picture of Priscilla in the room that I sleep in. It was the last photograph that was taken of her. She is sitting under a shade tree holding a small American flag. I can't believe how stupid I am. I can't believe the pieces did not come together for me before now."

They pick up their pace catching up to Connie, and the trio hastily make their way to the fairy ring. It looks to be undisturbed, but they walk around the area to be sure. There are mushrooms of varying shapes and sizes that form the ring. Will looks intently at it and turns walking away to look at the field and nearby woods. Preparations are being made for the fireworks display about a hundred yards away, and he checks to see if anyone saw the girls but has no luck.

"Hallie, take out your amber amulet and circle the ring nine times while you concentrate on the girls. Pay close attention to where you start. Do not take even one more step beyond nine circles and be careful not to step inside the ring."

She raises her eyebrows at him. "O…kay…" She takes her amulet out and starts to walk around the fairy circle. Connie stands by anxiously walking the edge of the woods looking for any sign of the girls. Will keeps count of Hallie's revolutions.

She completes the eighth turn walking the ninth with her head cocked as a sing-song tune begins to rise up from the center of the fairy ring. Her hand glows from the amber amulet. The words of the tune are not clear, but the sound begins to whirl and rise from the center of the circle. It hangs above their heads creating ripples in the air. The amulet grows brighter as Hallie finishes the ninth turn and stops. The tune becomes more of a buzzing shrill, as it spins and shoots away from the circle towards the woods edge where it blasts the undergrowth firing up dirt, leaves, and twigs at the base of a maple tree. A red satin ribbon floats up into the air.

Connie grasps the ribbon. "This is JT's." She steps closer to the woods edge and finds evidence of someone walking through the brush. Hallie and Will run over towards her, and they all step into the woods.

"Wait." Will stops. "Connie, do you have your spindle?"

She looks at him solemnly nodding as she pats the bag she has over her shoulder. They turn to move further into the woods coming up to a spot where there has been some sort of struggle and then nothing beyond that is visible. They each go to the periphery of the area walking slowly until Connie spots where the trail continues.

"This way," she whispers.

"Wait a minute Connie," Will says and turns to Hallie, "let me get my spindle from your bag."

She nods opening her bag and lifts up the cabretta bundle. He can see her muscles flexing over a tense jaw and reaches up to touch her cheek. "We will find them."

A tear runs down her cheek as she opens the sheep's skin cover. She rubs her face against her shoulder, and Will takes his spindle. There is a slight tremor of her hand when she grasps hers, and he meets her eyes with his to see if she is okay. She nods stepping in Connie's direction. His protective marks shimmer brighter. They are very close.

Except for their own steps, the woods are eerily silent. There is an area ahead of them where the sunlight glows brighter through the trees. He gives a whistle to Hallie and Connie holding a hand up for them to slow their pace.

The girls are to the left of the clearing. They are laying in the grass amongst wildflowers. Motionless. Lifeless. Connie tenses and starts to move into the clearing, but Will signals for her to hold her position.

The three of them look from end to end of the clearing and, remaining inside the cover of the woods, walk closer towards the girls. As they near them, blood on Sissy's shirt can be seen. It soaks the collar and upper bodice of the white eyelet fabric.

Hallie stifles a gasp.

Connie stands firm. Her expression is the same that Will

has seen during their many shared demon wars in Tartarus. He looks at her watching the sudden shimmer of her protective marks coursing down over her upper arm swirling towards her wrist and hand. Connie's marks are limited to her right arm, her most lethal weapon with sword in hand when in the underworld. She bears no demon's marks. None of Will's demon marks make an appearance either.

They remain motionless for several minutes waiting to see if Sariel lingers until Hallie breaks the silence with desperation in her voice. "Will, we can't stand here any longer. We've got to go to the girls."

Hallie and Connie maintain their positions in the woods while Will moves out into the open cautiously making his way towards the girls. As he walks towards them, there is a swing in the air temperature. It's cooler with a fine mist hovering over the ground. There is a shift in weight hanging over his back, and he brings his hand his shoulder grasping ahold of the hilt of his broad sword withdrawing it from the sheath. The blue jay feather that he had bound to it the last time he was in Tartarus brushes against his hand, and he extends his arms stopping to inspect his transformation. The leather wrist straps are on each of his arms. The three serpents, leather pants, and boots are all in place as well. He thinks of the McCaffrey house and Cercopes at the carousel. Pieces of the underworld have crossed over, and they are currently surrounded by one of its most evil presence. A place where innocent life has been taken. He knows if they do not settle this here and now, the consequences will be ominous.

He turns signaling Hallie and Connie to move forward, but they are already making their way towards him. Hallie's eyes widen as she draws near obviously feeling the change in temperature and seeing him through the mist as well as Connie's transformation to fury.

No threat from Sariel is evident, and he sheaths his sword. There is no sign of life in Sissy, and he goes to check JT when Connie comes to Sissy's side. He leans his ear over JT's nose tilting her head back to see if she is breathing, but there is no sign of life for the younger of the two either. His chest burns with hatred for the demon while starting to breathe life into JT's mouth when he sees the pearl. He removes it and leans in to give a breath seeing her chest rise.

"Oh God, not JT." Hallie sobs. "It can't be Will. She grows up and…and…she's my friend…she's our friend."

Connie begins to check Sissy seeing the blood on her shirt is from a wound extending from the side of her neck to her collar bone. "Will, Sissy's wound looks like one used for a blood sacrifice. It's not a mortal wound. I don't think her major blood vessels have been severed, but she is not breathing."

"Check her mouth. I found a pearl in JT's. Take it out and try to blow life into her with your mouth. You may need to compress her chest as well." Connie follows his instructions and begins working feverishly.

"Will." Hallie kneels facing him on the other side of JT's body. Tears trickle down her face. She opens her amulet pouch removing the willow's gift, the small feathered flower. "I can save one of them."

He stops for a moment resting his finger against the side of JT's neck. Hallie goes to open JT's mouth to place the flower inside, but Will gently takes her hand. "Then use it for Sissy."

She looks at him not understanding. "But…Will…the future…it is JT that survives…not Sissy."

"Yes, well that is going to change."

She looks at him opening and then closing her mouth when a smile comes to his face.

"JT is alive." He takes Hallie's hand and lays it over her

chest. "Her heart beats, and she is taking healthy breaths. She will grow up to be Joan, your family friend."

Hallie smiles with wonder.

"Go bring her sister back to her."

Hallie walks over to Connie who is stubbornly working to bring Sissy back despite no encouraging signs. Hallie lays her hand over Connie's to have her stop the chest compressions and opens the palm of her hand to show her the willow flower. Connie reaches up to wipe the tears from her face and sits back as Hallie gently opens Sissy's mouth placing the flower inside. They wait unsure of what else needs to be done. Several long minutes go by before bird song comes into the field. The three of them look around and at one another.

Will picks up JT and lays her next to Sissy. Their hearts lift when Sissy begins to breathe. Her cheeks glow with the flush of life. Connie leans over kissing each girl on the forehead.

From nowhere a bone-chilling roar cuts through the air.

Will's muscles tense. "Over there at the woods edge."

He and Connie respond drawing swords moving around the girls and Hallie until Sariel steps into the meadow. They turn moving towards him. Will tightens and relaxes his grip on the hilt of his sword. Air flows in and out of his lungs, and the oxygen saturates every cell of his body. His eyes narrow focusing on the threat before them, and his thoughts gauge the best strategy to counter each of Sariel's potential moves as he advances.

"How dare you defile the perfection of my sacrifice?" The gritty allegation fires from a transforming Dillon McCaffrey. His eyes are tawny and blazing. His thin frame barely holds in tense bulging muscles while his skin shines with a glistening film of sweat. Within seconds, his frame expands to a bulk of powerful muscles shredding the slender human form they had been occupying. A poleaxe appears in Sariel's raised hand, and he closes the distance between them while completing the transformation to the demon known to Connie and Will with a cloven hoof, fiery red skin, and braided hair hanging to the middle of his scarred back. A horned helmet crowns his head while a breast plate and spiked shoulder guards appear. Leather replaces the casual pants with a heavy boot covering his foot while lethal barbs circle above his hoof. The ground trembles under his weighted steps.

"How dare you reclaim my sacrifices?" He hurls the question at them again. "My pearl pentagram was complete. In moments, the ceremony would have completed, and I was to have her finally. How dare you? Melinda is mine." He is focused on Hallie charging straight towards her.

Time seems to slow as Will spins around blocking the way. There is a moment when they circle sizing one another up, but then the clash of their weapons rings across the wilderness silencing the bird song once again. Will's body reverberates with the blow, and the three serpents hiss striking several times, but they don't hit their mark. Sariel grabs Will by the neck and flings him to the side resuming his advance towards Hallie.

Will sees her stand with her spindle in hand. Her eyes widen and she shifts her weight with trembling legs. Connie runs forward with her sword, but Will recovers quickly bounding towards them while taking a leap to close the space more quickly. He swings his sword slicing into Sariel's arm. The demon swings around towards him.

"Connie, stay put," Will yells as he raises his sword to deflect Sariel's next attack. The demon is powerful, but Will's protective marks shine bright fortifying his strength. He turns and swings tightly to his left lunging forward slicing the demon's flank.

Sariel roars and ensues with a forward advance plunging

his pole axe with one blow after another sending Will back with each strike against his sword. Sariel turns and cuts an elbow across the back of Will's neck hurling him onto the ground.

Will's head hits hard and he loses grip on his sword. His ears ring, and he feels the sticky trickle of blood at his mouth. From the corner of his eye, he sees Connie advancing. "No!" He bellows.

Sariel turns on heel towards Connie. Will grasps desperately at the ground laying his hand on a large rock. He hurls it towards Sariel striking him on the back of the head. Sariel falls forward affording Will time to retrieve his sword and rejoin the melee. He holds his hand up to Connie warding her off the field. She paces holding her weapon at the ready. Hallie is just behind her gripping her spindle while casting side glances towards the girls.

"When I signal and not before," Will shouts towards Connie. Drew could not bear losing her, and Will knows he must work on wearing the demon down as much as possible before she engages.

He staves off several more blows from Sariel. His muscles are starting to tremor with exhaustion, and he fears he may not be able to bring the demon down. A mixture of sweat and blood stings his eyes, and he spats to the ground the salty mix that has accumulated in his mouth. He continues blocking blow after blow but makes little progress with the offense, and the demon shows no sign of slowing down.

He bares down hard on Will and roars landing a powerful strike hurling Will to the ground. The final assault from the demon threatens to crash down over Will's skull, and he looks to the side seeing Hallie and Connie looking on ready to engage, but he knows the demon has not been weakened enough for them to take him on. He musters his strength and raises up his sword overhead blocking the swing of the weapon. His arm shudders while he struggles to rise from the ground and keep Sariel's poleaxe at bay. His muscles burn and threaten to fail him. Connie moves forward distracting Sariel just long enough to allow Will to spin around causing the metal on metal from their locked weapons to screech with a sickening sound that abruptly silences when Will plunges his spindle into Sariel's side cracking through ribs and puncturing his lung.

The demon's arm falls downward, and he loses grip on the pole axe watching it hit the ground. He drops heavily to his knees with eyes wide rolling them towards Will while drawing in a noisy breath. Connie is at the ready rushing forward and thrusts the second spindle into Sariel's opposite side mirroring the damage already done crashing the demon to his knees. He turns his head to look at her with longing. Will almost pities him knowing the demon's feelings are unrequited and swearing he sees something like remorse wash over Sariel. He scrubs a hand over his face throwing aside the pity knowing the only remorse Sariel holds is that of his own defeat.

Connie takes pause for a moment transfixed by his eyes searching for the humanity that had once been there. Will lowers his sword and walks over to Connie gently taking her arm coaxing her to walk away. Sariel is immobilized, and his nostrils flare with each labored breath. His eyes' yellow glow begins to dim as his head falls back facing the clear blue sky. Black blood trickles from the corner of his mouth.

Hallie steps in front of Will. She looks at him for strength, and he lightly strokes the side of her face. She leans against his hand closing her eyes. A strong urge to grab her and take her away hits him but, before he can act, she stands tall taking him by surprise when she lifts the strap of the colorful patchwork satchel over her head and off her shoulder.

"Hold this for me?"

He nods still struggling with his emotions as she hands the bag to him. He grasps it by the strap, and she blinks, her lashes wet with tears. She clears her throat. "The cabretta is in there…you will need it for…later. I also put the pressed penny in there…you keep it. I put it inside the folded angel song verses from the other night. I want you to have them. Read them."

She turns to Connie. "When you go to see Drew, you need to talk to the sheriff. Something I thought about that may help prove he was not involved with the murders is the train ticket Dillon purchased to go out of town. Obviously, he didn't leave, so the ticket must be somewhere. In 2018 I found a book, *The Martian Chronicles*, and between the pages was a train ticket with yesterday's date, July 3rd, 1958. I remember it because the serial number on the ticket was the same as my birthday, 04042000…"

Connie's mouth opens, but no words come out.

Hallie flicks a smile at them and then looks over her shoulder at Sariel and takes a shaky breath. She turns back to Connie grabbing eye contact. "Connie, go to the '77 Restaurant, and see if it happens to be there. If they can trace it back to Dillon that may help prove that he never left town."

"Okay, but you can…"

Hallie cuts her off. "Yes, but just so you know." Hallie turns to Will and lays a soft kiss on his lips.

He blinks slowly and mechanically nods to her watching her turn and walk towards the demon. Their hands reluctantly let go only when their arms can no longer reach the other.

He squeezes the bridge of his nose. A muffled alarm seems to be sounding from deep inside him struggling to rouse through the exhaustion. He fights to process the warning just starting to raise his hand to draw her back when she kneels and, without hesitation, lays her left hand against Sariel's breast plate for support and plunges the long-pointed end of her spindle up and under his rib cage towards his heart. Will stops short seeing the blood flow over the skillfully carved wood, over Hallie's hand, wrist, and arm. The last bit of light is extinguished from the yellow eyes. Hallie puts her palm over the other end of the spindle grasping its sharp point. She takes a deep breath and forces its tip through her own flesh wincing with the pain as her blood begins to flow into the mix of demon blood and grit. Their blood courses down and around them onto the ground in a thin line, and within moments there is a flickering spark along the newly formed barrier of the blood which forms a circle around her and Sariel. Flames take hold and gradually rise.

It is as though Will is slapped across his face, and he jerks his head. *This does not seem right. Is the fire intended to engulf them?* He starts towards Hallie wanting to pull her free but the flames rush towards him keeping him away. The fire angrily circles Hallie and Sariel occasionally looking as though daring Will to try again. He sees the Sisters of Fate moving through the flames just as they had done in Odina's campfire. The fire's height and brilliance waxes and wanes as they circle. Atropos turns her head towards him wielding the same threatening look from that night at the Ridge's. Her glare quickly melts into a look of satisfaction. There is something else there as they dance among the flames…it looks as though they are conjuring a works of their own.

"What is this?" Will shouts and begins to walk around the circle. He stops near Hallie trying to reach through the searing heat and jerks his hand back.

Connie rushes forward as well.

Hallie turns her head to look at him through the wavy heat, and he sees a tear flow down her cheek, "I'm sorry for not telling you…"

"Hallie, what? Sorry for what?" She might as well be a million miles away. He isn't used to feeling so helpless.

Connie and Will look on in horror as crimson threads…the threads of life Will suddenly realizes…spin upward from where the blood mixes. They spin above their heads twisting together in several strands before lowering down wrapping themselves around Sariel lifting his lifeless body transforming him from demon, to tortured soul, back to human. He has a crippled left leg and had been a beautiful soul—a pure soul without doubt. Will wonders what had tainted his soul to demonize it, and he understands now why Hallie was chosen for the third spindle. Her blood is the only blood able to reclaim the pure soul that had been lost so long ago. *But, to what end?* His tormented thoughts are screaming at him.

Sariel's body is engulfed by the threads, they tighten, and suddenly there is nothing but dust. The threads dangle about swinging violently in a torrent of wind. They lower over Hallie. Again, the flames keep Will and Connie at bay when they try to reach her no longer willing to standby. Hallie is in a whirl wind. She remains on her knees with her eyes closed—her hair and clothing rippling about with a squall that only engulfs her.

She slowly turns towards Will opening her eyes and holding her hand up. He cannot find enough air to breath and his heart has moved to his throat. The tangle of threads covers her while the wind intensifies abruptly extinguishing the flames, and when they're out, only a glimmer of Hallie is there in the dust particles. As each particle moves through the air or drifts to the ground, she gradually disappears.

Will's chest explodes with emptiness. Hallie's bag remains in his grip. Glancing at Connie, he sees she has transformed back to her original summer attire, and so has he. All signs of their protective marks are gone. There is no sign that the fire, or anyone, had been there.

Connie has no comfort to offer him. Her face reflects his pain and loss.

"Connie? Will?"

Sissy sits up. Her blood-stained shirt looks out-of-place with her youthful and innocent face that is now so full of life. She notices the blood on her shirt and JT lying unconscious next to her. With a trembling lip her face contorts with fear.

Both Will and Connie rush to her side providing reassurance. Will hands Hallie's bag to Connie and picks JT up resting her head on his shoulder. Connie extends a hand to Sissy who calms and stands looking around the field trying to figure out how she got there. Connie engages her in light conversation occasionally looking over at Will. He walks supporting JT's head with his hand and keeps his focus straight ahead. He is desperately hoping that what they witnessed was Hallie's transportation back to her own time and not her demise. It will be sixty years, and an eternity in the underworld before he will know the answer.

When they reach the picnic grounds they are quickly surrounded by people. A picture is taken of them as they walked by, Connie holding Sissy's hand, Will carrying JT, and Teechee rushing towards them. Will answers a few questions, but Connie does most of the talking. He is spent and finds the intensity of the people around them too much to contend with. Sheriff Shively asks for them to come into Rocky Mount to speak with him, and they agree to meet him later that evening. Will searches faces in the crowd looking for Joe Tasker and Hester almost wishing the harvest would begin.

Instead, he is obliged to maintain control forcing himself to go through the motions to endure what needs to be done for the rest of the evening.

Before he realizes it, he is gratefully sitting in the front seat of Connie's car listening to the hum of the motor as they head back to Ferrum from Rocky Mount. The radio is on, but he is unaware of more than a rhythmic drone spilling from it. Drew remains in custody for now. Knowing Drew, Sheriff Shively is more convinced of his innocence then Deputy Hodges, and that is encouraging. Dillon's body will eventually be discovered. No longer possessed by the demon, his remains will be left for decay.

Will stares out the window lost in thought when he looks up over the tree line as they approach Ferrum. Fireworks are bursting into brilliant streams of color that scorch the night sky. They are a reminder of the day's celebration made sweeter for those in Ferrum by the rescue of two of their younger citizens, but it is still the darker side of the day's events that occupy his thoughts. What happened today will have an impact on the future that Hallie had known.

He thinks long about the images of Clotho, Lachesis, and Atropos within the flames. They had fashioned the spindles through Azure's alchemy ritual and reclaimed the demon that defied them. He has no idea what this means, but he cannot ignore the nervous twitch along his scar.

"Will, you okay?"

Connie's voice pulls him away from his foreboding thoughts. He suddenly realizes the car is parked at his apartment and nods. "Yes, fine. Thank you." He opens the door and looks back at her. "See you tomorrow?"

"Yes. We can go to the '77 before we go back into Rocky Mount. I want to check on that train ticket Hallie told us about."

"Alright."

She bites her lower lip. "You sure you're okay?"

He lies. "Yes." He lost Hallie. Again. No more. If she is there in 2018, he will take better care. Find a way and defeat the Demon King then and there. He takes Hallie's bag and gets out watching Connie drive away. The two cola bottles from earlier in the day are where Hallie had set them on the patio. He looks at them and leaves them pushing through the apartment entrance.

# CHAPTER 33
## Veneer

The night swelters with stagnant air, and the oscillating fan in his apartment offers little relief. Will sits at his small dinette staring at Hallie's bag while drinking a glass of water. A trickle of sweat makes its way down the side of his neck. He ignores the irritation and lifts the edge of her bag reaching in to take out the cabretta. He sets it aside and takes out the folded paper tilting it to let the pressed penny clink against the speckled Formica tabletop. Opening the paper slowly he begins to read the angel song that Hallie had hurriedly written down just last night.

*Once again, the threat draws near.* *–Demon King, but Sariel too*
*Stolen lives will be reclaimed while a lineage is at risk by*
*retribution*
*ill begot. –harvest, Will, Connie, Drew, Sadie*
*This is the moment for saving one of the line lost but not forgot.*
*–????*
*Take care the time is here.*

*Upon the back of trusted steed, --obvious, a horse. when? how?*
*A legend bore is a power gained that one must claim*
*and one must heed. –the key, Solomon's key!*
*The <u>one</u> <u>ahead</u> <u>will be</u> <u>left</u> <u>behind</u>. –me.*
*Liberation is found in memories newly made*
*haunting body, soul, and mind. ?Liam in 2018*

She must have stayed up most of the night going over the song trying to figure it out. They know now the one saved is Sissy, but Hallie was on the right track. She had written below the song:

*Melinda's lineage—all girls murdered so far look like her, but who is saved? Why the murders? Sariel trying to claim her for his own—how?* Under her jotted thoughts she had written *I DON'T GET TO GO HOME!!! Last verse—<u>last</u> <u>verse</u>!!! What's it mean?* He flips the paper over.

<u>**The traveler's end**</u> **comes with a <u>deed to be done</u>.**
**The decision is made with the lots drawn and the weapons won.**
**—the spindles**
**Thread spun and measured with cut denied will now find an end much the same.**
**Sisters three—are not we—but with a bond just as strong will soon reunite from**
**whence they came—Beattie, Dot and me!**

She had kept the last verse from him. The angel song told her more than she let on last night. His lips contort, and he balls the paper up throwing it in frustration. The table shakes when he pounds his fist down, but he quickly surrenders getting up to retrieve the crumpled paper from under his bed. Anger and frustration rule the moment before he calms down understanding why she had done it. She had to obtain the key, and she had to stop Sariel. She knew it. He knows it. It had to be done. Convincing himself, however, is difficult. Is there more that she had not written down? Searching his memories for any sign of her in his past is fruitless. There is nothing before 1928.

# CHAPTER 34
# Return

Will squints with a bright light shining on his face and rubs his eyes looking over at the clock. Twelve o'clock. He sits a moment shaking off the confusion from the deep sleep realizing he overslept. It's noon, and he missed meeting Connie at the '77. The Book of Lineages is lying open on the floor by his bed catching his eye. There is something odd about it.

On the page where he had sketched the watcher is the beginnings of another sketch instead. He picks up the book and flips the page. The watcher sketch and page of angel names are a couple pages in front of the new one that now occupies the last page of the book. It is his work, but he has no recollection of drawing it. It is a woman's profile as she turns to look over a bare shoulder with hair is swept back from her face and wet. It's unfinished. It doesn't matter. The slight curve of the nose, the glittering eye, the eyebrow, the ear…it is Hallie. He stares at the drawing baffled by how it got there. Although he has no memory of her from a time before Fayerdale, he still knows this sketch is proof that she is there in his past. A ray of hope sparks knowing the memories will eventually come.

Picking up the pressed penny from his night stand he lays it inside the book with the wrinkled angel song and sets it inside the box with the folded cabretta over it and lays the note for Azure on top. He grabs a clean shirt pulling it on when there is a tap at his door. "Come in."

The door opens slowly and Connie leans in. "Will?"

"Yes, I'm here." He walks towards her and stops short when he sees Drew standing next to Connie.

"Drew? What happened?"

"I've been cleared."

Will breaths his first full breath since yesterday afternoon. He walks over and shakes Drew's hand, and Drew pulls him into a tight hug.

"I'm glad, truly glad to hear that Drew, but how?"

"Will, I came by earlier when you didn't show up at the '77. Your door was unlocked, and I let myself in. You were out cold. I didn't want to disturb you, so I went on into Rocky Mount." She wrinkles her brow apologetically.

"It is okay. Go ahead and tell me what happened. Let us sit at the table."

"Well, Hallie was right. The book was at the restaurant, and the train ticket was in it. Sally said it was left sometime Thursday. She let me take it, and I went over to the depot to see if they could trace tickets. It happens that Mister Simms has a logbook where he writes in the name of the patron, ticket number, date and time of purchase. It's not an official railroad policy, but he has had problems with lost ticket claims in the past. It's his way of keeping track of things."

"Well that is a bit of luck." Will says.

"You bet. I headed into the sheriff's office and, when I got there, Cleo Adkins was there with Deputy Hodges from Patrick County and Sheriff Shively. He apparently had concerns about Drew's arrest. He heard the murder weapon was a hunting knife and asked if he could see it. They showed it to him, and he identified it as a knife that Dillon McCaffrey had in the back of his Cadillac when he brought it in for service not too long ago. Mister Adkins explained that he does an inspection of all cars that come into the shop before repairs are done in case there are any complaints by customers about theft or other problems."

"I worked on Dillon's car that day, remember?"

Will nods. "I remember you mentioning seeing the knife.

Do you think he set you up?"

"Yeah, the knife was on the floor behind the driver seat. I saw it and slid it under the seat to keep it out of the way. That must have been how my prints got on it."

"So, between the train ticket Connie brought in and Mister Adkins information they let you go?"

"Well," Connie goes on. "Actually, there's more. They found Dillon's body late yesterday probably just as we were leaving the station to head back here. They were doing a comb-through of the woods before the fireworks display making sure there was no evidence to be found that could possibly be disturbed. They suspect he died of natural causes oddly enough. Anyway, they found a silk pouch with pearls in it on him. They are going to see if they match with the ones found on the other victims and the ones we gave them from the girls last night."

Will looks on in anticipation.

"That's still not all. The coroner was there picking up some information for another case and overheard one of the officers talking about what happened at the celebration and Dillon McCaffrey's involvement. He asked for more details and reviewed some of the information they had, but he also called for records from Patrick County."

Connie draws a breath in letting it out slowly between her lips. "Will, he thinks there are some similarities in the deaths that happened in Patrick County and the girls here in Ferrum and at Shooting Creek *and* Dillon McCaffrey's sister's death. Not exact, but enough to suggest he may have killed his sister all those years ago. The coroner happened to be the same physician that was in charge of her autopsy." She chokes a sob back. Drew takes her hand.

She gives him a weak smile with trembling lips. "And, they think he may have even killed Missus McCaffrey. They are going back through his sister's, father's, and mother's autopsy reports. They plan to exhume Missus McCaffrey's body. Will, Dillon may have been a killer even as a young teenager. Way before his possession." She shudders.

"It would explain Sariel's attraction to him if it's true. The existence of evil would have been a beacon. It was not like Sariel was looking for the conquest of a soul. He just needed a convenient vessel to accomplish what he wanted, and an evolving serial killer would certainly be the means to the end Sariel desired."

"Will, I just can't help wondering what could have happened had Hallie not been here—not remembered about the book and train ticket. What else could have happened? Would Drew have been here and then lost to us again?"

"Well," Drew starts cheerfully. "Let's not think about that. A piece of history has been made right and, hopefully, Hallie has found her way safely back to her own time and perhaps even young William here."

Will wishes that was true, but he knows differently.

Drew offers a bit of distraction for the moment. "How about we head out to Fairy Stone? It's a holiday weekend. We're off from work. It will be a distraction. We can go over to the '77 and get some sandwiches made up. Sally can pack up a picnic for us. How about it Will?"

"Yes, let's, Will. I want to bring this book back anyway, so it's there for Hallie in the future." She holds up the copy of the *Martian Chronicles*.

Will looks from Connie to Drew seeing that child-like spark in his cousin's eyes that reminds him of better times and knows he cannot refuse. He gives a nod and heads out with them.

The '77 Restaurant is busy, but Sally is working the counter and gets their order going for them. They sit on the stools waiting. Will is quiet as Drew and Connie sit with their backs to the counter talking together.

The door of the restaurant opens violently, and everyone turns to look. There is a disheveled man standing in the doorway with a short barrel shot gun in hand. He is the man that was at the Fourth of July celebration who made threats against Drew. Most people are frozen in disbelief. First yesterday's events and now this! His eyes are wild as he scans the faces in the room stopping at Drew.

"There you are. You murdering son of a bitch. Don't know why they let you go, but I'm here to send you to your maker." His words hiss over gritted teeth.

Will turns starting to move from his stool towards the man, and Connie looks from the man to Drew as the blast sounds. Both barrels let go and the shot hits Drew in the chest. Will's ears pop, he turns watching in horror as Drew's blood spatters back over Connie, the counter, and beyond.

"Noooooo!" Connie keens in a painful sob. She holds onto Drew as he slides off the stool onto the floor. Will kneels down to support Drew's head, but he is already dead.

The man seems to be in a temporary shock at the sight of the blood and destruction he has caused.

"He was innocent. They let him go because he was innocent," she screams at him. "He didn't kill your niece or anyone else. He…" Her words are strangled by her sobbing.

Everyone in the restaurant stands frozen. Sally trembles behind the counter. The man drops his shotgun and turns walking mechanically out of the door onto the street. He steps in front of a cargo truck bringing a load to the train station triggering the groan of brakes applied a little too late and a shift of the truck's load as it spills onto the road. The entranced man dies instantly as the frontend grill strikes him with a dull thud. He catapults up grotesquely falling back to the ground striking his head solidly on the hot asphalt, eyes open, and blood pooling below him. There is a rippling of his skin at the base of his neck that quivers at first and then more violently until the claw of a scorpion breaks through expanding the tear and winning its escape.

It scuttles across the road dodging the on-lookers who hurry to see the chaos up close. The scorpion makes its crooked way to the road's edge where the Demon King stands. Hester is beside him with a look of determined disinterest. He bends over extending his hand to the scorpion allowing it to seek refuge up the sleeve of his shirt and under the skin of his shoulder where it comes to rest below the primitive scorpion mark etched into his flesh.

"Come Hester today is my day of reprisal. Time for the harvest has come."  His eyes are fixed on Will, splattered in blood, who is leading Connie out of the restaurant onto the street holding her close.

Will senses eyes on him and looks up fixing his gaze on the Demon King with an admirably brave intent to remain calm and collected. The Demon King smiles at him tipping his hat, as he navigates away from the gathering people. He walks slowly and deliberately past Will and Connie behind the buildings and towards the surrounding woods. He does not turn back. He does not have to. He knows that they are there. Following. Defeated. Subdued. With a sneer on his face, the Demon King turns coolly striking down the two remaining souls without ceremony. No need for more drama today. He inspects his hands and takes an appreciative look around him letting out a wistful sigh.

"Come Hester, it is time we return."

Hester winces looking at Will and Connie, but grateful their deaths were quick. Their bodies are already being pulled under through the forest floor, and she turns away falling in step with the

Demon King and together they fade from view.

# CHAPTER 35
## Truth

Will stands once more in front of the Demon King's desk. The room's décor has been updated to light wood finishes and clean lines matching the style of the decade he had just left. Oddly enough a telephone with a Bakelite finish sits on the ash wood desk almost bringing a smirk to Will's face as he muses about who the Demon King could possibly call. Chartreuse and turquoise dominate the color scheme with yellow and red accents. The window behind the desk has been augmented with a decorative network of vines made of black iron providing not just beauty but security as well. Will looks out into the garden seeing the remains of Persephone's tree. It was cut down and burned after his escape. Its absence creates a hollow barrenness that dominates the otherwise beautiful garden.

Drew stands on Will's right, and to his left are Luke and Jeb—all looking worse for wear. Apart from Drew's presence, Will feels as though he had never left the room. It feels as though the idea of crashing through the window to seek his freedom and find Hallie is a thought just now coming to mind, and his hand twitches wanting to grasp ahold of his sword, but he resists the temptation. He focuses on other things instead hearing the ticking of meaningless seconds come from a wall clock with a sunburst of chrome, and he glances around the room to see what else the Demon King acquired during his most recent appearance on Earth. Eurynomos lounges on a streamline-style sofa and the conquest Smyth is positioned near the back of the room with his blood-stained collar and poorly fitting butler's uniform.

One notable difference is Cercopes standing behind the demon's desk next to the window—one coarse-looking twin on each side. Cercopes on the right keeps darting its eyes towards Will as though it has something on its mind, and Will thinks about the carousel's gruff attendants. No one can be trusted—he will not acknowledge Cercopes' fidgety behavior.

The chair behind the desk sits empty, as it has for what must be hours now, yet the four human warriors continue waiting. They have already endured torture and torment, and now they stand without speaking, hands clasped behind their backs, and lost in their own thoughts. The bird creature fidgets on its perch until it eventually tucks its head under a wing and sleeps.

Finally, the side door to the room opens, but no one turns a head or diverts an eye to look to see who has entered. There is no need because that door is reserved for one being's use only. The Demon King flings the door shut behind him and walks across the room to stand in front of Will deferring his customary seat behind the desk. Will looks at him seeing the crimson glow seep into the dark irises of his eyes. Despite their long-term acquaintance, Will's soul is still highly coveted by him, and being this close triggers the red glow of desire. It somehow gives Will a sense of satisfaction to know that he affects the Demon King in this way.

He sneers as though he read Will's thoughts and shocks them all when he plunges his hand up under Will's rib cage grasping ahold of his heart. The bird creature flinches when Smyth drops the silver tray he had been holding and Cercopes cracks its statue-like stance while Eurynomus darts her eyes in their direction. Will gasps trying to breathe and remain standing. He has suffered much pain and torment at the Demon King's hand, but this is by far the worse. He has never been so completely invaded.

The Demon King holds him captive both physically and emotionally. With a firm grasp on Will's heart he cannot only read his soul completely but claim it with one swift motion should he choose. Drew, Luke, and Jeb reflexively spring forward at Will's defense, but one look from the Demon King, and a tighter grasp on Will's heart, holds them at bay.

Beads of sweat travel down Will's face, but he refuses to let any sound of suffering cross his lips. Ultimately the Demon King relaxes his grip and gives Will a thin-lipped smile.

"You have changed. I sensed it in 1928 that day in Pennymaker's store, but I could not put a finger on it. This—with my entire hand on *it*—however, is very effective." He pauses and tightens his grip again renewing Will's struggle to breathe.

He sneers. "This 'new you' had the audacity to make a destructive spectacle not so very long ago in this very room. Quite a different impact when you dare to behave defiantly…*here*… as you are only beginning to understand." He loosens his grip easing Will's struggle once more.

The Demon King pulls a breath in, his nostrils flare, and his eyes glow brighter. "The motivation for these changes was at a loss to me. Yes, I was quite perplexed until I saw the girl in Ferrum and remembered her from Fayerdale. Imagine that—seeing her in 1928, in 1958, and now here she is in your heart. So much *time* with so little change. Except one. One change indeed. It seems she has claimed a place inside you that was once shallow and empty. I had suspected such a change even way back at the original harvest, after our initial encounter in your father's barn, but how could that be? I asked myself that back then, but now…now I know who…she…is. And I believe you fully know as well." He is nose-to-nose with Will.

Will has no control over the increased rate with which his heart pounds when the Demon King alludes to Hallie. He feels like he is betraying her, and it begins to show on his face.

The Demon King's face cracks into a broad smile. "I knew that sparing your life would eventually pay off. That slight change of heart I saw in you at the original harvest was a hint to be sure.

My patience has proved most profitable. Of course, I have always thought you, the spoiled—proud—scared—colonist, would have broken and shed your humanity to join my legions long ago. That alone would have been a victory in itself. It was initially a disappointment I was forced to overcome when you staunchly maintained your soul, however, I have found advantage in maintaining our connection and the passage it provides me across the Mesu."

The Demon King gazes around his massive room of human collectibles before continuing his monologue. "Your perpetual existence has brought me many riches and increased my power. Now you secure a means for obtaining a pure soul to replace Sariel's—stolen from me by that troublesome fury."

A look of disdain comes to his face, but it is quickly supplanted with a menacing leer. "And not just any pure soul. No, no, no, you bring the means for my attachment to a traveler no less. And if my suspicion is correct, one from a powerful bloodline with connections to not only the mundane and celestial planes but Hester's stolen keys as well. Imagine the possibilities—all realms, all eras, and power over both demon and angel legions. I had been promised this alliance long ago, but through clever trickery it escaped me. You William, have renewed my enthusiasm for future endeavors, so I am choosing to allow you live yet again."

Despite the immense pain, Will struggles to lash out at Paimon. He doesn't care if his heart is torn out. He wants it to be ripped from his chest. He knows Paimon needs him to get to Hallie, and he will not be a part of anything that brings her anywhere near this despicable creature. Drew and Luke grasp ahold of him forcing him to calm down. Paimon smiles and then smacks his lips as though anticipating a delicious meal. He withdrawals his hand with a snap.

The wound on Will's abdomen heals and is overlaid with a

demon mark burned into the skin. He falls to his knees struggling to pull air into his lungs. The Demon King signals to Smyth for a cloth to wipe his hand, and the conquest clumsily responds. Paimon leans against his desk as he meticulously wipes each finger of his hand adjusting the gold ring with green stone. His gaze drifts down towards Will and his lips twist into a crooked smile.

*Benjamin's story about King Solomon was adapted, with author permission (Dec 2018), from Three Times CHAI:  54 Rabbis Tell Their Favorite Stories, by Laney Katz via Becker Behrman House.*

# ABOUT THE AUTHOR

SD Barron lives in the foothills of the Blue Ridge Mountains in Virginia with her family, including a feisty dog, grumpy cat, and two geriatric horses. Creative endeavors energize her, and Wings of Time was set to paper (or computer screen as it was) during a challenging time. The character conversations that helped develop the story were and continue to create a wonderful commotion in her life. She is awed by the beauty and raw splendor of nature, and spends as much time in its midst as possible. She deeply appreciates a good story that consumes her waking moments and hopes to give a similar experience to her readers.

## OTHER BOOKS BY SD BARRON:

Wings of Time: Breaking Darkness

Stay in touch: SDBarronWrites.com